Where Lies Our Hope

JUNE MASTERS BACHER

HARVEST HOUSE PUBLISHERS
Eugene, Oregon 97402

Scripture quotations are taken from the King James Version
of the Bible.

WHERE LIES OUR HOPE

Copyright © 1992 by Harvest House Publishers
Eugene, Oregon 97402

Bacher, June Masters.
    Where lies our hope / by June Masters Bacher.
        p.   cm. — (The Heartland heritage series : no. 3)
        ISBN 1-56507-035-6
        1. World War, 1939-1945—Fiction.   I. Title.   II. Series.
    PS3552.A257W48   1993
    813'.54—dc20

92-28302
CIP

Printed in the United States of America.

With deep appreciation to the countless persons who knowingly and unknowingly assisted with the creation of The Heartland Heritage Series, which spans a sometimes brushed-aside era beginning with the Great Depression of the 1930s and ending with close of World War II and its aftermath. This series has proven to be my most challenging and most rewarding. Were this book and the two preceding (*No Time for Tears* and *Songs in the Whirlwind*) plus one to follow a People's Choice awards winner, I should say humbly:

Thank you to my husband, George, who did all the legwork and bookkeeping details with nary a complaint nor expecting a word of praise.

Thank you to my son, Bryce, and his wife, Sun, who took pride in Mother's finished manuscript, though it often meant sacrifice of our treasured time together. Those two are *our* winners!

Thank you to my mother, Gussie Masters, whose keen mind furnished primary research from her endless collection of scrapbooks and remarkable recall of events. The grand lady remembers chronological order and feelings of the times as well—trying times, but made bearable because of love, compassion, and understanding.

Thank you to Arlene Cook, herself a professional writer with an overloaded schedule, who added the invaluable dimension of secondary research, checking accuracy of dates and names where "facts" entered into what is otherwise fiction. That service so aided the creative process that somewhere in the series fact and fiction merged. At that point the characters became their own people. So in "poetic justice," thank you, characters, for refusing to be pawns!

Thank you to the editors for their dedication and patience when the author's thinking pushed ahead of her fingers during the process of developing the story line. Added here must be the entire staff of Harvest House Publishers who go unsung while contributing so much to the finished publications and the morale of their authors. You are loved and appreciated by us all.

Thank you to the reviewers scattered throughout the country who alert others to this book and all previous ones. You are the supporting case who (in my opinion) upstage the writer.

Thank you to the faithful readers who make writing worthwhile and support me with your prayers . . . to the jobbers out there in the field who share the new with the bookstores . . . and to the bookstore managers who display that which we pray will be inspirational. You have helped me deal with some devastating situations in trying to rise above my humanness and reach for and find God's spiritual realm.

May He who is the Author and Finisher of our faith bless you all!

—June Masters Bacher

Contents

A Woman's Prayer

Keep us, O God, from pettiness;
Let us be large in thought, in word, in deed.
  Let us be done with fault-finding and leave
off self-seeking.
  May we put away all pretense and meet each
other face-to-face—without self-pity and without
prejudice.
  May we never be hasty in judgment and always
generous.
  Let us take time for all things; make us grow
calm, serene, gentle.
  Teach us to put into action our better impulses,
straight-forward and unafraid.
  Grant that we may realize it is the little things
that create differences; that in the big things of life
we are one.
  And may we strive to touch and to know all the
great, common woman's heart of us all.
  And, O Lord, let us forget not to be kind!

—Mary Stewart, 1904

Come Home . . .

Softly and tenderly, Jesus is calling,
Calling for you and for me;
See, at the portals He's waiting and
    watching,
Watching for you and for me.
Come home, come home,
Ye who are weary, come home;
Earnestly, tenderly, Jesus is calling,
Calling, O sinner, come home!

—Will L. Thompson,
1880 (hymn)

There is a destiny that makes us brothers—
  None goes his way alone,
All that we send into the lives of others
  Comes back into our own.

—Edwin Markham

1

The
Unseen Pull

I will remember this day always, she thought.

It was still dark the morning the Harringtons left Pleasant Knoll, Texas. But in the pool of light cast by the windows of her grandparents' boardinghouse, Marvel's stride was clean and straight—typical of her heritage. The cloud of amber hair framing the open-blossom face was still straight too, the mirror had said, except for the hint of curls hovering at the top of her forehead. But mirrors could be wrong. This one had betrayed the near-17-year-old girl. "You belong here," it might as well have said. But in a way the mirror was right, Marvel sighed, as she hurried to close the car door before the piled-high necessities for the long journey into the unknown spilled. There was a certainty of bearing, an elegance born of good breeding that spoke of *belonging*. This was her world. Here she belonged.

Now she turned and faced the house just once more. Grandmother Riley waved. Marvel waved back, careful to lift the corners of her mouth in a well-rehearsed smile. *But today was not a rehearsal....*

"I guess I would have been only a minor-league player," her father said, quite out of context. *His* father had said no to baseball.

But Mother understood. She always did. That's how it is with real love, Marvel realized, feeling again the rush of warmth she always felt for her parents. And that's how it will be with Titus and me. If only—if only there were no waiting period.

"You would have made it in the majors, darling," Snow Harrington said, "You *are* major league with me—us, our Marvel and me—"

The slight hesitation was the ever-obedient daughter's cue.

"Mother's right, Daddy," she confirmed staunchly. "You're no quitter. You faced life as it was. Gave up? Not you. *Grew* up? Grandfather would say yes to that. I guess," she said more slowly, "we're talking about life here—conditions. We had decisions to make and we made them—together."

"Yep!" Dale Harrington's voice strengthened. "You always make me feel better—you two. Sure your door's shut tight back there, baby? Hard to know when a man's a quitter or when he's a realist, when to stay put and when to let go. But was there a choice?"

Mother slid over the worn upholstery to put a supporting arm around her husband's shoulders. "None! So breathe free—"

Breathe free. It was Daddy's breathing, after all, that tilted the scales and convinced Marvel that go they must, no matter what leaving family, friends, her roots, her precious Titus—yes, most of all Titus—meant.

Dale and Snow Harrington were comfortable with their daughter's choice, but they would never know what the decision they had thrust upon her young shoulders had cost: no graduation...no proper goodbye to the boy she loved...no youthful years to be spent in the land of her roots. Still, it meant her father's health. So the choice was no choice at all. The doctor had said Daddy *must* have a change of climate for the sake of his cough....

They were called dust devils once upon a time—back when they were harmless. East Texas natives were accustomed to the minor whirlwinds that came in late summer. Dancing in hot-breathed glee, the miniature funnels meant no harm as they tore at ladies' hair and skirts, sent birds in backward flight, or picked up carefully raked-and-piled leaves innocently. It was sort of pretty really, causing the leaves to resemble so many fluttering butterflies, Marvel had thought.

That was before the winds grew stronger in velocity, causing the dust devils to become devils indeed! Across the fields they swept, enlarging their circumference to pick up the precious soil, carrying it higher and higher to pile it in unwanted places, invading the homes by poking beneath the doors, creeping inside windowsills, covering furniture with layers of dust, filling food with grit, and roaring from the four corners of the earth as if furious at mankind's folly. Now only waves of sand remained where once there was a Garden of Eden. And helplessly the people had watched as if receiving previews of hell.

There was hunger. The lands were poisoned. The cattle died, as did some of the men, women, and children. Daddy was more fortunate. Ill as he was, he survived. But there remained the verdict: "He *has* to get out of here!" Dr. Porter had said, as if giving an alternative to a death sentence. *Adventure? More like desperation.*

"Should a man as I flee?" Daddy quoting Nehemiah, was pondering now.

"Stop torturing yourself! This is going to be an adventure, remember?" Mother said lightly, sounding more like Grandmother Riley than she would have cared to be reminded. *Adventure* again.

Well, it was consoling to know that God would be with them no matter what their choice. He would be with those who went and with those who stayed. He would guide Marvel and He would guide Titus....

The great, rambling mansion-like house was gone—consumed by a lake of fire. Gone, too, was the sharecropper shanty the Dale Harringtons had tried to call home. But a home is more than a house. Mother, herself, had decided that—a shock since daughter Snow Riley, in making her emotional declaration of independence, had vowed to "settle down." Never in a million years would she live the gypsy-like life of her mother before her. It was wretched being pulled hither and yon in search of greener pastures.

But *home* to Marvel was the land, meaning the once-beautiful green roll of the pasturelands—yes, and more. It was security, family heritage, *belonging.* Now Marvel was torn between personal needs and honor and respect, the command to obey her parents and her own inexplicable dedication to protect them from all hurts. So she would be back, back to restore that land Daddy so loved and to give Mother the home she would never cease to covet—and back to Titus. Life would be perfect then. Both she and Titus would have found God's will in their lives and fulfilled it. Until then, there would remain in her heart the gentle tugging, yearning—that subtle, unseen pull like the moon pushing the tides out, only to draw them home.

Marvel looked back only one time once the caravan was underway. And that was to lift a hand in salute to Mary Ann. First she must don the smiling mask she had worn for her maternal grandmother. By prior arrangement, the Worth Harringtons and her own family would drive wedges between brothers Emory (in the lead) and Joseph (bringing up the rear). The reason was simple. The older brothers had better automobiles and were less likely to suffer a breakdown in the long journey to Oregon where Alexander Jr. (and still unmarried) had "made a fortune." "Nervous Nellie" Daddy had nicknamed the Essex of ancient vintage. The vehicle still shimmied in spite of efforts to repair it by Jake.

Jake. Jake Brotherton, her cousin's first love—how Mary Ann must be suffering, measuring her favorite cousin's grief by her own. But Marvel was the stronger of the two, so—burying her own grief—she gave a signal of support, as always.

"Okay, Mrs. Navigator. All set?" Daddy asked.

"All set, sir," Mother murmured, then busied herself unfolding the map Uncle Alex had made for them to follow.

The two of them went on talking, but Marvel did not hear. She was concentrating on a weathered billboard reading "Dr. Guertin's Nerve Syrup." The concoction was guaranteed to cure epilepsy, St. Vitus Dance, convulsions, hysteria, and a number of other maladies that there was no time to decipher before they left the sign behind. She wondered miserably if the medication promised to heal a broken heart.

Marvel's defenses commenced to crumble. The mirror was right. Her delicate features were unchanged. Her apple-blossom coloring remained centered by ripened-fruit cheeks, her blue-blue Harrington eyes wide and reflective. An outsider would have gasped at her rare type of beauty, only to see at second glance what Leah Johanna Mier Riley saw even as her granddaughter waved a too-brave goodbye. There was a bruised look in those eyes, a wondering. The gaiety of one so young was missing. In its stead was a longing for what might have been and never was. The dream was stripped away too fast, too soon, as if some cruel artist had stripped away the vibrancy of youth from a priceless painting. It was subtly done—so subtle was the alteration that the untrained eye would miss the substitution of a paler shade.

The artist? The artist was time, and Marvel herself—Marvel and her caring heart.

And now, leaving Pleasant Knoll behind and heading for the open road, Marvel knew she must say something before her parents took notice of her silence.

"So where's our first stop, most-able navigator?"

Mother checked the map and mentioned an unfamiliar spot. "And on and on," she added, "leaving the Dust Bowl far behind!"

Well and good, except that the map led away from home. The pool of misery deepened inside Marvel. And without warning the dammed-up tears gathered behind her eyes—morning-glory blue, Titus had named them—blinding her. These tears that were to go unshed lodged in her heart and froze into a lump that would melt only when she was back—back to stay, back to marry Titus according to her promise. Then neither time nor distance could separate them—so long as they both should live. The unseen pull would bring her home. . . .

Directly ahead, Uncle Emory made a right arm signal. They had reached the crossroad indicated on the map. Marvel sighed. In one way or another, she supposed, all faced that lonely crossroad in their lives. Turn right or left? Go into the unknown or stay and try to right all wrongs? What the young girl did not know was that there would be many such decisions with nobody declaring the winners.

And so for now Marvel Harrington checked to be sure the little box-style Kodak given to her by the newspaper editor was conveniently close. From here on the region was new since she had traveled little, and one never knew when a subject would appear. Best capture it before it was swallowed by distance like Dr. Guertin's Nerve Syrup. A pictorial review, Mr. Corey had instructed. But there must be captions, so where was the notepad? With the pad and pencil in her hand, Marvel felt stronger. Of course! She'd promised Titus a daily account, too. And suddenly the joy of yesterday and tomorrow were back. . . .

2

The
Huddled Masses

It is easy to imagine the emotions with which emigrants viewed the Statue of Liberty with all her promise after sailing the protesting Atlantic. Easy to imagine their undocumented misery of living shoulder-to-shoulder without privacy, adequate water, or more than a watered-down tin cup of soup and a dry crust of bread. Yes, it is easier to identify with that grand assemblage of brave souls—the Irish (whose potato crop had failed as our land has failed to produce); the Greeks and Germans; the Serphardic Jews hailing from Portugal and Spain... Poles and Hollanders... and Slavs from the crumbling empires of Austria-Hungary, Russia... Turkey...

Thus began grist for the mill of newspaper columns planned for the "Heartbeats of America, U.S.A." coauthored series by Titus Smith and Marvel Harrington. Or would Editor Thomas A. Corey decide to use the material she was seeing through the new view which, only heard about before, Marvel was now seeing? It would fit well into the syndicated column, yes, but in her own coverage, "Eyes of East Texas" (Would the *News Review* change its title to "Eyes of an East Texan" now?). Then Titus, Senator Norton's journalistic young aide who wrote "Ears of Austin" and his employer could put it to use as well. If ever the senator did make a bid in the gubernatorial race, it would be Titus who assured his winning. Not that Titus minded—not her Titus. He was above self-glorification. The man she loved chose only to glorify God. On that—as on all other matters—she and Titus agreed. That includes the woman—Marvel felt herself blushing—with whom he had chosen to spend the rest of his earthly days.

Oh my darling, her heart cried out, *will we ever get to write our book,* The White Flag of Victory, *together?* Of course they would! And before the tears stinging her eyeballs could course down to stain the work begun, Marvel resumed her writing. Her unflagging spirit must not be allowed to shrivel. She could not do that to those who loved her, needed her, and depended on her. Then "someday"—yes, she could live with the phrase....

> Now, after seeing the roads beyond my own shielded confines, it is as if I—along with the others seeking a golden door opening to a New World—were sailing with those emigrants who looked out on the horizon silhouetting the Mother of exiles, hear her chiseled lips whisper: "Give me your tired, your poor, your huddled masses yearning to breathe free..." for we, too, are the "homeless," the "tempest-tossed" to whom the Statue of Liberty lifts her lamp to the "golden door" of opportunity. We, too, are emigrants who left the "Old World" where others, equally heroic, chose to remain despite the bad conditions. It takes us all to keep America great...and so we must hold hands across the barren miles...for, ultimately, we are all striving for the same cause, a getting-back to God...a reclaiming what we have lost, our "Garden of Eden."

Daddy slowed the car. It had been obvious from the start that Uncle Emory's being the lead car put him in charge as to when and where the Harrington caravan stopped. Others' needs or desires had nothing to do with the matter. Marvel was not surprised, but she felt a pang of disappointment at being unable to take a few pictures. Maybe they would stop here. It was an interesting-looking little town—interesting after the long stretch of wasteland dotted by a few deserted houses. The drought had reached this part of the state, taken its toll, and pitched camp

instead of moving on. Where were all the people—sucked up by
incessant whirlwinds along with all their belongings? A battered
sign, still swinging in the wind, read: "And There Was No Rain!"
Beneath the crude lettering, a now-faded city limits sign was
partially visible. This—why this was a ghost town, totally uninhabited. In the days of its former existence there had been a
school, its doors and windows now sagging to meet the waves of
heaped-up dust, its halls empty and gaping as if mourning the
loss of childish laughter. There had been stores, too, as well
as a barbershop, a cafe, and there! There was a church, or its
remains. It, too, was without identity with the congregation
gone.

"I wish Uncle Emory would stop. We could all go inside, look
around, and *pray*," Marvel said wistfully, knowing he wouldn't.

The white line around Daddy's mouth tightened. She regretted speaking her thoughts—until Mother agreed. "We could
talk with God about the severity of this prolonged drought—how
it has withered our crops and our very souls. Oh, these poor
thirsty fields!"

"Don't you think He's heard all that before?" Daddy shook his
head. "We're God's people—and they were. I just can't understand."

Mother's pat on his shoulder offered comfort. "None of us do,
darling. Nobody's giving reasons or answers—not even God. But
let's not dwell on it. We're getting away!"

Snow Harrington was trying desperately to push through that
"golden door" for the man she loved—trying, as always to give
solace to another when she had to be feeling the same frustration, anger, and hopelessness. The child-of-the-covered-wagon
in her was coming through just as Grandmother Riley had said it
would, their daughter observed. And then she went back to her
own thoughts.

It rained on the just and the unjust. The Bible said so. The
same was true of the sweltering sun, Marvel supposed. Was it
possible that God had placed a curse on the thousands of acres
laid barren, and that He had reclaimed what was His after all?
Then they would be wise to beg Him to forgive their resentment.
If only they *could* go inside the deserted church. The inner urge
deepened. But Uncle Emory's pause was due to some confusion
with the map. It was easy to see that he and Aunt Eleanore

differed. If the boys joined in the debate, it could go on indefinitely.

Marvel saw with resignation that they were past the lonely little church now, but the crawling speed allowed her time to look around and make notes. "The remains lie prostrate with grief," she scribbled, then hastily she drew word pictures from the signs.

Ice Cream! Two scoops, 5 cents. (The sign had been crossed out and beneath the price was the single word "was.")

Bob's Barbershop. Shave 10 cents (includes bay rum and hot towel). Single haircut 20 cents, couple for 35 cents, lady's hairbob, 20 cents. Children's Buster Bob (boys or girls) 20 cents, trim, 10 cents. (This sign, too, bore the X, followed by the fatal word "Gone!")

Your Best Bet Cafe. Chili and crackers, 10 cents, (big bowl, half-size available. Ask us!). Hamburgers, 10 cents, 3 for a quarter. Breakfast special: 2 fried eggs, 'taters, biscuit and gravy, 10 cents. Sunday dinner: chicken-fried steak, all you can eat, choice of coffee, tea or buttermilk, 15 cents (preachers free!).

There was no time to read the remaining choices, but Marvel's practiced eye saw the bottom line of The Clip Joint, Building for Rent, Cheap! So the barber, too, had gone. Only faded reminders remained: an empty chair, overturned and sprawled in a carpet of sand; a broken window staring at the desolation with an unseeing eye; and a faded candy-striped pole, the barber's universally understood symbol of services offered. The winds had done this? Yet, even now, they were not to be satisfied. Determined to dig the Dust Bowl deeper, they formed a giant funnel, lifting an enormous tumbleweed which blocked vision momentarily, only to drop the bush in the narrow roadway before them and roll it into the deserted barbershop. There it halted like a bodiless head awaiting its turn to be groomed.

"It seemed only fitting," Marvel wrote with a shudder, "that a more recently erected marker should point to a side road, indicating the direction of the dead town's cemetery."

They were picking up speed again—not fast, but too fast for the old Essex which was wheezing and giving off a hot, metallic odor as if in need of water. Mercy! Water—*here*? Somewhere nearby there should be a graveyard for vehicles, too. The fumes caused Daddy to cough. He rolled the window down and then immediately back up, evidently thinking he could tolerate the fumes better than the dust.

"Here," Mother said, handing him a damp cloth. "Put this over your face. Don't cover your eyes, silly. This is no time to play games. So why am I smiling? Here's yours, darling," she said to Marvel without turning around. "My word! Look at those signs."

Marvel *was* looking. "Vote for FDR, our only hope!" one said. Propped beside it, as if someone passing by had arranged it for photographing, was another: "We waited and still no rain." Other signs, crudely lettered by those refugees who were stranded, begged for understanding: "California? Please, a ride. My wife's in a family way...kids are starving. Help! No handout—a job, anything. I ain't proud."

Sickened, Marvel squeezed her eyes shut, failing to see the cardboard warning some disillusioned hitchhiker must have lettered: "Go back!" Her mind, behind closed eyelids, was seeing the president of a starving nation—pondering as many men in his position had pondered before and would ponder afterward— what to do in times of great peril.

She was soon to find out and in a totally unexpected way.

* * *

"You're not to leave this place and go wanderin' around, you hear?" Uncle Joseph had an arm around each of his two older daughters. "And that goes for you, too, young lady," he added, looking at Monica, the youngest of the three, but letting his eyes pan the direction of his nieces. "You never know about places like this, or *these ramblers*."

"You mean boys, Daddy?" Erin asked innocently while looking around.

"Doesn't she *hope*?" Mary Ann whispered from the corner of her mouth after sidling her way to stand beside Marvel. "I need to stretch my legs," she said aloud. "Eating oatmeal cookies inside the car—well, there wasn't much exercise—"

"Every stop takes gasoline," Uncle Emory said shortly. "Yep! I agree with Joseph. And you boys stick around, too. You'll be needed."

"If it's so awful, why'd you stop, huh?" That was Billy Joe. "And what you said about the ramblers, Uncle Joseph—me, I *like* bein' a rambler. My mama usta be one—huh, Mother? And besides, we're not s'posed to look down on folks—that's what Mrs. Key said in Sunday school. That's, uh, *prejudice*," the child said triumphantly.

Joseph Harrington did not like having his ultimatums challenged. Neither did he take kindly to criticism. It was clear, however, that he was frustrated by his nephew's remarks. Trying to cover that, he boomed, "We'll have to take whatever accommodations we find—temporarily. So we'll be rubbin' shoulders with all kinds. But I could tell your Mrs. Key a thing or two. Just because a crow flies over doesn't mean we have to let it nest in our hair!"

"An' I can tell *you* something—" Billy Joe began.

Feathers. Surely he was not going to start that again—his ongoing claim that God and all His heavenly hosts wore feathers in order to fly everywhere at once. Uncle Worth was helping Daddy fill the leaky radiator of the old Essex. And Auntie Rae was relaying small containers of water from the windmill pump. Marvel saw that Mary Ann was enjoying herself, as yet unwilling to take over with her brother.

"I will have a word with your father, young sprout. Talking back to your elders—you should have your mouth washed out with soap!"

Billy Joe giggled. "I won't need soap for my *mouth*. I gotta—"

"Come on, honey," Mary Ann said, winking slyly at Marvel—her signal to follow.

"Defecate!" Billy Joe hurled over his shoulder as Mary Ann led him away quickly. Marvel, suppressing a smile, followed....

They had come upon the place suddenly. It bore the first sign of inhabitants in this desolate land of sage and hard-packed ground, overlaid by invasive sand, since leaving Pleasant Knoll. A sharp twist of the narrow road and there, between two stakes, swung the sign "Tourist Cabins, Family Rates." A cluster of small, bungalow-shaped structures, clustered together beneath a windbreak of sparsely needled salt cedar trees. Dilapidated and strangers to paint, the cabins were anything but inviting. But they offered shelter.

A woman in a shapeless cotton dress held onto what wispy gray hair she had left with one hand and flagged them to a halt as if some emergency lay ahead. "Better y'all stop—nothin' on down yonder fer miles. Old man's laid up with catarrh 'n bum legs. But they's uh pumpin station out back. "Better fill 'er up. Le's see, three—*four* cars. Say four bucks—bunk beds, hot plate, no dishes or—"

Uncle Emory bargained with Lucy (she said her name was Lucy but to "call me Luce") and got the four cramped-quarter cabins for three dollars. Luce pocketed the money and pointed out the public toilets squatting behind the one marked "Office."

"Make yer'se'ves right at home now. Lotsa folks here jest like y'all—all comin' or goin'—so ain't likely you'll git lonesome."

The woman was probably right, Marvel thought—in regard to hope for accommodations ahead, anyway. The last house— deserted, of course—was marked: "For sale, house and cow, cheap." It hadn't sold.

And now here they were—Marvel, Mary Ann, and Billy Joe— taking turns at the outdoor privy. Outside hung a string of red corncobs—probably the lonely woman's idea of a joke. But what caught Marvel's eye was a newspaper which had escaped from a nearby rusty barrel serving as a trash burner. Telling Mary Ann to go ahead of her, Marvel picked the newspaper up and was surprised to see that it bore yesterday's date. She was scanning it quickly when Luce reappeared.

"I jest happened t'be lookin' this direction," she said, carefully keeping her eyes averted, "so' seen y'all. I knowed y'all was kinda dif'erent—classier, y'know—'n my hunch is right. Gen'rally is. I kin read folks. 'N speakin' uv reading', I see y'got uh healthy in'erest in th' news. Well now, ain't that somthin'! Me 'n my ole man's like that 'n got us newspapers 'n magazines piled sky-high. If y'all wan'na come in—Well now, come on—lots to show yuh."

The inside should have been marked "Disaster Area." Mary Ann said later it must have been designed by vandals. Apt, indeed—tidy person's nightmare. The stacks of yellowed read-ing material was heaped perilously against walls papered with what appeared to be Christmas wrappings. On it some religious pictures with homemade frames clung crookedly to the walls and extension cords wound in dizzying mazes, with a few bare-bulb lights dangling here and there. A brownish daybed humped in a corner, looking for the world like a wandering buffalo had crept inside to die. Marvel was more amused than frightened until she saw Lucy McMeal's husband. Then, coupled with the news, she felt a prickle of fear.

"Th' Mister—McMeal's th' name, an' he likes folks t'call 'im Mac—he ain't a'tall well," the landlady whispered as she led the three young guests in to see him because he was "dryin' up fer compn'y."

The man lay humped like the front-room buffalo on a cot surrounded by bottles of patent medicine. All other furniture was draped against the dust storms by means of white bed sheets. Mary Ann suddenly bolted and ran, followed by Billy Joe. Later she laid the blame on her young brother but shudderingly admitted that all the shrouded objects looked like they'd been exhumed from a cemetery before Gabriel blew his horn (more like Arab tents, Marvel laughed).

Mr. McMeal's vague, blurry eyes attempted to focus on his guest only one time. Then he returned his attention to a small radio. There was a commercial ditty advertising "Jello that jells," followed by a special report. Luce put a restraining hand on Marvel's arm and the three of them listened:

> We interrupt this program to tell you that the FBI, aided by New York City police, have apprehended the notorious bank robber and kidnapper, Harry Brunette, in his West Side apartment, in a manner sure to spark controversy.... Word has it that Director Hoover took personal command in the charge to capture the gangster. In the ensuin' shoot-'em-up, the G-men set the building afire by lobbing in a tear-gas grenade. Firemen arrived but later claimed Hoover's men turned gunfire on *them*. So, although th' smoke from the fire has blown over, a cloud still surrounds the procedure. Was feds' watcher Jim Farley right in sayin' Hoover oughta be fired? A *Washington Post* gossip columnist thinks so. Just one more thing for the overburdened president to add to his concerns—as if Franklin Delano Roosevelt didn't have his crippled hands full

already! A still-empty-bellied society of once-prosperous people...sickness rampant, no cures, no arrangements for doctor's care...no jobs...no crops ...an' *no hope* what with this drought. There's more fist-shakin' between this country and Europe, too— not to mention Asia. Some new insights in later reports...but for now we return to our regularly scheduled programming.

"Now ain't that somethin'?" Luce McMeal said. "They's bound t'be war, mark my word. War's what taken my pappy—'n got Mac here, sorta shell-shocked 'im 'n busted up his insides. Just tears my stumick up thinkin' on it—I'm skeered—"

"We all are. We just have to lean on prayer."

The woman's eyes flickered with uncertainty—as if she wanted to believe and was afraid to. "I wisht I had some proof it he'ped."

"God offers no proof—not to you, me, or the prophets of old. That's where faith enters, Mrs. McMeal—Luce."

"Now, ain't that somethin'!" She was listening intently and giving her thin, frizzy hair some dangerous yanks in concentration. Marvel was sorry to hear a knock at the door.

The callers proved to be Duke and Thomas rather than a hoped-for customer in this lonely oasis. The cousins had dutifully come to check on Marvel's safety and to escort her back to the cabin. Luce interrupted.

"Here, take these—all uv 'em. Y'all give 'er uh hand. Don' jest stand there lookin' goggle-eyes. An' yeah, take today's paper, too. Bound t'have more 'bout th' upcoming' war. I been hearin' 'bout that feller talkin', sez he's got proof straight from Germany. Them hateful cusses! Shudda wiped 'em out 'long with Kaiser Bill!"

Marvel thanked her and gathered as many magazines as she could. On the way she would tear out items for the columns. Meantime, there was a picture of this place to take, light permitting, a note to Titus to write—and more. But first she would take a copy of the Bibles Brother Greer had offered back to the landlady. She, too, was among the "huddled masses"—starving for food, and starving for God's hope....

3

Lonely
at the Top

In the White House on Capitol Hill, the thirty-second president of the United States was indeed holding his head. Allowing himself in a seldom-moment's privacy the luxury of a sigh, Franklin Delano Roosevelt looked over a tired shoulder at his predecessor's frustration and shared it. Even as bitter charges and countercharges were hurled back and forth between himself and Herbert Hoover, the two men had understood and admired one another. Rome wasn't built in one day, but people were desperate and demanding immediate change. And it was lonely, so lonely, at the top....

All this and more Marvel Harrington gathered as she read from the heap of newspapers, *The Literary Digest*, *Time* Magazine, *Vanity Fair*, *The New Yorker*, and other sources. Words wavered before her tired eyes as the car slowly ate up the miles. Mother and Daddy had given up trying to talk above its groans of protest. Talking in so strained an environment served to make Daddy cough worse. The dust swirled and eddied up around them. It had been silver back home, rather beautiful when the moon shone on it—if one could forgive its transgressions. Here, however, the dust was dull—dull and gray in a gray world, like poor, dear Lucy McMeal's hair. "Dear God, help her," Marvel whispered. "Speak to her heart. Tell her to take the hand You so graciously offer to us all."

Marvel's eyes then went back to her reading. And what she

read transported her back to the lonely man now in office on Capitol Hill....

Hoover, FDR was remembering, had tried. Give the man credit for that. But any effort he made met with criticism. Plugging away won him no thanks from the hopeless millions. He must have spent hours on the telephone picking brains and seeking support for this idea and that, as well as calling meeting after meeting of industrial and financial moguls. It was the latter habit which prompted the Baltimore *Evening Sun* to deride one such gathering as the then-president's "new panel of honorary pallbearers." And still the man at the top had to maintain a calm he didn't feel, something the public mistook for "square-jawed self-righteousness." Sad, wasn't it, that the nation's leader must leave office scorned and ignored by most Americans? And it was sad, too, that his administration was so bitterly blamed for the Great Depression that his very name became an adjective for all the manifestations of the blight. How would *he* be remembered? FDR wondered.

He, too, had broken dozens of pencil points drafting proposals in trying to live up to his campaign promises here, maintain a balanced budget, and keep exports and imports on an even keel. On the latter issue, the president shrewdly juggled words which, hopefully, would serve as a soothing syrup to both foreign countries and the masses who looked hopefully to him for solace. Dare he make mention of the growing tensions abroad which—God help him!—*could* lead to more than the heated exchange of words? War must be avoided at all costs. There was nothing political in that conviction, say what people might. And so his wastebasket bulged with wadded notes to himself, words of comfort, and a bravado he failed to feel on occasion. But there was no room in his fireside chats for doubts or wishy-washy attitudes.

Marvel could envision him, hunched over his desk massaging his withered legs and chewing on a cigar—its ivory holder upturned—as he pondered the State of the Union address. Did he ever light that foul thing? She'd heard that the cigar went unlighted because smoke made him cough the way dust affected her father. And, she thought warmly, it was to families like her own that the president longed to bring hope for a better future. It was sure to come....

She scanned the president's accomplishments excerpted from the magazines and became increasingly confident. The printed pages danced before her eyes.

"Never was there such a change in the transfer of a government. The president is the boss, the dynamo, the works," wrote Arthur Krock in *The New York Times*, March 12, 1933. Well—yes.

When Franklin D. Roosevelt was elected, the country was scared out of its wits—more scared than ever in its stormy history—and with just cause. For that very morning, March 4, 1933, every last bank in the nation had to close its doors. The old leaders must have been ashen-faced with alarm according to the recorded statement of Charles Schwab, chairman of Bethlehem Steel: "I'm afraid. Every man is afraid." Marvel sighed. People were still afraid. Stark fear was more clearly etched on the masses out here on the roads than back in Pleasant Knoll, which now seemed so far removed. Only their second day out and already the desperate situation was reflected—either in the hope of those "escaping" or in the defeat of those "going home to die." And there were miles and miles to go. *Oh Titus, do you know how far away I will be?* Marvel swallowed hard and then returned to reading an account of that morning in 1933.

> On the high inaugural platform in front of the Capitol, the 51-year-old president-elect repeated the oath of office in a clear, deliberate voice, looked over the tense crowd covering ten acres and said: "The nation asks for action, and action *now!*"

Follow-up articles told how the man, wondering how he could justify increasing the strength of the armed forces to a nation bordering on hysteria—clasped his strong hands over his head in the traditional salute of a champion. The morning after, the report continued, rolling a wheelchair as he had been compelled to do since he was crippled by polio 12 years before, Roosevelt moved into the Oval Office of presidents. There he sat alone for a few moments—eyes closed as if in prayer for strength and guidance. Then with a great shout he summoned his aides in preparation for calling a special session of Congress—*tomorrow!* His emergency banking bill, designed to strengthen the nation's financial system, roared through the House unchanged in just 38 minutes. And when the banks reopened—those which *could* reopen—four days later, deposits exceeded withdrawals. The immediate panic was over. The nation's confidence was beginning to return. *Oh, a light of hope....*

"I guess I'd heard all about this before, but it is advisable to refresh our memories. People tend to forget so quickly," Marvel would write to Titus tonight and pin her letter to the heap of tear sheets—that and a description of the changing scenes around her, for they *were* changing. A glance told her that. Had it rained here? There was more greenery—a strange blend of dark and light greens. It was heartening, but a second look said these were struggling evergreens and that the ground beneath gaped open in cracks, like thirsting lips pleading for water. There were more people traveling, too, here in the westernmost edge of the state. In El Paso they would cross into Arizona, parts of which would be under irrigation. There should be more employment for those in search of seasonal work. But "searching" they still were. The haggard faces gave a grim report.

Everywhere battered cars stood along the narrow shoulders of the graveled road. Owners, ragged and dirty, tried in vain to stop passing vehicles—some men standing dangerously on the road itself in their desperation for help, while their families waited. Pitiful, heartbreaking, *frightening*! One such family group surely would wrench the heart of the most unsympathetic. Certainly there must be something more fortunate travelers could do. If only Uncle Emory would stop! But, if anything, the lead car picked up speed. The "banker" in him, Marvel thought angrily as she looked back at the pathetically thin-bodied mother, face pale and empty-eyed beneath the snarl of wind-ravaged hair, trying to breast-feed an undernourished baby. Older children, parched by the merciless sun, stood by expressionless, having forgotten how to smile. But Emory Harrington did not look back.

"Don't ever be a banker, Daddy—not *ever*!" Marvel said fiercely.

"I never will!" Dale Harrington answered his daughter with equal fierceness. "I care too much."

"There's no such thing as caring too much," Mother reassured him. "But I guess Emory felt there's little we can do—"

"We can care—and tell them so, Snow! Oh, strike that! I'll not take out my frustration on *you*. I thought we all cared more back home—even—even my brothers, the bankers. I guess it was just a dream—"

"There's nothing wrong with dreams, Daddy—only you weren't dreaming," Marvel began, only to be interrupted by her mother.

"That's right, honey. We weren't so lonely then, and we hadn't seen—uh—all this. Just a few passing through. Which reminds me, I must write home tonight. How shall I begin, you two? 'Dear Mother and Father' doesn't sound—well, appropriate. 'Mother Riley' would cause her to smell a mouse—so?"

"Try 'Dearly beloved,'" Daddy suggested.

"Are you teasing, Dale?" Mother's eyes said she hoped so, and that he was snapping back after the horrors of the scene just past. "I mean, isn't that premature? Like I'm assuming—or do you think—"

"I do!"

Mother laughed, relieved. "You *are* teasing—playing with words."

The look he gave her warmed Marvel's heart, made her feel safe, comforted. Strange, wasn't it, how she could feel so protected by her parents' love and yet so protective of them? Maybe God's use of "honor" covered both meanings. For the millionth time, she renewed her vow to care for her parents. Daddy *would* be well again. She could trust God and the change of climate for healing his body and his spirit. The supreme sacrifice was made. Hard work and faith would do the rest. They would work, scrimp, save, and somehow put together enough money to be free of the clutches of evil that had overtaken their homeland—temporarily. Dale Harrington would reclaim it—no more despair over the brutality of nature. *God help me*, her heart whispered, and felt a sudden singing in its inner chambers. No banking—just love of the land.

"Hang onto that dream, Daddy. We'll go back!"

"Yes, we will, baby—even if we have to pry your mama away from whatever quarters she sets up for us. Just joshin', Snow, darling."

The smile that passed between them was one of understanding. They had cast a cursory glance at the past and put it behind. Now Daddy's "three bears" could approach the uncertain future with courage. Marvel hoped they had forgotten the sacrifice it required of her. Not that she regretted it. Never! It would work out—somehow. In her own private dream, the young girl in love busied herself with chiseling diamonds from ordinary coal— wishing poignantly that the process of change did not take some 4000 years.

In the car ahead, Emory Harrington would be setting his watch back one hour, his mind undoubtedly set ahead to when the timepiece would be the golden one of retirement from banking. In his less-ambitious brother's car, Snow Harrington was saying something frivolous like, "Let's sing!"

And sing they did, the three of them. Mother's throbbing voice chimed out the first line. Marvel and Dale Harrington following:

> Jesus included me, yes, He included me,
> When the Lord said, "Whosoever," Jesus included me,
>   too....

* * *

Emory Harrington had set the pattern the first night on the road. The cabins he found the following nights offered better accommodations. There were more from which to choose, none of them crowded. But he needed no suggestions, thank you, this Moses of the Exodus!

Uncle Alex had planned the route well. The map avoided unnecessary mountains and big cities. It included only a corner of New Mexico, and suddenly they were in Arizona. That meant another change of time. "Unbelievable!" Daddy said of crossing the two time zones in a single day. "At this rate, I'll cave in before lunch."

He didn't, of course. If only it could have been that simple, Marvel thought later, how very different life would have been. For it was in the state of Arizona that a frightening thing happened, followed by a disastrous one which would lead to drastic results— a nightmare from which one tries to awaken and is unable because it is stark reality. Road maps can be changed, but the map for people's lives?

Still, one does not expect the unexpected. And with only Daddy's stomach to worry about, Mother handed him one of Grandmother's buttermilk doughnuts, and Marvel went back to her research.

Sensing opportunity, FDR held the lawmakers in session, another article told her. In the next 100 days the man rode herd on an uneasy nation with a firmer rein than he had felt his cousin, Teddy Roosevelt, held. The story used an illustration from a 1934 "Vanity Fair," recording the people's pleasure. "A self-assured Rough Rider," the caption read, "This man could tame the country." The caricature distorted the president's features, donned him in chaps and boots, and set him astride a balking steed (a map of the United States, with the New England states as the lifted head).

At any rate, Franklin Delano Roosevelt altered the conduct of American life in his 15 messages streaming from the Capitol. When Congress adjourned on June 16, 14 new laws offered jobs to the unemployed...a promise to develop the backward Tennessee Valley...support crop prices...repeal prohibition... stop home foreclosure...insure bank deposits...stabilize the economy—and more.

There was so much to pick and choose from, Marvel thought in awe. But uneasily she noted through the car window the wind was gathering speed and visibility before them was blurred, flecked with dust. Darkness would be delayed with the changes in time—comforting, as that would put them across the stretch of desert indicated by Uncle Alex's map before dusk. But the uneasiness lingered as she concentrated on the magazines. Titus would digest it all. He was better trained.

FDR called his program a "New Deal," Marvel read on. Yes, it was all coming back to her now. And these writers agreed that his programs went much farther. "We have had our resolution," said *Collier's* magazine. "We like it." The poor lifted their heads again. Even the well-to-do were delighted—at first. Why not? Roosevelt had noted their plea for action—any kind of action.

Alf Landon, then the Kansas Republican governor, admitted that "even the iron hand of a dictator is in preference to a paralytic stroke of the economy." Pierre Du Pont, the industrialist of untold wealth, bent to send FDR a downright friendly letter. And press lord William Randolph Hearst flattered FDR with the words: "I guess at your next election we will make it unanimous!"

History had proven him right. When Alf Landon decided to pin a "sunflower button" on his lapel and run against the president, he was soundly defeated. But much was to happen beforehand....

Marvel remembered that nobody in the early thirties ever said he just guessed FDR was "doing okay." People either loved or hated him with a passion. Now she was reading that the mail brought him from 5000 to 8000 letters each day, some warmly personal. That would be a tenfold increase over Hoover days. These writers saw Roosevelt as a personal savior. But the other side of the coin tarnished quickly. The more prosperous citizens began to view him as the very devil. And then the nation's press, 85 percent anti-FDR, went to absurd lengths to hand the devil what-for. Well, love him or hate him, the nation was more aware of Franklin Delano Roosevelt than of any previous president. That awareness reflected in excerpts from letters Marvel found. Gems, all of them—gems for Titus Smith who, himself, would serve his country in the political arena one day. And she would stand beside him as—who knew?—maybe Mrs. Governor, she thought dreamily as she ripped out the precious pages.

Dear Mr. President: This is just to tell you that everything is all right now. The man you sent found our house all right, and we went down to the bank with him and the mortgage can go on for awhile longer. You remember I wrote you about losing the furniture too. Well, your man got it back for us. I just never heard of a president like you. . . .

My Dear Sir: It is expensive and a headache to have a playboy as president. Wipe that grin off your face. . . .

Dear President Roosevelt: I'm proud of our United States and every time I hear the "Star-Spangled Banner" I feel a lump in my throat. There ain't no other nation in the world that would have sense enough to think of WPA and all the other A's. . . .

Mr. President: If you could get around the country as I have and seen the distress forced upon the American people, you would throw your (censored) NRA and AAA, and every other (censored) *A* into the sea, before you and your crooked crowd are in Germany, and that is just what you and the rest deserve. You are not for the poor nor the middle class, but for the rich, the monopolies, Jewry, and perhaps Communism. . . .

Dear Honored Mr. Roosevelt: I never saw a president I feel I could write to until you've got in your place, but I have always felt like you and your wife and children were as common as we are....

Dear Pres. Roosevelt: How's our dandy little quarterback tonight? Our little "plan that wayer," eh? What's become of the "happy days are here again" boys? F Depression Roosevelt. They tell me that you have no brains or mind of your own—that you are just a "Charlie McCarthy" for a couple of smarties called Cohen and Cocoran or Kelly or something. That's a terrible blow—to find out that our big, noble savior of the common peepul is nothing but a wooden-headed stooge.... Yes, FDR spells your grade, not A but F!

There were more cheers and catcalls recorded in the magazine, but daylight *was* fading in spite of new clock-time. That served as a warning which Marvel heeded. Quickly she ripped out the sheet and laid it on top of the growing heap. Then, as she folded the sheets for storing away, the day's newspaper fell to the floorboard. There was something important within it, Mrs. McMeal had said, "Somethin' more for our pore pres'dent t'fret over. Now, ain't that somethin'?"

Yes it was "somethin'," Marvel realized as she hurriedly scanned the words under the heading: "Reporter Foresees Hitler's Rise to Power." "Reporting for the *New York Herald Tribune*, foreign correspondent John Elliott, wrote in 1931 that 'the specter of dictatorship menaces the German republic.' He describes Hitler, the rising dissident, as a 'finery crusader' and a 'magnetic orator' but also calls the Austrian-born Nazi leader a demagogue 'aspiring to be a citizen of the country he may someday hold in his hands.'"

Was such a thing possible? Marvel shuddered. Could this man's predictions come true? Numbly, she skimmed the paragraphs. Elliott wrote a chilling follow-up assessment predicting the rise of a new totalism. It would begin in Germany... Germany was destined to begin the dread regime. Yes, it would become a military state... Nazis' rigid control would spread *unless it was stopped*... NOW! Growing persecution of Jews... one official there calling for mass castration of Hebraic men (*Oh no*!)...leading to an "extermination policy" (*Oh, dear God, please no*!). Sickened but fascinated she read on that German police, according to "reliable sources," were ordering newsstand copies of such "propaganda" be seized. Not true? Before dismissing it with a shrug, the reporter begged, ask your conscience why this madman is so enraged... "I am *here*...I see it unfolding.... Be forewarned that he and his butchers will sweep Europe... execute... purge...."

Small wonder the man at the top was so upset. How lonely up there, trying to protect our shores but shielding an already terrified nation. How could the president remain undismayed, relax, and radiate confidence with that famous head-back smile? "Psychoanalyzed by God," declared one of his awed associates. Lonely, yes, as was the Great Physician. "Oh, how lonely God must feel sometimes," Marvel would write to Titus tonight. "Imagine weariness with a skeptical people—"

And how lonely this road had become! Marvel came back to the present with a jolt. A strange yellow-tinged gloom had swallowed the road ahead and the wind was shrieking above the labored breathing of the zigzagging car. Voices! Were her parents talking in this storm?

Ahead, a yellow light gleamed dimly like an evil eye. A warning—

"Stop! Oh darling, *stop*—" Mother screamed. "Try—we'll be killed. *Try*!"

"I *am* trying—brakes won't work—" Daddy panted. And then it was too late.

4

Deadly Crisis!

The flashing amber light disappeared. A red reflector replaced it as Dale Harrington gained control of the careening car. Had they or had they not seen something—a bulk beside the first light—and heard screams, seen another vehicle stalled and blocking traffic?

"What was it, Daddy?" Marvel asked breathlessly.

But already he was attempting to put the old Essex in reverse. "We'll see," he answered grimly, both hands gripping the wheel. "We can't leave people stranded—"

There were no people stranded—nobody in need of help except themselves. Marvel realized the sobering truth just as a uniformed figure loomed out of the blinding dust. A road block. And the angry face against the window belonged to an Arizona state policeman.

"Halt!"

Stopping was easier this time. Daddy had backed slowly, cautiously. He fumbled with the crank in an attempt to roll down the window. When the glass yielded slightly, the officer leaned inside to make himself heard.

"Why didn't you stop when ordered?"

"I'm sorry, sir—I—I didn't hear and—"

The officer remained annoyed but motioned them on with a warning that another brake check was just ahead. Brake check!

Marvel heard her mother gasp. "Oh—oh Dale! Oh darling, you made the right answer. If that man knew we couldn't stop—oh

33

darling—and because you cared about others—Oh, the light ahead!"

Yes, because he cared, Daddy had backed up—another good impression on the man who was obviously hardened by working against nature in a futile attempt to make driving safer for people too foolhardy or ignorant to know when a car ready for the junkyard would never make it under conditions like these. Out-of-state license, wouldn't you know? Well, wave him on through. Get him out of here so the driver behind could proceed. That figured, another Texan—four in a row. *"Move!"*

Stopping was easier now at their snail's pace. And their stopping would help Uncle Worth. Daddy clutched and pumped hard at the brakes, made it, and moved on. With more volume than talent, Daddy belted out the lyrics of "Praise God from Whom All Blessings Flow."

The narrow highway was virtually free of traffic now, but they'd lost sight of Uncle Emory. Mother was frantically checking the map. "Oh, watch out! There's a sharp turn, best I can tell—and what are those signs? 'Dips Ahead'!"

Under ordinary circumstances, the three of them would have laughed when the car hit the first one, causing them to gasp as one does when pushed too high on a swing. But there was no cause for amusement as the car faltered in its attempt to climb the slight incline leading from the dip. Daddy spotted the curve in the nick of time.

Daylight was fading fast. "Still no sign of Emory. What now?"

Dale Harrington had asked the question with a kind of desperation. His wife was quick to reply. "The highway drops into a wider valley if I'm reading this map right. Yes, that's it—but—uh—"

"What's wrong, Snow?"

Mother hesitated, her tired face filled with uncertainty. "There's an old road Alex marked 'shortcut,' but he wouldn't take that surely—"

"Emory would take it to save time—and gas."

"But, Dale—" Mother's faint protest fell on deaf ears. Daddy had turned—turned into the sand dunes, heaped and piled by the winds, and already shifting into new contours. And once on the treacherous road, there was no turning back, for the only visible route was covered by rough boards, lined like railroad tracks.

A capricious gust cleared the windshield for a split second. But the wind's force was so great Daddy came close to losing control. Fiercely he gripped the wheel in an effort to keep the car on the boards. Marvel held her breath in an effort to overcome the panic rising within her. There surely would have been a warning sign, but who could see through this curtain of dust? She wasn't even sure Uncle Worth would be following unless—*oh please, God!*—those dim, bobbing lights behind them were his headlights! They were, but—

"Oh Daddy! Stop—stop! It's Uncle Worth—and they've run off the road."

He stopped too abruptly, an action which caused the old Essex to swerve. There was a sickening whine of rubber against sand. They, too, had veered from the obscured road. The abruptness of the stop threw Mother against the windshield and Daddy was pinned to the steering wheel. Marvel felt herself hurled forward as if her body were in a somersault. None of them seemed capable of moving in their sudden state of shock. Marvel tried to lift her head, only to feel a dull ache which developed into a stabbing pain with effort. Her vision blurred and she saw the still forms of her parents at a crazy angle.

The car—why, the car had lurched sideways and would have turned over completely except for the steep embankment of the dune on the left. The impact brought down an avalanche of sand. Soon the entire car would be buried. *So the shortest distance between two points is not a straight line—not always*, she thought foolishly. *We should have stayed on the main road, Mr. Phillips—*

Geometry! Instead she should be thinking about an escape. Still in pain, but fully awake now, Marvel leaned forward to touch her parents.

"Daddy—Mother! We'll choke—be buried alive—we *have* to—Daddy! Wake up—We have to back up—get away from the dune!"

Daddy stirred. "What the—what happened? I—can't remember—"

"We've slipped off the boards. Hurry, Daddy—I'll check on Mother."

Still dazed, Daddy pressed his foot against the floor starter. There was no response. He tried again, calling all the while, "Are you all right, Snow—Marvel? Snow, say *something*—"

"Mother's coming to. It's nothing—"

Dale Harrington, reassured by his daughter's words, pressed against the starter—hard. The car must have felt his reassurance. It choked a halting response. Then mercifully the engine started with an explosive backfire. He shifted into reverse, accelerated, only to hear the tires spin futilely in their failing effort to gain traction. The engine sputtered an apology. And then it died completely.

"Can you open the door on the right, either of you? I'm hemmed in over here. Snow—oh, thank God you're okay—can you open—?"

Mother was saying something incoherent and Marvel saw in the dim light reflected by the car behind them—*Uncle Worth's?*—that mother's forehead was swollen and bruised. But there was no time to check further on her mother. Escape—they must escape! She managed to drag her aching body across the tilt of the seat, noting that it had loosened from the back, and grabbed the latch. It refused to budge. Frantically, Marvel tried to lower the window, hearing the glass crack as it opened slightly. Sand stung her face, blinding her. Hastily, she rolled the window back up. What were they going to do, hemmed in as they were, *prisoners*? Surely they couldn't be in as much danger as they thought. They *couldn't* be.

"Somebody will come along—or Emory will be back," Mother was trying to soothe. "Worth and Joseph—where are *they*?"

Daddy tried the starter again. "Well," and his voice sounded as dead as the engine, "we're about to become a statistic."

* * *

Behind them Worth Harrington was in even more desperate straits. His car had spun out of control, and in its downward spiral had slid into a ravine of loose sand. With nothing to break its fall, the vehicle's back wheels headed downward. And now it stood, front upturned, not unlike a bucking bronco, with hoofs raised high and imperfectly trained to complete its springing leap.

Thank goodness, the engine worked. But the worn tires could not gain momentum in the axle-deep sand. How had it happened? How, oh how could all the windows be shattered, the windshield completely gone, and the car's body crumpled like a closed accordion, without harming his family physically? Of course emotionally they were destroyed. His wife was on the verge of hysteria, an emotion foreign to her calm, acceptant nature—not because of concern for their daughter and son. But because of fear of what had happened to those she loved so dearly in the car ahead, once she saw her family was alive.

"What can we do to save them, sweetheart? They could be bleeding, dying, or killed already. How can we get there? *How*?"

The wind was less ferocious on this side of the elevated side road, and their voices were heard—every word—by Mary Ann. It was she who recounted the nightmare in progress to her cousin later.

"Billy Joe was whimpering. And when nobody took note, he set up a howl, 'I want to go home to my Gran'mere and my Gran'pa' They *love* me—' 'Oh, shut up!' I told him firmly. 'Uncle Worth, Aunt Snow, and Marvel loved you, too—and now they're trapped—and may be smothering—'"

Mary Ann would regret those words for the rest of her life, she said. And that was easy to understand in view of what happened.

The child, frightened by big sister's words, managed in the confusion to scramble over the front seat and crawl through the gaping hole once called a windshield.

His scream alerted the family. Then, somehow, although their clothing was ripped by jagged remains of the glass, their faces, arms and legs scratched, the remaining three squeezed through. Driven by blind fear, they lost all reason. And, untrained in survival in the desert, they separated, losing all sense of direction—lost ... hopelessly lost ... and on a night like this.

It was Marvel who heard a scream, or thought she did. "A human voice—I know it was. Keep the lights on, Daddy. Honk the horn—"

How much time passed? Was it minutes or was it hours? Time lost all meaning for all of them. And how on earth had the wanderers found a downward sweep of the dunes, crossed through, and followed the sound of the car's now-hoarse horn, seen its flickering light, indicating that the battery was gone completely now? Those were the questions posed by a disgruntled man who had spent a long, hard day rescuing people who were stupid enough to take this shortcut in a freak storm.

He shouldn't grumble, the driver of the snowplow-like wrecker admitted to his latest victims. Stupid people were his only source of income. Put money in his pockets—yes, they did. Lucky, just plain lucky the patrolmen suggested he take just one more look-see on his way in. Roadblocks were put up now.

"Just a coupla miles yonder's uh garage of sorts. I'll pull these wrecks in, and then you take 'er from there on. Wife and kids'll be worrying as it is. Git uh move on, fellers—don't stand there like you was shell-shocked or somethin'!"

With surprising expertise and curt barking of orders, the man hitched onto both cars. The strange episode remained blurred in the minds of the two families. Marvel remembered vaguely that, while the men helped wordlessly, the women and children formed a human chain with Mary Ann hugging Billy Joe as if she would never let go. Now he had the attention he'd coveted. He was a hero—a Superman, sure to be featured on the front of not one but several cereal boxes.

One glance convinced Marvel of the inadequacies of the mechanic on duty. But his friendliness made up for the lack of skill and tools. "You ladies'll find shelter from th' wind behind that wall. Welcome to use that—er, facility, too," the man said with a nod from beneath a greasy cap. "Now men, let's see how we can patch up one of these cars. My, my! They took a battering."

What choice was there but to take a wait-and-see attitude? Marvel hoped Daddy remembered to ask for an estimate. She shuddered, remembering what the towing-in had cost. Nobody talked. They simply waited. Experience had taught them that. The verdict was sobering, but no worse than expected. Uncle Worth's car was beyond repair. But the old Essex had come through fairly well—considering. Good constitution. Could do with a new inner tube—and he just happened to have one. He looked hopeful, but Uncle Worth produced a patching kit. "About all I salvaged, far as the car goes."

"Sure is," the mechanic admitted, wiping his blackened hands. "I had to replace your battery in the Essex, mister, but she runs like a top. At least, she'll get you folks on into town."

How far? Walkin' distance in decent weather. "But on a night like this—" He hesitated, then seemed to reach a decision. "You, mister (meaning Daddy) can go ahead. Try it, but I'm guessin' that lizzie'll get you no farther—least, till that engine's cleaned. You folks from th' Dust Bowl, likely. Seen it hard, huh?"

Their numbed nods convinced him. "Rest of you pile into my truck yonder and I'll take you in. Leave your belongings—I live in back. Ain't likely there'll be thieves roamin' tonight anyhow."

His tone discouraged discussion. They offered none.

* * *

Ironically, they'd been at the very outskirts of Yuma.

"We *could* have walked, left both cars, not put you out like this," Daddy said regretfully. "Saving ourselves a little money," he added under his breath, as he groped for his billfold.

"No charge," their Good Samaritan said after scrutinizing the tense, white faces, "exceptin' for what it cost me—wholesale!"

"But the lift into town—we're not beggars," Uncle Worth hastened to say. He, too, withdrew a near-flat purse.

"I never thought that. My pleasure—just pass the favor on. Somebody meetin' you here?"

Somebody was. Both Emory and Joseph Harrington loomed out of nowhere, just as the dim lights had appeared suddenly around the curve from the service station. The mechanic saw, saluted, and drove away.

Uncle Emory made no effort to hid his displeasure. "How could you have missed my signal?"

"We were detained, and then I was disoriented," Daddy confessed. But Marvel was glad his voice was not apologetic.

Uncle Joseph's face showed disgust, but it did not reflect in his voice. "It *can* happen (to less intelligent people, he might as well as added), but how—? Hey, wait a minute—where's *your* car, Worth?"

The mood of both brothers altered slightly after hearing the story. They'd sleep on it. Meantime, yes, *of course* arrangements were made for tonight's shelter.

Billy Joe sidled up to Monica. "We'll probably buy a new one. Then *we* will be the lead car." Monica was impressed, so he'd better leave the conversation and be ahead. "Hey, look at that sign—says 'Free Gas on Rainy Days!' We can fill up tomorrow."

"Silly!" Billy Joe's same-age cousin hissed. "It *never* rains here." Then in her recently conducted wisdom, she cinched matters. "I don't believe in signs. I don't believe about that new car, either!"

* * *

The sound of a knock on the door awakened Marvel early the next morning. The wind had stopped, she thought, as she picked her way through the crowded quarters of the tourist cabin to determine the identity of the caller. Immediately she recognized the owner of the so-called "inn" silhouetted against a crimson sunrise.

"Daddy, wake up! Someone's waiting. Clear skies, no free gas!"

The owner told an amazing story. His friend the mechanic told him about the accident and he'd taken the liberty of driving out already. By special arrangement, the owner could assess the value, make an offer for a local garage. Yes, he was prepared—

In the end, Uncle Worth accepted the offer, shaking his head in perplexity that he had an offer at all. Just what next they would do, God alone knew. And He *must* have known, Mary Ann said, with a toss of her shining, black curls. Else how could they have been so fortunate?

Fortunate, indeed. Uncle Worth found a pickup of sorts costing little more than the parts had brought. Daddy helped him pack their belongings onto the bed and haul them back into Yuma.

There was no guarantee on the secondhand vehicle (more like a sixthhand, Uncle Worth said). But there were some words of wisdom.

"It's running, as you can see, but I'd advise you to cut across into California. You're near the state line. You'll be out of the desert—well, this *kind* of desert, find more services along the way—"

Daddy gasped at the words. "But—but we're on our way to Oregon—"

"Forget it! That crate would never make it over the mountains. You'd find yourself stranded. Familiar with *Tobacco Road*?"

All too familiar. Marvel felt trapped—trapped and helpless. This time there would be no decisions. There was nothing she could do to help her parents. Why then were their eyes seeking hers?

"We wanted to avoid California—most of it, the cities," Mother said in a low, wretched voice.

"And we will," Daddy promised. "There's nothing there for us."

The other Harringtons had busied themselves with packing and repacking, checking the maps and the time. Marvel found herself wondering if they had been aware of the decisions in progress. That was how it sounded when Daddy and Uncle Worth, after caucusing, announced that, of necessity, they must change their plans.

"Change plans? Are you out of your mind?" Uncle Emory spat out.

"Somewhat, but what would you suggest?" Daddy countered.

The two older brothers surveyed the situation. Then calculatingly, as if assessing qualifications of a man seeking a loan, they agreed. But they would be compelled to go on. Dale and Worth did understand? Of course. It was to be expected.

Dorthea Harrington cast a relieved glance at her husband. Erin, Lucinda, and Monica must have the best schools available. Alex, Jr. had recommended—what was that school of law? Oh yes, Willamette—private and expensive, but promising a wide variety of professional courses and up-and-coming young men. The two older girls would be ready by next fall, take a light load, and prepare themselves for high society where they belonged. Women had no need for careers, just proper husbands. Clever lawyers would fill the bill. Eleanore would share her feelings. Or would she and Joseph prefer the University of Oregon? The institution did offer ROTC.

Marvel and Mary Ann watched their aunts' exchange of glances. "I could read them like a book," Mary Ann was to say later. "Snobs, both of them—prim, money-proud, and on the lookout for ambitious dupes with fat bank accounts! Shallow—whoo-*ee*!!"

"Well," Marvel shrugged, "let them *hop* to it."

Good for a laugh. Uncle Alex had done well with the hop yard as well as with his other business ventures. Admittedly, the eldest of the Harrington brothers had a King Midas touch—a talent seemingly possessed by both Jake's Uncle Russ and Clarinda Thorpe—wasn't Thorpe the last name of the man their one-time teacher had married? Would Uncle Emory and Uncle Joseph do as well?

"Oh, Erin!" the cousin's mother was scolding. "I *told* you to be careful! You've broken a fingernail."

Erin had broken a fingernail, while our cars and our bodies are bruised and battered, Marvel thought in exasperation.

Mary Ann saw and understood. "Never mind, honey. 'Parting is such sweet sorrow'—isn't that how Shakespeare put it?"

"Close enough. They just don't *feel*."

"Sometimes I wish I didn't," Mary Ann said, "I'm lonely—"

"For *them*?" Billy Joe asked in surprise. "They're nothing but sillies, even Monica. I'm three months older and a lot smarter, but she won't listen. Oh, I know, you're lonesome for Jake, huh, Mary Ann? But he's comin'!"

"Jake's coming? He told you that? When?"

"Night before we left," Billy Joe said with a smirk.

His sister was in no mood for his stalling. "You tell me or—or I'll take you back to those dunes. When's Jake *coming*?"

His big eyes widened momentarily, then narrowed. "Soon as he makes his first million. He'll buy a big car we can all ride in and—"

"The dunes," Mary Ann reminded. "You'd like being *left* there?"

Maybe he'd better not chance it. "He's comin' even if he hasta swing a freight train. That's what he said, Mary Ann—honest. And you'll keep me close, so I'll not wander off, remember? You promised."

"Pest!" Mary Ann said. But she reached out and gathered him close. Her eyes were shining—so were Billy Joe's. He loved being a "pest."

Mary Ann wanted the whole world to be happy now. When was Titus coming? What did Marvel mean they had no specific plans? They could have a double ceremony and—honeymoon in a boxcar? Marvel asked.

She was relieved with the scramble said that good-byes were in progress. There were promises of letters—yes, as soon as they had addresses. Meantime, there was Alex Jr.'s address. There was a bad moment when Uncle Emory offered a few dollars—an offer Daddy and Uncle Worth promptly refused.

And then they were gone. Dale and Worth Harrington faced their hard decisions alone. No, not alone—with their families, *and with God*. He would lead. Their loved ones would follow....

5

The Road to Nowhere

"Which way?" Daddy asked to no one in particular.

He and Uncle Worth had experienced little difficulty in loading the dilapidated truck. Auntie Rae had never been one to toss in unnecessaries to roll around in disarray. Everything was boxed, labeled, and stacked. Marvel admired that and took note of one box in particular. "Quilts," the lettering said. The word took her back to the coverlet presented to Mother, Daddy, and herself the memorable night neighbors surprised them with a "going-away" present. Their departure had come too suddenly for the top to be quilted, but it bore embroidered names of the donors, bless them all. Oh, she mustn't dwell on that. It was too painful. Yes, they would return. But that dream diminished in size with the distance. And each turn of the wheels would take them farther and farther away on a meaningless road that led to nowhere.

Yes, repacking their belongings had been easy. The decision before them was harder, more challenging. "I—I just don't know," Uncle Worth said uncertainly. The two men turned once more to the map of California that the service station attendant had given them.

"Can that be?" Mother gasped, spotting a roadside fruit stand with a sign saying, "Large Arizona grapefruit, one cent each. Buy here!"

The plump, golden fruit smelled of sunshine, promising ripe goodness. Mother and Auntie Rae filled a sack excitedly. Then, laughing as if it were a joke, they counted pennies cautiously. Such a small matter, but big enough to determine their route—and their destiny. Why not? Yes, why not head toward orchard country, indulge their wives, and—well, look around? When their families returned from the "wild shopping spree," the men had reached the decision. Salton Sea? Yes, low elevation.

Marvel had taken a picture of the sign at the roadside stand and posted two letters, one to Titus and the other to Editor Corey. Mary Ann mailed a picture postcard to Jake, and Mother stuffed a fat letter to Grandmother into the chute at the post office. It took little time, but in it Marvel's trained ears picked up the sounds of fluently spoken Spanish. She supposed then that the presence of so many Mexican men was due to the proximity to the United States-Mexican border. Later she was to learn these were laborers.

The drivers were eager to get underway. Daddy and Uncle Worth had planned tonight's destination. They could make better time now. The mechanic had adjusted the timing on both cars. But there was no way to set the timing for the sudden, unexpected delay ahead.

Just after leaving the city limits, there was another flash of yellow lights. "Oh no!" Daddy gasped, slowing quickly to a stop.

"Checking station!" A squat, uniformed man, sharp of eye and voice, informed them curtly. "Step out of the car please—*all* of you!"

"I don't understand," Daddy said. "We were checked—"

"Open the lid please, and the suitcases. Ladies, leave those handbags! I'll need to go through those boxes, so untie the ropes."

The search took over an hour. A man in a waiting car explained everything to Daddy. Entering Arizona was one thing; entering California, quite another. Just looking for folks to pick on, that's what, the disillusioned man said. As for him and his brood, they would be heading back to God's country, that's what. Yeah, he was headed for home. Shucks, so what if spuds cost just two cents a pound—onions, three! His old lady could grow them free in Kansas if it rained—and it was sure to. Preacher-man said so. Wished he'd listened, that's what. But some wag up and told him tall tales. Wanting to hold the land, he'd been silly as a gander in a flood, turned up his nose, drowned in lies.

"My man's right, sure enough," his wife told Mother and Auntie Rae. "We ain't able t'pay what's agin' th' land, but this robbin', thievin' hell-hole learnt us sum'pin', sure enough. Iffen them feds come tryin' t'take our farm, we're a-gonna fight. Ruther be kilt outright than give uh inch. We may die uv starvation, iffen that preacher-man *ain't* right. But afore we die, we're a-gonna set fire to what crops we got. P'izen th' cows, too. We got ourse'ves a shotgun—"

Marvel tried listening to both conversations at once. "What are they after here?" Daddy asked the other man anxiously.

"Ah-h-h, ever'thang, pilgrim. Ever'thang y'all got—"

"Cotton!" the inspector barked. Marvel heard her mother's gasp when the man slit the "Dutch boy" quilt Grandmother had made. "This will have to go. Let's see the others. Make that all of them! Plant life, fruit—have to guard against disease of our precious fruit trees. Citrus fruit—Here, grapefruit! No way. I'll take these, too!"

That was too much for Billy Joe. "You can't have them. That's stealing and that's breaking a commandment! The Bible—"

Auntie Rae rushed from the truck, turning her ankle in the leap, and pulled him back. If the inspector heard, he was unimpressed.

When the ordeal was over, the Harringtons had lost all their food and most of their bedding. White-faced and speechless, the four parents stood as if dazed, having parked just beyond the station.

"What'll we do?" Mary Ann whispered desperately.

"We," Marvel said slowly, "must *not* give in to fear. We *can't.* We—we can't be the storm. We have to be their port!"

Numbly, Mary Ann followed her to their parents. "Let's go. We don't need cover here—and this is the land of fruit, remember?" Marvel began.

" 'Sail on—sail on and on—', isn't that what Columbus said to his men? I can't wait to see this state. It's *beautiful!*"

There was a catch in Mary Ann's voice, but her parents did not hear. "God bless you both," Daddy said. And they reentered their cars. "So, Mrs. Navigator, let's 'sail on' to the Salton Sea."

The sea stretched on for miles like a fallen sky. The land was barren, uncultivated and uninhabited. But skies arched overhead, brilliantly blue and uncluttered by clouds. The air was dry, without dust or moisture. And Dale Harrington had ceased coughing!

Marvel was relieved when a small oasis appeared in the distance. A cluster of palms seemingly reached leafy crowns to brush the sky with their 15-foot, jade-green leaves. In the palms' midst stood a quaint thatched hut, inviting guests with the sign: "Valerie Jean's Date Shop." If Daddy would only stop. He did.

Inside a pale-faced lady welcomed the travelers with a warm smile. Seeming eager to talk, obviously hungry for company in these lonely surroundings, she answered questions and volunteered other information.

"You folks must wonder what a woman alone is doing out here. Well, I'm not alone, not exactly. I have a sick husband—at least, he *was*. But this dry climate has healed his lungs completely. I like to think of him as healed. I guess tuberculosis isn't *cured*, just arrested—"

"Arrested!" Billy Joe interrupted. "They arrest *sickness* here?"

Mary Ann was embarrassed, but the lady smiled. "Sort of. I think you'd like one of these, sonny." She handed him a dried date. "Are you folks looking for work? Most traveling this way are. Something seasonal like picking fruit? You don't look—well, like most. Uh, no offense, but they're called fruit tramps—"

"We are not fruit tramps!" Uncle Worth said defensively.

"Oh no—I knew that at a glance. It's unfair anyway. But," she sighed, "life's not always fair. I—I've had my struggles, believe me. Leaving the big-city life, coming here as the doctors ordered. But I found no welcoming committee, so I know how you feel. I wish I could offer you employment, but I have two Mexicans willing to climb those steep ladders. See how they're nailed to the rough bark at dizzying heights to propagate and harvest the fruit? I'm unable to pay—just feed the men. But any day they can move on, leave me stranded. No, I'm afraid there's nothing here, but I'll tell you where—"

Feeling far away and a little frightened, Marvel idly picked up a pamphlet devoted to dates. Fumbling through it while the concerned lady offered suggestions (even sketching a map), directing the two families to more prospective areas nearby, Marvel pretended the pamphlet was one of utmost importance. It was, she discovered.

"Dates," she read, "are no longer found wild today. Their original home was near Mesopotamia, dating back to biblical

times...probably grown by Babylonians some 8000 years ago."
She began jotting notes:

> ...cultivated in North Africa, Egypt, Syria, Iraq,
> Queenland (Australia), and North India...now in
> United States...principally Coachella Valley of Cali-
> fornia (here!). Good production where summers are
> hot and dry...but drink 100 gallons per tree...irriga-
> tion or oasis essential...must keep "head dry and
> feet wet." Used symbolic of Palm Sunday and the
> Passover...propagation by seed impossible....

Now in control, Marvel skipped through uses of date palms
other than for food. The others were preparing to leave as their
hostess (Was *she* Valerie Jean?) was sacking a small amount of
fruit—very small, but what could one expect for a dime? More,
she found out, as the thoughtful woman handed Billy Joe an
additional large sack of "culls."

> Male and female flowers borne on separate trees
> ...male must be near female...wind unreliable...
> female clusters of yellowish blossoms either tied to
> male...or must be hand-pollenized as in California
> ...mortality rate high if offshoots transplanted...
> whereas, above method gives likelihood of 100 years
> of production....

"You needn't take notes," the woman said. "Take a handful of
the pamphlets. And here's today's newspapers, too—"
Marvel smiled at a cartoon on the front page. It featured the
wild-eyed Adolph Hitler as a toilet brush, hair springing from his
scalp in tufted bristles. A caption read, "The Fuehrer Brush
Man." Luce McMeal would appreciate the caricature. "God bless
you," Marvel said, as she'd said to Mrs. McMeal. "I see my family
has gone, so—"
But the woman detained her. "I *thought* you were Christian. No
churches around and I have a niggling problem—trouble han-
dling Matthew's ruling out the possibility that everybody'll be
saved. Chronicles tells it differently—sounds like everybody
will. I don't know—"

48

"I don't know either," Marvel said slowly. "We have the promise of God's mercy and love—and *hope*! Hoping the majority will be saved is better than hoping it won't." The woman's face lighted as Marvel rushed out.

Daddy and Uncle Worth had debated over the map. Redlands—there would be a high school. Yes, but work? Well, Riverside? Maybe, but to be sure San Bernardino looked promising for both...railroad center.

"San Bernardino, here we come," Daddy said. "All roads lead to a Somewhere—always ahead there's the promise of the road!"

Yes, the road led somewhere. In this case, nowhere would have been better. But for now Marvel said, "God will never lead us from His reach."

6

The Lost Colony

It was in San Bernardino that they met Tansy Gordon.

Darkness had fallen when the Harringtons—tired, weary, hungry, and afraid to use the yardstick-measure to check either vehicle's gasoline supply—saw the lights of the city. All breathed a wordless sigh of relief after the endless parade of warning signs: "Sharp Curve. Honk Your Horn!"... "No Accommodations"... "Next Gas 50 Miles"!

"That one concerns me," Daddy said. "We have to be low—"

"Oh, piffle!" Mother had brushed the idea aside as if fuel were but a trifle. "Remember what happened when I bought all that grapefruit?"

Dale Harrington had made no reply. But relief spread over his face at sight of "Willie's Filling Station" He made a left arm signal and turned in, stopping to wait for his brother. The two talked and checked their billfolds. Marvel shared her father's relief when he inched the Essex closer to the pump. His brother pulled in behind them.

As Willie filled the gas tanks, he answered questions. Lodging in back. Cabins generally went for two dollars, but he would settle for a buck and a half if the seven of them wanted to bunk together. When the men hesitated, he said, "Got a good garden in back, more than my family can do away with—good garden country. I'll share if you want."

They wanted! Mother and Auntie Rae exchanged excited glances.

School? Sure—elementary school just three blocks north. Good high school not too far past. All overcrowded, lots of new people.

As to work, word had it that there might be something where the road construction was underway across town. Otherwise, try the groves....

Marvel and Mary Ann had listened with interest—as had another girl, they realized suddenly. Marvel was struck by the beautiful face before them. The girl was young, about the age the two of them were, she thought—middle or late teens. The red-brown hair framing her creamy face waved in thick skeins to reveal large green eyes opened wide like those of a lost, frightened child. She looked vulnerable, hurt.

"I'm Tansy," the girl said in soft, musical tones, "and I—I'm stranded. Oh, I do hope you're goin' to Hollywood. Both of you look like stars. I play the guitar and Grandmammy says I'm headin' for instant success if I can just get there. I promised her I'd do anything—*anything*—and I will if you're willin' to let me ride—"

Marvel was touched. It was hard to tell Tansy they would be remaining here instead. But they *would* talk to her? the other girl pleaded.

Her full name was Tansy Gordon, she volunteered as, without invitation, the girl helped them unload. Tansy lived with an elderly grandmother who had sacrificed her life savings for this trip to Hollywood. Nibbling freely on the dates, again without invitation, Tansy Gordon commented from time to time that they must have been born rich. "Me—I was born poor as a church mouse. But that'll change in the movies."

Only once was there a problem. "I've never seen such a violin—"

"Don't touch that—please! It belongs to my mother," Marvel said.

She studied the priceless instrument thoughtfully with an unreadable expression before continuing her story. "Ever hear about the lost colony that just disappeared without a trace?"

"Only in legendary accounts," Marvel answered thoughtfully. "Back in the fourteenth century, I believe. You're saying it's true?"

Oh, it was true all right. It had been Grandmammy's birthplace—a little island fishing community on the banks of the

Atlantic, just a piece from North Carolina's mainland. Most never heard of the place—sort of stayed to themselves all these generations—

"If your story's true—" Mary Ann said a little doubtfully.

"It is, cross my heart. And you'll be hearin' more on it when I make my mark. Grandmammy has pieces of glass that'd make your eyes bug out. Says more's buried thereabouts. I've got some I'd sell. I'll bring it—it's in the boxcar down on the tracks with my guitar—"

"*Boxcar!*" Billy Joe dropped a kitchen utensil with a clatter.

Tansy preferred not to dwell on that, saying only that there were nice people there. They even asked her to go along tomorrow when loading of fruits and vegetables was finished—lots of hoboes, down on their luck, but nice. She shifted quickly back to the lost colony she claimed to be a part of: peaceful back in the 1500s till food got short . . . Indians stopped sharing . . . root of the trouble between colonists and Indians. The girl had her story straight, so there seemed no need to doubt her. Still, the lost colony? It seemed so unlikely.

And it was. The next morning the men's billfolds were gone.

"We should have listened to Emory, after all!" Uncle Worth said angrily. "Look what trusting strangers can do—rob us of—of hope!"

Daddy was equally grim. "Yep. Lost colony, my heel! *We're* the lost colony. Lost our senses—and every red cent between us and starvation. So what do we do now—wait for archaeologists to come dig us out?"

* * *

Standing before the principal the next morning, Marvel felt an overwhelming déjà vu. She must impress this preoccupied woman in the few minutes allowed her. One hearing was all there would be.

It had been important in Pleasant Knoll, urgent in Culverville. Here it was *critical*. Deep in the heart of Texas, they had been among friends, people who cared. Now, in San Bernardino, California, they were alone, stranded among strangers who, she was beginning to find, for the most part wouldn't share the time of day.

Stay calm, Marvel willed herself. God would apprehend desperation, bent though it was on breaking and entering.

"You just came into town, yet expect to graduate this year!"

"Yes, ma'am—yes, I do."

Something in this girl's tone of voice caused Ellen Welch to look up over her frameless glasses. Never before during her 25 years in education had she heard such grim determination in the voice of so young a student. Undeniably she was impressed, but in *six weeks*?

"I'm sorry," the principal said briskly. "There should be exceptions—courses of study designed for migratories—"

"I am not a migratory. Neither do I need a special course of study—just an opportunity. If you will look at my records—"

Mrs. Welch sighed. "Time won't allow. Admittedly, I'm too busy—"

"Then I will help you!"

Marvel had her full attention now. "Yes, you heard right," she rushed on. "I'm accustomed to working hard. School is easier for me than for some. And besides, I welcome challenge! Please Mrs. Welch, just one look at my records. I won't disappoint you, I promise."

"You leave me little choice," the woman said, looking at her for a moment, then reaching for the sheath of documents. Marvel saw the eyes behind the unadorned glasses widen. "Office work...teacher's assistant...newspaper reporter...extracurricular...church work. My word! All this and more while carrying such heavy a load in school, and you managed to make the honor roll, be a likely candidate for *valedictorian*! Then—then all these scholarship offers! That's unbelievable. Tell me, Marvel Harrington," she leaned forward to look deep into those widely spaced, blue-blue eyes, "what made you leave?"

"Circumstances."

"I can't believe what I'm reading, seeing—hearing," the woman murmured, drawing back to her former position. "Yes, I can use you. I see you have a camera. We're behind on the yearbook. Teachers need help with their registers. I need help in the office. Not much pay, but a little—textbooks and school supplies furnished in California. Meantime, I'll have to check. Not that I doubt your word, understand—"

"I understand." Marvel rose and stood erect, her rounded chin lifted, in an effort to repress the urge to sing. She had made it!

What's more, she would receive money—money she dared not refuse.

"Come back tomorrow, Marvel. We're overcrowded, but I'll find a way to work you in. And I can't help saying you're unusual, special!"

Unable to trust her voice, Marvel smiled, then hurried out, almost colliding with a frightened-looking girl. Her dusky loveliness spoke of Spanish blood. Another new student? Probably. Marvel took a chance and greeted her in Spanish. The reward was a brilliant smile.

At her desk, Ellen Welch shook her head in wonder. So this Marvel Harrington—whoever she was—could speak Spanish in addition to all other achievements. What a godsend! Each day brought a wave of here-today-gone-tomorrow Mexican children, offspring of transient laborers, and schools were unprepared—another job for the girl she had almost turned away....

Just wait until I tell Mary Ann! But it was Mary Ann who did the telling. Marvel found her cousin pacing back and forth, impatient in her waiting. Oh Marvel, she'd struck it rich! Admitted without question...landed a job...a teacher of sorts...helping students— Could Marvel *believe* students couldn't read in high school? Mary Ann supposed it was because they never stayed in one place long enough...and teachers just kind of gave up... reckon? But wait, there was more.

"Oh Marvel, I'll be paid—did you hear, *paid*? Won't mother and Daddy be pleased? And on top of it all, wow! You can skip the junior and senior years here—just take a test and go into junior college! Sorry 'bout that, but I'll be ahead of *you* for once!" Mary Ann gloated.

Let her gloat, Marvel thought happily. The mood was a far cry from Mary Ann's usual self. A far cry, too, from their morning's conversation. Both girls had shared their parents' feelings of desperation and exasperation at being "suckered in," as Uncle Worth called the encounter with Tansy Gordon. But there was one thing she had seen more clearly, Mary Ann had said: the need for helping her mother and father. And (reluctantly) she guessed that meant more schooling. But in the meantime, what? A day at a time, Marvel had said haltingly.

Billy Joe had found his way to the tourist cabin alone. School was a drag. He knew more than that stupid teacher and told her so. She didn't like his attitude she told him . . . "And I don't like your *smell*, you're choking me!" he told her . . . That zombie said it was perfume. *"Perfume?* You mean you smell like that on *purpose!"* She threatened to . . .

"Leave it to him to make a favorable impression!" But Mary Ann was repressing a giggle. Her face sobered at sight of the loaded cars.

They were leaving? Again? "Oh no, please Lord," Marvel gasped.

Moments later the two girls were hemmed in by parents, the four of them talking at once. Both men had jobs with the construction company—not much, just serving as temporary flagmen some three or four days. The regulars were injured when a truck ignored the barricade. Same accident damaged flashing-light warnings. Campsites furnished, and just take a gander at the vegetables! The women had stocked up well.

Marvel couldn't believe her eyes. Snow Harrington was smiling—actually smiling. Against that pale apricot skin—inherited from the Mier side, Grandmother said—her eyes glowed like jewels.

"My covered-wagon days weren't for naught," Mother said, her voice sparkling like her eyes. "I can make the tastiest vegetable stew in that black dinner pot—some relic, but Mother was right in putting it in. Rae'll make drop biscuits. You do remember how?"

"I certainly do," Auntie Rae laughed, with a toss of her dark hair, so characteristic of her daughter. And for a moment she looked as young. "Learned that in the orphanage. There *is* a barbecue pit?"

The mood was festive. Gone was the morning gloom. Except—

"Be a little guarded, like Emory said," Uncle Worth cautioned.

On the way to their new quarters, Marvel would have preferred time to examine her feelings, sort them out, find a way to cope with these alien surroundings. But Mary Ann, who had wedged herself into the backseat of the old Essex, had other ideas.

"I wish Daddy would stop talking about Uncle Emory. He reminds me more and more of that—that awful person, you know, Frederick Salsburg. Are you sure they weren't brothers, Marvel?"

"Uncle Emory's a brother to our fathers. Uncle Fred was a stepbrother. That shouldn't bother you."

Mary Ann shrugged. "Have it your way. You should know—you—why," she shuddered before going on, "you were with him when he died! Oh, it had to be awful. And that terrible fixation Fat Elmer had. He was dangerous. I hope you never hear from him again. You don't, do you?" A look of sheer panic passed over Mary Ann's lovely face.

"I haven't heard recently, but I must get in touch. I promised Uncle Fred, but it has nothing to do with you. Don't think about it if it upsets you, Mary Ann. As for my being there, no it wasn't awful—not awful at all. It was rather beautiful. Oh, I guess we've arrived. The place looks clean. I guess we sleep in those tents?"

Marvel guessed right. But it was only temporary, Daddy hastened to assure her. Then with a frown, "like the work," he added. "I—I guess nothing's guaranteed—" he twirled the car keys in concentration.

"Stars die, and stars are born; suns burn out, and new suns emerge" Marvel murmured, remembering having read that. "Does anything in the universe endure forever?"

"Well?" Daddy looked straight at her. "Does it?"

"Yes," Marvel answered in a steady voice. "God's love."

* * *

In the next few days, the lost colony of Harringtons adapted, each in his or her own way. The life they were living was not what any of them wanted, but there was no choice—temporarily. Marvel alternated between the hope of tomorrow and the hopelessness of today. She had never known she possessed so much of either. She didn't fit in here—never had, never would. But she must pull herself together, force it, fake it, do whatever it took to face the *now* of it. Others were depending on her in a growing number. That included the teachers now.

With a sadness that threatened to overwhelm her, she wrote to Titus, making no mention of the sorry surroundings and concentrating on the agricultural productivity. Of course, farmers all relied on irrigation here, but it pointed up something both of them knew: what water could do for an otherwise arid region. Tucking in a sheath of clippings, she licked the glue on the envelope's flap and secured it, then opened it before it could seal. "Oh Titus, I miss you—miss you and love you! I resent the miles and the years that separate us. But each day shortens them—as we work toward fulfillment. . . ."

Marvel slipped away from camp alone to the corner mailbox. Ignoring the whistles of male bystanders, she kept her eyes riveted on the horizon where the sun was lowering. The sky softened to a lilac-pink, streaked by fingers of vivid rose. How lovely! The soft breeze was Titus' gentle fingers stroking the curve of her cheek, pushing her hair from her face to capture radiance in the fading light, then—with something akin to reverence—gently brushing the curls at her forehead with his sensitive lips. She was his angel, his impossible dream—*for now*. But for now there was stark reality. "Someday" lay ahead.

With renewed courage, Marvel prepared reports for Editor Corey, wrote a quick note to Kate Lynn as she had promised Dr. Porter, and another to the institution where Elmer Salsburg was a patient. Then she attacked her schoolwork. She must graduate. She *must*.

Both cousins were revelations to their teachers and the principal. There was no time for socializing and the girls, after looking around, felt no sacrifice in that. Mary Ann experienced only one real difficulty: concern over a required paper she must write to qualify for possible entry into junior college the following year. What did she know about *local industry*?

"Never fear for I am here!" Marvel laughed and handed her the pamphlet brought along from Valerie Jean's Date Shop. "All but done for you—and I want to include the data in one of my columns back home."

The columns! It occurred to Marvel then that she'd given Titus no address, no means of contacting her. But "General Delivery" sounded so *transient*—a bad word here, another dragon with claws and teeth and an appetite for the human flesh and spirit. But true love must endure, be brave, face the wrath of those hungry dragons—if it hoped to conquer. And conquer she would. Yes, with God's help. He understood that anything clean and purposeful would have its foes.

And so she would take pictures and write articles about this tent city marked "Blaire & D'Agosto Construction." Their dwelling in the place had nothing to do with the account.

Mother wrote to Grandmother. Auntie Rae wrote to Aunt Eleanore. And both gave "General Delivery" without explaining. A fine arrangement, as the temporary jobs extended well beyond the expected "three or four days." In fact, the Harringtons were able to organize a little prayer group in which Marvel felt peace return to her bleeding heart. Neither she nor Mary Ann could help, of course. School demanded their every moment...school—and Billy Joe.

For a time, B.J.—as he insisted on being called again—was indeed the pest his sister had named him in jest. Mary Ann, seeing Auntie Rae's frustration, took full charge. He became too much for her, too. "Marvel, I need help. My school work will suffer—"

Billy Joe caught up with them. Usually he lagged behind on the way to school. "Talking about me, I can tell. So does *she!*"

"Your teacher, B.J.? Doesn't she have a name?" Marvel queried.

Kicking sand with a worn shoe, he looked thoughtful. Miss Dragness—only they spell it wrong. Should be Miss *Dragon*—only I don't call her that."

"I would hope not."

"You see, it's because she likes me now—*really* likes me. Says if things keep on, she'll just have to keep me another year!"

Marvel looked at the child gravely. "We may not be here."

The words stung her tongue, her heart, her very soul. She saw Mary Ann wince, while the lad for whom the words were intended darted away without hearing—or so the two girls supposed.

However, B.J. proved them wrong. He and Miss Dragness—stupid name, but he did *not* want to get stuck with her again—had called a truce. Yep, he up and told her they would be leaving....

"Billy Joe, you *didn't!*" Mary Ann gasped. Her voice said *smart aleck.*

"*B.J.*," he corrected. "And I did. I told her all about our rich uncle in Oregon—about the hops and the grass-eatin' geese, sayin' they laid golden eggs. And she swallowed it—the story, I mean, finally. At first, she was madder than a wet hen, bound on takin' me to the principal. And *then* I told her Uncle Alex was single and looking for a good wife. Wow! So I'll study now!"

Mary Ann had turned palms up in resignation. She and Marvel laughed then. Let sleeping dogs lie....

The busy days flew past, marked only by the paychecks which came weekly. Daddy and Uncle Worth whooped at the welcome sight. Accustomed to studying by lamplight, Marvel and Mary Ann gave school their all without complaint. Mary Ann's research paper came back marked "Excellent!" And the men used the same adjective to describe their wives' meals, largely created from the chapter "Camping Out" of the *Stretching to Survive* cookbook they had helped put together. Marvel noted her mother's once-lovely hands, fashioned to produce the music of the spheres with her violin as she stood in some grand opera house, were bruised and blistered from cooking over the open fire. And God alone knew how she and Auntie Rae managed to do the laundry on rub-boards, the ironing with flatirons heated on red-hot coals—and with smiles, always with smiles. But, achingly, Marvel saw beyond their masks.

They were all getting along fine, they reassured one another, counting their meager savings daily, then sleeping with it tucked safely beneath their feather pillows at night. And then Marvel was summoned to the principal's office.

"I took the liberty of asking your former school to help resolve the problem of your final exam in Spanish. Downright tragic that we don't offer the language here. And it so necessary. French! What a waste of time. Anyway, your Mr.—uh, Phillips—responded by Western Union, a first for us all. We'll wire the results. There's so little time—"

"I know," Marvel whispered in relief. "Oh, thank you—I'm ready any time. And ma'am, I'll repay you—"

The woman waved the idea away. "I owe you more than that. Mr. Phillips said the same—and more. Neither of us would require this, except that you'll need the credit to enter a four-year college."

Marvel took the test, breathlessly awaiting the results. After all, she'd had no textbook. But she had no cause for worry. She made a perfect score. Now, if they could hold on another two weeks....

They did—barely.

Two days before school ended, Daddy and Uncle Worth found themselves jobless. The regular flagmen were back, lights were repaired, and no, there would be no more work. Sorry, but the tents must come down, overcrowded as it was. Health Department made no exceptions. Rules were rules. Two days? Okay, but keep it quiet. Then get going!

Marvel fought to control her emotions, a rage gathering within her heart. Who or what caused such needless misery? Never had she seen her father so beaten, her mother so broken. *Yet I must go on pretending, be valiant, bear my own heartache alone*. No—not alone. There was God. Always, there was God.

The words of comfort Marvel offered almost choked her, but she managed. "We *will* go on—not because we want to, but because we must. So much depends on it. Think of the land, Daddy—our *home*, Mother! We'll make it. Nothing can stop the three bears! Do you think bears pray?"

Away from their parents, Marvel took note of Mary Ann's white face, her deeply furrowed brow. "I can't go on," her cousin said in a small, helpless voice. "I'm not strong like you. I—I've never been without Jake before. Oh, why isn't he here—and why isn't *God*!"

"What kind of talk is that?" Marvel asked firmly. "God *is* here. We're the ones who have drifted away, giving energy to the overload we're carrying—energy that belonged to *Him*. But God understands, He cares—and so does Jake. He'll come. I promise you. Just pray."

Mary Ann shook here head in denial. Then, to Marvel's surprise, she lifted her chin. "Thank you, Marvel—just two more days—"

Poor darling. Mary Ann couldn't go on breathing without Jake any more than Marvel could without Titus—Titus and their dreams.

Marvel's thin facade of bravery threatened to crumble completely as she explained her situation to the principal. Fighting to control her emotions, she said truthfully that graduation exercises meant nothing—nothing at all. Just her diploma mattered—and if she could possibly have it early?

"Of course," Ellen Welch promised. Just how to honor such an unusual request she had taken no time to work out. One look at the girl's agonized face chipped away at all objectivity. "You can't know what this is like for me, sitting behind this desk. You *can't* know."

Marvel shook her head. No, she could not know, could not imagine. The flash of anger which crossed the woman's face might mean the loss of her job. And Marvel would be responsible. It would never have occurred to her that the principal, who knew so little about her, could care so much and feel so helpless, or that Ellen Welch was so tired and angry she could shake her fist at the very heavens for withholding rain. It was forcing young people, the hope for tomorrow's world—such as it was—to be torn from their homelands. Never again would she meet the likes of Marvel Harrington. Yet she, like the rest of the masses, was slipping through her fingers. *Hope*, the president said. Bah! Hope was as empty as the hot winds that stole the soil. *Pray*, the preacher said. Why utter meaningless words to a being who wasn't listening? She turned aside to brush away a seldom tear. Tears made one look weak, feel ill—a waste.

And yet this girl, whose secret life she knew nothing about, turned grateful eyes her direction—blue, blue eyes, as blue as the skies should be—and said gratefully, "Oh thank you. You're so kind."

One day ... two ... Hiding out was over. Marvel, gripping the coveted diploma, rushed from the school, praying that she would meet no inquisitive students. Time spent here was history. And the future? She was too tired to care. There was only one safe place to put it: in God's hands. A Father would never forsake His children. The thought served as a sedative. Life was hard, but—

Marvel's thoughts trailed off at the sound of Mary Ann's excited voice. "Oh look, look," she gasped breathlessly. "I ran home ahead—just hoping—and he—he did—he sure enough did—"

Marvel was surprised to find the strength to laugh. "Wait a minute! You've lost me. *He?* And just what did *he* do?"

In reply, Mary Ann waved a sheet of paper. "Jake—Jake *wrote*!"

"Wonderful!" Marvel said, feeling happy for her cousin. "Good timing. Any news?" Oh, how could false pride have kept her from giving the general delivery address to Titus? They had never kept secrets.

"Just—uh—personal things. Oh Marvel, I wish he'd mentioned coming. Archie's missing you still. I wish—but never mind—"

No, never mind. Marvel loved only Titus—*only* Titus, for always.

Mary Ann sobered suddenly. "It wouldn't have mattered—I mean if Jake had come. There are my parents to think of. All else must wait."

Yes, there were Mary Ann's parents and Marvel's—in priority, and in the flesh. The cars were packed. All was in readiness. The lost colony was soon to be underway. Marvel could not bring herself to ask where.

7

"Ex Nihilo"

Silently, Marvel glanced out the window. It was late June. The air was heavy with a bittersweet mixture of wild daisies dozing in the fierce sun and waxy white blossoms of the several orange groves. Hills in the distance were painted yellow with head-high wild mustard as if in defiance of the relentless sun in its attempt to set the very land afire. She concentrated on the pale beauty of the orange blossoms, hoping that Mary Ann had noticed—dear Mary Ann, so filled with dreams of that beautiful wedding. The dream was enough for now.

There was no time to examine her own feelings. A sharp, shrill whistle of a passing train pierced the silence. It lumbered past, followed closely by another. Both were loaded with citrus fruit and hoboes—migratory workers or professional tramps?

Then, without warning, Dale Harrington made a sharp turn and headed back toward the city. Marvel looked back. Mary Ann waved as their car followed.

"Dale! What on earth?" Mother's voice registered surprise.

"The railroad—why didn't I think? This is a railroad center—"

There was no time for discussion. Both men had hurried into the depot where a sign "Register for employment here" invited.

Moments later they were both back—with jobs! Miles and miles of rails to be laid...repairs to be done...hauling gravel ...loading....

Of course, there were some drawbacks. But it would be worth it in the "long haul." Daddy laughed at use of the phrase.

"Such as?" Snow Harrington asked cautiously.

Marvel watched the excitement in her mother's eyes fade with Daddy's explanation. He and Uncle Worth must join a union, take a driving test. Yes, drivers were required to pay a fee, like they did in Texas to vote. But there was no poll tax here. Nice? Worst luck! Wouldn't you know the man in charge of hiring saw the out-of-state licenses? So unless they were just passing through? But the work would last, and Marvel could go on to school. Wasn't it all good news?

Mother swallowed. "But that will take our cash, won't it?"

"Well, I thought about that, but the pay's good. Only we'll be forced to—uh—cut corners temporarily, camp out again. You *will?*"

Mother questioned Marvel with lifted brows. Numbly, Marvel nodded, a million troubling questions unasked. And dampened though it may have been, the fire of adventure returned to Mother's eyes.

A strange evening followed. The sun slipped below the horizon, training a retinue of shadows over the designated "camp." Camp was just clusters of people totally unlike themselves— men unwashed, unshaven, and not caring...women, devoid of expression, having succumbed to despondency as their husbands attempted to shave without soap or water...children, sitting in silent circles, hunger's story etched on the gaunt little faces. Yet from the ugliness of it all came the soft strain of wild-sweet music.

"Gypsy music!" Mother exclaimed. "There has to be a band of gypsies somewhere out there. Toss the feather bed on the ground, Dale, and bring my violin. I can match them!"

Auntie Rae was checking the food supply: wilted apples, a few forlorn vegetables remaining from the tourist-cabin garden, a package of corn flakes, and some stale bread. But, bless her, she smiled?

Mary Ann clenched her fists, set her jaw, and shuddered. "How can they be so blind! We can't stay here—you know we can't. *Billy Joe, get yourself back here this minute!* Oh Marvel, what can we do?"

Marvel fought down her own frustration and the ever-enlarging sense of rebellion. "Do? We'll stick by them. They need us. And our mothers aren't blind. They're sticking by, too."

"I'm sorry, it's just—just so hard. And Daddy's not up to this himself. So what about Uncle Dale? You *know* they can't—"

Yes, Marvel knew. But men feel a need to prove themselves—to their families, yes, but to *themselves*. If Daddy lost all self-esteem— Oh, he mustn't. Sorry and pity filled her heart, but with it was admiration and loyalty—a loyalty that bordered on fanaticism.

Closing out the sorry sights and smells around her, Marvel listened to Snow Harrington's music—soft and sweet, but the notes were full and clear. Her eyes blurred with tears, she played on and on. Then the mood changed. At first the rich, warm notes of Mozart flowed from the instrument. Now the music was wild and sweet as only gypsy music can be. The violin had found its own voice, and now it filled up the twilight like an invitation. A few ventured closer. And suddenly there was a crowd. Would she stop in embarrassment?

Mother surprised them all then, including herself, Marvel thought in wonder. Without a pause, she moved among the masses, leaning down on occasion as if playing for that person alone. The audience blinked as if exposed to sudden sunlight. Faces were no longer blank.

When she approached the gypsies, Daddy moved to stop her—too late.

One of the women—dusky-skinned, ripe-olive eyes flashing, and heavy black hair partially covered by a scarlet kerchief—approached Mother bravely. The rest of the band stood back, speaking one of their several tribal languages. Moustached men's golden earrings flashed as they surveyed the newcomers.

"Itinerants—all of them," Daddy muttered. "Deep pockets, too—"

"Stew?" the woman inquired with a flashing show of pearly teeth. "Nothing like it, save music—or silver. This in appreciation—"

"Of my wife's music or the silver you obviously expect?"

"I expect nothing, sir. It is I who offers a gift. Nothing compares to my cat's-eye stew—"

B.J. broke free of Auntie Rae's restraining hand and bolted forward. "Cat's-eye stew—does it really have *cat's eyes*?"

The gypsy's laugh was low and mellow. Leaning forward, while hugging the countless strands of beads surrounding her throat,

"Just a name," she confided. "We're destined to be thought of as barbarians."

Barbarians? Marvel had taken note of the perfect English, the mark of a European accent. British? She would know about the threat of a totalitarian political party—

But already the "cat's eyes" were explained as chicken. No, they did not raise the fowls. No more questions. They were *donated. While the owners slept, no doubt*, Marvel thought wearily. But her young cousin had set up a howl for cat's-eye stew. And then they were all eating hungrily of the delicious brew. What's more, Mary Ann was helping serve. For like the loaves and fishes, the supply seemed to multiply. At one point a man left the band of gypsies to hand his waitress what appeared to be a new book, shaking his head to communicate his inability to read the contents.

"More preachers than we need, but nobody brings a Bible. We're never around long enough before being driven out," their self-appointed hostess said of their nomadic life-style. "But I could translate."

A look of understanding passed among the Harringtons. One crone, stooped and withered, made a last-ditch stand, even as uniformed law officials came to herd the brightly garbed band away.

"Cross me palm mitt silvah. Stars 'ave—der sek-rets—"

"This book holds the secrets, goes beyond the stars," Daddy said hurriedly. Then, turning to the younger woman, he added hastily, "You will read it—tell them—"

Uncle Worth cinched it. "We know about lifelines and all that. But here you find a lifeline that lasts forever," he promised, handing her another copy of Grady Greer's Bibles.

"Music, too—beautiful music in the words," Auntie Rae said, her usual shyness seeming to have vanished.

Mother continued to play her violin even as the pitiful lot departed. Hauntingly beautiful, the strains of "God Be With You Till We Meet Again" trailed after them—wanderers of the wastelands. Sad—

"Oh, thank God, we have work!" Dale Harrington said.

His wife nodded dreamily. "And even if we, too, must move on, I can leave a trail of music."

"A word in due season, how good is it!" Daddy quoted joyfully from Solomon's proverbs. And all seemed well again.

Mother's music, Uncle Worth's gift of the Holy Book, and the kindness of the wandering gypsies was to set a pattern—a badly needed pattern—in the trying days ahead. Marvel and Mary Ann found comfort in the book the man who could not read had placed in the hands of a young maiden he so obviously admired:

> God created everything—every color, every texture, every living creature, every planet, every star, every speck of stellar dust in the most forgotten backwash of the universe. And He did it all from chaos, from nothing—nothing at all. *Ex nihilo!*

* * *

Dale Harrington collapsed the first day on his new job. It happened just before noon, his brother reported, when he brought Marvel's father, pale and shaken, back to the campsite.

"Oh, the man administering first aid was nice—doing it for Dale's own good, he said. Listened to his chest and said he'd need rest and sunshine. Well, we've got the sun. That's what laid him out—that and trying to heft loads needing a block and tackle—"

Daddy tried to smile. "Well, hon," he gulped, looking into Mother's concerned face, "first the car, then me. Neither of us can climb 'them thar hills'. So?"

Marvel's mind whirled in a fog of desperation and despair. But she mustn't surrender to these emotions. Mother's stricken face no longer held delusions of finding security in a house. Now she had awakened, and awakenings can hurt. How well Marvel knew.

"So we *don't* stay here, Daddy," she smiled bravely. "Where to?"

* * *

Some 20 miles west a wide valley opened. Here and there citrus groves patchworked melon fields together. The aroma of ripe cantaloupes harvesters sorted and overripe watermelons cast aside to split and fall to ruin filled the car. Their sweetness was intoxicating.

"Oh Dale!" Mother gasped, inhaling deeply. "The smell's like music!"

Daddy needed no urging. Moments later he and Uncle Worth were trying in vain to make themselves understood among the Mexican workers. *No ingles, no ingles* the men said repeatedly without looking up. Marvel wriggled from the car. In halting Spanish, she inquired regarding the whereabouts of the owner. The men pointed him out, and she rejoined mother. Shortly afterward, Daddy was with them.

"Good news of sorts. Melons all came on at once. Worth and I can work until the rush is over. And darling, *anything* will help!"

"Of sorts," he had said, which translated into "reservations." There was no housing. Laborers slept in the groves. Union cards meant little. When harvest ended, that was it. Pay? By number of boxes harvested and packed for shipping, but they would be welcome to the culls.

"Oh, but the fr—fruit's good news," Mother gulped.

And they all rushed out to gather it up. Nobody was hungry afterward. Mother, ignoring the other problems, took out her violin and fearlessly moved from group to group of the laborers. Nobody looked up. But the owner, looking fresh from a shower and shave, appeared. "You're wasting your time, lady, except on my wife. She heard and suggested you two families might like to occupy the little guest house back of us for two or three nights. So follow—out of here!"

They followed. Mother, again misty-eyed, played on. And the Mexicans, squatted on their heels, went back to their dice and beer....

All too soon, the harvest was finished.

* * *

"No Help Needed!" greeted the travelers repeatedly as they rode on. But the gas tanks were full, as were their tummies. And there was money enough to lay in staple supplies from a small grocery store. There would be work—of course there would. So they drove on.

As they paused at one point to get their bearings, a young, prematurely wrinkled woman came forward eagerly to greet them. She carried a babe-in-arms, while two other scared toddlers clung to her faded dress.

"Oh, we've been downright lucky in California," the migrant's wife said with pride. "One more piece of pipe and our water tank'll be finished." Spotting Marvel's camera, she offered to pose before a single-room box-shape building, identified as a house only by a narrow door and a square covered by mosquito net while waiting for glass.

"Bought ourselves an acre for a song—made the money picking prunes. I worked right beside my man—even helped nail our house together. It all takes teamwork and patience. Ain't it great?"

Marvel looked at the flat, lifeless land surrounding the "home" and felt a surge of pity mingled with a kind of admiration. But life here for Mother? For *any* of them?

Daddy took care of that. He thanked the lady graciously and asked how much farther it was to the grape vineyards he'd seen mentioned along the way. A day's drive? Very good!

"But a hard one," the gaunt woman warned over the throaty growl of the exhausted Essex. "Takes you over the Grapevine—hilly, and talk about steep! Better save them brakes. Just put 'er in second gear after reaching the summit—if you do. Good luck—tough road—"

Her dire predictions proved to be an understatement. The road twisted and turned as if writhing in pain. Fortunately, the incline was gradual. Even so, the eight-mile climb was tortuous for older vehicles. To the right and to the left were the near-unrecognizable skeletons of cars which, overheated, had burned for lack of water. Abandoned, they'd been pushed aside. One had to wonder about the owners.

Marvel sat tense and silent. "We'll have to keep going," Daddy said at one point. "If we stop, the radiator'll boil dry—"

And our car will burn, he might as well have added. The radiator was steaming already. Ignore it. Ignore the burned cars, too.

What a welcome sight the sudden appearance of white-on-red signs promoting sales for a brushless shaving cream was! The barren hillsides came alive with color. True, the first two concerning safety were sobering. Spaced some 20 yards apart, the lines read: "Hardly a driver...is now alive...who passed on hills...at 65! *Burma Shave.*" Ha! 65! The Essex would be flattered. "From bar...to car...to gates ajar! *Burma Shave.*" Marvel missed a line on the third and had to look over her shoulder to unscramble it. The turn backward held its own reward. Uncle

Worth was close behind, and they were all laughing and pointing at the signs posted on the straight stretches.

So they were making a game of the folksy humor. Well, why not?

"He had the ring . . . he had the flat . . . but she felt his chin . . . and that was that. Burma-Shave!" she sang out.

Marvel's mood was contagious, she saw at once. Mother and Daddy clutched it as a drowning person clutches a straw. "Within this vale," Marvel began. "Of toil and sin," Mother's voice continued a little uncertainly until Daddy read lightly, "Man's head grows bald . . ."

"Your turn, Marvel—hurry and finish. Suspense is killing me," Mother said then.

"But not his chin!" Marvel chimed out triumphantly, her fear gone.

It was a game then, each trying to spot the signs dotting the distance first. And even when curves interrupted the parade, the three of them tested their memories at remembering the jingles.

Marvel suggested saying the words in unison. And then Mother went a step further and made them into a musical ditty. They were singing as they reached the top. And there the hissing radiator blew off its cap and what remained of the water went up in steam.

Stifling heat from the steam filled the car's open windows. The moisture was sucked in by dizzying heat immediately. It would be easy to give up as the radiator had done. There was certainly reason enough to be dour and grim. The journey had been trying, disappointing and frightening. But it was unfinished.

"Well," Marvel said, hoping to sound sincere, "rest time—so we can get the old zing going or," she tried boldly when neither of her parents responded, "do we declare a National Worried-Frown Day?"

Daddy laughed—actually laughed. "Talk about being frivolous. That's our Marvel. Sooo," he said crawling out a little sheepishly, "we throw a party. I need some practice."

"Mother always said to list your blessings—count what's *right* when everything's wrong," Mother recalled. The lilt in her voice did not find reflection in the lovely eyes, but she gulped and stumbled on. "Said troubles were like—like cockroaches. I hate the beastly things, but they can't take over your life unless you let them—not that we can get shut of them—not entirely."

"Still, this radiator— It's hard being Papa Pollyanna!"

That's when the miracle happened. At first, Marvel thought she was hallucinating—the heat, the exhaustion. But no! It *was* real.

"The sign!" She pointed, but Mother and Daddy paid no attention. Probably thought she meant another Burma-Shave bit of wit.

"Water! Daddy, *look*!"

And there it was as big as life. A faucet extended from an underground pipe—part of an irrigation system. Who cared about the source? The *real* Source was God Himself. He always sent light when clouds were darkest. Grandmother was right. Count the blessings....

The men filled the radiators. The women checked for losses. Some bedding had blown off the pickup, but it wasn't worth risking a stop. Who needed covers in California? Auntie Rae smiled cheerfully. "It's such a relief to be on top—to have found water. We learn to stop taking things for granted. The orphanage taught me, but I forgot."

"Oh, true! No need to worry. It's all downhill from here."

Mother was right—all downhill. The uphill climb was long and challenging. But the downward plunge was all too easy. Who could have foreseen the destruction that lay in the wide, green valley below—have foreseen their personal universe more battered and torn than their cars, invaded by cockroaches in human form? Marvel could find comfort only in remembering that God created from those *nothings*.

Ex nihilo.

8

"Trampling Out the Vintage..."

Miles and miles of citrus groves, leaves blindingly green to eyes grown weary of monotonous sun-baked hills, stretched ahead. Between the rows of trees, well-manicured and moist from irrigation, stood boxes heaped high with bright-orange market-ready fruit. It was like the Promised Land. Here they would find security. Here they would find peace.

Teamwork—work beside your man, the migrant woman who felt herself "downright lucky" had said. Well, that was happening here. Bonneted women scurried like mice among the men.

"We'll all work—make a killing!" Mother cried excitedly.

"And gorge on oranges. And lookit the kids, oh boy!" B.J. leaped from the pickup and headed for the nearest group of children. Very appropriate, Marvel and Mary Ann were to agree later, for it was he who was responsible for their departure the following day.

Marvel had a strange feeling about the place from the beginning. It felt tainted, as if Satan had paid a recent visit. If he had fled, he must have left his helpers behind. Grizzled, unwashed men smirked and gaped at any passing female and let out coarse laughter, tittering remarks punctuated by oaths. Was she the only one to feel it?

Fortunately, the grove's manager set the Harringtons to work in an area apart from the brawlers' paradise. Daddy and Uncle Worth gathered oranges, barely able to keep ahead of Mother

71

and Auntie Rae's sorting. Marvel and Mary Ann labeled the crates. And then they all filled cardboard boxes with the culls.

That night, in a state of exhaustion, Marvel scarcely noted the sweat-soaked, big-bellied men who licked their lips while eyeing the women from a distance. Mother and Auntie Rae put together a picnic-type cold supper and suggested that the girls keep an eye on B.J.

When summoned for the meal, he came obediently, then turned back to his ragged, unkempt playmates. Stabbing the air with his forefinger, he whispered for the girls to look at "Buzzie's mama, a 'night crawler.'"

"What's that supposed to mean? Night crawlers are worms," Mary Ann told him. But Marvel wondered if there could be a deeper meaning when she caught sight of the tawdy, overdressed woman. No older than Mother or Auntie Rae, she appeared to be 20 years their senior, if one could judge from the slathered-on makeup, mostly around the worldly-wise but weary-looking eyes—lovely eyes at one time, but now garish with red-purple eye shadow and lashes spiked with mascara. But the thick lips, painted a brilliant red, kept laughing as her eyes roved the surrounding grove. Dancer? Circus performer? Or what?

Marvel shuddered. Was the pathetic creature, dragged West, struggling to survive while her man "made it big?" What lay underneath that paint, privation?

And then they saw! The woman was slipping from one make-shift tent to another, her mission painfully obvious even before Billy Joe's announcement. "A night crawler—see? I told you about Buzzie's mama!"

Then came the drunken yell of rage. Buzzie's father? "I'll kill you—you cheap, filthy hussy! And you—you *whoremonger*—"

"What's that, Daddy—a wh—?" B.J.'s eyes were filled with curiosity—a curiosity never to be satisfied.

"What do you mean, you're leaving?" The manager was furious. "I should have known. That's the way it is with you fruit tramps."

"Never mind the name-calling," Uncle Worth said, his voice dangerously calm. "I will not have my family exposed to this."

He would pay them later, the man said sullenly. They could mail him their address—providing such as they ever settled long enough. He would pay now, Daddy said firmly. Two against one—

oh well, why bother? the man's expression said. Texans, Okies, Arkies—all alike, the whole trashy lot. But squirrel-eaters did have a good aim. He paid.

A killing, Mother had said trying so hard . . .

* * *

Dale Harrington tried hard to lighten the somber quiet he felt responsible for. "Sorry, precious," he said, "but I should have warned you, Snow White, that marriage is not a *word*—it's a *sentence!*"

Mother's smile was feeble. "Check with our grammarian. Is Daddy right, Marvel?" *A life sentence*, Marvel could have teased, but didn't.

There was no time to answer. Before them an ancient car, square-top piled with dirty mattresses, wooden-spoked wheels now riding on rims, had stalled in the road. A hapless man, hands on hips, looked grimly across the harvested field and back to the disabled vehicle. Doors were wired shut. And on the back a homemade contraption carried their few possessions: dented pails, a trash barrel with fragments of clothing trailing out, a mop, and two cola bottles fitted with limp nipples. The bottles were empty, and the baby inside the dilapidated car was crying, destitute.

Oh, thank God, Daddy stopped! "Yessir, we're starved, stalled, stranded. The land of milk and honey, they told us—now, I'm uh *Okie*," the man said helplessly.

Marvel would never forget the blank face of the woman staring back at her from the stalled car's window. The weary eyes were fixed, unseeing, the lips chapped and bleeding. Drudgery and privation had robbed her of feeling—even for her three children, whose tangled hair and smudged faces told the same sordid story. *I can't bear it, Lord!*

Somewhere from out of this barren ugliness, a mockingbird sang its song of eternal hope. And for one blessed moment, Marvel was hoisted away. Transported by mind's magic carpet, she was back in the "someday" world. The morning air was calm, hazy with sunlight, rich with fragrance, and ripe with promise. Nature's peaceful harmony was at its most lush. The bad dreams were over—dreams of the Great Depression, the Dust Bowl, this journey to nowhere. There was only reality in that Garden of Eden where she waited for Titus beneath their tree. And in that delicately beautiful moment he drew near, his outstretched arms extended. "Marvel, my brave Marvelous—"

Brave. It was God's reminder.

"Oranges," she said. "The children must have fruit."

Dirty, claw-like hands grabbed their treasures wordlessly. They had finished eating the oranges—unwashed and unpeeled, with only juice forming sticky rivulets down tiny chins—when other cars stopped behind Uncle Worth. Some could help. Others could not. But all could offer similar stories of despair.

"Out in the Texas Panhandle we wuz hit harder'n most. Dust blowed in from Oklahoma, Kansas—an' agin Colorado 'n New Mexico ways. Fierce—how them towns blacker 'n th' walls uv hell…"

"I seen it!" a school-age boy broke in. "Cou'dn see les'sen th' lights wuz on. School bus kep' headlights on—teachers made us'n wear dust masks. Folks said th' world wuz comin' to uh end. One po' woman got down on her knees in Amarillo 'n prayed out loud: 'Dear Lord, please give us'n one mo' chance'—'n we're still lookin' fer it!"

Yes, a man who only identified himself as a migratory worker, withdrew a small notebook from his pocket—his log, from which he hoped to write a book when men regained self-respect. "October to December—cut Malaga and Muscat grapes, Fresno, $40…December—left for Imperial Valley…February—picked peas, $30 for entire season on account of weather, fortunate to break even…left for Chicago, haunted employment agencies, about 5000 ahead, hired 100, lined up for soup and fresh water— returned to California, odd jobs, cut lawns, fixed radios…June picked figs. Fruit played out, me, too. Where to now?"

Marvel, feeling her sweat-soaked skirt clinging about her bare knees, braved the heat to snap pictures and take notes. Her compassion-filled heart was breaking, but what greater service than letting a world which had forgotten them know of their pitiful condition?

Ragged but tough, a small South Carolina farm girl dressed in boy's clothing remained unintimidated. Chin high, she swaggered up to Billy Joe. "We work from 'can see' to 'cain't see,'" she boasted.

"I'm writing Jake," Marvel heard Mary Ann say at her side, "and I—I feel so uncertain. We'll have to change plans, won't we?"

"We'll do whatever we have to. I'm writing Titus, too."

Oh Titus, I only heard about all this before. Now I know....

"We have to stick together—folks like us," a woman from the coal fields of West Virginia said to Mother and Auntie Rae, who appeared to be collecting a few food items to share. "Can't let our spirits sag, bitter lesson—but God keeps us steadfast. We'll win!"

A man beside her laughed. "Right, lady—come hell or high water. Down home, we got ourselves doing what folks here with Texas and Oklahoma backgrounds are bound on doing: tuckered selves out prayer for *water*. Gol-*le*, oh! I tell you all, I'd seen that old river come up, but when she reaches the rooftops—*mankind*! Needed us some kinda ark. City folks came trotting with soup kettles—hypocrites! Poked fun at us Tennessee squatters and plain insulted us. 'Do you think them people's got little enough sense to come back to them shacks when the river goes down?' We got our pride—we got *guts*, but let 'em growl, we don't welcome charity. And yes Sir, Lord, we'll always go back to Shantytown till the river rises someday and forgits to go down...."

People around him agreed with a rousing "*Amen!*"

His family was going home, too, an Oklahoma farmer said happily. Never should have left. Used to be a *farmer*. Now he was an *Okie*. Wished he'd kept his family to stick it out. Had to scratch to live, of course. Go into town, peddle tads of sour cream for nine cents a pound (if they could find a town big enough and far away from the dust) and eggs a dime a dozen. Despite all that dust and wind, they were putting in crops, only they never "made," so had to live out of barnyard products. Five crop failures in five years. Still they owned one thing: *identity*. But, God willing, they'd find it.

Think that was bad? Try Detroit! "Before daylight," the unemployed auto worker said, "we'd be off to Chevrolet. Police just waiting for us, waving us away, 'Nothin' doin'! Nothin'!' So we were tramping through iced-over snow, bound for Dodge. Big, well-fed men in heavy overcoats stood at the door, waving us past with a loud 'No, no!' as we passed before them. So on the tramp again...."

"A man's got no right having kids.... My God! Why have you forsaken us?" a desperate voice rose above all others.

Marvel turned away then. She could stand no more. They came from the four corners of the earth—these human beings referred to in newspapers only as "a substantial number." There had to be a turning point. There *had* to be. Mary Ann must have seen the deep hurt within her. They understood one another so much. For when only a short while ago Mary Ann had registered frustration, now it was consolation she offered. "God will see this suffering and stop it!"

Was He doing so already? Marvel noted with pride that others were following Mother and Auntie Rae's example—sharing what they had and, shaking their heads over the sad state of the stranded family's car, loading their belongings into other vehicles, offering them a ride on "a piece of the way." Soon now, all would be "tramping again."

Almost recklessly, Mary Ann grabbed the Kodak and snapped a candid camera shot of Marvel. It was that unposed picture which went to Titus Smith later and inspired him to write the words which would linger with Marvel to sustain her in her deepest hour of sorrow. "My darling, my darling—the photograph of the only girl I will ever love is framed and resting on my desk, framed in my heart as well. It is as you were and always will be: so open, so honest, so true. And those eyes—oh, those eyes beneath the wind-tossed hair (innocent, yet questioning and filled with expectancy), wear that look of excitement as they gaze into mine. It is as if those eyes probe into my soul—and then beyond, envisioning something neither has seen before—our miracle!"

But for now Mary Ann returned the box camera and said, "Now, my turn. Take one of me—for Jake. Who knows? Anyway, hold this roll so I'll have it to surprise him. Don't send it for developing *please*, Marvel!"

Marvel honored her cousin's wish. That night she mailed the other exposed rolls of film and her numerous notes to the office of *The News Review* and a hurried letter to Titus. "I feel so far away, so isolated, out of touch. I have had no opportunity to hear the news or read the daily paper. Oh, how I miss it all—and *you*. There'll be so much to catch up on...a *lifetime*—a lifetime together. I am your Marvel."

* * *

The Harringtons must face it, they agreed. Poverty had found its way into every region. Their own misery was no longer the exception. It was the rule. This they discussed in a huddled group. What they did not discuss were the poignant yearnings within each heart. They, too, were wanderers now—immigrants, tramps, gypsies, members of the legendary "lost colony." Yes, all of those—without family status, respect, or legal residence. And they all felt the pull of home.

But disguising their raw emotions, they pushed on to meet one rebuff after another. "We will survive," Daddy gritted, never saying how. "What's more, the Brothers Three are not to hear one blessed word of this: Alex, Emory, Joseph. We'll walk, we'll crawl—but not to *them*. Let's say all's well, and with God's help, one day it *will* be!" Uncle Worth declared.

Not a word—all right, not to them. But others would know—not by accident either, but by plan. For Marvel Harrington was determined that the world should see, feel and yes, accept responsibility for these bleeding bodies and hearts. She would fulfill her destiny, capture the very soul of the Great Depression. The words and pictures she gathered would spell out a new definition of faith....

"Oranges harvested—try the plums. Orchard farther on."

"Peas? First picking's finished. Awhile yet before second crop..."

After each unsuccessful try, they drifted on, still following a westward direction. Once hope flickered briefly. Figs were ready. Mother took one look at the shanties called "migratory housing" and shook her head. They were cardboard, papered over with distasteful billboards advertizing tobacco, beer, and women's most personal sanitation needs. And the stench was unbearable. Without toilet facilities, human waste lay uncovered in the glaring sun, courting disease. Mary Ann retched, but Marvel covered her face with a towel and snapped a picture, hoping that the swarms of flies did not obscure the view. *God help them all.*

"Cotton fields—now hiring." Cotton they knew about, all of them—knew about, and hated. Nevertheless, the sign was good news. They would endure—and gladly!

"What do you think?" Daddy asked uncertainly. "You first, Snow."

"I think," Mother said without hesitation, "that we're down-right fortunate. Not that I like it—"

Daddy exhaled as if he'd been holding his breath a long, long time. "I don't exactly, let's say, *cotton* to it—but Marvel?"

Marvel's attempt at a laugh was fairly successful. "My witty father—telling himself jokes. Well, sir, I don't take a shine to it either, but—"

"Like the man said back there, 'When the Depression has pups on your doorstep'—" Uncle Worth said as he joined their parked car, "'beggars are not choosers.' So we're all for it—"

Brave words—for around them, all the horrors they'd here-tofore witnessed were rolled into one: the stench, the luckless legion of homeless moving and shifting as the sand dunes of Arizona had done. Dirty, filthy, unkept, sunken of face and spirit, the hired hands no longer tried to maintain sanitation. Life had knocked them down too many times.

Don't look, Marvel willed herself. But even behind closed lids, her heart would see. Mary Ann closed a supporting hand over hers. Love must be brave. "I'm proud of you," Marvel said, meaning it. For Mary Ann was growing, gathering strength and sharing it.

"'My strength is made perfect in weakness.' Paul's words seem written for us, don't they, Mary Ann?" Marvel said warmly. "So, come on, my strong one. Let's take a squint at our new quarters."

"Before I puke," B.J. said from behind them.

"You know better than to use that word, young man." But his sister's rebuke was gentle. "I know you hear such language—I'm sorry."

Moments later, Mary Ann took one look at the inside of the first shack and muttered that maybe little brother used the right word, after all.

Entering was easy. There was no door, just a burlap sack protecting the gaping entrance and the one room's only source of light. Walls were papered with sections of newspapers—pages from such magazines as *The Saturday Evening Post, True Confessions,* and *Movie Star Scandals*. Crisscrossing at dizzying angles were empty cereal boxes—opened and spread flat to help cover the roughness of the boards beneath. Furnished, the field boss had said. Furnishings included a rickety iron bedstead, an unvented brick burner for cooking, and orange crates for tables and chairs. What appeared at first to be rumpled rugs was dirty clothing—the overpowering odor of ammonia could only mean unwashed diapers.

Taken aback, Marvel and Mary Ann could only gaze at one another in stricken silence. And for once B.J. was at a loss for words.

Not a sound, and yet there was the unmistakable feel of another presence. Too late they realized that the place was occupied.

"Dear God! Oh, dear God!" Mary Ann whispered, unable to move.

Marvel saw them then: two dirty, frightened children—two little girls . . . stark naked . . . no longer looking human, but more like the skeletal remains of some starved-to-death animal. And left unattended!

It was a temptation to turn and bolt out the hole through which they had entered. But what if the waifs had been abandoned, left to die? By unspoken agreement, the girls moved toward them—both thankful that Billy Joe had fled. At first the children sat silent, neither shrinking nor responding to gentle questions. At last, however, they pointed to a heap, covered by a man's worn coat. One spoke in a monotone: "Mama, she sick— baby died. Go 'way 'fore our daddy come. Him drinks stuff—"

The door darkened. Mother and Auntie Rae! "We must do what they ask, Marvel. We'll check on—on the situation later," Mother whispered.

"No! Don't—don't touch anything, Mary Ann," Auntie Rae cautioned in guarded tones. "I—I saw a rat. Your daddies will check this out!"

They were right, of course. And so the four of them tiptoed out, leaving behind a ghostly silence. None of them spoke of the troubling situation as they scrubbed themselves and the similar shack they would be compelled to occupy. They would eat out- side, even though there were flies and hornets to deal with. The air was fresher, cleaner. And they *must* stay clean. Water? All they had must come from an irrigation ditch, but fortunately it was a canal—the main artery to neighboring tributaries watering nearby fields and groves. A government project, the field boss

had said with pride, leading right into the city system for puri-
fication. Of course, it was wise to boil it for drinking—unless
they preferred beer like some. Boil it? Of course, they would.

Dale and Worth Harrington settled the matter regarding the
children and the sick mother left alone. They were to be avoided
at all costs, the men said by way of command. Eviction notice on
the way, the field boss had said (Eviction, ha! From that place?).
The head of the household had been unable to work... whole
family down sick... goodness knows from what... man of the
house trying to find other work... scarce as hen's teeth... drunk
all the time trying to drown his troubles. They weren't to breathe
a word of this, the field boss said—that is, if they hoped to work
for *him*. One word might bring the County Health Department!
No jobs...

In the grueling days ahead, there was no time for dwelling on
the problems of others, no energy for caring. In that white-hot
world of cotton, their hands became scratched, pricked, and red
with baked-on blood. Their lips blistered and cracked, and gradually their faces bore the same gauntness of those around them.
The polluting cloud bank that shrouded America settled over
themselves. Marvel overheard her mother comment to her
sister-in-law that people who rambled in covered wagons fared
far better. And Rae Harrington responded that the same held
true for children in the orphans' home.

Marvel Harrington herself was remembering something she
had heard about, never dreaming that the gloomy words by
broadcasters would touch her own family: "The Bull Market is
dead. Not one breath of life remains.... Billions of dollars' worth
of brokers' loans liquidated.... Thousands upon thousands joining ranks of homeless, unemployed.... *The market has crashed!*"

But the broadcaster had summarized by saying nowhere did
there remain even the slightest ray of hope. Not so! Dale and
Worth Harrington picked up weekly paychecks for their wives to
"salt down." When it was time to move on, there would be
money—their ticket to where?

Small wonder men had blown their brains out in the twenties.
Maybe that accounted for the name the Roaring Twenties. The
roar of gunfire, Marvel thought dully. She knew there was much
to be thankful for, but the dragons of doubt were back in her
young heart. The same dragons that blotted out the light that

saved their money, and more. The Lord had chosen to use them for His purpose, and they had fulfilled it!

The itinerant preacher, in a brief exchange of words, revealed his own financial condition. Compelled to divide his time between physical labor and spiritual pursuits, he depended on donations—usually small as his congregation was "the needy of the fields" whom he chose to serve. He had recently passed through vineyards—work there, but he felt called on eastward. God never made mistakes. Oh, he was glad to be here in time of need. His own hunger would pass as he satisfied theirs. Daddy told him hurriedly that the Dale and Worth Harrington families had three days' earned wages to be collected from the arrested man. "It is yours—our donation. See that he pays it!" Undoubtedly, it was the largest contribution the dedicated minister had ever received. His eyes said so.

Mother, whose heart ached to play her violin music to those despairing around her, knew circumstances would not allow. But she could and did remove a new Bible from the hastily packed car and place it into his grateful hands. Opportunities would come for sharing her talent later.

And, Marvel realized suddenly, she herself *had* saved two lives!

She remembered the English teacher then—how he had chosen to criticize and embarrass her to the point of persecution. If the predictions she had read were true, if the Germans were on the march toward brutal totalitarianism, she knew what it felt like to be called a "Jewish pig." With a shudder, she imagined the sound of marching boots, row after row in an otherwise silent world of fear.

Aloud, she said to her parents as she had said to the despotic man at Culverville High: "We can feel sorry for them. We've learned it is better to bear pain than inflict it. Pity the field boss—*do!*"

Daddy spoke in awe, as if he'd seen a sudden, near-blinding light: "Yes, I understand now: 'Blessed are ye when men shall persecute you.'"

Marvel's heart soared skyward like a small bird once caged and now liberated, lifting on a breeze. "Matthew said that. Remember what else he said we must do, Daddy?"

"*I* do, you two!" Mother chimed out. "Pray for them!"

Pray for them—the suffering they'd left behind and the evil man who had caused it. Marvel Harrington would pray. So would her parents, for they had learned as she had learned before them the divine truth in the parody: "More blessed be the beaten than he whose hand holds the whip."

* * *

Frightened and bewildered, but feeling a deep peace within their hearts, the Harringtons had driven all night. Now a pale dawn broke over the far-distant mountains. Marvel watched the colors change into shimmering pastels. And then the sun rose triumphantly.

"Watch the map, Mrs. Navigator—the one the lady sketched back at the date shop, Valerie Jean's. We should be coming to the crossroad."

Mother squinted, then said quickly, "Oh here, I see. And there's the sign just ahead. The one to Sacramento means vineyards—"

"And the other goes to Los Angeles—no city life," Daddy said tiredly. "The minister had found work in the grapes. So will we."

Mother began chatting animatedly about her near-forgotten world, once she'd promised to watch for a pullout with a trash can. Yes, they must eat, but first she must feed her undernourished soul. Stroking her chin where the violin loved to nestle, she told of the concerts in which she dreamed to play: first to a captive audience in the vineyards, later in some great symphony— they all needed comfort.

Daddy winked when he and Marvel caught one another's eye in the small rearview mirror. *Let her run down, she needed the release.*

"Such understanding between mates," something within Marvel whispered as a gentle reminder—then more fiercely, "Apples fall close to the tree (Grandmother's voice!), and you will settle for no less."

Right, Grandmother dearest. If only—if only that man (what *was* his name, the reporter—that prophet of doom who said war clouds hovered over America?) *is wrong, like Lindbergh claims.*

But no, the writer probably was to be nominated for the Pulitzer Prize. Franklin Delano Roosevelt was among those prophets. She was sure of it. But that lonely man at the top must keep his feelings under wraps. He couldn't afford the luxury of giving voice to worry to a hungry world at home, and neither could Marvel Harrington. Others depended on them. So the president of the United States and the now-itinerant slip of a girl numbered among those who gazed across the stormy Atlantic but gave no voice to forecasting that the clouds might reach here.

Until someday—yes, someday when she and one Titus Smith would expose the truths as they saw them, *dare* expose their sometimes-dark souls in their book. "Then we, too, shall win that coveted prize!" she would write Titus tonight, while wondering what columnists were saying now.

"And now my stomach?" Daddy said with a playful grimace once Mother paused. Marvel came back to earth. Mother remained in the stratosphere.

"Oh *you*! How could I have forgotten my mother's words of wisdom: 'Best way to a man's heart is through his stomach'? Oh, a trash can!" But even as Daddy slowed the car, Mother dreamed on. "Oh darling, if only we *can* find work—and we will! We'll rise above this. I—I will make music, maybe even compose. You'll make the big leagues one way or another. Marvel will go on to school. I'll *play* on and on—"

"I should have brought my opera glasses, but I'll settle for some coffee and a kiss!"

* * *

The minister was right. People were gathering grapes. Marvel gasped at the beauty of the enormous vineyard where first they stopped. The green leaves looked cool and inviting in the hot sun. The purple of the grapes clustered heavily to parent vines, breathing out a heady wine-ready perfume all their own. It was magnificent and so clean.

B.J. leaped up and down with childish pleasure. His sister was equally impressed. "Look, Marvel!" Mary Ann whispered, pointing at a two-story house in the distance, complete with balconies adorned with swinging baskets of trailing scarlet vines—a near-villa and totally charming.

Their parents, naturally, were totally absorbed with the wine harvest. It was clear the fruit was intended for wine only, as the multi-windowed factory with its vats and barrels stood close enough to the vineyards to fill the summer air with an intoxicating headiness. And for its purpose the Italian-born owners made no apology, their families were to find. It was their way of life—a part of their culture from the Old Country, one of the several men in managerial positions explained. Clad in expensive twills, he approached the newcomers with raised eyebrows. His was a position of power, his eyes said.

"Are you here to seek employment? If not, you're trespassing!"

"I'm sorry—I didn't realize. We, both families, were admiring the vineyards. But yes, we *do* need work," Daddy said hastily.

The man relaxed visibly. "Very well then, it will be my pleasure to show you about the premises. I am sure you have heard of the De-Mure family. None other in the area can lay claim to such fame. The De-Mure family has been here for generations. Allow me to escort you."

Marvel and Mary Ann looked on in wonder. They—why, they were being treated like royalty. A tour, with no embarrassing questions? Surely they were dreaming. They trailed along in silence as their host, who identified himself only as Gaston, pointed out the accommodations. The buildings were sturdy and whitewashed. They would share a duplex, quarters separated by bathroom facilities—toilet and shower. "How long will you be staying?" he inquired as if he were their host.

"Until the harvest ends—as long as there's work," Uncle Worth said eagerly, glancing quickly at the rest of them for an approving nod.

He received it. The look, though only momentary, was not lost on the all-seeing Gaston. "Very well," he said. "There are only a few rules. You *are* to remain until the grapes are harvested. And we wish permission to inspect the building you occupy. It is to be kept clean at all times. The De-Mures require total dedication— hard work and decent behavior. Bear in mind this is their ancestral home. Treat it all with respect, perform well, and you'll be amply rewarded."

None of them could believe their good fortune. Unloading quickly, they set to work in the appointed vineyard at once and remained until it was too dark to see—a long day's labor. No sleep to, in Shakespeare's words, "knit the ravell'd sleeve of care," Marvel realized in amazement. Yet, now showered and

changed into clean garments, they were elated—so elated that
they lingered long over the bracing coffee, plucking often from
the great clusters of succulent grapes arranged in a charming
centerpiece.

"I'm almost afraid to sleep," Auntie Rae said a little uncertainly. "What if—what if we wake up and find this was just a
dream?"

Uncle Worth rose to put an arm about his wife, holding her
close. "It's unlikely, hon. Just dream about the house you're
going to have when all this—this drudgery is over. You and Snow
deserve that!"

B.J. shook his head. Grown-ups were hard to understand—
telling him there weren't any bears under his bed, so sleep. And
they were scared too? "Where'll we build the house, Daddy—
here or in Oregon?" he inquired practically. It deserved a practical answer, Uncle Worth's eyes said.

"We aren't going to Oregon, son. Your Uncle Dale and I have
talked this over, and we can't because—Well, we just can't, that's
all."

The men explained then, breaking the news—which wasn't
really news at all, just something they hadn't talked about. The
cars would never make it. Conditions might be no better there
than here. And frankly, they preferred to make it on their own.
That is—

If they agreed? Of course they did!

Joining hands tightly, the Harringtons prayed a round-robin
prayer then—praising God for employment in these respectable
surroundings, begging comfort for those unfortunates they'd left
behind, and asking His holy guidance here leading them to serve
others.

The days following passed quickly. Inspired, they found truth
in Isaiah's prophecy: "They shall run and not be weary. . . ."
Marvel found strength to write Titus. They would have a permanent address soon now, she promised rashly, and oh, to receive a
letter from him! Mother and Auntie Rae wrote glowingly to the
Oregon relatives, leaving reports back to Grandfather Harrington temporarily to his sons. And surprisingly, Mary Ann
reassured Jake that delay would make no difference in their love.
"But I still want the grand wedding," she read aloud to her
cousin. "No matter what it takes to bring us together, I ask God to
let it happen!"

Days blended into weeks just as harvest of one variety of grapes blended into another. July passed. Then as August drew to a close, Gaston paid them an unexpected visit. "You are to be commended," he said. "Seldom have I seen such dedication. You have accumulated a goodly amount, but I hinted at bonuses. There will be a sizable one by way of financial reward. However," he said, fumbling with his gloves and words, "I think it only proper to extend an invitation to the annual festival the De-Mures hold at the harvest's ending. Attendance is usually reserved for townspeople and neighboring husbandmen, but would you not enjoy observing a true *vendage*?"

Vendage? It was Marvel who repeated the word questioningly. The rest of the family was speechless with surprise.

"Ah yes, Miss, I should have explained," Gaston said without hesitation. "There are cylinders which crush the grapes in the large vats in these days. Nevertheless, the De-Mures disregard the practices of others at the celebrations. They prefer to preserve the ways of their native Italy, just as it was done centuries ago—fireworks and fair maidens treading barefoot. Providing you wish to come?"

"Oh, yessir, we do wish to come!" B.J. exclaimed, doing a fair job of imitating the voice and manner of Gaston. "Daddy— Mother—please say yes. The gentleman is waiting. Say yes, *please!*"

Someone or several of them must have said something in agreement. Gaston was smiling slightly, an expression of pleasure on his face. "Then we shall see you there." And then he strode away.

A flurry of excitement followed. What to wear? Ah yes, sort of *fiesta* dresses, like the gypsies wore! But how? Then they recalled some colorful remnants intended for quilts. There was plenty of lace Grandmother Riley had found at a fire sale. Pieced together—

The men smiled indulgently—wonderful to see the women-folk smile again and really mean it. They, too, were excited, calculating their earnings and trying to guess what the monetary bonus would amount to. Marvel fought down a mixture of regret that they must move on, away from temporary security, and an unexplainable feeling of apprehension. Always this place seemed to hold a secret, fascinating yet distasteful.

Mary Ann noticed her quietness. "Aren't you excited, Marvel? I know you're wishing our fellows were here. It's no real celebration alone. But, you know, we can tell them—*Marvel?*"

Marvel started. "It's something I can't explain—"

"You're *scared*?"

"I guess you could call it that," Marvel admitted.

As always, Mary Ann understood. "I think I am, too, in a way. I mean, I get gooseflesh—first thinking how thrilling, then something happens. I—I kinda feel like Elmer's lurking here—"

Marvel laughed then and felt better. "No chance. You can forget nightmares of the pitiful stepcousin. And forget what I said, as well. Don't let it spoil our fun. You're right. We'll write Titus and Jake. In fact, I'll write every detail, send Titus a copy and Mr. Corey one, then record it all for our book—"

"*Book?*"

Marvel laughed again. "I've told you about it, only you were too head-over-heels in love to hear."

"I still am! But I want to hear."

Mary Ann listened raptly as Marvel gave her a briefing on *The White Flag of Victory*. No, not the red flag, the white. One wins by losing when surrendering to God. It would be history . . . fiction, in a way, but factual . . . an actual account of this journey based on history . . . a picture of life. But why black and white? Wasn't life colorful? Just look at what they'd be seeing at the *vendage* compared to the ugliness of reality seen and experienced before . . . like Mark Twain, Ernest Hemingway. . . . And now there was talk that the journalist, John Steinbeck was using his exhaustive research to weave into a novel.

"Then there'll be more!" Marvel said excitedly, once again caught up on the wings of her dream. "Titus and I want to do some books for children, books that let them *imagine*, actually *see* the characters. And oh, something else—did I ever tell you that I've taken notes for years now on folk sayings? You know, the kind of vocabulary we used back home? It's colorful, picturesque—and Mary Ann, it'll all be warped out of shape when younger historians lay hands on it. Already there are those who laugh at us until we are ashamed of our heritage. So we work at changing ourselves—"

It was Mary Ann who was laughing now. "You mean like my carrying a cow up the stairs? You told me it couldn't be done—"

"It could though," B.J., having sauntered up beside the girls unnoticed, reasoned. "If you started out with a calf and practiced ever' day, then one day it would be a cow—"

"Oh, off with you!" Mary Ann laughed again, and then—with a roll of her eyes at Marvel—pleased her young brother by saying, "The only way I can *get shut* of you is to call you what you are: a p-e-s-t!"

"I couldn't resist that," Mary Ann said, sobering. "But you know what? I found some stuff that's apt to help you. I owe you so much, and will keep calling on you for help. But surprise! I kept this for you. So now, let's talk about the celebration ahead!"

* * *

Harvest of the grapes had passed, and without mishap. Not once had there been a signal of warning to prepare Marvel and Mary Ann for the beauty and the horror lying in waiting for them on the eventful evening ahead. Snow and Rae Harrington oh-h'd and ah-h-h'd at sight of their finished handmade garments as they had their daughters practice walking as Grandmother had taught them to walk. They were straight, tall, and beautiful as princesses—Mary Ann with her wealth of heavy black curls secured with a scarlet ribbon to cascade far below the scoop of the lace-ruffled dip of the dress's neckline, and Marvel, in contrast, looking so angelic with her delicate coloring. Her china-doll fairness of skin and corn-silk-fine hair seemed to reflect light where there was none. But did angels ever possess such blue-blue eyes, such apple-kissed cheeks as if she were forever flushed with happiness? On impulse, Marvel's mother brushed back one side of her daughter's hair and pinned a pink velvet rose above her ear. "Beautiful," she breathed. "Just beautiful."

The Harrington men were saying the same of their wives. "We mustn't let these two out of sight, Dale," Uncle Worth said with a wink at Daddy. "Not on your life!" was Daddy's quick reply.

With a word of caution to B.J. to stay close by, the party of seven hurried toward the sound of the revelers coming from somewhere between the factory and the castle-like house said to be occupied by the De-Mures. They went as spectators, little dreaming that they were destined to become participants, central figures in a life drama.

There was no moon, but finding the pathway was easy, guided as they were by torches and swinging lanterns. The air, after the heat of the day, was softly warm and balmy. It added to the dreamlike quality of the evening. There was only one interruption. It came when guests, unaccustomed apparently to the De-Mure traditions, broke into folk songs of celebration. Gaston, himself, looking more suave in his black cloth coat, held up a restraining hand. Soon afterward there came the soft notes of a single flute. Otherwise, all was silent.

Suddenly, the small group was not alone. A man whose dusky skin spoke of Spanish descent approached Snow Harrington. "You will pardon me, Madam, but you are the lady who played to my Mexican laborers, no?"

Flustered, Mother murmured, "No—I mean, yes—yes, I played my violin. But I thought nobody noticed."

Marvel was equally surprised and became more so as the man explained. He was a distant cousin of the De-Mures, he said. As such, it was proper that he invite her to join the flutist. Daddy hurried back for the musical instrument. Moments later, the violin had found its home on Snow Riley Harrington's shoulder.

Mother played then, first softly with her eyes closed. Not so with her ears, for she was in perfect harmony with the clear, mellow notes of the flute. Enthralled, Marvel listened, realizing that the music came straight from her mother's soul—as if the violin were the mouthpiece of her heart, saying in music what she could never say in words. Haunting, pleading, inviting, hoping, like a whispered prayer.

This, then was Mother's unwritten song—the cantata, opera, or musical symphony of her dreams. And Marvel's heart responded in words:

> Oh, Lord, my God, You who have divided the light from the darkness, hear this, Your song. For Your Holy Presence is here among us—here to wipe away that darkness for all who prefer Your heavenly light to the worldly darkness because their deeds are evil. Sing with us, use us. Keep Your song on our lips as we speak Your Word.

The mood of Mother's music had changed now. Notes of triumph soared to the vault of stars overhead. She was moving among the crowd now, her face aglow in the flickering light of the lanterns, swaying gently as she looked into the expectant eyes of her spellbound audience. Daddy wisely followed close behind, not altogether comfortable with some of the unbridled approval men were giving by way of stomps and whistles as she brushed past. Where were the others?

A quick survey showed Uncle Worth was holding B.J. in his arms in order for him to miss no part of the theatrical pageantry around them. Auntie Rae held her husband's arm, as if suddenly afraid.

But Mary Ann? Where could she have gone?

Then suddenly, Marvel was not alone. Beside her stood a striking-looking man, the type one seldom saw outside the moving picture houses. The dark eyes and impeccable manners told her immediately that here was one of the De-Mures, holders of these vast lands.

"I gather this is your first glimpse of such *vendages*, Miss— uh?"

"Harrington, Marvel Harrington," she supplied quickly, while wondering what a man of such importance could want of her. He spoke the English language fluently, yet there was the slightest hint that it was not his native tongue.

"Harrington—Harrington. Have I heard the name before?"

"I doubt it. You see, sir, I am only—"

He bowed. If Mary Ann were here, perhaps the bow would be comical. Alone, it caused Marvel to wonder if he were mocking her—a peasant in his life-style, a common laborer in his vine- yards.

"Ah, a guest. I thought so. Then you are most welcome to come to one of my balconies. The view is better from there."

The invitation frightened her. But it was such a short distance away. And she *could* see better, just as Billy Joe could watch from Uncle Worth's shoulder. The man was older and seemed kind.

He laughed at her hesitation. "Come with me, Miss Har- rington. I assure you that I do not eat little girls. I prefer sweet cakes and wine. Allow me to introduce myself. I am *Señor* Henri De-Mure."

And *Señor* Henri De-Mure was used to being obeyed. Already, he was shouldering his way through the spectators and expect- ing her to follow his lead. For a moment she could imagine a whip in his hand. Marvel dismissed the thought. She was being melo-dramatic.

On the balcony, Marvel felt even safer. From her position near the vine-entwined railing, the singing, swaying revelers appeared to be within reach. And yes, there was Mother—seeming in the shadowy brightness to be so near that Marvel could touch her cheek. She relaxed and watched in fascination as her mother twirled among the other guests, thinking briefly that the music she'd played to the Mexican laborers was not lost, after all. Nothing was when it served the Lord's purpose. What a beautiful thought, fitting for a beautiful evening.

For beautiful it was indeed—so beautiful that Marvel forgot the presence of another. She was alone up here, with the unfold-ing pageantry below so close she was a part of it—yet, so far removed she could reach up and gather the stars. Instead, she gathered memories to share with Titus. Then, surrendering completely to this once-in-a-lifetime event, she watched the dancing which seemed to have grown more frenzied . . . heard a loud announcement (but missed the words) . . . saw an explosion of multicolored fireworks as they showered about her . . . and realized that a young girl was being lifted to the pavilion holding the grapes to be trampled by her bare feet.

The beautiful illusion was gone then. She had glimpsed the dancing girl's face. *Mary Ann*!

"You know the girl, I gather?"

The man beside her had changed, as had the tempo of the revelers. He was a stranger, an intruder, someone apart from her life, her world.

"My cousin—this must not be. I—I must stop her!"

"My little guest need have no fear," Henri De-Mure said, too close to her ear. "Your cousin is in good hands—my trusted Gaston."

Trusted, indeed! Marvel had caught a glimpse of Gaston's face and it showed clearly that he was certainly *not* to be trusted. In his eyes there was naked desire as his practiced eyes roved her cousin's bare legs beneath the lifted skirts. And he—why, he was licking his lips as if he, too, enjoyed sweet cakes and wine.

The crowd was rowdy now, obviously having taken too much wine. Anything could happen. *Anything*!

"You will excuse me, Mr. De-Mure. Mr. De-Mure, please let me pass!" Marvel gasped when she saw that he had barred her way from the door onto the balcony with a reach of his arm. His sensuous mouth was close and drawing closer. She was his prisoner!

Marvel's sense of panic heightened. "You've made a mistake—" she gasped. "I am not who you might think I am—"

"I know exactly who you are! What would you think Gaston's duties are? He has found many charming ladies for me—and himself."

She must escape—bolt and run if necessary. Her attempt was futile. Henri De-Mure was enjoying the game. He saw her terror and took pleasure in it. His manner had grown cruel now. In his effort to gather her in an embrace, he caught at her dress. She heard the sickening tear but ignored it. This evil man sought to spoil more of her than her garments. He wanted her flesh!

Wildly, she beat at his chest. And then Grandmother's "gypsy" in her came out. She bit his roving hand, heard his scream of rage, followed by insults and curses. Ignoring it all, she fled, praying until she was safely on the ground and had found hiding in the faceless crowd....

Mary Ann was totally destroyed—destroyed and disoriented. In an effort to comfort and console, Marvel gained strength and courage to overcome her own burden of shame and the overwhelming sense of guilt—the conviction that she, herself, was at fault. They had been foolish, but that gave the hateful men no right to take advantage of young girls' innocence.

"I feel so soiled, so dingy. Jake will hate me—" Mary Ann sobbed. "And they—they'll never trust us again!"

"Our parents? They'd never hate us no matter what," Marvel soothed. "I feel unclean, too—and responsible. We behaved unwisely, but we can learn from this—and we *will*. Nothing happened, did it—I mean, nothing that means you—uh, *have* to tell Jake?"

Mary Ann looked horrified. "Oh no!" she shuddered, "not *that*! I ran away screaming when I saw. He ran after me, and that drunken mob laughed—'specially the men. That's when I—I clawed his face—"

Marvel, now calm, shared her own experience. She felt objective, removed from the terror. God had heard the prayer sung by her heart as Mother played the notes. He had protected them both, kept them whole and pure for His purpose. He would forgive their poor judgment and make them clean again if they would trust Him.

"And the rest is up to us, I guess," Mary Ann said slowly. "Aren't we supposed to forgive ourselves? But—but our folks, what about them?"

Marvel shook her head. "I—we, Mother and I never talked about, you know, such things. Strange, but Grandmother and I could."

Yes, strange, Mary Ann agreed. They decided then to say nothing to their parents. It would not mend matters. They had too much on their minds already. And besides, why spoil their happiness?

It seemed a wise decision. Mother was ecstatic with pleasure. She had brought joy she said. She had brought hope. And the crowd had loved her, appreciated her concert. The evening's memories would never fade—never! Daddy was as proud as a peacock. Billy Joe had fallen asleep, still smiling, against Uncle Worth's shoulder. And Auntie Rae's face remained alive with wonder. None of them had seen their daughters.

The men talked then. The bonuses had been high—very high (and obviously paid before the episodes they would never know about, Marvel could only suppose). In that mood, it was easy for them to discuss the future. Grapes were finished, no other crops ready for harvest, no going on to Oregon—so why *not* the City of the Angels? Yes, why not?

Marvel felt resigned. There was evil in the high places as well as the dins of iniquity. Never mind the "vintage of the wicked." Jesus was the true vine, and Him they would follow.

10

A Single Step

"Well, Mary Ann, what did you think of the grand celebration back there?" Daddy called over his shoulder, once they headed toward Los Angeles. She had chosen to ride with them so B.J. could rest.

"It was very—interesting," Mary Ann gulped, and relief spread over her face when Mother and Daddy engaged in an animated discussion all their own. Mother was still entranced, it was plain to see.

It was equally plain to see that Mary Ann remained troubled.

"You've not been able to put it all behind, have you? What's troubling you, Mary Ann?" Marvel asked in guarded tones.

"I know we're supposed to forget—"

"Not forget exactly. More like face ugly facts—know there *aren't* any of Billy Joe's bears under our beds. You're not smiling, Mary Ann. What is it? What happened that you didn't tell me?"

Tears filled Mary Ann's eyes. "I—I'm scared—like I was about Elmer. I'm afraid that awful man'll follow. He—he told me I'd regret this—that it would haunt me, turning down a chance of a lifetime. It was a threat—I know it was. He'll follow. It *was* a threat?"

"No," Marvel said thoughtfully. "No, I think it was a promise in a way—a hint of what we dumb-but-beautiful, in his scheming mind, would grab. Those men had something in mind—maybe to take advantage of our ignorance one night and then throw us away. Or maybe more—*pay* if we insisted, or be their mistresses, lovers, concubines—whatever they have in his land. *Tradition*, bah!" Marvel bit off each word in disgust.

"But what if—what if they'd forced us to give up?"

Hearing the agonized tone, Marvel reached for her cousin's hand. It was cold, clammy. Mary Ann would have nightmares over this. Marvel forced a certain serenity. She must help as always with others.

"There's an ugly word for that. The law is on our side—both God's and man's," she said reassuringly. "But if they had? I hope you would have remembered our bodies can be ravished, but not our souls."

Mary Ann lifted her chin then. "You're right, Marvel. You're so smart and so brave. Yes, you *are* right. Our souls belong to God. But our hearts belong to Jake and Titus, wouldn't you say?"

Marvel laughed, feeling better now. "Yes, I think God would allow that. But we'll be more careful now. That's our responsibility."

Yes, "abstain from all appearance of evil," Paul had said. God had warned them now. Why bother Mary Ann with details of women who chose to sell their bodies? One step forward was enough for now. That was how every journey began—with a single step. . . .

* * *

Dale and Worth Harrington bargained with a heavily rouged woman and were able to get a two-bedroom apartment for almost nothing. They had accumulated a sizable amount of cash during grape harvest, but it must get them by until they could afford better arrangements. One look at the seedy building caused Marvel to tremble. It was shabby and, she was sure, in a red-light district. Although she'd had no experience in such things, instinct warned of evil. Men staggering about had to be drunks. And behind those cheap green windowshades she could feel hopeful eyes looking for business. *Prostitutes!* But she kept still.

They would be careful—very careful. And, she reminded herself, the dark, dismal quarters were only temporary. There would be work!

And there was. It happened so fast, so unexpectedly. Marvel was helping Mother and Auntie Rae clear away the filth while debating inwardly whether to write from such a place when, with a whoop, Daddy and Uncle Worth were back with them. Yes, they had work—both of them. It was true what people along the way reported. The defense factory was hiring men. Their being untrained made no difference. Some of the applicants standing in the line stretching from here back to Texas—fellows who'd been suckered into here-today-gone-tomorrow schools—said these two were out of luck, didn't stand a prayer.

"*We* prayed. But go on, you haven't told us: wages, how long, *everything*!" Mother interrupted. "But wait! I have to wash my hands."

Daddy laughed, then looking around him, sobered. "How long? It depends on lots of things, I guess—mostly overseas. But long enough to get us out of *this* hole. We're paid every two weeks—"

"So don't unpack much, lovely ladies. My sakes, Dale! This place smells like a manure pile." Uncle Worth almost gagged with revulsion. "Wages paid by the hour. We'll be gone before this thing collapses. It's propped against the building next door. Ugh! I could puke!"

"Vomit!" B.J. corrected. "We gonna eat in this outhouse?"

The men made good their promises. Mastering the skill of riveting, driven by sheer need, they had made an impression on the overseer of their department. It was he who told them of a simple, but clean apartment house in a better neighborhood. The man also told of carpooling—oh yes, essential here, cheaper, too. He could arrange for both, providing they wished to stay on? Indeed they did!

"Well," Marvel confided to Mary Ann, "I'm thankful for everything, and laugh this one off: thankful the walls *are* thin as paper. Radios are blaring—*listen*! There's the news now."

Both girls pressed ears to the rough walls with thudding hearts. The defense plants meant preparation for war *somewhere*. If the United States helped with weapons, wasn't it possible the country could send *men*? The president promised, but what was this man saying?

"We in America today are nearer to the final triumph over poverty than ever before in the history of any land." Sound familiar? They came from the mouth of a man called Hoover. Herbert Hoover, made the daring declaration. The then-president may have believed his words. The nation did! You see, that's why the Great Depression came as such an earthshaking jolt. Men considered to be great thinkers had led us to believe them. We had achieved "a permanent plateau of prosperity," they said. Fourteen months after the Hoover declaration in 1928, the crash of the Great Wall of New York sent shattering reverberations throughout the Western world. You know the rest: by '32 American industry operating at less than half the '29 volume . . . one car rolling off assembly line compared to four . . . building halted, naked girders left to rust in open air . . . foreign trade slumped . . . crop prices plunging . . . farmers watching labors of a lifetime wiped out, fields, houses, equipment put under the sheriff's hammer. Result? Thirteen million unemployed . . . so many enlisting in the "vagabond army" that otherwise-empty freight cars overflowed. . . . Cities became garbage dumps, haunted by the hungry, air heavy with stench and flies . . . yet desperate men probe the dumps for a single crust of bread. That, then, is what our present president inherited! Along with a nation palsied by fear. Maybe these names will sound more familiar: Rud Rennie, Babe Ruth "The Babe?" They are of the thirties' vintage . . . and sportswriter Rennie said it well, recalling his journey north with the New York Yanks from their '33 training camp: "We came home by way of Southern cities which looked ravaged by an invisible enemy. People seemed to be in hiding. They wouldn't even come out to see Babe Ruth and Lou Gehrig."

"We've heard all this before," Mary Ann said, relief spreading over her face. "Like he said, 'We have nothing to fear but fear.'" As if he had overheard, the commentator continued:

"So what good is a rehashing of history?" you asked. Plenty, in view of today's fast-breaking news. FDR said of our current Depression he would deal with it as if we were in fact invaded by a foreign foe. Now, indeed such foes may be hammering upon our very doors. Electrifying words? Close your eyes, as America dared do, soothed by Hoover's words, if you dare join the ranks of isolationists! Remember, however, that journalists never sleep. John Elliott didn't! Could his glaring headline, "Reporter Foresees Hitler's Rise to Power," prove to be correct? Today's news carries eyewitness reports of having experienced the beginning in Berlin in '33. . . .

"That magazine article—the one that lady gave us—" Mary Ann whispered in white-faced horror.

Marvel nodded, whispered "Mrs. McMeal," and returned to the news:

> . . . and so he returned to the AAA, restricting acreage devoted to certain agricultural crops in a "parity" formula, admitting that it was inspired by the similar program of the Word War. *War!* Always comparisons to war. The plan might not work . . . but what was the president to do? So here we are in '35—off the gold standard for the first time since 1879 . . . a plus, only people remain destitute . . . and, in the warning words of financier Bernard Baruch, "Maybe the country doesn't know it yet, but we may find we've been in a revolution more drastic than the French Revolution!" But now President Roosevelt may be facing a far greater enemy than the Great Depression. The man is smart, he listens. He knows what's going on across the seas. But how to break the news to the American people or gain support of Congress are problems. The man's shackled by isolationists, and he knows the pitfalls of interventionism. Remember Hoover and Coolidge before him? He's taken care of Cuban waters. There are the "isms" to deal with: Fascism . . . Nazism. Will America remain neutral? *Can* we? *Dare* we? He has promised. . . .

An unseen hand turned the radio off. A creaking on the stairway said someone was leaving or arriving. "Daddy and Uncle

Dale!" Mary Ann said with enthusiasm born more of relief to close out the news than excitement over her father's return. Marvel followed her to the thin door and helped her grapple with the resistance of the rusted knob. The door yielded with a sudden swing, causing both to tumble into the dark hall in near-somersault. Under ordinary circumstances, it would have "tickled the funny bone," as Mary Ann said later. But the circumstance was not funny. That thin, pitiful, white-washed face underneath marked the woman "prostitute." Clutching the cheap paisley kimono in shame, the young woman fled.

"Is she one—one of B.J.'s *night crawlers*?" Mary Ann's whisper sounded ghostly in the tomb of darkness, a darkness filled with the trail of cheap perfume left behind the frightened woman.

"Prostitute? Yes—yes, I guess she is—"

"I thought so," Mary Ann gulped. "I saw what must be her boss—what's the word—*madam*?—made up like a vampire and madder'n a wet hen, shapeless as a cow and, of all the nerve, looking at *us* like we caused it all! Hard as nails—or did she think we wanted jobs? Ugh!"

Marvel managed to pull her horrified cousin back inside the door. "I know—I know. Business is probably booming. But, we'll be here such a short time. Try to think of this as a picture-from-life's other side. Remember when we heard the evangelist's song back in Pleasant Knoll?"

"A million years ago—back home where we belong. Oh Marvel—"

"I know—I know. But we'll go back. We have a future—something to work for, somewhere to go. Let's not look down our noses at these pathetic people. They've lost hope—nothing to live for, just surviving. I'm beginning to believe people can be driven to anything when nobody ever cared enough to look behind all that powder and paint—"

"You—why, Marvel Harrington, you're *defending* them!"

"Pitying is more like it. That's why we have to offer help—leave a trail of hope, like that pitiful girl left the cheap perfume—"

"You mean we're supposed to *worry* about people like this?"

"Not worry," Marvel said firmly. "Worry's a work of the devil."

"Well, he got his claws in here! If not worry, then what?"

"Feel concern. Yes, that's it—concern would come from God!"

"Have it your way," Mary Ann shrugged. "Now *that's* Daddy—I know his step. But—but *you* open the door!"

* * *

The apartment was simply-furnished but cool, clean, and inviting. Mother and Auntie Rae were delighted to find such a bargain—and with a washing machine in the basement for tenants to use! There was a sign-up sheet posted as well for using clotheslines on the roof for sun-drying clothes. No, of course they did not have to sign up to use a toilet, the landlady assured B.J., who had nosed into the conversation. Each apartment had its own bathroom. They must be new here? The one defense plant was bringing in so many people. Housing might present a problem later—particularly in this area as it was near a market, several churches, and only two miles from an elementary school. Junior college? The apartment was near a bus stop—unless one could walk two miles! Rent was 25 dollars, *in advance*. Refund if the two families left the place as clean as they found it. Garbage chute here . . .

"It's like a dream after what we've been through," Mother said excitedly. "I just feel something wonderful's bound to happen!"

Marvel studied her mother's face. The strain of the trip added to all that preceded it had taken its toll. Her eyes, behind their new brightness, reflected sadness—as if they'd seen a millennium of dark.

Struggling with tears, Marvel vowed again that she would wipe away that sadness, take care of her parents—no matter what the sacrifice. She and Titus would be together! He would be with her in her dreams, she thought wistfully. Oh, what strange and wonderful things were dreams—God's gift, His promise for this world and the next.

With renewed hope, Marvel turned to Mary Ann. "Tomorrow you and I shall take a two-mile hike. We are going back to school!"

The next week was most eventful. Everything fell into place. The world was no longer upside down. And God was in charge. Everything went well with Dale and Worth Harrington. Their wives listened with animated faces, hanging onto every word. Billy Joe entered school and fell in love with Teacher. "Miss

Houser says I'm far ahead of the California kids and—*listen* to me!—I can skip a grade like Marvel!"

Like Marvel. Marvel began to wonder, as she spoke with the registrar at the junior college, if Marvel wouldn't have to skip a year's schooling! The harassed registrar shook his head as he told her the bad news. The school was overcrowded, enrollment period had passed, and out-of-state residents would have had to pay tuition anyway. Now if it were employment she sought, he needed an efficient person, but—

"Oh, but I could do both!" Marvel hurried to assure him. Only then did the man make eye contact. With a start, he raised now-enlarged pupils to stare at her over half glasses, looking amusingly owlish in his surprise.

"I failed to catch your name. You *what?*"

"My name, sir, is Marvel Harrington. It's on the folder I laid on your desk. Please take a minute to look at it. You'll see that I'm capable of attending classes and performing whatever duties you wish."

"It's against the rules. Oh, I'm Mr. Towers, Miss—uh, Harrington. What you ask is out of the question. You are out of state—"

Against the rules. Then why did he bother to look? Marvel's heart fluttered with hope, hope which enlarged as this Mr. Towers shuffled through the pages and muttered an occasional "hm-mm-m." Seizing the advantage, she recklessly pointed out her achievements: her grades as indicated by her candidacy for valedictorian, followed by a record number of scholarship offers. Not to mention the awards, the double promotions, the extracurricular activities. And working—all the time working. And, oh yes, please note all her newspaper columns. Then and now for, yes, she continued to write. And suddenly she was telling the registrar about her ambitions, her dreams—one day a book, for sure!

"And Mr. Towers, I *am* a resident. I mean, we have residency here. My father has his California state drivers' license, and our car is properly registered. We have no plans to leave. It's *so* important!"

Had he heard? In the silence, Marvel heard the ticking of a clock—or was it the pounding of her heart? She jumped when he spoke, beginning in mid-sentence as if there had been no pause.

"—and one of the scholarships can be transferred out-of-state to the college of your choice. Unusual, but then the whole situation here is unusual. You are a persuasive young lady." His grin revealed another side to the stick-by-the-rules personality. "Sort of a witch, are you, filled with magical powers? Tell me, what brings you *here?*"

She had won! "*Le roi le veut!*" she sang out. "The King wills it!"

Mr. Towers leaned forward in obvious admiration. "You speak French?"

"No, sir, just Spanish—haltingly."

"Much more practical—needed here," he said, ignoring the last word.

* * *

Did her feet touch the floor in her exit? Marvel ran once she was on the sidewalk, feeling lighthearted and giddy. First she must pick up a newspaper, see what the Associated Press was saying, get her finger on the pulse of this faraway city, read about the Depression, the possibility of war in Europe, the general feel here. Yes, she must know, even though some of it would cause her throat to constrict with fear. What she'd seen already had set a new pattern, one so foreign to her upbringing, without roots and groping for stability. People seemed so open, falsely so—yet so closed as if shielding themselves from others, from the world. The melting pot of the nation, she had heard said of California— no common ground . . . *too much of everything . . . or nothing. . . .* Without vision the people perish, the Bible said. But what happened when they envisioned the Apocalypse, the four horsemen?

Oh, stop it! Marvel scolded herself as she paid the newsboy. Her hand trembled slightly, but she was in control. She was behaving like a newspaper reporter. That could wait. Oh, she would write. Of course she would! People must know the truth. And there was the answer—God's answer: "And ye shall know the truth, and the truth shall set you free." *Le roi le veut!*

The reunion of Marvel and Mary Ann was joyous. It had been easy for Mary Ann—amazingly easy. Her admittance was more or less routine. She, after all, was completing high school, in a sense. But there was more. "But you first. Tell me, then I'll spring my surprise!"

Marvel told her. The registrar hadn't made things easy, *but* he was impressed favorably with her records. Would check them out, of course. Meanwhile, she could attend class on a kind of revolving-door basis. And work—she had work! That, too, was on a trial basis, but it paid remarkably well. And oh, Mary Ann, they needed an editor for *The Bellringer*, the campus newspaper—work piled high, no applicants, and she was it! Now she could combine all her newspaper work and—

"Oh, why didn't you stop me? Tell me about *you*!"

Mary Ann hugged her tight then. "Stop you? Oh, I was worried—no, not worried, *concerned*," she corrected roguishly. "Concerned about *you*! Now I can be excited for us both. I have a job, too! I—imagine *me*!—I'm going to help students with reading difficulty. And I owe it all to you—y-o-u! It's paying off now. Wait till I tell Jake!" Starry-eyed, she handed Marvel a picture postcard. "I picked up two."

That night Marvel scanned only the headlines of the news. Then bunching them with other materials, she sent another bulging packet to Editor Corey. Proudly she wrote her new return address on the envelope. The picture postcard of the college went to Kate Lynn with only a hastily scrawled note. The rest of the evening was spent on the long letter to Titus. Now he could write *her*, she said triumphantly, letting her heart and the pages fill to the brim with love. . . .

* * *

Marvel plunged into her work, adapting quickly to the new schedule and its heavy demands—just as, she was proud to note, her father and uncle had adapted. All fell into place as if by design. Lost in the work she loved, days blended into weeks in a kind of perpetual calendar. Teachers noted her achievements in silent awe.

Professor Simon, her advisor, said, holding her finished layout for *The Bell Ringer*, "All this underscores faculty agreement that you're a gifted young lady—one with expertise coupled with rare humility. But aren't you going just a little overboard? What's driving you so?"

"Driving?" Marvel asked innocently. "Nobody's driving me. I—I love my work. My records show this is nothing new. You did check?"

"We checked. You're for real, but—well, it's *your* future."

Mr. Simon sounded dubious. He was shaking his head, but why wrestle with trying to read his mind? Here was a strange one, he might as well have said—so young, so beautiful, but clinging leechlike to some kind of conviction, committed to a secret purpose with such fervor that she was near condemned to fulfill. She'd battle failure tooth and nail—and, he suspected with *prayer*. Something whispered faith.

Marvel Harrington saw matters differently. Committed? Yes, she was that. But it transcended duty or moral obligation. It was a sacred obligation, a *privilege*—to God, to her parents, and yes, to Titus.

"Oh! I remembered something else," she said suddenly, as a reminder to herself to notify the sanitarium where Elmer Salsburg was institutionalized as to her whereabouts. "I'm sorry—I must go now."

"Another job? What *are* you trying to do? Penance for a heinous sin somebody else committed?" her advisor said in exasperation.

"Something like that," Marvel murmured and hurried out.

Two weeks later she was named student of the month. And her editorial concerning an overall view of wounds inflicted by the Great Depression turning the heartland into a "heartless" one had sent shockwaves farther than she knew.

* * *

The family came home one evening to find Snow Harrington nearly doing cartwheels with joy. "It all started out so simply and turned into a miracle—just a single step from here to something gr-*great*!"

"Tell us, darling, before you burst or I cave in! Is that *roast* I smell?" He sobered. "All great journeys begin that way."

Mother told then, her words tumbling out in a single breath. Everything was shipshape in the apartment. Auntie Rae had shopped. Dinner was underway when she sat down to play. Her violin? Of *course*, her violin... and the old joy came back. She could see gardens of flowers, *smell* them, touch them—and roses, especially roses, climbing to the top of sky-touching spirals of great cathedrals . . . iridescent colors twisted into rainbows above. And the melody came—the melody for the beautiful symphony she would write one day. . . .

"Maybe I played it. Yes, I must have, for when I looked out there was a crowd of spectators—women in pretty dresses, men in pants—"

"Well, I should hope so!" Daddy said straight-faced.

Marvel bit her lip. If she looked at Mary Ann, they would laugh. But her mother did not laugh. She didn't so much as hear.

"That's when he came—the minister, I mean—Dr. Harmon, pastor of the First Baptist Church. And he gave me the address," she said, fumbling for the scrap of paper she held in her hand (Marvel noted with pleasure that Mother's lovely hands had healed). "There's a choir, choir practice, all that. And now he wants *me*—do you understand, *me*—to come. Never mind practice—never mind their voices or my voice. My voice is in my hands, Dr. Harmon says. I'm to play *Sunday!*"

"And she agreed—if—if it's all right with you all. We've been needing to find a church home. Oh, please say yes!" Auntie Rae pleaded like a child.

"Yes!" they sang in unison.

The church was large yet there was standing room only for late worshippers. Ushers rushed the Harringtons toward the front, and seated all except Mother. Mrs. Harrington was to join the choral group, one explained in a hushed whisper. She hesitated only a moment before following, clutching her violin as if it were a needed shield. Marvel knew the apprehension would pass once she placed the bow to the strings. As the other members of the family clenched and unclenched their hands, Marvel relaxed and looked around her. The walnut-paneled sanctuary reached up to join a high-beamed ceiling. Curved, cranberry stained-glass windows, through which the sun now streamed, cast a warm glow to the carved smoothness of the pews. Home. She was *home*—home in the house of God and home in Culverville. The elderly minister Mother had spoken of as Dr. Harmon was Dr. Holt . . . the choir, graduates of two years ago . . . and among them, Titus, her Titus. . . .

The fantasy must pass. It *must*. But it clung, for how could anything beautiful fade when Mother played as if with a band of angels circling the very throne of God? *Home*, Marvel had thought. It was now Snow Harrington who was home. No longer seeing a church, she was in a great cathedral she had envisioned. Once more the music came from her very soul, swirling and echoing against the rafters as if to appeal release to soar through the gates of heaven. Mother's eyes were closed so she failed to see the spellbound faces of the congregation. When she lowered the bow, the audience stood in silent ovation. As she played an encore, there were tears in her eyes—but behind them there were brilliant stars. Marvel knew that her mother's music would live on and on in the hearts of those who heard. She had taken that first step....

* * *

Daddy and Uncle Worth pretended to stagger beneath the weight the day the mailman delivered a high stack of letters to the Harringtons.

"Well, let's see what all the good news is—undoubtedly news of our newly acquired wealth has spread, so people will be asking for loans," Daddy teased, then added, "but I've lost my audience—"

He was right. Everybody scrambled for the letters, scattering them up and down the hallways. There was laughter as they bumped heads as each tried to collect envelopes bearing his or her name. There would be an equal eagerness to share news contained within those envelopes soon. But for now there was silence punctuated by gasps. Marvel shut away all sound, concentrating on her own mail: a letter from Editor Corey...one from Kate Lynn Porter...the Sanitarium for the Insane...and *oh, thank God*! There was a letter from Titus. In her rush to open the bulky envelope, she cut her finger, feeling no pain, ignoring the blood which dripped on the first page.

Titus had written daily, keeping a sort of diary, Marvel saw at a glance. He was responding to her daily letters. How thoughtful. But temptation overcame her. She needed to read his most recent words. Some people, unable to wait for the plot of a novel to unfold, skipped to the end. Why not with a letter? She could read the diary and accompanying clippings later. But the last could not wait:

Oh, my darling, my darling! You're there—off that awful road—safe. How I prayed—oh, *how* I prayed and God heard. He always listens. How can people bring themselves to sing the hymn, "Hear My Prayer, Oh, Lord . . ."? But then, how can people bring themselves to make such a needless sacrifice as I made in letting you go? I even mesmerized myself into thinking I was being noble. God doesn't require that of a man—doesn't even require it for Himself. He prefers obedience! If I had those days to relive, I would behave more rationally (no, *ir*rationally!)—figured out a way for us to do His bidding *together*. Forsaking all others, I would have grabbed you by the hair and dragged you, caveman-style, into some secret cave of mine . . . whatever it took—yelling, roaring. Oh darling, how much I've learned! A person can make graven images of the wrong things. Am I making sense? I'm only trying to say I love you, *love you*—LOVE YOU! Your T.

Hugging the letter close for a more thorough reading, Marvel tried to concentrate on the choral-verse choir of those around her. Daddy read excerpts of Grandfather Harrington's letter aloud. Texas economy was still in the doldrums, but a few trains were back "on track," and business was booming for himself and the Duchess due to overnight stays of the drummers. And would they believe that Principal Wilshire was no longer a confirmed bachelor? Yep, Cupid up and took good aim, so he married a fourth-grade teacher. And they now were boarders. Pleased as punch with his boys, Alexander Jay Harrington, Esquire, penned . . . but they *would* come home?

Grandmother Riley wrote somewhat the same in her long, chatty letter to Mother, except for a quote from Samuel Clemens which captured Marvel's attention. She nudged Mary Ann to whisper as much. But her cousin, eager to share news from Jake, said irritably: "Who's he?" "Mark Twain," Marvel told deaf ears and listened to Auntie Rae.

"A detailed letter from Eleanore," she said, waving it like a flag, "and another from Dorthea, not as long but newsy. Mostly, Dorthea talks about the girls, how popular they are: Erin and Cindy, Lucinda now, turning all heads—boys' heads. They're taking required exams for entrance into Willamette. No matter—a large donation would talk. And wow! Were they ever making a fortune!"

"A letter here from Alex, Jr. makes her more believable," Uncle Worth said tartly. "He still thinks we should join them—"

"I don't want to!" Billy Joe objected loudly. "They're hateful—and *irreverent*! Always calling me 'Sinbad' or worse. Once that silly little one, you-know-who, called it 'Sin-more' instead of Seymour. Where'd I get a name like that, and why did I have to be named *Joe* after Uncle Joseph, the uppity one?"

"Mind your mouth, B.J.!" Mary Ann answered. "Stop interrupting! For your information, Mr. Question Box, you're *not* named for Daddy's brother! You're the namesake of Mother's father, the grandpa we never knew. He was William Josiah Seymour. And stop poking fun at the name! Mother—Mother never saw her daddy. You are all she has of him. You should be ashamed of yourself—proud to have the name."

"I am now," he gulped. "I—I guess I'm just a pest."

"You are that all right, but we'll keep you around, if—" Mary Ann smiled while pushing back his cowlick, "you'll comb your hair!"

"...so I guess that's all, except what Eleanore says about the boys. Duke's in the university—not interested in fraternities, but was able to transfer into ROTC—still considering the RAF.... Thomas drills with him but has high school to finish. All sound happy."

The conversation continued. One thing was certain, they were not going on to Oregon. Neither were they going back to Texas now.

"But that doesn't keep Jake from coming *here*," Mary Ann whispered once they had slipped away unnoticed. "Only," she frowned, "Jake sounds worried—uh, *concerned*—about something. Says things are uncertain."

"These are uncertain times," Marvel said, feeling sober.

"Don't remind me! Oh, he's certain about *me*—it's not that. We'll work the future out. Anyway, I have my hands full, too." Mary Ann tried to laugh. "Nobody ever listened to *us* in there—not much to tell, only I was going to say Annie Pruitt's married to some farmer. Farming was all she knew. And Ruthie—Ruth Smith—moved away. Arch doesn't care. He's still mooning around over *you*. Hear from Titus?"

Oh, yes indeed, she had heard from Titus. Tonight she would write her heart out, dare to dream, be his "beautiful lady in blue," and begin their book with Mark Twain's quote: "Travel is fatal to prejudice, bigotry and narrow-mindedness, and many of our people need it sorely.... Broad, wholesome, charitable views ... can not be acquired by vegetating in one's little corner of the earth" (*Innocents Abroad*, 1869).

Marvel's light burned late that night. Once she paused to smile tiredly that it was a good thing their electricity was included in the price for the apartment. Dawn would be dimming the city's flashing neon lights before she finished the letter to Titus for, once inspired by the Twain quote, it seemed essential that she reacquaint herself with his biography, his literary works, and the secret of his lasting success. The letters from Mr. Corey and Kate Lynn lay unopened. Those she would attend to later.

The ache for Titus was almost unbearable as she read and reread his entire letter. For there she found the same hint of wrestling with decisions Mary Ann had found in Jake's.

But in work there was solace. Marvel pitied the rich!

Born in poverty, she read of Samuel Langhorne Clemens, whose pen name was Mark Twain... printer... self-supporting ... apprenticed himself to a printer... then to a river pilot. Licensed, Twain continued the lucrative profession until the Civil War closed the Mississippi. But he was widely traveled. "In that brief, sharp schooling," he recorded, "I got personally and familiarly acquainted with about all the different types of human nature.... When I find a well-drawn character or biography I generally take a warm personal interest in him, for the reason that I have met him before—met him on the river." (*Oh, how true! Marvel, who had moved to the old typewriter Editor Corey gave her, wrote to Titus. Which brings us back to our being "literary journalists," weaving together the power of historical fact and the colorful drama of fiction.*)

He teetered between rags and riches... ever the humorist, *albeit* oft crudely so in frontier journalism... married a gentle, fine-spirited Victorian-notioned wife who eliminated the Twain-crudities... humor, his natural mode of expression, proved to be his strength and his weakness.

And then came *Tom Sawyer, Huckleberry Finn*, and *Life on the Mississippi*, all planless, but every person within them is a recognizable human being, and they

> record imperishably a perished epoch in American life. In these books the man who began his literary career as a comic journalist takes his place among the masters.

Biting her lip in concentration, Marvel drew a quick mental comparison between the "then" and the "now" of the nation. Different age, different era—however, a likeness was there. The man whose works became classics posthumously had struggled through the Civil war and then the depression of the 1890s....

War! Did Titus know more than he talked about? Could that be the underlying cause for the small innuendos she had sensed in his letter? Titus, after all, was very much in touch with the global situation, serving as he did as Texas State Senator Norton's aide. So much had happened, and she had been shut off. What had happened to the foreign trade disagreement with Japan, their silk, our scrap iron? And what about the rumor concerning the German dictator whose megalomania led him to think himself possessed with some supernatural power? He sounded possessed all right—possessed by a devil! Had the shadows of darkness stretched longer, made him feel he could conquer the world? It was a nightmarish thought. "Oh Titus, my darling, if only we could talk—if only we could be together! Yes, yes, I understand about the cave. Only you wouldn't have to *drag* me— I'd run with you. Together we'd hide away from this ugly world. But could we escape our feelings, our concerns for others? The time will come, but for now— Oh Titus, *always* be open with me. Tell me your concerns and I'll understand. I'll always understand, for I am *yours forever*! M."

That would prove to be the most lengthy letter Marvel would be allowed to write for some time because her own world was whirling at an ever-increasing speed—whirling so fast that she scarcely realized the speed took the other Harringtons whirling as well. Vaguely she remembered that one step they'd discussed, for the journey was long....

11

Sudden Success

Time lost its meaning as Marvel engrossed herself more and more in work. Exhausted, she frequently fell asleep in her clothes. In class, although her eyes burned in their sockets, her mind remained as clear as her driving purpose. It showed, the mirror told her—a sort of haunting sadness in her eyes. Shrugging it away, she fluffed a frame of hair about her face. It was longer now and more becoming, she decided, and thankfully it had lost none of its silver sheen. And the round spots of color remained in her cheeks, sometimes glowing feverishly. *But face it, Marvel*, she reminded herself with a smile, *you're a reporter now. News knows no clock.*

Success had come suddenly. Never had it occurred to her that *The Bell Ringer* would reach beyond the junior college campus, that there were so many subscribers that places of business paid well for advertising. Complimentary copies went to other newspapers. And the first editorial "From the Heartland to the Heartless" captured attention of a wide reading audience. Some had never known, never dreamed how cruelly the Great Depression had dealt with those who were driven from the land they loved. Others had traveled that road with this heretofore unknown young writer. Editors, calloused though they had hardened themselves to be, were struck by the sincerity of this Marvel Harrington's writing. It needed no polishing. The words held a shine all their own. And where on earth had a nonentity like "a sheet-metal school," a last resort for lesser students, found so skilled a feature writer? They were bewildered.

". . . so, all in all," Professor Simon said, his eyes gleaming with the trophy he'd garnered for himself (just wait until the Board heard about *this*!), "you've made a hit, Miss Harrington! They're whooping and stomping with approval. 'More, more!' people are yelling. We don't *dare* disappoint them. Our futures are at stake—the school's I mean. Of course, the *school's*!"

"I know exactly what you mean," Marvel said quietly, hating herself for blushing. Here was the man who, just months ago, had been concerned for her welfare, insisted that she slow down. But now that her writing concerned *him*—How transparent could an advisor be?

Mr. Simon recognized the look. Reporters—*real* reporters, the gifted ones—could probe a subject's soul and find a story. He began an apology. "I—I'm sorry. I have no right to ask anything—"

Marvel closed tired eyes to collect herself. She felt embarrassed for him and ashamed of *herself*. Why, she should be grateful.

"You needn't apologize, sir. It is a good break for us both."

He leaped from the swivel chair and for a frightening moment Marvel thought he would leap over the desk and embrace her. Instead, "You will?" he exulted, unconsciously rubbing palms together. "You *will*?"

"Of course I will," she said tonelessly, not sure to what she agreed.

Two weeks later a copy of the editorial appeared "by special permission" in the city's two leading newspapers. From there it traveled to the hometown she had mentioned in the article like a homing pigeon, ending up on the desk of *The News Review*. Editor Corey forwarded it to the Associated Press immediately. And so began the account of the journey to the West the editor had asked for. Marvel found no particular joy, no sense of achievement. She'd simply had a job to do and done it. Why should an audience be applauding before she performed?

Unaware that her words—like the notes of an unfinished symphony—echoed to stir up memories or awaken once-sleeping hearts nationwide, Marvel went about her work objectively. The new state of automation was foreign to the heart within, but essential. Days danced past in a white maze, and nights differed very little except for the dying light, because her heart had died a little, too. Carefully, on occasion, she removed the tissue wrapping from the treasures so dear to her: Titus' letters—all of them, his precious valentine, the blue dress, and the pearls. Biting her lip to control anguish, she would kiss the keepsakes and pray at each viewing: "Dear Lord, protect him for me. Bring us together again. Renew my faith that it will happen—"

It was a strange prayer. But something larger than herself had whispered a warning—something Marvel was unable to understand. It was as if her dreams would never materialize, that she would never know that first gentle kiss she had dreamed of... never run into those strong arms that waited to hold her... take those sacred vows....

Then she quickly folded the souvenirs away, and the tender memories along with them. Work! She would work and be grateful for the blessed solitude of her room. With a brave smile, on one such evening she clipped the heart-to-heartless editorial from its first source and sent it along with the picture Mary Ann had taken—the one which Titus Smith would keep before him as he struggled with decisions of his own—to the man she had asked God to bring back to her.

* * *

Christmas had come and gone, marked only by Mother's concert at the church. Beautiful—so beautiful, the notes restored hope and peace to a groping world. Music was Snow Harrington's gift. It was to her what words were to Marvel. Both gifts must be used to glorify the name of the Giver. They would try—were trying, Marvel recalled thinking as she caressed each of her fingers gently for the sheer joy of feeling the soft comfort of the kid gloves, Titus' gift.

Shortly after the holidays, Mother appeared unexpectedly at school. A committee of several men and one woman—the college board—had summoned Marvel to the surprising conference. What was this?

The chairman, whose name Marvel missed, stated briefly that Professor Simon had been in attendance at the Christmas concert at which Mrs. Harrington played. Since they knew her daughter—

"The situation is simply this. We are in need of an instructor and wondered if you would wish to consider helping us out?"

The male speaker was looking at Mother.

"Me? Me teach?" Mother gasped. "Surely you can't mean—"

"It would be necessary, of course, for you to prepare a complete resumé of education, experience— But I'm sure you are familiar with the routine."

Mother looked touchingly like a child as she turned to Marvel for encouragement. This time, Marvel was at a loss for words. This—why this was incredible. It had to be a dream. Could *two* dream such? Helplessly, Marvel stared back. If only somebody had prepared them—

"Mrs. Harrington?" the lone lady reminded her softly.

"I—I've had no preparation," Mother began, only to be interrupted by Professor Simon who had appeared at the door.

"Like mother, like daughter," he smiled in his new confidence. "They are a becomingly humble pair, simplicity being one of their charms."

There was a jumble of words. . . . Mother had played all her life, yes . . . and she *did* teach, well, under an adult program . . . concerts, yes . . . her mother taught her at home . . . she, herself, having been trained by Franz Heinloin . . . yes, private tutelage, if that constituted an education. . . .

"Excellent!" Did they all chime out the word at one saying? At any rate, they would check. Mother would be notified, if she wished. . . .

If she wished! Marvel was sure she saw her mother sprout wings and sail gracefully from the building. Two weeks later she was employed.

Still dazed, Snow Harrington walked around in a sort of spiritual silence. "Just wait until I tell Mother" was all she could say.

* * *

Auntie Rae took over the domestic duties for both families without complaint, even found time to volunteer for church work. Nothing much, she shrugged it off, letting her loved ones dominate the conversation. They seemed to have so much to say, and what were cookies and cakes in comparison? Oh, there were times when she managed arrangements for weddings and receptions. And goodness knows, the drapes in the reception hall needed brightening. Why settle for less than needlepoint? And that led to the mural. But nobody was listening—

"Can you believe it? About Mother, I mean?" Mary Ann, skipping to catch up with Marvel, asked breathlessly one March morning. "We've all left the nest—"

"What about Auntie Rae?" Marvel asked absently, her mind busy with a news report heard this morning over their newly acquired radio.

"She's working at the church. And you're such a slave driver—you and that bonehead reading class I try to teach. I didn't even know. B.J. spilled the beans. My mother," she said, chest out with pride, "has a *paying* job. She went through the same screening that board subjected Aunt Snow to, with just about the same answers. And get this! Not only is she among the employed, Rae Harrington has total charge of the kitchen *and* the redecorating—thanks to all that work with Mrs. Sutheral, now the Reverend Mr. Grady Greer's wife. She resigned—"

"Who?"

"The lady doing Mother's job—not Mrs. Greer!" Mary Ann laughed, then sobered. "Nobody would ever resign from being a wife. Oh Marvel, it will happen for us, won't it. We'll have that double wedding—"

"Of course we will," Marvel said with more certainty than she felt. And why remind her cousin that people did divorce? Mary Ann had come such a long way, was working so hard. *And why not face it, Marvel? You feel the same shakiness. The fellows sense it, too.*

With a bright flash of her red skirt, Mary Ann was gone. Marvel stared after her, the news report coming back to haunt her:

Where did it all begin, anyway—this Great Depression in America, heralded the world over as the "land of plenty"? On Wall Street? Not exactly—except indirectly. Wealth—*agricultural* wealth from the rich, virgin soils of America's heartland—was of great importance to Wall Street. "In God we trust" speaks well of the Western world's convictions of a persecuted people... but in paradox, Wall Street might well have said "in agriculture we trust," so numerous were the corporations whose stocks were listed there... enormous harvests... bumper crops... upward of 350 million acres under cultivation in '29, a figure unchallenged to this day. Oh, not that Wall Street cared about the man behind the plow . . . not with farms and farmers, but the mechanical equipment it inspired. That meant big business in the farm-implement industry . . . food processors . . . packagers . . . refrigerated cars . . . one day—who knew?—maybe *frozen* foods. In anticipation of a bright future, investors went hog-wild, using little foresight, else they might have guessed economy is like a balloon: Squeeze it here and it's bound to enlarge elsewhere—or burst! The farsighted sought havens in banks . . . ruthless, self-serving, and money-crazed. Listeners know the story in these Depression-ravaged thirties! Our once-wealthy farmers are now the "little" customers . . . unable to go back to their drought-stricken farms . . . seeking havens in the defense plants for weekly pay to "invest" not in the banks—for existence!

So much for where it all began. The critical question is, *Where is it all leading*? True, there have been revisions in the banking law, Federal Reserve Board holds tight reins on Wall Street. But are we examining this fragile thing called "new prosperity"—looking at it beneath a scientific microscope? *Should* we become so enthralled with our less-Spartan surroundings that we are led down the primrose path, blinded to the *why* of what we are producing in these new-sprung plants? Look overseas! If the crash *was* caused by the too-hasty withdrawals from banks, then it's safe to say what lies ahead would come under the heading of withdrawal of *brains*! Maybe the Soviet Union is facing facts more than we are—industrializing, yes, but with a purpose . . . aimed either at attacking our capitalism with communism or protecting their own coasts . . . concentrating less on rebuilding Moscow, Leningrad, and Stalingrad and more on building up merchant marines and navy. Our president clings to his good neighbor policy, refusing to intervene. After all, Franklin Delano Roosevelt inherited a strange American attitude when he took oath of office—a curious mixture of arrogance and missionary benevolence toward the Orient . . . fear of the "yellow peril" . . . illusory hopes for more trade mixed with sentimental concern for China. But Japan? Ah, that opens up a new can of concerns, policies, and problems. "We *will* stay out of war!" FDR has assured us. Good! But have we become a nation of isolationism? Who will be first to touch off a new arms race? *Fortune* Magazine is digging deep under our cuticles with its charges that the World War was maintained by weapons made in England and France. America doesn't want a repeat performance, and so the Neutrality Act—restrictions on loans to belligerents. But this will come as news: Extra, extra! "Italian Forces Have Invaded Ethiopia! Our President Has No Effective Way to Check Mussolini!" "I have seen war," he says, "on land . . . on sea. I have seen blood running from the wounded. The agony of mothers, wives, sweethearts. I hate war. Our boys *must* stay at home!"

And yet, there's a rumor coming from the Hill that he is asking Congress to amend the Neutrality Act to cover "specific points." Does he refer to Spain? Is this the *why* of our speeding up production right here?

Marvel had been happy to hear an amusing rhymed commercial break in.

* * *

A tinkle outside the open window said the "Good Humor" man was peddling his wares. Someone should do a story on that, Marvel thought fleetingly. Lost in the annals of time, like so much else—Mike Meehan, the ambitious young entrepreneur, invested some 500 thousand dollars into an ice cream company. With the crash, down went his disastrous investment. But he protected himself by claiming a name for it: "Good Humor"!

"Good Humor." Would that be an appropriate title for the collection of phrases which all the "Tex's," "Arkies," and "Oakies" were ashamed to use? Just yesterday one of the professors of speech made a snide remark concerning "Dizzy Dean," the "kid from Oklahoma who butchers the English language. The million-dollar arm—ho! That Dizzy is just what his name implies, and his mouth outruns his feet!"

Marvel had felt herself stiffen in defense. Not that she cared for baseball, except that Daddy loved it, but to poke fun at him because of the way he talked was unfair. She'd heard Daddy discuss the young star, saying he had a remarkable sense of humor, that he—like the "Good Humor" man—had helped the country through a rough time.

"Want me to help?" Mary Ann asked when Marvel mentioned the wanderings of her mind. "I like the 'Good Humor' title—stick to it. And remember I told you about some ideas I'd share? Yep! I *do* have something up my sleeve. 'Up my sleeve'—know where that came from?"

"No, not really, but—"

"No buts about it. That collection of phrases needs some peppering up—say, some ethnology. Ha! Didn't know I knew the word, did you? We have to know the origin of people. Well, don't we?"

"I'm listening," Marvel said, amazed at Mary Ann's interest.

"That way we can understand these, well, peculiarities—like the 'up your sleeve.' We think of that as meaning a kind of secret plan. But it all started when starving students wore those long, big-sleeved robes, like for graduating. Well, they stashed away food in those sleeves like squirrels hide acorns. Here, *you* read."

Taking the sheaf of papers, Marvel read aloud, and they shared some good laughs. "Blockheads"—blocks for wigs for bald people ...hundreds of years ago slang for dumbbells. Oh, "dumbbells"—weights used for muscle development...now stupid, dense, *dumb*. "Creeps"—crawl ("Like in the Bible?" Mary Ann had asked of Noah's animal collection. Yes, so much of the language went back to the Bible, another source to investigate)...now cold *creeps*, gooseflesh. Again Mary Ann interrupted to say, "Or like—those awful men in the vineyard. Oh, go on!"

"Bootlegger"—people used to hide bottles of alcohol in their boots..."eat crow" "pull your leg"..."beat you to a pulp"—

Mary Ann whooped, drawing her knees beneath her chin as the two had done when little girls. "Try 'beating the tar out of somebody.' Remember how Fanny used to threaten Sula Mae and Casper?"

Marvel laughed with her. "I thought Fanny's expression was to 'beat the whey out' of those bottomland people. Makes more sense."

Immediately, both sobered. Mary Ann spoke first. "Oh Marvel, I miss them all so much—them, Morning Glory Chapel, the First Baptist Church, Grandfather Harrington, Gran'mere—"

Heart aching inside her, Marvel tried to tease. "Not *Jake*?"

Mary Ann, who first trembled uncontrollably, rose suddenly to bang a suntanned hand down hard on the table beside them, sending papers fluttering across the carpet. Then her lovely face crumpled as she gave way to tears. "Oh, how could I have given him up, left him—the boy I've loved to the exclusion of everything else in this whole sick world? But, no, I chose *duty*... shredded my heart to pieces... deserted him—the one I wanted to marry. People get shot for desertion!"

"You haven't deserted Jake," Marvel whispered, feeling the familiar wrenching ache inside—the desire to weep until she fell into a heap along with the papers on the floor. "We'll go back."

"We won't. Something's going to happen," Mary Ann said with a terrible finality. "But," with a lift of her chin, "we did what we had to do. And we *do* have to make dreams—come back for our parents. But we could have all been so happy—without that drought and—"

"The crash and the Great Depression. It would be so easy to drown in self-pity, wouldn't it? We've had this all our lives, but it happened. Don't look to me for an answer. And it's not our parents' fault. I just know that we couldn't have taken our vows, then disappeared from the world—although I admit the temptation's there. Just beg God to bring them back safely, no matter where they go."

Mary Ann's sad little smile was like a fragmented rainbow. "Well, where's a tissue? We'll be rich anyway—rich and famous!"

"Famous? I doubt that—not our purpose in recording. But always remember we're rich in love already. Nothing—*nothing*—can take that away! Now about that book—" Marvel said, but Mary Ann dreamed on.

"No 'nigger jokes'—that's what they're called at the plant where our daddies work. I'd thought California would be more enlightened, but no! They claim Daddy and Uncle Dale are from some jerkwater town, call Southerners, 'chitterlings.' Why, I never ate one of those hog guts—er, swine intestines, if you like—in my life."

"Forget it, and don't be too hard on California. Remember it's the melting pot, attracting people from all parts. I guess they feel more comfortable with a sort of pecking order. Chitterlings, no thanks."

If she had hoped for a smile, Marvel received none. "Don't go too easy on them either. Now listen, Marvel—you're the smart one. No, no objections! You just are! But sometimes you're blind. Right here in this section there's a kind of local option—you know, like Texas had on liquor. Colored people can shine shoes and all that, *but* they have to head back for the city before dark! Tell me they're not facing prejudice? They can fight in a war—oh, why did I say *that*?"

"Because history says so, and we might as well look ahead," Marvel said, choosing words carefully. "We may be building up to another in time. Could be that's what's concerning our fellows."

Mary Ann nodded. "I'm glad you came right out and said that. Truth hurts sometimes, but it's always best to face it. I think I borrowed that thinking from you. Here you go, still trying to pull the wool over my eyes." She laughed again, tension lessening. "And I know where that came from: English courts when pranksters pulled those silly wigs over the bigwigs' faces. I have more— lots more. It'll all come in handy. You'll see. And we'll *all* have books—some talented family. Mother did so much on that recipe book, Aunt Snow'll write her symphony, you and I'll do this 'Good Humor' thing. Hey, you know what? It's a sort of history. We keep finding new facts, so we—I'm getting all excited—like you said, we look ahead, but never ever stop looking back."

"So you 'hit the nail on the head'!" Marvel smiled pensively. "And we know that nothing is immune to change. But we *must* preserve the old before Americans forget who they are. Let our older generations read and remember, yes, but to inform those too young to be aware. Titus and I will do that—*are* doing it with our writing—"

* * *

Correspondence was kept to a minimum because of Marvel's heavy schedule. Her letters to Titus were briefer than she would have liked, but she managed to tuck in copies of her editorials. Demands on his time were greater, if that were possible. Senator Norton (himself "facing decisions"—*what decisions, Titus? Tell me!*) needed ghost-written speeches. New bills were coming before the House as a result of the Ethiopian invasion . . . and now rumors from the Far East, but the ambassador to Japan didn't favor strong measures against Tokyo yet (*yet?*). "By the way, I'm sending a copy of your AP write-up taken from your campus editorial. The senator is impressed, so am I, my darling. I'm so proud of you—so proud. And I love you so much. Benny Goodman's playing here and I'll not go hear him. Nothing's fun without *you*. ALL my love, T."

Titus added a P.S. then: "You're a sudden success—I mean, a *real* success, the 'shot heard 'round the world.'"

Sudden success. It had happened to them all—the Harringtons, at least. But Marvel wondered about the rest of the world. And Titus, her beloved Titus, warm and loving though his words, avoided her questions. . . .

12

Bust, Boom—
Bedlam!

The New York Times solemnly suggested that tension had ushered in a craze. Quoting a psychologist, the magazine called it "a dangerous hypnotic influence—a tempo faster than the human pulse." Marvel Harrington noted the item only because it made mention of Benny Goodman. Not that she cared for band music. One week of school remained, and heretofore she'd supposed the air of tension had multiplied only in her own small world. Certainly, few looked overseas.

Little did she realize that the passage of time could be marked by such trifles, that she was standing on the brink of total change.

In reality, swing music seemed to loom from out of nowhere. But Negro groups back in the twenties had developed something called "jazz" in more sophisticated circles. It was a driving rhythm and improvised solos, but few whites heard of it. Either it was too "common" for them, or people who knew and loved the bottomland folks preferred their soft, throaty crooning and their "shouting out the glory" in the cotton fields. During the height of the Depression, the authentic jazz disappeared—going underground for safety, some said. The record industry had "gone bust" along with the national economy. A few jazz musicians resorted to bland music in radio studios—supposedly to soothe jangled nerves of a desperate world in need of solace. It was understandable.

One week later, like a clash of cymbals in celebration of numerous surprises when Marvel completed the year, she read that Benny Goodman and his jazz band had come to California.

> Benny Goodman, 24, who has formed a band to play real jazz to mass audiences, will play at the Palomar Ballroom in Hollywood tonight, after his cross-country tour was a series of beads on a string of disasters. Those audiences in popular music circles will be interested to hear that the budding young group of musicians has given up that hope of revival and gone back to innocuous dance music.

Titus might like to see the item. Why not clip it for him? The following day, a follow-up review appeared.

> Benny Goodman was here! So it's back to the old, in with the not-so-new, or is this a marriage between the two? Goodman was so disgusted with the thick-syrupy music at the close of last evening that he ordered members of the band to "let it swing." Swing, they did. The ballroom filled up with the strong beat of drums, the resonance of brass, precision saxophones, and improvisation of hot soloists. The crowd went wild.

Marvel showed the clippings to Mary Ann, who only tossed her black curls with a "So what? Another research project? I'm too busy with our book. Wait till you see what a grade I got on this term paper! You can recycle it for your master's degree. You'll want one!"

The next day Marvel was summoned to the Office of the Dean. Forgotten, the two items were tucked into her note to Titus. Little did either girl know that balmy summer evening that the "swinging sound" would take the country by storm—that within a matter of months the revived form of jazz would pass into the mainstream of American culture, elevating blacks in a sense, but leading to riots, a feverish sickness. It was a medium to drive some to the verge of insanity, while rescuing others from the brink of despair, preserving their sanity. Faster, faster than a pulse—yes, 72 bars to the minute in music.

* * *

The dean? There was a group, all rising to greet Marvel. Introductions over, there came the all-too-familiar scene. Except that this time it had enlarged—enlarged tenfold.

A distinguished-looking middle-aged man, suited and face florid from the temperature of the small room, stood. "The college board recommends that you transfer to a larger institution such as ours. If you wish to take certain prescribed courses this summer, you could make the move this fall, Miss Harrington."

"Move?"

"To the four-year college," a younger man explained. "You would be able to retain residency here by commuting."

"I am Dr. Horner," the third of the visitors reminded her. "There are details—no sudden decision on our parts, none at all, so have no reservations. Boiled down, it means simply this: You may complete two years in one, as we have you scheduled. First, however, it is prudent that we pose this question. Do you consider completion of the bachelor of arts *terminal?*"

Marvel felt a wild desire to laugh. *Yes*, she wanted to burst out, *just find me a final resting place.* Aloud, she said, "To my education?"

Yes (in arm's-length agreement), if Miss Harrington wished to become a candidate for a master of arts degree, the general consensus was that she should devote her thesis to the Associated Press releases. The accounts were told in simple, understandable language, giving insight to those who lacked imagination...powerful...persuasive—factual accounts which could be written only by a credible witness...new slant on human nature...worthy of preservation.

The first speaker rose to leave. Extending his hand, the man said, "Congratulations, Miss Harrington. You have said very little, but your manner shows humility and appreciation for the honor. Naturally, there will be scholarships to cover everything. Too, this seems a good time to capsulize this interview in a single sentence. Which is to say that, in your case, it is entirely possible to work at your own rate, but given your record, you can complete both degrees in two years. That is, if you wish to work? It would require sacrifice."

Sacrifice? What else had she ever known?

She shook hands with the gentlemen and thanked them. It was all such a shock, such a blur. Then, she—like her mother before her—felt herself floating away. Oh, which one to tell first? *Titus...*

* * *

Fashion-minded ladies of the land paid close attention to the changing styles. Either they were too occupied with the "new prosperity" within their own homes now that most were members of two income families or, never affected too much financially by either the crash or the Depression, they danced and sang their way on shopping sprees. In reality, the changing styles reflected the attitude and atmosphere—always an unexplained barometer. The miniskirts of the Roaring Twenties had given way to the midi of the early thirties. "Two inches below the knee," designers declared as the rolled-down hose (leaving the kneecap exposed) had been discarded. The entire silhouette differed completely, hips and busts were back, "The hour-glass figure of Grandmother's day may be next," fashion magazines sang out, delighted that women were slaves to fashion. This was correct for the cocktail hour, that for at-home entertaining, another "little number" for bridge (the card game which was no longer new). Those who remembered tried to forget, donning dark glasses (so popular in Hollywood circles, giving celebrities an escape from a public-gone-mad) to shut out the sights and sounds that warned that this decade, so wildly hailed, might one day be written off in history as a blacked-out period, a refusal to see.

Adolescents, hypnotized by the big band rhythms, screamed in frenzy—long, flared skirts twirling and saddle shoes tripping to the Benny Goodman "swing." Often they sang Duke Ellington's "Oh, it don't mean a thing, if it ain't got that swing" lines as the craze continued into 1936 and 1937.

The Harringtons heard little of this, saw little, and cared less. Theirs was another world—one of work, looking back while looking forward, busily storing away for the future "back home." They no longer talked about it, just knew it was there. Marvel would have preferred more time for serving in the church but felt secure in her pursuits. Hadn't God said "study to shew thyself approved unto God, a workman that needeth not be ashamed?"

"Do you remember the reference on this?" Marvel asked of Mary Ann one evening as they were writing together. "I'm mentioning it to Titus." And she read the partial quote aloud.

"Sure do. Funny you'd ask. That's the very Scripture I used in last night's note to Jake. Second Timothy—uh, verses 15 and 16, I think. And I added more—just so he wouldn't think this silliness in Hollywood's rubbing off on me—us . . . that part about shunning profane and vain babblings. I wish I had time to write longer notes—"

Mary Ann's voice trailed off wistfully. "I do, too," Marvel agreed. "My notes are so fragmented. And Titus' are, too."

Yes, it was true. And letters meant so much. Thank goodness, letters *were* coming from home. They, not the music, kept them "swinging."

Grandfather Harrington's letters were those of a banker, written by a man of authority—and that included parents. No tittle-tattle kind of thing. But knowing Alexander Jay Harrington as recipients of those letters knew him, they could feel the pain of parting with his sons and the unspoken warmth of his love. And for good measure there was the light touch of wit. "Do I still have granddaughters in Oregon?" he asked testily. "Oh, Dorthea paints them as wingless angels, so sweet they ought to be sold on a stick like this 'Good Humor' ice cream the Duchess and I read about. Me? I think the stick should be applied to the part nature intended—even give Mama a swat or two!"

"It's true," Mary Ann said. "Angels, my foot! Erin and Cindy are more like demons. Aren't demons self-centered? They should write."

"Don't write *them*! I double-dog dare you. See, I wrote Monica that you and Marvel were celebrities—and you *are*. Only she'd swallow a fish hook, so she s'poses you all are big-time kids!" Billy Joe admitted. "Don't look at me like that, Mary Ann. I'm a *pest*, remember?"

Aunt Dorthea did do a lot of bragging, but Marvel found nothing new in that. Uncle Joseph's wife lived for the day that her daughters found suitable mates. Neither was she surprised when the newspaper clipping came announcing the engagement of Miss Lucinda Harrington to John Roosevelt Strong, "rising young attorney." Aunt Eleanore put her stamp of approval on the upcoming marriage. Duke and Thomas would serve as groomsmen

(Wasn't that for *horses*? B.J. wondered). Wasn't it just too bad that Marvel and Mary Ann were too far away to be bridesmaids? "By the way, you may be seeing Duke. He's in ROTC and probably will attend camp in Monterey."

"Too *far* for us?" Mary Ann had sniffed. "But close enough for Duke?"

Mother and Auntie Rae were untroubled with their sisters-in-law. After all, they wrote vivid descriptions of Oregon—a country they would never see. And they wanted no part of alienation. They were family. Daddy and Uncle Worth spoke of their brothers' obvious success with pleasure. This was no contest. And hadn't *they* been promoted?

Grandmother's lengthy letters received greater welcome by them all. Leah Johanna Mier Riley prided herself on her writing, said Marvel inherited the same gift. "You too, Mary Ann. No matter what science said about genes through bloodline, it appears to me that sometimes the mysterious things have a way of rubbing off on others."

> I've changed my outlook (Grandmother wrote). There comes a time when "chickens come home to roost," like the Squire says. He's patient with me and sort of sighs and tries to indulge my grandiose ideas. You see, he knows my calendar is in my growing plants. He lets me dream when the seed catalogs come . . . knowing that's when I miss all of you, especially you, Snow, because you loved your flowers so much. Deep down, I get weary of mothering all those plants—wondering if the geraniums would feel better if I pruned them . . . if the chrysanthemums can stand another year without dividing them . . . and if the sweet peas will wither and quit just in time for Decoration Day. The Squire offers to help, but he'd end up stiff and sore and secretly use up all my Watkins' liniment.
>
> Speaking of secrets, Alexander Jay Harrington, Esquire, is not hiding one thing from me. I pick up the mail for the board house. How could my unwithered eyes fail to see the trial packet from a "famous doctor-chemist?" Who else would waste a two-cent stamp for a magic compound guaranteed to grow hair

in a single night? What tomfoolery! Well, it allows for individuality! I grow my plants and the Squire grows his hair—both of us taken in by colorful advertisements. Dreams know no boundaries. I can no more plant a forest, border this enormous rooming house with mildew-resistant plants, put in a fish pond, and design a vegetable garden without rain than my partner in crime can grow a wealth of hair on a balding head. But I reckon he keeps a kind of mental journal, listening to my dream gardens—and that, he, too, marks the passing of time by the seasons. May wakes us up, says "Get spading, weeding, and planting" (Casper and Sula Mae have other fish to fry now). Then by early July the surviving plants are rewarding there in their hanging pots, never having been transplanted. Come Thanksgiving, we move the survivors inside. "Never again!" I say . . . and keep my promise until, say, February. It would work if those seed companies would lose my address. But you, my darlings, are closer to me in every way. We wait. . . . I want to mother *you*—not a garden . . .

Dear, wonderful Grandmother. It was easier, hearing news of the two aged boarders' deaths from her ("just dozed off with ribbon-cane syrup dripping off their chins"). Shortly afterward, she wrote that Old Uncle Ned had "passed to his just rewards," followed by Hezzie. Fanny was understandably lonely ("losing first you and now them"). Would they want to consider allowing the rest of her family to occupy the house Brother Grady built? Morning Glory Chapel had closed, united with Culverville Baptist.

Kate Lynn Porter's note was more disturbing than the usual infrequent ones Marvel and the doctor's daughter exchanged. What, Kate Lynn asked, did Marvel make of all this "fascism" business? "I read in one of Titus' 'Heartbeats of America' (Wow! is your fellow smart, or is he smart!) that while President Roosevelt did not start all this, he would be blamed. This scares me—read the quote."

Marvel read the clipping and it scared her, too:

The leaders of the Western democracies face three difficult tasks: maintaining peace, containing fascism, and restoring the international economy. Is it still possible to check fascism *without war*? Failure to do the latter must be charged largely to Britain and France. FDR will shoulder blame . . . and there is little he can do to alter it. Prime Minister Neville Chamberlain sought to prevent the war which is spreading now. Fascists view the democracies as weak and blind . . . so, thinking they have nothing to fear, launch another aggression. Prospects of another war in Europe grow darker. . . .

Laying the article aside, Marvel returned to her friend's letter. Bill had returned to school, as she supposed Titus had written. "Oh Marvel, remember when Bill Johnson was Titus Smith's cocaptain in football so long ago? What if it happens again, in the nightmare of war? Airmen *do* have cocaptains, and Bill has said that it was a toss-up between the Air Force and Navy if—Oh no!"

Then, blessedly, Titus' long letter came, Hungrily, she read:

Oh, my darling, sometimes we set our goals too high—so high they're impossible to reach. I have learned that doing what one ought to do does not always make one happy. Are you and I called to sacrifice our love in order to keep order in society? All I know is that earthly life is meaningless without you. But we know the answer, don't we? We must serve God and country—and I'm struggling with the latter. I guess my letters have reflected that concern. But no matter what happens, love is stronger than death. The Bible says that loud and clear. And we *will* get back to one another. As our president says: "We can. We *will*. We *must*!"

The only thing that keeps me breathing is our future together, and it is reflected in all the clippings I'm sending in pride. Oh, what reviews! They open the door to our plans. . . .

Yes. Yes, they did. Oh, the book she and Titus would write, Marvel dreamed, holding the precious letter to her lips before pressing it to her heart.

* * *

Marvel Harrington is well-named, for indeed the
young writer's work is "marvelously uninhibited." The
artist—for that is what she is destined to become—
weaves accounts of the journey from the drought-
stricken area westward in a way which takes readers
along. Skillfully, she manages to maneuver sudden,
sharp angles of reality as one manipulates curves in
the road, expecting the unexpected. Thus, this promising writer makes the journey from Texas to California
a journey of life. With an arm's length passivity, Miss
Harrington weaves together the world of today and
that of yesterday, making them a sometimes-painful
reality. The reader senses and accepts the netherworld of both, and something more—a separate reality
which condenses and purifies like a well-concealed
still, concealed even to herself. There is an endearing
quality to her work, a protectiveness of self and those
left unmentioned. Sincere and open, yet with a certain
reservation as if saying, "I have been hurt in my short
life....I have learned to accept it, but never will I
wallow in my hurts or inflict them on others." No
wounds show, just the feel of still-tender scars. While
the scope is restricted to the peoples and the places
featured, the feelings are both timeless and universal.
Characters come alive on the printed page, charm-
ingly and appealingly. The budding author reveals,
unknowingly, that she cared for each of these characters—cared deeply. There is no presumption, no hint
of condescension, a certain humility which reaches
out and grabs. The outcome is that readers fall in love
with the writer as well as her characters.

Awesome—frightening, really. Marvel felt dazed by the words
of premature praise. Through simple newspaper articles she had
made an unprecedented leap to national recognition? "The
trouble with their painting me perfect," she whispered in a sort
of prayer, "is *they* set my goals and leave me nowhere to go. And

yet the public, like teachers, looks for constant improvement." Thoughts jumbled together in breakneck pace—a crazy clockwork, whipping her past, present, and future into an *Alice in Wonderland* unreality. Her thinking was rapid, breathless, like Alice's White Rabbit spoke.

Great? Did she want greatness? Fame? Forget it! But in some faraway corner of the mind, Marvel Harrington sensed that issues were coming to the fore. Whatever lay ahead, she and Titus would share.

In a captivating style, Marvel Harrington leads the reader leisurely, while rushing to catch up with herself. One wonders if the young writer made some appointment with destiny a long time ago and hurries now to keep it. She is open, yet closed. Private, as if reserving the something for fear of being stoned. When the inevitable book appears, she will no longer be confined by rules that bind other writers to reality.

Subject to hurt (another wrote)... vulnerability typical of a generation subjected to the Great Depression and parental talk of "that awful war."... No hardness about this young writer... a sort of journalistic style which would fuse together with fiction, with a bit of fantasy tossed in. No matter who her characters chance to be in that bestseller the world looks forward to, Marvel Harrington will live inside them all, making a composite of her unique personality.

Simple... unadorned... but here is a young girl blessed with a sensitivity which is rare: the ability to bring to the printed page small-town empathy for large-city detachment. There is a chessboard structure to her writing... strategic moves toward a climactic end we have yet to witness... an extraordinary girl living in extraordinary times and recording the sort of historical accounts which could be lost. Marvel Harrington's work is of textbook quality, with a flair.

There is a kind of honesty here that commands empathy and understanding usually reserved for those walking on stage. For that is what the young writer does with words:

walks through life in a crumbling society, patching the lives of others while mending her own. "I was there," Marvel Harrington says in her understated simplicity, "and I *saw* misery written on the faces." One picture is worth ten thousand words? She paints with one word, making the inverse true . . . mirroring life. One wonders what childhood was like—certainly dream-filled, in a culture which has forgotten how to dream. There is a deep spiritual commitment here . . . mortality with a kind of immortality which brings eternal hope and inspiration to those struggling to survive.

More than a little disturbed by the glowing praise, untainted by the slightest negativism, Marvel was unaware of Mary Ann's soft rap on the door. "Knock, knock!" Her cousin's call went unanswered.

"*What* on earth!" Mary Ann gasped, picking up the scattered clippings. "Oh, sorry I made you jump. I thought you heard. My sakes! 'A kind of Armageddon, the final battle between good and evil,'" she read aloud. "Did Titus send these? Oh, feast your eyes on this one!"

Marvel had feasted her eyes too long. "I feel overstuffed, sick. This is outrageous. Why, these articles are making me sound too complex, mysterious or—or worse, they make me feel undressed, naked!"

"Oh, stop being so humble. I think it's great—a bestseller!"

"See what I mean? These so-called critics have implied here that I have no free will. I'm putty—"

Mary Ann laughed lightly. "Well, aren't you putty in the hands of Titus. He's so proud, and here *you* are looking like rain."

Titus. He deserved better than this, Marvel told herself. But reservations persisted. "They've made this my moment of glory—made me too all-seeing, like an umpire when Daddy plays baseball—"

Mary Ann laughed again, this time with a note of triumph. "See? You're doing just what they say here—using metaphors to embellish. Oh, *forevermore*! Enter, the *country cousin*!" Raptly, she read aloud again.

Out of the heartland and into your hearts is this picture, done with the aid of a cousin by the name of

Mary Ann. Never again will readers resort to dangerous generalizations—that all who had to seek life's basic needs of food, clothing and shelter elsewhere demand grits ... that the Southern accent is the equivalent of a low intelligence quotient ... a tribe of slope-browed ridge-runners shaken by (in the words of Marvel Harrington) "the results of a last 'time out.'" Theirs is a tradition of God-fearing, law-abiding citizens, clinging to family values they are committed to preserve—their thinking, caring, and their language. ... More powerful than magnolias, moonlight (or moon-*shine* if you will), sweet as a mint julep, they undo the ugly stereotypes they've been compelled to wear—that of rednecked, black-hating bigots—*The Big Dumb*! This chapter, which in itself might well become a book (Mary Ann rushed on breathlessly). How's your own I.Q. y'all? Think a water witch is a black-robed creature of Halloween? Read this and see. A "bootlegger" peddles booze while dodging the Revs? A "blockhead"? ...

"Oh, Marvel! This *is* our shining hour! They've stopped blaming *us* for the stumbling economy, stopped pointing us out as WPAers. This is worth a trillion bucks. Oh, read these again. *I* did the research!"

"A trillion bucks," Marvel laughed with her. "Well, I 'reckon as how.' *Why trouble trouble till trouble troubles you?* Grandfather used to say."

* * *

Somewhere outside the confines of the Harrington world, a radio blared nonsense songs which had swept the country. The Andrews sisters were singing "Three Itty Fishes" and "Flat-Foot Floogee." Lyrics were obscure, but fans faked the words as *"Bei Mir Bist Du Schon"* became "My Mere Bits of Shame"! Nobody noticed or cared. Neither did they listen to FDR's "quarantine" speech which slapped sanctions against Japan. *Absurd.* They danced on as the big band rhythms led on to bedlam....

13

"Long-Distance Calling!"

Graduation was close. Marvel's thesis lacked only a proofing and a bibliography, but she must keep an eye on the clock. The two-degrees-in-one hinged on timeliness of submission. Finish, she must.

"So I know what I *should* do," she whispered, shaken by the sudden impulse to turn away from it all, just as she had turned away from listening when Mother, Daddy, Auntie Rae, and Uncle Worth discussed the hiring on of larger crews. This meant enlarging facilities, even starting another plant—which, in turn, meant another move. Why not a house—or should it be two houses? It was a family decision, just as the newer (but still used) cars should have been. Marvel's mind was elsewhere.

"I feel guilty," she had admitted to Mary Ann, "but this writing, school, the degree—" Marvel said disjointedly. "I'm afraid I've started something I may be unable to finish."

Breezily, Mary Ann had said, "Oh, you'll finish. I'll eat my hat if you don't. Oho! See? You got *me* doing it. Know where that ridiculous expression originated—*Eat my hat*? Not a straw man's hat—I mean a man's straw hat—or felt. It goes back to pilgrim days when sugar came in cones—you know, like witch's hats? Good but expensive—"

Something else to include, Marvel had answered vaguely then. But tonight was different. Never mind what she *should* do. There was something between her and Titus she didn't *want* finished. Ever!

Guilt fled. With an overwhelming sense of rightness, she shoved the papers aside, opening her heart in a way that scared her.

My darling: (Titus Smith was to read five days later) My heart overflows with words I wanted so much to say back there beneath our tree. At first, the comments of reviewers shocked me—made me angry, in fact. How dared they try to analyze me. My writing, maybe, but they had no right to pry into the writer! And how could total strangers be of one mind? Had they all sat on a jury, made a case of Marvel Harrington? As if God revealed my problem to me, I know now what undid me. The reviewers were right! Truth hurts. I *have* withheld words, feelings, situations, telling myself you understood. No, that's not true either! I put a bridle on my tongue because I was taught to be proper, say the right things, do the right things, never be forward. You had your goals, obligations, your calling. I must not be a stumbling block but a stairway to your success. Inside me was a wild desire to stand on tiptoe and scream the good news to the wind: *I love this man . . . want to spend the rest of my life with him . . . become only one thing, Mrs. Titus Smith.* Oh, Titus, how beautiful that title looks! I never saw it written before! I feel bold . . . released . . . close to you—so close I could reach out and touch your face, run my fingers through your hair, smooth away every line of that profile of your face I carry within my heart. How would you have felt if I had let go—just up and said, "Titus, I want to marry you!" before you asked? Right now, wherever you are, can you feel me trembling within your arms, see me reaching up with closed eyes, lips pursed in invitation for a kiss? Oh, how bold, how brazen I sound! But how good—how *Marvelous*! Yes, *yes*, YES! I will marry you. Didn't I say, "So long as we both shall live?" And marriage means sharing. We will be as one flesh . . . sharing our innermost souls. Until then, I will be sharing what life was truly like for me then and what I have suffered along the way. But for now, I am shaken by my release of emotions, my darling. After all, this is a first rehearsal for that oneness-to-be. It is only natural that I would have stage fright. So I dare not reread this disjointed love letter which would be a real shocker to Mother and Grandmother—and to *me*. Although I long to write on and on, I'm going to stop and run to drop this into the nearest mail slot while I have the courage! Let's take a sacred vow to never again hold anything back, Titus—*never again*! I look forward to setting the date! LOVE! M. P.S. Reviewers were too generous with praise. I am no ambitious genius. God has given me a gift, if gifted I am, so it is my sacred obligation and privilege to return that gift to Him through my writing. That means that I go ahead with our mission through our columns. Here are the inevitable clippings.

Laying the pen down to massage her cramped fingers, Marvel was surprised to find that she could not bring herself to feel uncertain about the words so openly expressed. "There's no way I can argue myself out of this. It's right!" she whispered. Skipping all the way to the corner mailbox, Marvel Harrington loved as she had never loved before.

The thesis was in, accepted, and the name of Marvel Harrington, Bachelor of Arts and Master of Arts, *cum laude*, appeared on the list of those graduating with distinction. But the recipient did not appear to accept the parchment. Just another trophy, all honor and glory going to the university, she shrugged. She wondered briefly if her high school trophies still occupied a place in their glassed-in case in the hallway. Education was her reward. It must be used wisely.

"Aren't you ever going to give up—I mean stop some of this studying? Me—I'm tuckered—'*plum tuckered*.' Tell you what—there goes the Good Humor man. Let's have something that will spoil our supper—make that *dinner*...something sweet and toothsome and talk girl talk. Oops! His cart's stopped. Here I go." Mary Ann rushed out, scattering Marvel's papers as she slammed the door behind her.

Marvel smiled as she bent to collect them. Their parents were still talking of buying a house. One or two? She couldn't help hoping it would be a single dwelling. The cousins needed each other. Yes, and her smile blossomed into a laugh at the sound of Mary Ann's singing for her benefit, "Oh, I'm the Good Humor man with a frown on my pan...."

When she reappeared it was with a breathless "Whew! It's hot. Grab this bar-on-a-stick before it melts. We must live in the torrid zone. *Marvel*, now listen! I'm older by one hour. I order you to stash that stuff!"

"This isn't *stuff*, and it is *not* work. It's signs of the times."

Mary Ann's mouth was full, but she managed to mumble a disagreement, tell Marvel it was time she built a life for *herself*. Marvel took her by surprise, telling what she had written Titus.

"You did—you really *did*?" Mary Ann choked in her pleasure.

"I really did. Ummm, this is good—thanks, Mary Ann. My treat next time. We have to hang onto those dimes, you and I, getting ready for that double wedding. Meantime, these clippings take on a new meaning...."

* * *

Five days going. Five days coming. Marvel counted time on whitened knuckles of clenched fists daily, scarcely able to wait for Titus' by-return-mail response to her love letter. His reply would come—she knew it would. They were older now, more mature, but their love would never age. There had never been the squeaky-cute bon-bon adolescent in Marvel Harrington. Perish the thought! Neither would life harden her, make her uncaring. The two of them would move into their middle years together, accept others' differences, and eventually grow old, secure in their special world. Mellowing, yes, but love would remain ever fresh and new—giving, sharing.

Yes, *sharing*. Implicitly, she had promised that sharing, hiding nothing. Why hide her hurts? Most people of culture did not discuss pain and hardship. *Did* not or *could* not? Marvel asked herself now. Well, this "artist" (as reviewers chose to call her) would. Society would be horrified. So be it. She wasn't writing for society, but for the man she loved. It was fitting and proper that they discuss feelings others kept private, locked away unexpressed.

That reasoning kept up her constant flow of letters to Titus, even as she counted knuckles—the research, too, for *their* book.

Big bands had become big business—so big that their leaders became stars. Benny Goodman appeared in "The Big Broadcast of 1937"...Bob Crosby in "Let's Make Music." As with other celebrities, the big band leaders became fair game for gossipmongers. The hot-tempered Dorsey brothers feuded and split—

big news! Other hot items included the marriage of band leader Kay Kyser to his svelte blonde vocalist, Georgia Carroll. And Benny Goodman, whose days were supposed to be numbered, played on.

The most dedicated swing fans are following the exploits of their heroes in *Downbeat* and *Metronome*, trade journals of these popular band musicians. This year readers are invited to write in names of favorite bands. The magazines will conduct the two polls to make a distinction between "sweet" (bands playing the schmaltzy sound popularized by the likes of Guy Lombardo) and "swing" (the hard-driving beat and improvised solos). Choices are hard, you can bet. The clarinet-playing Goodman will likely be number one since, in similar polls, Benny has surprised the older generation—the diehards—and wears the crown "King of Swing." Number two? Most likely Artie Shaw—not as hot as Goodman on the clarinet, but in there swinging! Tommy has Jimmy outswung. The trombonist created a brassier sound after the Dorsey brothers split. We all know and love the one-and-only "Boo, boo, boo" croon of Bing Crosby. Now, kid brother, Bob (remember him back with the Dorseys?) has come up with a Dixieland Band which is raging out-of-control. And be on the lookout for the yet-new Glenn Miller—fine arranger, trombonist, noted for fast tempos and lead clarinets. Don't count the Count out— Count Basie that is. Great vocalist (throaty, "Sleepy Hollow" throb tattling of Southern heritage) chooses to stick with his droll piano style and let other great vocalists do singing for him: Jimmy? Versatile—plays both alto sax and clari-net—if he makes up his mind which way to go after swinging between Dixieland and the more modern swing. 'Way back when, Harry James was with Goodman, but talk is he'll be starting his own group. Could be, but chances are it would depend on Benny's backing. Then there's Jimmie Lunce-ford in his double-breasted swing. This leader has showman-ship coupled with a bouncy beat which is contagious and very well may rise to the top as one of the decade's most dynamic bands. And to make ten, folks, lend an ear to a gifted composer called Ellington. The Duke has managed to create a sophisticated style—a jazz sound with a beat he calls the "Duke Ellington Jungle Music." So get those cards in. Take it from the top and, as Larry Welk says, "One uh, two uh, three uh—Won'erful, won'erful" . . . and hope it will last.

Marvel made notes before including the clipping in Titus' letter. *Hope it will last*, the writer had said. Textbooks had demanded so much of her that there was no time for reading much else. Would current trends in musical preferences fade into the past like clothing styles? She had salvaged the item because it mentioned Benny Goodman. But, in reading, she decided it might be of historical value—on the lighter side. Too, one could almost feel a kind of doubt, helplessness, in the printed words of the columnist. It was as if—as if he thought something unmentioned here could be waiting in the wings. Bands *did* play in wars. . . .

Mother's style was different. It was classic, timeless. Marvel smiled at the memory of Fanny—dear, wonderful Fanny whose vocal chords matched the soloists of Count Basie, Jimmie Lunceford, and Duke Ellington bands—who would fade with the whirlwinds of time. But not in the hearts of those who knew and loved her so-called "washer-woman" blues. Confined by the rules of society peculiar to that era, the ebony-skinned woman never once complained about her lot. She was too busy loving and serving. Yes, the era would fade, but it was that very "fading" which brought Marvel's wistful smile. "Now, honey-chile, we gonna sep'rate dem—those—blues an' whites, les'sen de—th'—colahs fade." Grandmother Riley would have told Fanny by now about the new preshrunk fabrics, newest of which was the guaranteed "Sanforized, sanitized, colorfast." Yes, of course she would. Leah Johanna Mier Riley, Grandfather Alexander Jay Harrington, Esquire's "Duchess," was a woman ahead of her time. Hadn't she written Mother about the availability of nylon hose?

"Oh!" Mother had clapped her talented hands together with delight. "Think of it, Marvel—no more of those baggy rayons and tight garter belts. Silk is scarce for some strange reason—always snagged anyway. I wish (wistfully) we could shop together, look for nylons—"

Marvel resolved then and there to reserve more time for her family. All this work had inevitably led back to her original purpose in life anyway—that of preparing to care for her parents. Love meant quality time!

With renewed energy, she thumbed through the remaining stack of newspapers and magazines. Music led to songs, so best check on singers of the day. Something told her to rush, although several knuckles remained uncounted. And here they were: "Canaries and Their Hits"!

Most of the big bands, swing and sweet alike, feature vocalists, usually female. Their hot voices—or cool looks—often upstage orchestras in making songs click. *Variety* Magazine lines up the canaries from '36 to the present with a sneak preview for the future . . . some of the most popular not strictly swing even in this swinging age (shall we say *crazed* age, age of *escape*?). . . . One wonders, too, why some canaries go unsung—example: Wee Bonnie Baker (wee little thing, so wee band leader Orin Tucker had to lift her to a box to reach the mike). So why didn't that canary make *box* office with the baby-voice, remnant of the twenties, lisping "Oh, Johnny?"

"Liltin' Martha Tilton' (Benny Goodman's canary) now cutting record apt to make big hit of "And the Angels Sing" . . . Helen O'Connell (Jimmy Dorsey vocalist) sure to be voted top female, dimples and all, one day) . . . Billie Holiday (Artie Shaw's orchestra, unknown until the two teamed up—now *the* great jazz vocalist) . . . Mildred Bailey (husband Red Norvo's top attraction, singing ballads such as "Willow Weep for Me") . . . Marion Hutton (up-and-coming Glenn Miller's blonde canary, not to be confused with big sister, Betty) . . . Ella Fitzgerald (Chick Webb's discovery, found in an amateur show at 17—Now here's one to watch, this dusky-skinned canary is the *big* gal with the big voice and heading for the big time with "A-Tisket A-Tasket"). Blow our troubles away, girls!

1936 Hits (partial list), "Chapel in the Moonlight," . . . "It's a Sin to Tell a Lie" . . . "Lights Out" . . . "Moon Over Miami" . . . "The Music Goes 'Round and 'Round" . . . "Red Sails in the Sunset" . . . and "Just the Way You Look Tonight" . . .

1937: "Boo Hoo" . . . "Harbor Lights" . . . "It looks Like Rain in Cherry Blossom Lane" . . . "Little Old Lady" . . .

"That Old Feeling"... "Vieni Vieni"... "When My Dreamboat Comes Home"... "You Can't Stop Me From Dreaming"...

1938: (Getting that old feeling, readers? Stick around, there's more!) "Alexander's Ragtime Band"... "A-Tisket A-Tasket"... "Bei Mir Bist Du Schon"... "Cathedral in the Pines"... "Love Walked in"... "I've Got a Pocketful of Dreams" ... "Music, Maestro, Please!"... "My Reverie"... "Rosalie" ... "Says My Heart"... "Thanks for the Memory"... "Tip-Pi-Tin"...

And 1939? Dare we predict, in an age of uncertainty as to where the musical world is going? A lot depends on the direction of the world at large. Music reflects the age, and there is always the late-breaking news of both! Here, then, is a sneak preview—less than that, a wild guess: "And the Angels Sing"... "Beer Barrel Polka"... "Deep Purple"... "My Prayer"... child-singer Judy Garland's "Somewhere Over the Rainbow"... "Three Little Fishies"... and "Wishing Will Make It So"... newcomer "You Must Have Been a Beautiful Baby," etc.

1940? A whole new decade? Who can say what the forties hold? Recovery from the Depression should be complete by then, and maybe, just maybe Wee Bonnie's breathless "Oh, Johnny" will have become a theme song for us all—our victory song! Kate Smith's "God Bless America" or something lighthearted but frivolous, say, "When You Wish Upon a Star" or "Playmates." There's a heart-tugger in the works, but not for a national anthem! Title? "I'll Never Smile Again." Sing on, America!

"I will not be depressed by this, I will *not*! Lord, please let me stop reading between the lines, trying to foresee a future which belongs in Your hands. Remind me to be patient—wait upon You."

And wait for Titus to answer, Marvel could have added. Somehow she was sure the Lord wouldn't mind. Their once-in-a-lifetime love was wholesome and pure. With a lighter heart, she thumbed through *Time* Magazine in search of an item to tie together this frenzied swing that spoke of a world which, robbed of its sweetness, had gone mad.

She found it:

> The Big Apple! Amid a crowd of well-bred dancers in proper evening attire—tails and long gowns—come the hefty rule-breaking intruders. Completely swept up by the Big Apple, they go center stage, firmly planting saddle shoes in wild-eyed spraddle, a maneuver called posin'. "Praise Allah, wiggle, wiggle—praise Allah, wiggle and dance; do that stomp with lots of pomp and sweet romance! Big Apple, Big Apple...." Lee David and John Redmond conjured up these lyrics in 1937 for a swing dance which quickly became a national craze: the Big Apple. Although the Big Apple remains a total mystery to conservative adults, they did their inadequate solemn best to explain with some condescension. (Excerpt below):

> Danced in a circle by a group, the Big Apple is led by one who calls the steps, as in a Virginia reel. Fundamental step is a hop similar to the Lindy Hop. In the words of *Variety*, "It requires a lot of floating power and funnying." In groups or singly, the dancers follow the caller and combine such steps of the Black Bottom, "shag," Suzi-Q, Charleston, "trucking'" as well as old square-dance turns like London Bridge, and a formation which resembles an Indian rain dance. The Big Apple invariably ends upon a somewhat reverent note, with everybody leaning back and raising arms heavenward. This movement is called "Praise Allah." Through it all, the "caller" shouts continuously—"Truck to the right...reverse it...to the left...stomp that right foot...swing it! *Praise Allah...praise Allah...praise...praise...praise!*"

Sickened, Marvel Harrington dropped her head wearily in her arms, letting fair hair swirl in the breeze of the electric fan. Small wonder Grandfather had warned of the evils of the road. Temptations to resist? That was easy! Was this the view others had of California? An unfair generalization—such as that applied to Southerners. The danger was far greater than the glitz of Hollywood. Why, this Big Apple had its core back in New York! But

"Praise *Allah*?" She was more frightened than sickened at that. Praise this, praise that...false gods...money...power...*everything* but God Himself.

And there was the *real* danger—like that which came threateningly from far distant lands, and could come closer....

The doorknob was rattling. Earthquake? Marvel wondered in the confusion of half-sleep. Where was she anyway. Even in the darkness, the room seemed unfamiliar—as was her curled-up position. Both legs were sleeping as soundly as her brain.

Gradually, last evening came back. The Harringtons—both families—had talked about everything, then nothing at all. They simply dreamed together of the houses they would buy here, beginning with small, affordable ones and working upward—as they'd done with the cars...continuing to save money for that wonderful time when they would all go home...build back together, all of them, and reunited.

"But meantime we'll *live*," Daddy had said positively. "Take time out to live, see each other more often, do some shopping—"

"Yes, oh, yes!" Mother had sung out. "Picnic, sing—I'll play—"

"That violin you've kept silent because of books!" Marvel said with regret. "I know—I know, you wanted me to finish, but now—"

"We'll make up for it—all of it. And we'll let you all know about our book we're writing—" Mary Ann said excitedly.

More silence, none of them quite able to say all that was in their hearts. More talk—another silence. That must have been when an exhausted Marvel fell asleep. She remembered something about Auntie Rae's needlepoint...Daddy's second promotion...B.J.'s demand for ice cream...then nothing. Nobody had courage to awaken her.

And now the rattle again, louder this time, more insistent.

"Long-distance call for Miss Marvel Harrington!" The manager's wife spoke softly but with ill-concealed excitement. "Call for—"

Phillip Mor-ris! Marvel thought foolishly, remembering the pint-size page in the red, tailored suit cigarette ad on radio and billboards. And then she stumbled forward, realizing that she'd been sleeping on the living room couch. "Yes ma'am, I'm coming," she murmured.

"For *me*?" Marvel asked uncertainly at the door.

The lady urged her into the lighted hallway. "This way, dear—there on the wall. Your party's waiting all the way from Texas!"

Grandfather? Grandmother? Only in an emergency would anyone call long-distance, particularly at this hour. Vaguely, she recognized sounds of a stirring neighborhood and heavier traffic outside, which spoke of coming dawn.

With trembling fingers, Marvel accepted the black instrument. Her heart pounded unmercifully as she murmured her name and heard the metallic voice of the operator say, "Go ahead, sir."

"Marvel? But of course, it is—*Marvel!*"

"Titus!"

Over the long stretch of wires came his deep, resonant laugh, so intimate it could have been a caress.

"Did I disturb you? Oh, I forgot the difference in time. No, actually, I was watching you sleep. Did anybody ever tell you you're as beautiful asleep as awake?" That laugh again. "Am I embarrassing you—being too personal?"

"I—I'm not used to compliments since—since we're apart—"

It had been so long—so *very* long. And here she was stuttering.

Titus Smith was unbothered. "Apart," he repeated her word. "That's what I called about. I couldn't wait after your letter came."

Happiness filled her slender body, robbing her of the power of speech. Love had come so suddenly back in high school when the wind blew them together—two strangers who weren't strangers at all. In the twinkle of an eye they had known one another better than either had known life-time friends. There was no newness. They had known each other before. How long? All their young lives. And yet, love like theirs *was* new—always would be. And it was that newness which struck her dumb. Writing had been easy. But *say* such things?

"Still there? Yes, you are—I hear you breathing."

"You can't, because I'm not," Marvel stammered like some silly schoolgirl on a first date. It struck her then that time and distance had stolen that opportunity from them. But, with or without a formal date, Marvel Harrington and Titus Smith had made the most of each moment.

"I'm not either. I *can't* breathe. Men in love are like that—"

"And so are the 'objects of their affection.' Remember that song, Titus?"

"I remember them all—everything about you and me. But I'm remembering something more recent—your letter. This *me* you talked about, this person you wanted to be—Who would she be? Tell me—"

"I—I told you," Marvel whispered shyly. "Mrs.—don't make me say it—"

"Mrs. Titus Smith! You meant that? You're really in love with *me*?" Now Titus was stammering. "You love me, but are you *in love*?"

"*I'm really in love with you*," she said in a small voice.

There was a jarring whoop at the other end of the line, followed by a deep intake of breath. "Oh Marvel—Marvel—I wish—"

"Your three minutes are up, sir," the operator said impersonally, as if two lives didn't depend on this. Marvel wondered about herself later. Did she breathe at all as she waited while Titus deposited additional coins? Mercifully, the operator told him to go ahead.

"I wish I could hold you close. I never have, you know. And I need that for courage—" Titus began. "I—want to ask you something—"

"Go ahead, like the operator said, before I die!"

"Marvel Harrington, will you marry me—*now*?"

It was her turn to gasp. "*Now?* I mean, we can't. Can we?"

They *were* holding each other. Time and distance made no difference. She could feel his heart beating against her own.

"We can find a way. I'm too much in love to be apart. But first things first. Fair lady, you've been proposed to. I await an answer."

"Marry you? Oh Titus," she cried exultantly, "yes, *yes!*"

"My darling," his voice was humble, the words muffled, "we'll be happy. I'll spend my life at it—"

Misery rose up inside her, the dragon always in the lurking. "But how—how *now*?"

"How now brown cow?" Billy Joe! The little rascal had overheard and now was invading their privacy—their brief, sacred time.

"Go away," Marvel hissed, wishing he were close enough to kick.

Blessedly, a door opened and he was jerked inside. "What in Sam Hill's wrong with you!" Mary Ann said furiously.

"Pre-puberty," B.J. said smugly. "Ouch! Stop pinching me."

In the telephone, Titus was saying, "Go away—?"

"Not you, darling. Don't *ever* go away—without *me*—"

"That's what we're talking about—never being apart. I can't for I love you more at this moment than ever before. I promise—"

"I promised too, Titus, but circumstances change things. And there's Lucille—I promised Miss Ingersoll." The words were torn, ragged, wretched. Marvel was dangerously near tears.

"That was unfair of her," Titus said angrily. "I heard about that. And there are your parents—our hopes and dreams and theirs. But we can make them come true together—for everybody. They'll understand. We'll find a solution, but I just *had* to hear your voice. Just say *yes* to life!"

Marvel squeezed her eyes closed. "Yes—*yes*—God willing."

"God willing, my darling. Now it's proper for the gentleman to let the lady hang up."

"I can't. I don't want to say good-bye. You'll have to do it—"

A click said the operator had made the decision for them.

14

Callings and Contradictions

In a state of euphoria, Marvel ran lightly to her bedroom and closed the door behind her, then locked it. Privacy—she must have privacy, a time to pull herself together, making sure, absolutely sure, that it was true. Titus—Titus Smith—had proposed to her and wanted to marry her *now*. It had happened! *Or had it?*

Try as she would, thinking was impossible. Marvel could only hug herself tightly and waltz around the room, first whispering a prayer of thanksgiving and then, turning her small table radio on low, she danced to the soft strains of "My Reverie."

Tactfully, Mary Ann had allowed her the time alone. In another situation, Marvel might have wondered why. Now she could think only of Titus' low, intimate voice, and the words she had waited so long to hear. In truth, neither of the cousins felt like sharing. Each was buried in her own private world. Which was just as well, since the curtain of time shielded them mercifully from a surprising future—one which neither girl was prepared to face.

*   *   *

Just two days after Titus called Marvel, his letter came. At first, her happiness doubled. Air mail, special delivery! It *was* real, after all. Titus, feeling as giddy as she, had found a way just as he had promised—a way in which they could be married and go ahead with their other commitment together!

With trembling hands and pounding heart, she ripped into

151

the colorful air-mail envelope. Then, dazed, she let the single sheet of onion-skin paper drop to the hallway floor. *Titus was going away!*

My darling, (the words surely intended for someone else to read) Here is a letter I am not supposed to write, a forbidden fruit. This must be our secret—ours alone—because my mission is secret. Nobody must know where I am or what I'm doing. Just know that the assignment came suddenly and unexpectedly—and that it's of short duration. Yes, assignment! The call came this morning (after our wonderful, wonderful talk!) and I'll be gone when this reaches you. Associated Press is sending me to cover the story in Spain. There is no doubt that General Francisco Franco is Nazi-backed. Never mind reports that it is confined to an internal uprising, a so-called "Spanish Civil War." And Marvel, our American boys are there ... not understanding. We must know the truth. Senator Norton has contacts and the AP is furnishing more. Think what insight this will give us, what it will mean. Now, no worrying. Praying is better. God will bring me back sooner than a cat can blink its eye. Americans will come to know they've been had ... and yes, our president knows. What rewards! Not to mention the monetary one—the answer we looked for, paving the road to our immediate marriage when I return. Oh Marvel, I'm glad you're not here, looking up at me with those *Marvelous-blue* eyes (I still like my word better than yours, for I plan on changing Harrington to Smith the day I get back!). I couldn't go if I looked into those eyes. I'll be taking that adorable photo you sent—the one with the look of expectancy that something wonderful is about to happen. It's going to! You'll be Mrs. Titus Smith forever and a day. We're *engaged!* Oh, I love you, love you! T.

When the first phases of shock and disappointment passed, Marvel realized that she must live with her future husband's decision. Titus' future, which was *their* future now, depended on her acceptance of his chosen way to reach life's goals. Proud of him? Of course she was proud. This was the big break. It was unworthy of her to question his response to such a great opportunity. This way Titus Smith could serve his country and his God. For God had a plan for him—for them both, and who could know the mind of God?

Somewhat restored, but still in need of privacy, she picked up the letter and hurried back to her room. Her memory needed restoring. Not that the explosive situation in Spain was new— more that it had been shelved because of other demands.

When was it that the Daughters of the American Revolution had allowed themselves to be duped into joining forces with the zany YCL (nobody realizing that the letters stood for Young *Communist* League)? Oh yes, 1937. Patriots, they called themselves—loyal Americans. "Why, some people have the mistaken idea that YCLers are politically minded, that nothing outside of politics means anything. Gosh, no! We attend shows, parties, all that like other people." It was a sorry matter.

That was only two years ago. Actually, of course, roots went farther back—1935, Marvel believed. She searched for and found supporting information in the scrapbooks of her columns:

The sudden transformation of the local Bolsheviki commenced in Moscow, of all places. The Soviets, realizing that Adolph Hitler intended one day to attack Russia, put an end to their anticapitalist dogma and ordered Communists the world over to unite to protect the Red motherland. For all its contradictions, the changeover was a serious matter. In an about-face, the country put on a homespun exterior and began waving the U.S. flag, whisking under the carpet all bias against the American social system....

Not that the D.A.R. was alone. Other organizations joined in, designed to appeal to the "ordinary American" of all persuasions. A sort of wooing followed and, blind-mice-like, Negro churches fell prey...medical groups...folksingers...theater buffs, and book clubs, to name a few. Hollywood, hearing that the "fronts" (as they came to be called) had attracted over seven million members, decided it was good publicity. So

Tinsel Town really kicked up the dust. The place came alive with activities of "enduring value." After studio hours, Beverly Hills buzzed with activity, blissfully unaware that "cause" was dangerous, opened their hearts and swimming pools to the "common American" in one-big-happy-family style. Social climbing and do-gooding went rampant. Where but here could the lonely liberals rub shoulders and "fronts" with the likes of Joan Crawford...Myrna Loy...Edward G. Robinson...James Cagney...and other celebrities? The film industry welcomed the sensation of being involved with real history and gave generously time and money.

Marvel, recalling all the hullabaloo, glanced out the window at the restful blue of the California skies and smiled. "Hello, Lord," she whispered. "Thank you for love—and keep my love safe."

Safe? Was anybody safe when it came to war? Frightened suddenly, and knowing God would understand her human concern, she returned to the newspaper clipping. And there, sure enough, she found the awful truth staring her in the face:

"Great fun while it lasted," one might say, except for the possible tragic history yet to be written. Bear in mind that American boys are there. When the Fascist General Franco, supported by both Hitler and Mussolini, marched in to overthrow Republican government, our red-blooded young American men— idealistic and misguided—rose to the cause. Over 3000 volunteered to fight. For naught? What is to become of them there overseas? Let us hope and pray that all are home safely, but it is impossible to do a head count since the men were not in Spain at the order of our government. Hollywood has awakened. America's so-called "common people" cringe with embarrassment, realizing they've been had. For there has been another about-face. Russia signed with Germany a Nazi-Soviet pact...Stalin toasted Hitler's health ...and those who thought they were pursuing good causes realize they were doing so beneath a Red banner. Who is to say what will happen?

Who is to say? Titus, for one. The Associated Press had dared send him into *this*? How could they? *How could they*? No, not even Titus, brilliant thinker though he was, could answer what would happen eventually. He could tell only what *had* happened and what was in progress *now*. And, Marvel realized miserably, she would know nothing except what she read. Unless—

Yes, that was it. She must recap the items for Editor Corey, write more articles, stay in closer touch. That way she and Titus would be working together until their "someday" came.

It occurred to her then that she had failed to read Mr. Corey's most recent letter, as well as the one from the mental institution where Elmer was a patient. She must organize her time, check on gainful employment, become more active in church (even though it was not like home, she thought wistfully), *and* see more of her family.

Ready to close the notebook, Marvel's eyes caught sight of some excerpts she had clipped from another newspaper and planned to include in one of her columns. The collection taken from actual letters was written by a Wil Mendeleson (member of the volunteer group then in Spain). The excerpts had touched her deeply then. They were even more heartbreaking now that Titus—her Titus—was there:

> I am writing from the training base of the Spanish People's Army. Last night we marched into the nearby town. Older women, careworn faces, thinking of their own sons and husbands at the front, cried. The young girls smiled or raised arms in the popular salute. Our 4000-mile journey was being understood, appreciated.
>
> —June 3, 1938

> About myself, I am doing fine, a good shot really, like a Coney Island range expert. This summer may well seal the fate of world peace. Everybody must be brought to the realization that every day Spain continues in its efforts time is gained for peace forces all over. In this light Spain is holding the fort for America. If America does not rally it is cutting its own throat.
>
> —June 22, 1938

I've seen a magnificent cathedral rising through Barcelona completely stripped...but that can convey nothing to me. My brain says "bombers." I know it, I see it, but the terror just isn't there.

—July 15, 1938

Looks like any hour now we'll be off. While our forces are tremendously strong and we confidentially expect victory, accidents do happen. Don't show any of this to my parents. I love you. I love you.

—July 23, 1938

Footnote: Wilfred Mendeleson of Brooklyn, New York, was killed in action July 28, 1938.

A warm breeze playfully lifted the lace curtains, but Marvel shivered. Half expecting to see dark clouds, she scanned the sky. But the window revealed that the arch of blue overhead was still in place, broken only by the ever-increasing number of experimental planes from the aircraft factories. Somewhere they were dropping bombs....But no, she was not going to allow such thoughts to become another dragon of worry—the dragon of speculation as to the whereabouts of Titus. This was Saturday, a perfect day for shopping. The family needed her and she needed them—and she no longer wanted to be alone.

"Mother!" she said moments later, "how about some shopping—"

Snow Harrington's face lighted with pleasure. "Oh, some nylons—I'd love it! And Rae spotted some black-eyed peas at the farmers' market—that is, if she and Mary Ann are included?"

Daddy laughed. "How could you ask, my love? And I vote for the peas. Hey! Look for some okra! Ummm, does that *Stretching to Survive* cookbook include Mother Riley's down-home cornbread? Wait, add two more items: ham hocks for the black-eyes and a fryer. We're going house-hunting tomorrow. No reason why we can't ride on down to the beach—"

Mother clapped her slender hands in little-girl glee. "Oh, could we, Dale? Could we *really*? We've never been— Imagine living this close and not seeing the ocean—"

Yes, imagine, Marvel thought with a twist of her heart. *And imagine my never having seen a football game and Titus was captain.*

"I agree. Let's not postpone that," she agreed quickly. "And Daddy," she said with a forced laugh, "I'm guessing that you are ordering fried chicken for a picnic—"

"'Down beneath the sheltering palms—'" he crooned with a grin.

* * *

On that faultlessly blue, clear Saturday the Harringtons stole from the apartment like truant schoolchildren. Too many of them for one car, they agreed. It would take one vehicle just to haul Marvel's camera and notebooks, not to mention all the heaped-high blankets and bulging picnic baskets, the men teased.

"I'll drive," Daddy volunteered. "I know exactly where to go. I've done a sneak preview. So hop in and see our dream house!"

B.J. stopped abruptly, disappointment written on his face. "I thought we were going to the beach, go wading, picnicking— have fun." He yawned, his mouth open like a cave. "*You* go. I'll stay—"

"You'll do no such! Get in like Uncle Dale said." Mary Ann's command was sharp, unlike her. "What kind of haircut is *that*?"

"It's a Dracula," he said with adolescent sullenness.

"That figures! Dracula must have cut it himself—with a jack-knife. Stop stalling and get in the car," she said fiercely.

It was unlike Mary Ann to be so ill-humored. Something was wrong, Marvel realized immediately. Come to think of it, wasn't it strange that her cousin had made no mention of the long-distance call? Marvel had been relieved, of course. Anything to avoid questions—questions she longed to answer but must not. But now?

"I'll go, smarty, but I won't be nice," B.J. sulked.

"I believe you!"

B.J. stuck his head inside the door, then stopped to hurl back over his shoulder, "Gran'mere told us we were of royal lineage, so we're the style setters. I can wear my hair however I choose. You're bloody lucky I don't assert my rights, make you address me as 'your grace'!"

"Well, Grace, my boy, get your hind parts loaded in," Uncle Worth intervened jovially, giving Daddy a wave of any-minute-now.

He had missed the exchange of words between his offspring. So had Mother and Auntie Rae, how busied themselves with picnic materials. Marvel was glad. Nothing should spoil their day. She herself was having to force brightness, not that it was easy—particularly when Billy Joe muttered his wish for a gun so he could play Russian roulette with his life....

Dale Harrington, obviously enjoying the mystery he had created, ignored all questions. "Ask me no question and I'll tell you no lies," he quoted Grandfather Harrington's old saying glibly.

Past the apartment houses they drove, past the surprisingly large plant where he and Uncle Worth worked (still silent, he pointed it and other sprawling factories out), and into a crowded but attractive cluster of modest cottages. They would stop here probably.

Only they did not. Instead, Dale Harrington drove on until houses began to thin, to a more secluded area, with more acreage, where houses were Victorian—aging but well-built. The residents of this neighborhood had unquestionably said a firm *no* to the urban sprawl which would have swallowed them up if money could buy peace.

Marvel caught her breath. Surely Daddy would not think they could afford anything this grand. Why, the asking price would be terrible. But he was slowing, then pointing to signal Uncle Worth. And suddenly the car stopped before a corner lot, in the middle of which stood a white, multi-windowed two-story house. It was beautiful in spite of the peeling paint on the clapboard siding, the sagging of the quaint cactus-green shutters, and a few red tiles missing here and there from the roof. There was a wide expanse of cool green lawn, with great pepper trees fanning the breeze in front, while along the fence was the most colorful display of zinnias Marvel had ever seen. A curving flagstone walk led invitingly to the heavy door. Fascinated, all the Harringtons were talking at once—except for Marvel and Mary Ann. Each sensed the other had a problem, but there was no time to talk. B.J., his pout forgotten, led the way to the back.

"Let them investigate," Mary Ann, white-faced, whispered, desperately tugging at Marvel's sleeve. "I *have* to discuss something. I—I'm *miserable*. We won't be missed—"

But already their families were calling. "*Hurry, girls!*"

"We *will* talk, Mary Ann," Marvel said hurriedly. "I need it, too. But try to show some enthusiasm. We have to for their sakes."

Yes, she needed to talk. There was very little she could reveal about Titus, since it was classified information, yet he was the focus of her mixed emotions about buying a house—any house, and particularly this one. It would be overpriced, payments would run high, and—worst of all—such an investment would hold them here longer than she had hoped to stay. She wanted to go home to Titus.

Mary Ann, having turned palms up in despair, sighed. "Let's go."

Although Marvel nodded, she took another glance at the house. It held a strange appeal, regardless of all else. And then she knew! Of course—she was remembering the Harrington mansion, as neighbors called the East Texas home. Only fragments of memory drifted in since it was so very long ago, buried as it was in the ashes of time. If only this house had remained there. Well, she would restore it all.

"Oh, it's a dream. I love this house!" Mother was saying excitedly. "And look at this backyard: oranges ready to juice—"

"And still blooming!" Auntie Rae joined in. "And an *apricot* tree!"

The backyard was fenced by hedge to guarantee privacy, although there could be no problem with prying eyes. The lot was too big. Daddy followed Marvel's gaze. "There's room for baseball!" he said.

Uncle Worth had eyes only for the three-car garage. "My shop!"

"Look at the concrete slab—room for one-on-one basketball for me and the guys. And this is the first garage I ever saw with an upstairs!" B.J. pointed in amazement. "What for? A *fort*?"

"Guest house maybe," Daddy speculated. "Or servants' quarters? But it will make a fine workroom for our girls, Worth: Rae's artwork—a studio for Snow, you know, her practicing or teaching violin lessons. And there'd still be space for Marvel's writing and Mary Ann's grading papers, her books for teaching reading—even a den for you and me. There must be three or four rooms up there. Let's go in. I have a key to our new home—"

Their new home. Marvel swallowed the lump in her throat. Her parents, whom she loved more than her own life, would never change. They were born to dream. Never mind that it was impossible.

Even as Dale Harrington unlocked the door his wife was furnishing the house. "The Windsor chairs should be grouped around the fireplace, and the marble-topped tables close by. The willowware—" she began, her face bright with expectancy. "Agreed, everybody?"

Marvel gasped, almost tripping over the welcome mat. "Mother, you—you're speaking of the things from the Harrington Mansion. You know they're stored with Grandmother un—until we go back."

"We'll have the furniture shipped. Oh, look at the interior!"

Marvel *was* looking. Grudgingly, she had to admit that the inside was all Daddy had promised. Everywhere big-eyed picture windows panned the sprawling countryside. It took very little imagination to see the blue of the ocean. Surely those palm trees were close. It was both spacious and gracious, deep-pile carpeting, a million electrical outlets, and a kitchen so huge anybody could cook up a dream. The house was large enough for *ten* families. Two would be lost in a luxury of space, architectural glory—and debt!

"Worth," Auntie Rae said in a little aside, "I *love* it, but—"

"Wondering about price, sugar? Dale says it's a steal."

"That's against the law," Billy Joe piped up, "but I'm above the law. We'll take it!"

"You'll take that 'For Sale' sign back, that's what," Mary Ann told her brother fiercely. "We don't own this house."

"*Yet*, honey," Daddy said. "Look at your mother's face!"

With an intake of breath, Marvel asked the dreaded question. "The owners—how much have they asked for this place?"

He quoted a figure the heirs had named. Real estate was high and going higher, so they would be wise to grab it. "We can't swing it alone, but with Worth going in with us, it's a sound investment. You," he sobered, "don't like it? Don't want us to have it?"

"It's not that," Marvel gulped. "It's still a lot, but something else is bothering me," she admitted. "What about going back? Our plans?"

Daddy put a comforting arm around her shoulders. "Oh, we'll go, little one—in time. But there has to be lots more rain. And if we build up an equity while we have work— I forgot to mention that bigger orders are coming in all the time for planes. We're putting on a night shift, and something in between called a swing shift."

Uncle Worth tapped him on the shoulder and drew him aside. That afforded Mary Ann an opportunity to whisper, "I don't go along with this. You know we can't afford it—not even together—and—"

"You have other reasons, too. And I have reservations. This is not how we planned it—And, oh, Mary Ann, you know how hard it is for my mother to let go of a house. But it's all cut-and-dried."

She was right. The commitment was made. And they must hurry, *hurry*. There were papers to sign. The house was available for immediate occupancy. Rent was up at the end of the month ...so much to do.

Before the hurried move, shocking events were to occur— among them, other callings of a different nature, adding up to an overload. But first the beach, although Marvel's enthusiasm had waned. The sea was flat, glistening like pewter in the lilac-pink of the lowering sun. But it felt windswept, desolate, dark with wrack, the still palms whispering of a great beyond where the tides had gone....

15

Those Unexpected Events

In the midst of frenzied packing there seemed no time for Marvel to sort the magazines and newspapers used in her writing. Of necessity, she had neglected a multitude of tasks. At least there would be space in the new house, places for storing, and hopefully time. Until then she must postpone organization.

Moments later there was a change of plans. To her embarrassment, three unopened letters dropped from the heap, each addressed to her. One came from Kate Lynn Porter, another from A. Thomas Corey, and the third bore the return address of the institution to which Elmer was committed. The postmarks bore last month's date. Probably routine. No, they deserved attention.

Kate Lynn's letter was brief but filled with heartbreak. "Oh, Marvel, Bill has enlisted in the service! Keeping up on the news as you do, I know you listen to Fulton Lewis Jr.'s talk of drafting all the young fellows. So he's a jump ahead—thinks it's best to enroll in officers' training (eligible for a rating with his education)."

Draft? Marvel realized then just how much of the news she had missed. What did it all mean? Something like conscription in the *war*?

Feeling apprehensive, she read the two paragraphs remaining. Kate Lynn was worried sick about Bill ("and we'd planned to be married!")... and yes, about her dad. Doctors were called into active duty during the other war....

Other war? Did she mean—? "Oh, dear God, wake me up. Shake me! I'm dreaming this—another war? And Titus there. We need You!"

The words wavered before her eyes, but Marvel forced them to focus. Kate Lynn would go to Bill as soon as he was commissioned. And Marvel, where was Titus? Bill's letters had been returned.

Biting her lip, Marvel hurriedly ripped open the envelope from the mental institution. Miss Harrington would wish to know that Elmer Salsburg was near death. Her services would be of utmost importance when the end came. It was imperative that she stay in touch at all times. Miss Harrington would respond immediately?

First, fear. Now, guilt. Her unicorns had slunk away....

It was hard to breathe. Air—she needed air. No, she realized, it was not oxygen she needed. It was hope restored. Surely Mr. Corey's letter would have cheering news, revive her dreams. It failed miserably.

My dear Marvel (the editor's letter began): It troubles me that I must be the crepe-hanger, the bearer of bad news, but I'm elected to that office without notice. It all happened so suddenly in this rapidly moving world. One day we were a small-town newspaper (growing because of you and your young colleague who seems to be out of touch. Can you help on that?)... the next, the *Titus County News Review* (for perhaps the same reason, that they've recognized your worth) has become a tributary of an as-yet-unknown widely syndicated biggie. My future? Who can say? I'm a nonentity, you know—just an aging editor with ink on his hands and egg on his face! A downright shame for the area—a landmark being razed. But there's a great opportunity out there for you. Strange, isn't it, that one guy's adventure can be another's misery... opportunity or bondage? I guess Marvel Harrington, level-head that she is, would say God had a hand in this. I'm still wrestling with that. I fail to see His taking a part in this drought... Depression... or this merger! So I'm waging my own battle, I guess, asking myself, "Where in hell is heaven?" Stumps me... hits me right between this fact-fiction idea you refer to as a search for truth. One question and one suggestion. Question: Got yourself a Christian geography book so I can see where Mother Earth fits into the scheme of the kingdom? Suggestion: Keep those creative juices flowing. Follow your stars! Don't stop now. We all need you so much. Thank you, dear young lady, you're just what Titus Smith calls you: Marvelous! ATC

P.S. Hope these clippings help, but bet you're onto it.

Under different circumstances, Marvel supposed she would have paid less attention to the first of the items clipped haphazardly together without regard for subject matter or date. As it was, a growing concern gnawed at the shelf of her mind where she had tried in vain to tuck it away. How could it stay shelved when both Kate Lynn and Editor Corey mentioned Titus' dropping out of sight so suddenly?

"What lies in back of Amelia Earhart's disappearance?" (the caption queried). Just two years ago the famed avaitrix's sleek Lockheed Electra dropped mysteriously from the sky, supposedly crashing onto some unknown atoll called Gardner Island, aborting the famed flyer's mission—whatever it was. Personal or secret? Who knows, and who is to say what happened or why? Search followed, along with a kind of hush-hush secrecy. Was Earhart on a spying assignment as some believe? If so, by whom was she commissioned? The search for clues continues ... whereabouts ... reasons. Speculation varies, and now there are claims of spottings ... of capture by a hostile enemy ... or safety under a new identity. Several reporters came up with what was thought to be signs of life, and such rumors are sure to continue until some questions are answered. But in this world of unrest, the mystery becomes more and more important. *What is going on?*

There was more, but Marvel buried the article from sight. Maybe if she read on she would find a direct report from Titus. Associated Press would give priority to his on-the-spot reporting. Then her mind would be set at rest. Oh, if only ... if *only!*

Shuddering, Marvel found item after item of disturbing information, but nothing from Titus. No more of this. She would not give way to her emotions, fearing the worst. Packing must be finished. But no amount of reasoning helped. The news drew her back.

An item on Social Security caught her eye. "Don't wait—register now if you have not done so already!" the piece cautioned. Daddy and Uncle Worth had their numbers, but what of Mother and Auntie Rae? Here was something to look into. She and Mary Ann must apply, too.

The article reviewed the history of President Roosevelt's proposal for the Social Security Act back in 1935. Herbert Hoover before him had declared, "Social Security must be built upon a cult of work, not a cult of leisure." And decades before Hoover's presidency, Germany and Great Britain had provided for the aged and the jobless. FDR's plan was far more reaching: old-age security . . . care for dependent mothers and children, the crippled, and blind . . . and public health services—too long deferred, he said. The bill had squeaked past conservatives. Then in 1938 the persuasive and seemingly open Roosevelt (inside, a very private individual known perhaps only by "Fala," his Scotch terrier) appeared before Congress to say:

> Government has a final responsibility for the well-being of its citizenship. If private cooperative endeavor fails to provide work for willing hands and relief for the unfortunate, those suffering hardship from no fault of their own have a right to call upon the government. . . . We have had to take our chance about old age in days past. We have had to take chances with depressions and boom times.

How well Marvel remembered—how well. The president who concealed his private feelings behind a mask of cheerful gregariousness had kept his promises. But most of the rewards came too late for the Harringtons—and millions of others, she realized now, just as they themselves were too late in realizing that occupants of the vast heartland had grown overzealous, careless, greedy. Urged on by soaring prices for grain and cotton brought about by the boom following the war, farmers had overgrazed the land, put it to the plow, and ripped off the protective grass-matting ruthlessly. Then came the payoff—not in dollars and cents but in dust storms which scalped the land, reduced it to powder. And the food-and-clothing land became the Dust Bowl, scene of the Great Depression.

It was easy to identify with the president. Marvel, too, had for the most part concealed her own feelings for so long. "But I can be myself with You, Lord," she whispered now. "I'm sorry—so sorry. But I beg of You, please protect us from evil—and a fresh disaster. Let us not be too late this time—if war must come. . . ."

She squeezed her eyes shut to discourage a would-be tear. But behind closed lids there came the painful memory of lead skies which refused to shed tears on a land laid barren and useless . . . fill the pools and wells . . . water the dying cattle.

Home was gone—literally and figuratively. Debt-ridden, none could pay mortgages . . . banks foreclosed. And farmers, broke and disillusioned, crammed their few belongings into jalopies and headed for California—only, in most cases, to collide with new disaster.

Dusted out, flooded out, tractored out, tillers of the soil went West as their ancestors had done in early-American history— except for one big difference. Those migrating to the Northwest long ago had dreams in their eyes. Present migrants had dust! It would be easy to grovel, wallow in self-pity, place blame. Or as John Steinbeck's mouthpiece said, "Who can we shoot?" Marvel had read only reviews of the writers' *Grapes of Wrath*, but she resolved to read the entire fact-fiction novel the minute time allowed.

There was more, much more. Would the world believe her? She was glad now that she had preserved a day-by-day account of the trek to California. Who would believe that laborers—dirty, hungry, anxious—were compelled to work for 45 cents a day? But then, who would believe their ultimate victory over poverty? Marvel was glad now that Daddy and Uncle Worth had bought the house. They deserved it! And somehow she and Titus *would* be together. They would find a way, he had promised. And that way, of course, was through God.

* * *

Well, the last box was packed, Marvel thought with a sigh of relief as she straightened to massage her back. The movers could be here anytime. The driver had been vague about his schedule. "So busy, you know, what with the man on the hill relocatin' them Oakie and Arkie sharecroppers, cleanin' out the slums, and doin' his darndest to cram 'em all in here. All that resettlin' is downright *un*settlin', puttin' up low-cost housin'. Move in, move out—"

Ignoring his ethnic slurs, Marvel had turned away, feeling faint with fatigue. A man that busy should spend less time talking. Now she wished there were time for a shower. She felt like a melting-down candle. But what was *this*? Earthquake? Gripped by the hand of sudden fear, she waited as the door rattled as if loosed from its hinges. And outside was the sound of a voice in panic.

"Let me in—let me in this minute, Marvel! I *have* to come in!"

Mary Ann!

In her rush for the door, Marvel tripped over the stack of boxes, righted herself, and with hands still trembling, turned the knob. "What on earth?" she mumbled, still in a state of confusion.

"Another letter—this one worse. Oh, you don't know about the other one. I—I haven't felt like talking, no time either. *Look!*"

"Is *that* all—a letter?" Marvel felt a twinge of annoyance.

"Is that *all*!" Mary Ann burst out in near-hysteria. "Yes," she said, leaving the door gaped open and dropping into the nearest chair to cover her quivering face. "All, yes—just the end of my life."

Marvel's hands continued to shake uncontrollably as she accepted the letter, knowing that she would be unable to comprehend the message which had shattered her cousin's world. Closing the door hurriedly, she made an effort to skim the contents, at first seeing only Jake's signature. The page continued to shake, but she made out a few words—enough to know that Jake Brotherton reassured his intended wife of his undying love, saying he would miss her. Oh, how he would miss her in the long, terrible days...months...*years* ahead. Paragraph after wrenching paragraph followed. He didn't *want* to do this. He *loved* her...wanted to marry her *now*! But how?

"I don't understand," Marvel said cautiously.

"I don't *either*." Mary Ann's words stopped with a dry sob. And then she shouted in desperation, "I hate him! Hear me? *Hate him!*"

This was no time to reason. "Why, Mary Ann? Why do you hate Jake?"

Weak from the outpour, Mary Ann said with heartbreaking finality, "Because I love him so much!"

Marvel folded the letter she had no right to read. It was too personal, too passionate with yearning, torn as he was between two loves. Two loves? Then Mary Ann's childhood sweetheart found another?

"He's a traitor, that's what he is—cutting my heart to shreds, then *deserting* me. Oh Marvel," she groaned pitifully, "why didn't Jake let me stay when I begged so hard? *Why?* We could have been so happy—"

Marvel sat down opposite the suffering girl and fanned herself before returning the envelope with a gentle toss. "You mentioned another letter. Want to tell me about it so I can put this together?"

Chokingly and with many a pause, Mary Ann obliged. The "other woman" was his country! War was inevitable, he said. And he had chosen duty to country over duty to the woman who loved him. He was deserting her in spite of all *her* needs and his pledges.

Biting her lip, Marvel managed a question. "Is Jake enlisting?"

Mary Ann nodded without lifting her eyes. "Volunteering when there's no war, no need—not even this draft thing yet! I begged him not to. Country to the exclusion of all else? I *hate him!*"

With that, she lifted her head, wiped her eyes, and shook the wealth of midnight curls from her white face. "I'm going to have this mop whacked off! We'll see how the patriot likes *that!*" she said defiantly. "There's a new cut called the victory bob. Oh Marvel—"

Suddenly all the pain came back to Marvel's own heart. It would be a mistruth—an out and out *lie*—to say Mary Ann should not care. Of course she cared! As did Marvel. Even now, Titus stood before her, his gray eyes turned black with gentle devotion to her, but leaving all the same.

"I understand, I really do," Marvel said through numb lips. "I'll never stop caring—not today, not ever." And her own voice broke.

Marvel told about the telephone call then...the proposal ...the change in plans. "Don't ask me where Titus is. I don't know where he is or what he's doing. I only pray that God will bring him back into my arms. You'll have to do the same—"

The cousins embraced in the echoing silence of the emptied-out bedroom, each in silent prayer. It was brief, because of a knock. So the movers had come?

* * *

It was not the movers. Instead, at the door stood a tall, handsome young man in uniform. Both girls, in their mutual sadness, sprang forward in greeting. How could prayer be answered so quickly?

"Hey, cousins! I never expected such a welcome!" the surprised guest laughed while reaching out arms to encircle them both.

Duke!

"Oh!" Marvel said excitedly, "I never would have known you! Come in, come in, Duke. How tall, muscled out—and an officer!"

Duke Harrington, handsome in his royal blues, smiled. "At your service, miss!" he said saluting smartly. "Yes, Marvel—an officer, first lieutenant. No longer a shavetail."

Mary Ann remained speechless, but Billy Joe had darted from the shadows. "*Shave*tail!" he exclaimed, wide-eyed.

"Well, look at who we have here. Talk about growing, young man. Show me that muscle—wow! You'll be ranking captain before me—"

"Don't tell him that," Mary Ann said fiercely. "I'm sorry. It's just that—I want you to come home safe and sound. That's your first order: healthy, no injuries or wounds. Oh Duke, must you go?"

He nodded and began a futile attempt to rationalize his decision, not that it was new. But Mary Ann cut him short. "We're moving."

"I would have guessed as much. We'd better see everybody. My time's short before reporting to Her Majesty the Queen."

"Still with the Royal Air Force—I should have known by the blue uniform," Mary Ann said raggedly. "Oh Duke, if you can go there they can come here—"

Newly commissioned Lieutenant Harrington looked puzzled. "There's no interruption in air travel. Of course the English can come here."

The enemy, other hostile countries, Marvel knew the other girl had meant. America was still sleeping, afraid to wake up to danger. She shuddered and was glad to have the rest of the family join them.

Yes, time was short. But, sitting on packing boxes, they made the most of it—asking rapid-fire questions and receiving rapid-fire answers. Duke's parents, Uncle Emory and Aunt Eleanore, were caught up in activity—as were Uncle Joseph and Aunt Dorthea. Both men were in banking, investing with Uncle Alex (no, he wasn't married, but Cousin Lucinda was—brilliant marriage. And wow, oh wow—what a wedding!). No plans for returning to Texas. They had broken the news to Grandfather and had no word since. Duke frowned slightly and asked about Daddy and Uncle Worth. They told about the house, all their activities. Then, meeting their daughters' eyes squarely, said they *would* return one day.

With a promise to write, Duke was gone—waving and trying to smile.

Passivity was no virtue, but Marvel wished life could have been different....

16

Brief Moments of Glory

Mother and Auntie Rae were wonderfully happy after the move. Marvel, feeling a kaleidoscope of shifting emotions, wished she could be caught up in their sheer enjoyment of those golden days, that she could be totally at peace without measuring the latitude and longitude of the world scene. It distressed her to observe sadly that the majority of Americans seemed to be intellectual lightweights. In school she had reviewed the pictorial documentaries, "The Plow That Broke the Plains" and "The River." The President had taken that approach to exposing mistreatment of a vast area of the country. Using federal relief funds, he had utilized the services of Pare Lorentz to complete the dramatic features in an effort to acquaint the nation with the dire conditions of those caught in the Dust Bowl, because of man's mistreatment of the land. The films were vivid and memorable, sure to strum the heartstrings of all who listened to the haunting strains of American folk themes and the factual account of the Great Depression.

Mary Ann had shrugged. "I saw enough in real life. As for reports, enough of that, too. That's your craft, like music's Aunt Snow's and needlepoint's Mother's. Me? All I can do is *love*. And don't go making something out of that either, Marvel. You're the smart one, the philosopher. I'm just a problem-solver, and I'm trying to work out how to convince Jake that we oughtn't wait—"

That had been in 1938 when Marvel viewed the films. Now, a year later, her cousin continued with added vigor the attempt to

171

convince Jake. She alternated between dark days of depression and exhausting anger. How could men be so insensitive, so thoughtless . . . inconsiderate . . . uncaring . . . *calloused*?

Marvel, watching Mother as she lovingly sifted soil with those delicate fingers, transplanted already-blooming flowers, and tamped fertilized sod around bulbs which would bloom in early spring, shook her head. She had no answer, no solution—just a sense of foreboding.

"This is hard on the fellows, too," she said lamely.

"Is that all you can say?" Mary Ann demanded, hands on hips as if Marvel had put the feeler before Congress concerning a possible draft. "I'd think you would be trying to solve the mystery of the Titus Smith disappearance! Well, have you heard another word?"

"No," she admitted, her own heart twisting inside, "I haven't."

"You make me sick!" Mary Ann burst out, readying for another of her tirades. "Don't you feel angry, embarrassed, let down?"

"At times I do," Marvel surprised her by saying. "But (wistfully) deep down I know Titus loves me, did the pursuing, made me feel *desired*. What is there to do but pray for their safety—"

"I can do more. Oh, wait a minute," Mary Ann gulped. "Did—did anybody think to leave a forwarding address? That's it—that's why—"

"You may be right, but don't build your hopes up—not for a few hours. We'll walk to the post office and attend to that. We couldn't change addresses. Streets are being renamed, remember? I just must answer some letters to take along."

Mary Ann was not listening. "Duke can't write like he promised either, and he—he's gone. Something else to worry about. Well, you may be willing to stand by and wait, but I'm not!" Mary Ann was remorseful then. "Forgive me—I'm sorry. I guess our cousin's coming did me in, and I *don't* want Jake to go. If there's no mail, I've got a plan—for me. But your case is different. Let me reach for a laugh. Remember Gran'mere's saying you can't grow hair on a bald head? I can *try*—"

"It won't work!" B.J. said knowingly, having grown tired of yard work. "She told us Grandfather was trying with that stuff."

Marvel, trying to smile, left the upstairs deck where they had been standing to watch the neighbors' children splash under the sprinklers. Somehow their innocent play took her back to the old oak tree where she and Titus had dreamed young dreams so much, sharing so much—and missing so much: a first gentle kiss that should have been his... a football game that should have been theirs. She stopped herself in midthought. The sweet days would come again. They *had* to. Else how could she go on living?

Back in the privacy of the big sunny room assigned to her, Marvel searched through the drawer of the writing desk, a replica of the great mahogany desk they had left back home. They had been happy then—happy in spite of the hardships. They had been together. And Titus, she thought with a catch in her throat, had been within reach....

Locating the last of the sheer lilac stationery Editor Corey had sent a lifetime ago, she hastily penned him a reply. She was sorry he was leaving. One day, yes, she promised, Marvel Harrington *would* write that book. Meantime, her writing would continue in some form. The world needed a firsthand account of history in the making. Had he read *The Grapes of Wrath*? She planned to. But Titus? Holding back tears, she told Mr. Corey truthfully that she was unable to say. *Oh, if only I could, Lord*, she whispered, knowing that she must forgive the harshness of reality and remain strong in spirit—in every sense of the word *His*.

Marvel had paused to pray. Now again she lifted her pen. She must write to both the mental institution and to Kate Lynn Porter. She dreaded both, for entirely different reasons. Looking back from the perspective of a young adult caused wonderment at the patience of herself—so young, so untried, yet called upon to do a task her elders would have shunned, even had Frederick Salsburg chosen to put the burden of his deranged son in other than her hands. Surely she would have been justified in rebelling, refusing outright, or throwing up her childish arms and escaping to wail. Instead, she had said "yes" to the dying stepuncle's last wish. Actually, Marvel thought suddenly, she played little part. It was God's decision, a high honor.

The letter came easier then. Yes, Miss Harrington would keep in touch, she wrote to the man whose signature appeared at the bottom of the letter. Here were her new address and telephone numbers. Yes, in answer to his question, she would be of service. She wondered how or what. Elmer's late father had made all the arrangements. Time would tell.

With Kate Lynn, Marvel was vague. While admitting that all the draft talk could be just that, it was a distinct possibility. Even back in 1937 (and it began earlier in the thirties) their leader had tried to alert Americans to the menace of Hitler. But Congress balked, while the rest of America had a new pastime: Turn the radio on and forget it! Titus was deeply involved with work. The senator could have sent him anywhere, she wrote ambiguously. In fact, if Bill had an update, Marvel would appreciate knowing. "Tons of happiness to you and Bill, Kate Lynn," she finished. "I know how wonderful you must feel. Titus and I plan to marry, too. That could be anyday. You know how he loves to pop in unannounced! And, like you, I'll follow him to the ends of the earth. Anything can happen, we say. Oh, true! Why, then, can't we believe it may be something *beautiful*?"

Even writing the words lifted the darkness. Of course! Happiness was only a thought away. And once more there came a moment of brief glory. Her heart became a cathedral and within it rose the triumphant strains of Mother's unwritten song. The room spun around her. At any minute a knock could sound at the door, and there he would stand. Blue, she must wear blue—and the pearls. Frederick Salsburg had left her a more priceless gift than he would ever know. Or *had* he known? Nothing happened without a purpose—nothing.

All this she would write to Titus, and more. Follow those stars, Mr. Corey had begged. And Marvel had promised that she would. Yes, she would write a long letter to Titus tonight. Included would be a digest of the clippings she should have finished before now . . . keep on with the work they had begun together . . . plan for that someday which was such a vital part of their lives. Titus would never have left her without a cause bigger than themselves. He was not one to toy with her heart. He *loved* her, wanted to *marry* her!

Any minute—any minute, her heart ticktocked with joy, beginning its own countdown. In her burst of elation, Marvel realized then that she should have contacted Associated Press. Who would know better than they of Titus' whereabouts? They had sent him—would tell her. Marvel Harrington was still a member of the AP team.

"I have prayed for God's wisdom during these lonely hours," she would write Titus. "And I feel it now as my soul soars up to meet Him. I can write again, let my words reach out again as we have done before—and will continue to do. God will watch out for you, bring you home. In fact," the words flowed out like Mother's music, "you said the assignment would be only for a short time. You may never receive my letter—"

She was right. Titus Smith did not receive that letter.

* * *

Warily, Mary Ann had refused to accompany Marvel to the post office, saying she had something much more important to do. Too bad, for completing the change-of-address card led to spotting the announcement posted above the counter. "Apply Now!" it commanded.

A man wearing metal-rimmed glasses and a collar which must have fitted too tight the way he kept tugging near the Adam's apple shoved an application across the counter. One more duty done, the gesture said.

"Agricultural Conservation Association, just around the corner. Read instructions, see if you qualify, and take it in person," he said, giving another yank at his shirt. *"Next!"*

Minutes later, Marvel had a job. The county board was holding its monthly session and hired her on the spot.

"Looks good," one of the pipe-smoking men said of the application. "Rural background, hmmm? That helps. Used to be these forms had to be processed—government business, you know. Not anymore—too apt to be a manpower shortage. Not that women can expect equal pay (Marvel bit her lip in restraint). Eight-hour day—six days a week. If you could report at eight tomorrow?"

"Oh, just a second, Miss—uh, Harrington. Got a Social Security number? Not that the government offers it to their workers yet, but we need some kind of identification," another man said, tamping his pipe.

Holding her breath, Marvel said haltingly, "No sir, but—"

"Don't matter. But better get one, so the New Dealer says. How about California state driver's license? That'll do."

There had come a churning in her stomach. "No, I plan to get both," she said meekly, then gulped. "I *do* have a birth certificate."

"Good," a third member of the august body said. "Bring it with you tomorrow. And I *would* get some I.D. the way things look. Lunch time!"

Another moment of glory! Thanking the men, Marvel hurried out with a second application in her hand. Mary Ann would appreciate that.

But, as Grandmother Riley would have said, Mary Ann had "other fish to fry." She was watching for Marvel's return from the upstairs balcony, periodically parting the baskets of red-purple fuchsias Snow and Rae Harrington had hung with such pride. Any mention of work would go unheard, Marvel saw at a glance.

"Up here!" Mary Ann called. With expertise, she wrapped the towel she held turban-fashion about her head. "Be right down. I did it—I told you I would!"

Marvel stopped in her tracks. "You didn't—oh, how could you?"

It was her cousin's turn to stop. "Didn't what?"

"Have that beautiful hair cut in one of those—what's the name of it? Oh no! Not a Dracula cut you accused B.J. of getting."

"I shampooed my hair," Mary Ann said calmly, her threat obviously forgotten. "I sent our new address to Jake by wire. It's faster. He won't enlist—that'll change his mind. Wait and see!"

Wait and see. That might be like waiting for a river to run dry in order to get to the other side.

*　*　*

Marvel rose early in hopes of leaving without disturbing the rest of the family. The entire household must have had the same idea. The big house was ablaze with lights, smelled tantalizingly of freshly brewed coffee, and abuzz with talk. At 4:00 A.M.?

"All factories are expanding, putting on new hands, and other companies opening," Daddy was saying excitedly. "I can get time-and-a-half for working the graveyard shift, Snow—an adjustment, but—"

Her mother was clapping? Apparently, and Auntie Rae was joining the applause. "Worth's told me—and I'm all for it. The big grocery markets have extended shopping hours—open all night to meet the demand. You and I can teach nights, all have breakfast together. It'll work!"

Marvel felt confused as to the goal. Mortgage here—or going home?

The hall telephone shrilled. Having left a hurried note, Marvel was ready to close the door behind her, planning to take an early-morning trolley to her former school to get a copy of her transcript. Fine print on the application stated it would be required. Before she could silence the phone, Mary Ann had rushed to pick up the receiver.

"Jake!" she exclaimed excitedly, then lifted a hand in signal for Marvel to stay put. "Jake—oh no!"

"You *what*—where?" Then silence. "Jake Brotherton you couldn't. You—you did though—oh, how cruel, you—you t-t-*traitor*!"

The talk went on and on. Obviously, they were experiencing difficulty in hearing. Which was just as well, for Mary Ann was now remorseful, busy berating herself, begging forgiveness. And either Jake did not hear or was asking that she listen. But happiness had taken over.

"All right, darling. I—I'll be quiet," Mary Ann whispered.

Marvel could all but see her cousin's face glowing in the dark.

"Oh yes, *yes*, YES! You know I will. Speak louder, I can't hear! *Turn that radio off*! No, not you—and not you either, Marvel! Stay—Jake, you talk on—I'll hear. Yes I can do that...."

Mary Ann's voice faded as the radio blared on:

> "We are facing a peril," the president has warned, and still quoting, "it must be treated as one treats an epidemic. In case of an epidemic of physical disease, we quarantine to protect the community." The word "quarantine" has been interpreted as a new turn in his foreign policy—abandonment of isolation...not only toward the German Fuhrer (will the Czechs be gobbled up?)...but our commander-in-chief has cautioned Japan as well. The draft is all but sure.... Reserves called in...other military units alerted. Stay tuned!

Someone had turned the radio down. Marvel, heart pounding in her ears, strained to hear. But now Mary Ann's shrill tone of uncontrolled excitement drowned out the hoped-for news from Spain.

A flurry of excitement followed. Marvel, mind on the new position, could make little sense of Mary Ann's rambling, except to know that she was to marry Jake—marry him *now*—pending minor details. Blood tests and the like, the bride-to-be said airily. Jake was in officer's training already...not allowed to leave. They would have a proxy marriage, "a marriage celebrated in the absence of one of the contracting parties," she explained with newly acquired wisdom. Honeymoon would have to wait, but she would go wherever her husband (Mary Ann tasted the word as if it were new honey fresh from the hive) was ordered.

"Hive" was a good word. The entire family was buzzing about like a swarm of bees, uncertain which flowers to sample for colonizing. Marvel, familiar with crop rotation, depletion of soil, and parity pay, had little problem with differences between the state of her birth and her adopted home. She could communicate with Mexicans, Negroes, and—by means of sign language or through an interpreter—the newest immigrants from the Philippines. Men from the islands could not own property, but their American wives could. A sorrowful situation, Marvel realized immediately, heartsick over the blatant philandering of less-than-honorable gold-digging women. Painted like Jezebels, the designing wives brought memories of the "night crawlers."

The deep involvement helped. Marvel had received no reply to the long letter to Titus and decided to postpone listening to news. There was a hurried trip to the university where she completed her master of arts degree, the outcome surprising her greatly.

"Why, Miss Harrington!" the dean of graduate studies greeted, rising to extend her hand. "We've wondered where you were—had a new job opening, one which the Board of Educators felt only you could fill. I will instruct my secretary to prepare your transcript. What a record! And then I want to pursue the matter. Please sit down."

How many times had she been through this? A waiting Marvel asked herself. Noting the girl's fidgeting, Dean Colton switched on her small desk-radio in the midst of a news broadcast:

And just three weeks after our president's warning regarding Japan, the League of Nations Assembly proposed a conference...a dismal failure. Japan didn't even attend. Then came the swept-under-the-rug Japanese air-bombing and sinking of the U.S.S. *Panay* in the yellow waters of the Yangtze River in China. Two Americans died... 14 injured. Congress indignant but anxious to avoid trouble. "Pull out of the Orient!" they command, while the Japanese foreign minister says, "So sorry, please." A showdown was averted, but why do we hear of alarming events a year late? And golfers, have you noted disappearance of rubber golf balls from market shelves? The tone of Japanese spokesmen is changing. A New Order is in the making, they declare... a tightening of the belt for the long haul? Unless we choose to believe one military commentator who claims it is foolish to consider strikes. "Japanese attack is absurd... a virtual impossibility."

In Europe, Fascist powers continue to march. Hitler occupied Austria... continues to take the Jews as prisoners. And, in an about-face, the mad ruler has swallowed up Czechoslovakia. And after Franco's successful conquest in Spain, Mussolini has seized Albania. "Never have I seen things moving so fast, with more crosscurrents," our leader says, knowing that he's accused by his own people of being a warmonger. But gradually the truth surfaces. Bravely, our commander-in-chief, says this: "We are dealing with two madmen who respect force and force alone... and we are woefully ill-equipped." This explains the quiet talk of possible draft and the increased military and naval appropriations... the buildup in service personnel and equipment... *now*!

Dazed by the news and terms of the agreement made with the university, Marvel hurried home. Dean Colton was right. It was an undreamed-of opportunity—one which would take planning but Marvel could do later. Now she longed for the peace and quiet of home, a time alone to think and pray. She needed God's guidance as never before. And He needed *her*. "I must rearrange my priorities, Lord," she said aloud. She had managed to juggle her time at home, and she would *here*.

Peace and quiet? An olive-drab Jeep passed as a reminder of the news. And at home the bedlam continued. Daddy and Uncle

Worth would go on double-shift next week. Wasn't it wonderful? Mother and Auntie Rae would cooperate as planned. B.J. was turning somersaults for attention. And Jake called again! Let Mary Ann have her moment of glory....

17

Weddings—
To Be and Not To Be

It was difficult to enter into Mary Ann's happiness. Asked why, Marvel would be compelled to murmur the truth: the suddenness of her cousin's plans brought painful memories crowding back. She and Titus were the ones who made those hurried plans. How long had it been? A lifetime ago. The girl planning a hurried marriage was Marvel Harrington. "*I* will be taking the vows," she would declare. It had almost happened. *Almost!*

Oh Titus, where are you, where ARE you? her heart cried over and over until blessedly, she entered the beckoning world of unreality—a world in which one functions as if programmed.

Vaguely, it occurred to her to wonder what Mary Ann's parents thought of the arrangements. Uncle Worth and Auntie Rae seemed to say little—at least that Marvel had heard. But there had been no time for talk.

"Aren't you happy for me, sweet cousin?" Mary Ann asked time and time again. Then, answering her own questions, "But of *course* you are!" she would resume planning.

It would be a beautiful wedding. She would wear the wedding gown stored away for so long, with orange blossoms—real orange blossoms right from their own yard! "Already laid out and pressed . . . you'll be my maid of honor and carry a bouquet of those golden California poppies from the backyard. Absolutely no zinnias," she had laughed. "Sometimes called *old maids*. Oh Marvel! I'm sorry. I didn't mean—well, your day'll come and I'll be your *matron* of honor! You can wear my dress then. I'll wear the something blue then, but you'll wear it—"

"My blue dress, the one Erlene gave me?" Marvel managed to gasp. "No—no, absolutely not. That's for Titus. It and the pearls—"

But Mary Ann was not listening. "Daddy'll give me away. The mother of the bride'll have a new floral gown and those nylon hose. Aunt Snow'll play the violin... Uncle Worth and Billy Joe witness... whopping big wedding cake. Oh, had the blood test ... wear Mother's ring... later Jake and me—I—will choose one all our own and he'll put it on for me when I go be with him... real soon. Have I left out anything? What's the matter, Marvel—*have* I?"

"I'd hope not," Marvel said, forcing a laugh. "Jake's taking care of everything else?"

"Oh yes, yes! He's so wonderful! We're *so* much in love—knee-deep. Arch has a leave... be best man like we planned... and the chaplain'll perform the ceremony. Oh, I wish things could have been different. We could've been married in the Wee Kirk O'the Heather here... better yet, go *home*. Oh, I wish everything were normal again—"

Normal? When was the world into which the two girls had been born been normal? Or even before? Aloud, Marvel only said wistfully, "I do, too, Mary Ann. Someday—"

Normal? When downstairs a newsboy was hawking: "Extra! Extra! Read all about it! Prime Minister Neville Chamberlain warns Great Britain of approaching war!"

"War, war! Oh, I wish they'd shut up—go home and take an aspirin like their prime minister—what's his name? Oh, Eden—no, Anthony Eden told Chamberlain to—when was it?"

"Two years ago—when world affairs were different, Mary Ann. And it was the other way around. Mr. Chamberlain was the one who refused to listen. A lot has happened since 1937."

"I'm sick of the mess! When will it all end?"

"With Armageddon," Marvel said with painful finality.

"Don't say that—don't *say* it! Don't even think it! Well, it's not gonna—going to rain on my picnic—spoil my wedding gown—"

"No, don't let it," Marvel said with a catch in her throat. "Remember Clarinda's words about grabbing onto happiness before it passed."

From somewhere in the house beyond Mary Ann's bedroom, a radio continued the story the newsboy had begun. The timing was unfortunate for Marvel, but her cousin did not seem to hear:

> Even then Great Britain set about to win the good-will of the United States . . . back when King George VI and Queen Elizabeth visited North America. One does not touch royalty, but the King tolerated a slap on the back from Vice President Garner . . . placed a wreath on Washington's tomb . . . rode the grounds of the World's Fair in New York in a miniature train . . . and on their last day in our country picnicked with the Roos-evelts at Hyde Park. The American way—but British royalty? The king removed his necktie . . . ate hot dogs. And now three months later, our president has said: "Gentlemen, I regret that Congress signed the Neutrality Act. I regret equally that I signed it." *It is now inevitable that England will go to war!*

But people will go on marrying, feasting, and merrymaking as they did in olden days of the Bible in the face of destruction, Marvel thought with a shudder. Oh, she must turn full attention to Mary Ann—shut out thoughts of impending disaster. *Alas, as prophets had foretold. . . .* Alas, Babylon!

The wedding took place on a blue-ribbon day touched by the gold of August-turning-September—the day before Daddy and Uncle Worth were to go on double shift, and Marvel would begin work at the university (evenings, by special arrangement). It was a day to hang onto, never letting go, for more reasons than the radiant bride could possibly envision. She took her vows in a little-girl voice which made her sound too young to consider marriage.

The chaplain read of the earth's first marriage in a voice loud enough for all to hear: "And the Lord God said, 'It is not good that man should be alone; I will make him an help meet for him.' And He created Eve from Adam's flesh, Jake and Mary Ann. At the completion of this brief ceremony, you—like Adam and Eve—will be of one heart. Like Adam, Jake, you shall look upon your beloved wife as bone of your bone, flesh of your flesh. As your Creator commanded, you must follow the words of Genesis:

'Therefore shall a man leave his father and his mother, and shall cleave unto his wife; and they shall be one flesh.'"

Above the soft, sweet strains of Mother's violin, a dog barked. The sharp yelp set a nervous B.J. into a spasm of laughter. Auntie Rae rapped him sharply with the heel of her new sling pumps. He let out a sharp, "Ouch!"

"No, no—I'm all right, darling—" Mary Ann murmured reassuringly into the telephone. "Go ahead with the ceremony, sir."

"Sir? Yes, I can hear. I'll repeat after you, 'I, Mary Ann Harrington, take thee . . . oh, I'm sorry—*Daddy, you're* supposed to say something. I say that later—but first—you're giving me away—Dad-*dy*!" Uncle Worth moved obediently.

The ceremony went on uninterrupted. Until Auntie Rae began to sob, followed by Mother, and then Mary Ann. "It—it's all right," the bride hiccuped. "The mother—the m-mother's supposed t-to cry. And—I'm c-c-crying—be-because I-I'm happy. We *all* are!"

Which may have been true. Billy Joe let out a piercing wail. And a usually serious Marvel stifled a giggle even as tears stung behind her eyeballs. She felt an overwhelming relief when Mary Ann said, "I do—oh, I do!" in a rapture-filled voice.

Seconds later, Mrs. Jake Brotherton turned to her family triumphantly to announce: "We're now pronounced man and wife! Marvel—Marvel, where *are* you? Lift my veil so my husband can kiss me!"

The family tiptoed out. The bride and groom must have a moment of privacy. That moment lasted longer than the ceremony. While Marvel helped arrange cups for fruit punch as Auntie Rae brought out a three-layer cake, she heard muffled sobbing from the hallway. The sound in no way resembled Mary Ann's crying because she was happy. Something was wrong, very wrong.

Mother and Auntie Rae realized it shortly afterward, for Mary Ann's voice had risen in shrill protest. "How could you! Oh Jake, it's not fair! We married t-to be to-together—and now, you're saying *no*! Then why did you marry me?" she demanded indignantly. "What! Insurance—G.I.? What's that, for goodness' sake? What did you say—government issue? But that—oh Jake, that's in case—in case of *death*! I don't want money. I just want *you*—and we promised—"

There was a pause. Then Mary Ann was saying meekly, "We were to cleave to one another, forsake all others—and choose this country. Jake Brotherton, you didn't marry the United States. I—I see—"

"Oh, I must go to her," Auntie Rae cried. But Mother reached out to restrain her. "Mary Ann's married now," she said a little sadly.

Inhaling deeply, Marvel realized that her own attempt at lightness would be totally out-of-place now. "A gala affair," she had planned to say, "particularly coming from a bride who *hates* the groom!"

Not that the opportunity presented itself. Mary Ann, her eyes red and swollen from weeping, rushed up the stairs without a backward glance. The family stood speechless. And Marvel thought fleetingly that her cousin had forgotten to toss her the bouquet. Maybe the old maids would have been a wise choice. She shuddered.

* * *

On the following morning, Mary Ann delighted the rest of the Harringtons by appearing at breakfast. "I'll have that wedding cake now," she said brightly—too brightly. "And coffee," she added. "Lots of coffee—this'll be a busy day. Daddy, don't you and Uncle Dale start the double shift? And me," she turned tragic dark eyes to Marvel, "I've decided to *hop* along to work with you. Wait, I guess that's Oregon's crop. But I know about dates, grain, cotton—ugh!—and (more slowly) more than I want to know about gr-grapes—"

Marvel hurriedly steered her from the painful memory. "You can complete the application there. Oh, I see it's finished. Good!"

"Found it when I—I couldn't sleep last night—all but the date. Look at the calendar, somebody."

"September 3, 1939," Billy Joe scrambled up to announce.

"Look again. Is this *Sunday*? Nobody works on—"

"Where've you been, big sister? Somewhere in outer space with Flash Gordon? Everybody works on Sunday these days. When they're on essential jobs, that's what they're called," B.J. said.

"The Sabbath," Mary Ann said palely. And then she shrugged. "Oh well—break one commandment and you break them all.

Jake and I can't—c-can't cleave together. He says it's unwise. That's another thing: We women are told to obey our husbands. So what difference does it make if this is a red-letter day?"

September 3, 1939 was a red-letter day indeed—the day Great Britain went to war.

Loudspeakers amplified the terrifying news once the girls, with B.J. sauntering behind them for no apparent reason, reached the busier streets:

> Earlier this less-than-peaceful Sunday morning, England declared war! Just three short months after the royal couple's visit to the United States. Prime Minister Chamberlain announced immediately to the people that their country was at war with the Third Reich. There has been a German invasion of Poland. Americans may expect our president to call for a repeal of the arms embargo. A Nazi-Soviet pact of nonaggression in August shattered world illusion that fascism and imperialism have Soviet Russia as a foe, yet so far our country remains wedded to isolationism. How long can we out-Hitler Hitler? We *must* come to the aid of the Mother Country—and *England is at WAR!*

Speechless and white-faced, the two girls faced one another. A trolley bus clattered by unnoticed. When at last they spoke, it was simultaneously.

"Jake," Mary Ann whispered.

"Titus!" The name caught in Marvel's throat.

"Duke!" A frightened Billy Joe had caught up with them. "Duke—he's the one over there. Oh, I could claw their eyes out like—like Tyrannosaurus Rex—"

"Oedipus Rex," Mary Ann corrected absently. "Oh, what can we do? What can we *do*?" Her piteous gaze fixed on Marvel, but B.J. replied.

"Pray!" the maturing boy said. "Come on—here's a church!" And, shoulders high, he took the lead. Without question, Marvel and Mary Ann followed. It was early. They would not interrupt. Nobody would see.

But somebody did. The pastor, entering noiselessly from his study, walked down the long, plush-carpeted distance to sit wordlessly beside them. All bowed their heads in silent prayer.

"God bless you," the gentle man said in the half-light of an early-morning fog. "If you have no church home—"

"We have just found one," Marvel whispered, accepting his outstretched hand. That God had led them here there could be no doubt. He had a purpose. He would reveal that purpose in His time. And she would be ready. Meantime, there were needs to be met, others to serve.

So, Marvel realized through the layers of pain, Mary Ann had had her wedding. But she had not. It still felt unreal—all of it, just as England's shocking declaration of war. Unreal—although she had known, just as the world had known. For truth is difficult to face. But face it, Marvel Harrington would! She would find Titus. . . .

18

The Searching Heart

People spilled onto the streets, literally stopping traffic, feverishly ignoring whistles of policemen. "Did you hear? Will we fight England's war again? It's got to stop!" they cried in riot-threatening voices. In confused contradiction, a brass band passed through the mob, blaring a stirring march. And through open doors of every small cafe, a new crop of Americans—too young to understand or care—was overcome with excitement. "In the groove" truant teenage boys and girls plugged nickels into the jukeboxes and rocked the floors in wild jitterbug dance, as if celebrating a victory, screaming, "Jive, man, jive!" " 'Be a rooty-tooty—find yourself a cutie. Why should you be snooty?' Jive, man, *jive!*"

Marvel and Mary Ann elbowed their way to the ACA office, only to be greeted by solemn-faced realists, who spoke in the subdued tones usually reserved for a funeral. They, too, were stunned by the turn of world events. "Looks like a stalemate. The United States can be a kind of quartermaster. That's right, no need getting more involved. Let those Communists, Fascists, and Nazis do their own fighting. England, well, that's something else. We'll have to furnish weapons, but keep some ourselves, just in case. In case of *what?* Well, there's still the Japs to deal with—and goodness knows, they own half this city already. Peace-time draft might be smart. Well, one thing's sure, we have to stick together. So, what's on the day's agenda?"

Item one was the hiring of Mary Ann Brotherton.

The same spectacled man who interviewed Marvel asked a single question. "I see your application lists teaching reading. University needs some assistance. Guess we'll all be more— shall we say in a kind of war effort, undeclared as yet. You may want to work nights?"

Still having trouble with a too-tight collar, he stretched his neck to peer at the applicant questioningly. Mary Ann, looking lost and forlorn, promised surprisingly to look into the matter. Marvel squeezed her arm.

Streets were less busy as the two girls went home, making conversation easier. "Everybody's talking like we're in it already. Oh Marvel, Jake was right. There'll be conscription. I guess we're no longer a land of the 'free and the brave,'" Mary Ann said, looking toward the sea with yearning in her storm-dark eyes.

"We're free so far. And *brave* we'll have to be."

"I'm trying, but I'm a leaner. I need you—and *Jake*," Mary Ann gulped, then turned anxiously to Marvel. "Any word from Titus?"

"You know I'd have told you. But I'm starting my search tonight!"

And it was she, instead of the weeping bride, who ran up the stairs when they reached home. There, in brief solitude, Marvel— struggling against the awful tightness in her chest—wrote a brief note to Associated Press. She was an "insider," she reasoned, and any information leading to the whereabouts of cowriter Titus Smith would be helpful and considered confidential. Her letter to Senator Norton's office said somewhat the same. Both inquiries were marked "by air."

Downstairs, all members of the family were talking at once. Even so, excited radio announcers' voices boomed above the conversation:

> Britain may very well prove to be America's line of defense, but it is too early to decide.... What did our president mean by *aid*? It may be unclear in his own mind... too soon, too shocking.... He knows the nation does not have enough planes for its minimal requirements to keep our own shores safe. Of course, we're working overtime to remedy *that*. But what about our Army? Third power... and the Navy has its hands full... committed more deeply than we realized to the Pacific.... People in the know say Britain

has only a slim chance for survival without help...
Congress won't buy that. Still, one American diplomat
notes that Ambassador Joseph P. Kennedy is right on
the beam saying, "He is a realist, and he sees England
as gone!" Stay tuned for late-breaking news.

The fire of frenzy lessened, but nowhere was overseas war
declared dead—just a bed of ashes. The blaze of reality changed
the American life-style too much. People were working harder
and longer. And nowhere was that change more evident than in
the Harrington home.

Dale and Worth Harrington, looking tired but determined,
adapted to the double shift quickly. Earning more money than
ever before in their lives, they declared proudly—just too bad it
had to come because of war. Still, it was for a just cause, wasn't it?
Thank God there were no old debts to pay off, no teeth to be fixed
in their families ("We Harrington men always look out for our
wives and families," they said with no small amount of pride),
and so they could pay off the mortgage in nothing flat. "And have
unlimited steaks," Marvel's father said with the familiar twinkle
in his lovely blue eyes.

Marvel, more tired than she cared to admit, favored him with
a smile. "There's my girl," he said in pleasure. "And now if my
other girl will come stand on the opposite side— Come on, so I
can hug you both. You two are doing your part and more! I'll tell
you my other plan."

Daddy's other plan was to spade up the back lot (baseball
would have to wait until the Lockheed aircraft quota was met).
Prices, in step with increased earnings, were climbing, and
wouldn't fresh vegetables taste "larpin' good?" Mary Ann looked
at Marvel and managed a crooked smile. *Another phrase for the
book I put away*, her eyes said.

Just as Marvel had done, too, since correspondence between
her and Titus had stopped. The topic was too painful for discussion, even with Mary Ann. Like the unfinished books, the cousins
had left plans for their private lives unfinished. There had been
only one sad discussion.

"My heart's shot in half—without warning," Mary Ann had
said, tears in her voice along with a kind of hopelessness. "I—I
guess there's no harm in keeping souvenirs of a broken heart, is
there?"

"None that I know of," Marvel said in a near-whisper as the bright hope within her own heart was waning. "But," she said with renewed courage, "remember Grandmother's hope chest? We'll store souvenirs temporarily, hoping that someday—"

Mary Ann nodded, tears spilling over then, "'Someday my prince will come' Snow White sang. But I'll store my heart in the chest, too."

As Mary Ann folded the wedding gown away tenderly, along with the veil she insisted Marvel would wear soon, and a sprig of orange blossoms, Marvel went through somewhat the same ritual in her own room with the near-sacred blue dress, the precious pearls, the sentimental valentine, and the kid gloves. Then, fighting back tears, she tucked in a poem to share and added the stacks of letters, refusing to yield to the temptation to read them one by one. That would only add salt to the open wound....

The garden plans materialized, although Marvel wondered how on earth Mother and Auntie Rae managed to find time— even to read the fine print on the seed catalogs, for that matter. Print had grown smaller and smaller as there was a whisper of paper shortage. It must be more than rumor, she decided, as magazines had fewer pages and newspapers were either merging or discontinuing circulation.

But manage they did. And in California's warmth, seed germinated and promised an abundant fall and winter garden. They found time between the adult classes they taught to accept part-time office work at the aircraft factory— partly because of the amazing pay, partly because it was said to be "patriotic," but mostly to be with Daddy and Uncle Worth. Otherwise, they would scarcely see their husbands at all. After all, Auntie Rae reasoned, B.J. had declared his independence, welcomed no help with his homework, and accepted a job on his own as clean-up boy at an open-all-hours market. And their obligations did not end there.

Mother insisted, after attending one early-morning worship service (between shifts) at the First Baptist Church where their children had gone to pray the day the world picture changed, that they transfer their memberships there. With the "members of good standing" letters from the previous church had come records of the families' varied incomparable abilities—"talents not buried beneath a bushel."

The minister, whose speech pattern tattled of the South, won the hearts of them all when he said simply, "My name is James Murphy, and the congregation calls me by a passel of names, some with titles. But please, if you folks feel comfortable with it, just call me Jim or Pastor Jim. I've no recollection of the disciples claiming more."

"Well," Daddy had grinned, "we feel mighty comfortable with the name, Jim. Now, you'll make us feel more at home by doing likewise."

"Go ye and do likewise," Billy Joe smiled, drawing himself to full height which—Marvel noted with surprise—was almost that of his father. "I'm B.J., and that's my uncle you're talking to."

Pastor Jim extended his hand. "Welcome, B.J. I remember you," he said, treating him like a *person*, Billy Joe boasted later.

Uncle Worth was to make a different kind of observation. "I'm all for joining that church, such a down-home atmosphere. But," and he grinned, "I knew right away our Pastor Jim had something up his sleeve. Remember, Dale, how Father used to say, 'Boys, you catch more flies with honey'? He's a good leader—put us *all* to work!"

Dale and Worth Harrington accepted the inevitable. "Once a deacon, always a deacon," according to the faith and order of their church. Since records showed that Deacon Dale's wife was a talented musician . . . Yes, Mother said with stars in her eyes, the violin was her ministry, her calling. She would play for the church, her loved ones, and her Lord and Savior . . . *yes*! And Deacon Worth's wife *would* join the ladies' organization ("They're so in need of leadership in putting together a women's recipe book"). Well, yes, if Pastor Jim felt her qualified. Pastor Jim did.

"I should be," Auntie Rae said later with a sigh as gentle as a sea breeze. "Goodness knows I'm packing enough sack lunches. And there's that *Stretching to Survive* book we can use as a guide—"

"*We?*" Mother laughed. "Of course, *we*—and flowers for the altar—"

Mary Ann looked at Marvel and grimaced. "Stop looking at me like that! Okay, I might as well volunteer. You'll see that I do." With an exaggerated sigh, she tossed her curls with near-grim determination, "They need Sunday school teachers. I managed at the Morning Glory Chapel. But between you and the pastor, I'm being pushed!"

"By the Lord perhaps?" Marvel suggested gently, certain of it.

"He does look after the simpleminded. The hymn, 'He Included Me,' fits the bride and the bride-to-be—*service*. How did we get into this mess: days at that conservation office, nights teaching, trying to write books, and—and—letters we know won't get answered? Oh Marvel, if I could hear—if only a word for my hope chest!"

Only a word. *Yes*, Marvel's own heart cried out—a word from Titus or a word *about* him. But there had been no response from either Senator Norton or Associated Press. Unable to wait, she wrote to Kate Lynn again. But all the while there was a gnawing away at her heart, a knowing that letters were useless. She had to be too cautious, make questions sound unconcerned, unrevealing. The mission was secret, supposedly short. Short—over a year had passed!

In vain Marvel tried reminding herself that Titus enjoyed surprising her. He, why he could show up at any moment. As moments crawled by, adding up to days and months, she searched every face in the ever-increasing crowds of city streets. She could spot him anywhere, single him out by his long, straight stride, the gentle line of the sensitive mouth, and those achingly beautiful gray-turned-black-with-caring eyes in expectation of singling her out. He would find her. He *would*. Titus had promised. And they would be *married*.

Gradually, all reminders lost their power to comfort. Reassurances turned to doubts. Bad things *did* happen to good people. Faith—she must cling to faith. *But where was he?*

The knife of pain cut even deeper when Mary Ann received her first letter addressed to Mrs. Jake Brotherton. "From *him*, Marvel, him. Do you hear? Jake, my *husband*—he's all right, has been under quarantine—meningitis case. Wasn't supposed to write, but did. He loves me—he *loves* me. Don't look so stricken. You'll *hear*, you will—"

"Of course," Marvel said tonelessly.

* * *

Responses came from Marvel's three sources the same day. With trembling hands, she opened the letter from the state office first.

>We wish to inform you that a complete search of our files indicates that the parties mentioned, namely, Senator Norton and Titus Smith, serve in no capacity for the Texas State Congress. The senator retired due to his health prior to the recent election. Titus Smith unknown....

Shattered by the words, Marvel could scarcely comprehend the cool, noncommittal note from Associated Press. Such information would be considered "classified." As to news contributions, Miss Harrington might wish to contact the editorial department, let them know of her interests. It was, Marvel thought dully, as if she, too, had dropped out of sight. Disappointment turned to a kind of bitterness—a bitterness which reflected in the letter from Kate Lynn:

>Dearest Marvel (she read dazedly), The long delay is due to the awfulness around us. We, Bill and I, are away out here on the East Coast...together, thank God...but for how long? Marriage should be more than this kind of uncertainty...and poor Mother's going through the same. Yes, Daddy was called as doctors are much in demand...possible that both will go overseas. Oh, I'm scared...so scared. *No, Bill has had no word from Titus...a scared world....*

* * *

Yes, a scared world. Franklin Delano Roosevelt had hoped the despised Mussolini might serve as a counter against the hated and feared Hitler. At dawn on April 9, 1940, Hitler's troops had crossed the border of Denmark, sweeping widely through the coastal low countries. Denmark fell in hours...Norway in nine weeks. The Netherlands was overrun in five days...Belgium in 18. Within three weeks, the Nazis drove all British armies out of France. And on June 22 the Third French Republic surrendered to the Executioner. Adolph Hitler was bent on becoming world dictator. Americans were stunned. It had taken less than three months to destroy what a saddened president thought they should have sensed years before: their illusions about the outcome of the European war and their own impregnability. Walter

Lippmann wrote then, "our duty is to begin acting at once on the basic assumption that before the snow flies again we may stand alone and isolated—the last great democracy on earth."

For the moment, even Roosevelt's severest critics rallied to him as the national leader in time of crisis. He called for a vast increase in armaments and moved to create a crisis government of national unity. On June 19 he named two prominent Republicans to the chief defense posts in his cabinet: Henry Stimson as Secretary of War and Frank Knox as Secretary of the Navy. Mussolini had *not* met with the hopes of the American president. Instead, he became a utensil of the blood-thirsty Nazi leader.

Newspapers screamed the headlines, while, fighting mad, Roosevelt ad-libbed a burning sentence: "On this tenth day of June, 1940, the hand that held the dagger has struck it into the back of the neighbor!"

Congress continued their fierce debate over a bill for peacetime draft. Tempers flared. Exhausted, confused, and jarred into reality, two members exchanged blows. "Enact peacetime conscription and no longer will this be a free land." "Oppose it and we will become slaves," a majority hurled back. Riled Americans inundated the White House with letters and telegrams favoring the bill. In mid-September 1940, Congress voted to conscript men between 21 and 35.

* * *

Leaves of the shady Elm Street turned gold but clung tenaciously to the trees, trembling in the ocean breeze as if afraid to let go. Inside the Harrington home, faces grew more haggard, its members' pace more harried. They held hands in silent prayer, giving no voice to fear. Like elm leaves they clung—to one another ... to God ... and to *faith*!

"I will not give up. I *must* not!" Marvel cried out to Mary Ann, who was hearing regularly from her husband now. Having completed officers' training, Jake had his commission. Soon they could be together.

Marvel wrote a lengthy letter to Leah Johanna Riley. Grandmother would understand better than Mother. The older woman did not disappoint her. The loving reply came immediately. *The News Review* was gone ... syndicates published local statistics.

She would check all. "And let that young heart of yours keep searching, my pet. You'll find your Titus. *We* trusted—and the rains have come!"

19

War!

The morning was bleak, matching Mary Ann's mood. Still in her twenties, slim and graceful, the wide, dark eyes told an age-old story without words—the grim story of loneliness and bewilderment.

Marvel, misery roiling behind those Harrington-blue eyes, recognized the look. Hadn't she seen it written on the vast sea of faces of women everywhere? When would the tension end, those faces asked—or was this only a foretaste of what lay ahead? But Mary Ann being Mary Ann added yet another emotion: that of rebellion. Today was one of those occasions.

"I'm sick to death with all this waiting around for the world to blow up!" she declared with clenched-tight fists sweeping back her equally rebellious curls. "I've worked my—well, the sitting-part of my anatomy off. And for what? I don't see the world any happier! How can you go on like you've got your wagon packed to journey on *forever*—never fuming, letting off steam? *How?*"

"I hold it inside," Marvel said in an off-guard moment. Her voice lay dead.

Her cousin, remorseful now, had hurried to put comforting arms around her in the morning quiet before the rest of the family was up. "I know you do. Oh Marvel, I'm sorry—*so* sorry. Tell you what. Let's skip breakfast and take a quick detour by the ocean. It'll help us both."

It failed miserably.

A storm at sea was brewing. Low clouds scudded inland trailing skirts of rain in the distance. Beyond the beach, Marvel saw the usually tranquil-blue water whipped high with dirty-white breakers. And still farther out, she spotted a rocking ship. A battleship, or was the color camouflaged by the drab sea? The tightness came back in her chest. Involuntarily, she stood on tiptoe, as if to catch a glimpse of Titus. How would he be traveling when he came?

She must have spoken aloud for Mary Ann, suddenly amused, laughed, "Why, on a white charger, of course. You'll be married, Jake will come, and (triumphantly) we'll live happily forever after!"

"This foolish heart has betrayed me again," Marvel murmured in despair. "Oh, something has to be wrong. Shouldn't I go look for him?"

"Like where?" Mary Ann said practically. "You stay put so Titus can find you. He'll be here. He's honorable—the way you describe him. Hey, we'd better run for it. Looks like rain." They had turned when Mary Ann panted breathlessly, "Have you ever—ever thought of swingin' your hair 'way up like Betty Grable? You'd look— Oh, listen, that's *for me!*"

The song, Mary Ann meant. Inside a little ice cream parlour, not open for business yet, a clean-up boy was swinging chairs from their overnight rest on the tables to the rhythm of the jukebox:

> Careless—now that you've got me loving you,
> You're careless in everything you do,
> You break appointments—and think you are smart—
> If you're not care-ful, you'll break my heart...

But from somewhere else came the hauntingly sweet strains of "I'll Never Smile Again." And Marvel, knowing the next lines, bit her trembling lower lip to hold back the tears:

> What good would it do?
> For tears would fill my eyes, my heart would realize
> That our romance was through.

* * *

The world grew more tense. The presidential campaign of 1940 had stepped up debate over Roosevelt policies. Dramatic events in Europe assured the president's nomination for a third term, which he received on a first ballot at the Democratic convention in July in Chicago. When Roosevelt dropped Vice President Garner and chose former Republican Henry Wallace as a running mate, news broadcasters had a field day, chortling over such trifles as:

> "No one wanted Wallace—absolutely no one," claimed a Louisiana delegate to George E. Allen. "Just name me one man who did." Allen replied drily, "Brother, that I can do—and that one man was Roosevelt!" Developments in Europe revived hope for the tousled, hoarse-voiced lawyer from Indiana who tried to convince Republicans he would offer a real challenge to Roosevelt... receiving not one vote... even on a sixth ballot manipulated by a group of part professionals led by Harold Stassen. Undaunted, Wilkie announced that he was eager to take on "The Champ," a challenge completely ignored by the commander-in-chief. Oho! Shaken, one Republican Congressman protested helplessly: "Franklin Delano Roosevelt is not running against Wendell. He's running against Adolph Hitler." Aren't we all!

America needed a laugh, so—eyes closed momentarily to darker news—they chortled along with the reporters. Too, they needed a boost to their morale—something to let them whistle in the dark.

They cheered at the landslide victory of the incumbent in November's general election, again shutting out sour-grape cries that the Roosevelt administration was inviting war. FDR *wanted* it.

Opponents were right about one matter, wrong about the other. After election day, events abroad moved swiftly to bring war closer to America's doorstep. But the troubled president did *not* want it! Still wrestling with the Great Depression, fully aware that trouble was brewing with the Japanese, his hands were full without further involvement in the European war. But how to stem the tide?

On December 9 Roosevelt received an urgent message from Churchill. Britain was in "mortal danger"... in need of vast quantities of American arms... and running out of cash. The president responded swiftly. On December 17 he unveiled a plan whereby America would lend arms directly with the understanding that they would be returned when war ended. Again, news reporters chortled over the air waves:

"Lending war equipment is like lending chewing gum" Senator Taft protested. "You don't want it back!"

They said more. But this time America did not laugh. The popular tide had turned. At election time, polls showed an even division of sentiment on whether to help Britain would increase risk of war. By mid-January 1941, 68 percent favored taking that risk, according to the new poll. The Senate approved lend-lease by 60-31. By the end of March, Congress had voted seven billion dollars as first installment on the huge program to arm the Allies. All pretexts of neutrality had vanished like vapor. By April 1941 American naval vessels were patrolling far into the Atlantic. Our own shores must be safe.

America was humming with activity, humming as well the sentimental British war song: "There'll be bluebirds over, the white cliffs of Dover, tomorrow when the world is free...." *That tomorrow must begin today*.

On May 27, 1941, the president proclaimed an unlimited national emergency. In June he froze German and Italian assets in America and closed their consulates. On June 22 Hitler brutally invaded his ally Russia. Americans gasped. And then on September 4 a Nazi U-boat attacked the United States destroyer *Greer* off Greenland. A week later in a national radio broadcast, the president denounced German "piracy" and declared he had ordered the Navy to shoot on sight these "rattlesnakes" of the Atlantic. That fall Congress repealed sections of the Neutrality Act of 1939. Henceforth the president could arm merchantmen and authorize ships to sail into combat areas.

* * *

Throughout the world-shaking changes, the Harringtons read newspapers and listened to radio broadcasting with indrawn breath—Marvel, in particular, for all efforts to find any trace of Titus had failed.

Each reply to her queries brought less information. Associated Press ignored her letter. The state capital sent a form letter: To Whom It May Concern. Fire had destroyed previous records, they regretted to say. Interested parties might wish to inquire at their respective county seats—exception being Titus County, since fire had destroyed most records in Culverville as well. Fire, *fire*! The information did nothing but serve as a painful reminder of Elmer's mental illness. There should have been further word from the institution.

Grandmother tried to be helpful, but she could no longer make out the fine print of newspapers. Perhaps Marvel could make heads or tails of the columns enclosed. Of course, the whole world had taken leave of its senses. Anything could happen, *anything*! For example:

Wouldn't you think agriculture would take heart from the continued rain? Well, maybe mankind will take heed of the prophesies someday. Can't say Joel didn't warn us that plowshares would be beaten into swords... and it's happened sure as shooting. But the Squire, bless him, says we *have* to go on believing that the pendulum'll go swinging the opposite direction. Your grandfather's right... Isaiah foresaw a different world... promising just peace one day: that swords will be beating into plowshares. That'll be the day! All lush and green like before. He's all bottled up inside— like you, my darling Marvel. You're a Harrington through and through... easy for me to see through you both, loving you like I do, so I know he's worrying about Duke. And your Aunt Eleanore never writes a word. Oh, about farming, folks here have gone crazy since oil's scarce as hens' teeth in Europe... probably accounts for those bloody invasions, causing human blood to flow like the Bible tells us it will. Big companies aren't here... but there's wild-catting—another spoiler of the land. The Squire takes comfort in your owning the vast acreage. You *will* come back? Silly me, of course you will! Meantime, sweetheart, didn't you say this young man of yours had a sister hereabouts? Let this be our secret: *Call her!*

Why, of course. How wise of Grandmother! But the long-distance operator's metallic voice said that the telephone had been disconnected. Then, Marvel's letter came back marked "Unknown."

But she, like Grandfather, must go on believing....

It was on that golden September morning of the president's announcement of arming American vessels aimed at "shooting on sight the European pirates who sank the *U.S. Greer*," that the Harringtons managed a togetherness for coffee—a rare happening indeed.

Marvel was unaware of the beautiful portrait of herself—so eloquent in its grief, the classic bone structure more visible now beneath the flawless ivory skin. The naturally arched brows lifted above the startlingly blue eyes, but other eyes would have seen the suffering in their luminous depth, the paler-blue shadows beneath speaking of lack of sleep. But other eyes were focused on the dining room radio and on each other questioningly. Worth Harrington was first in breaking the horrified silence.

"Well, what do you think?" Uncle Worth asked at large.

"That we will be in war soon," Daddy said in a strained voice.

"Don't *say* that! How could you be so cruel!" Mary Ann's lashing out was intended more at the enemy than her uncle.

"And don't *you* say that either—sassing your uncle. Got your mind on nobody but yourself—you and Jake! Me, I know somebody's gotta teach those Nazis and yellow devils. I'll join up soon as I'm older and give those (and B.J. used a forbidden word to cast reflection on the circumstances of their birth) what they asked for!"

"And don't *you* say *that*!" his mother cried out in anguish. Disregarding or failing to hear her son's colorful language, Auntie Rae was bent on protecting her own—an attempt known only to mothers throughout the world.

"More coffee, everybody?" Mother asked cheerfully. "There isn't going to *be* a war! Let's switch off such talk and enjoy this coffeecake."

"What do *you* think, honey? You haven't said a word," Daddy said.

What did Marvel think? That she was tired—tired of caring so much, trying so hard... searching... waiting... grieving... trying to cling to hope where no hope existed except in her own heart.

"That we're fighting a battle of nerves," she said woodenly. "Maybe Mother's right—" but there her voice broke.

Mother was *not* right. She wasn't right at all. But Mother was Mother, trying to cheer away gloom, or pretend no gloom existed—never quite facing reality because it hurt too much. But Marvel loved her with a passion. She would protect her as Auntie Rae would protect B.J.

Snow Harrington reached out to smooth a strand of ripe-cornsilk hair from her daughter's upswept style. "Of course I'm right, baby. I love your new do. Suppose I could wear mine like that? What's wrong, Marvel? You look so fragile—worrying over something in particular... something we don't know about?"

"Naturally she's worried!" an anguished Mary Ann answered for her. "Just the way I'm wor-ried. Jake sure to go into the thick of it and (her voice rose) Marvel—un-unable to find Titus—"

Mother's china cup clattered into its matching saucer. "Titus? Haven't I heard that name? But that was long ago. I thought you—"

Had forgotten? Mother had married the man she loved when she was as young and certain as Marvel had been when Titus, the only man who could ever possess her heart, pledged to Walt. But for the first time in her life, Marvel wished for her mother's ability to shut out the unpleasantries of life and make the world go away...

* * *

While America worried about the danger of involvement in Europe's war, the country's commander-in-chief worried about the trouble brewing with Japan. Always strained throughout that fateful year of 1941, relations deteriorated rapidly. On July 25 Tokyo announced that it was establishing a joint protectorate over Indochina with Vichy France, the Nazi puppet. The move threatened the Philippines. The following day President Roosevelt froze Japanese assets in the United States. A single stroke of the pen cut the island empire off from the source of 80 percent of its oil. Both sides began to prepare for war, although American military men urged caution and delay. People wondered.

President Roosevelt wanted peace, but not at the price of major concessions to the Japanese. He took a strong line. The empire *must* abandon the plan, withdraw from China—after the costly four-year war.

Yet Japan continued to invite distrust. "Peace, we want peace!" was the hue and cry while presenting to the world a bloody spectacle of government by assassination. By autumn of 1941 the Japanese militarists were impatient for war. Franklin Delano Roosevelt bore the terrible burden of knowing since a team of Army cryptologists had cracked Japan's secret code. His few confidantes were privy to threats from Tokyo. Ambassador Grew whispered a warning: "Sir, there *could* be a surprise attack on Pearl Harbor." But such an assault seemed unlikely, American naval experts said. Japan lacked necessary resources. An over-burdened president grew more so, his face haggard from bodily pain and his mind busy with questions. What was best for America? Should his people bear his burden of wondering which front to handle: the European or the Japanese? And had he not pledged that American boys would never be sent into war? He prayed for peace when American observers spotted a Japanese expeditionary south of Formosa. But even then those observers assumed it was heading for Indochina, Malaya, or the Indies—hardly worth worrying the president about.

On December 7, 1941, most of the country awoke to a beautiful sunny morning. Churches were crowded, newspapers filled with ads—one by the Matson Line offering a vacation cruise to Hawaii. In Washington, Cordell Hull went to his office in the State Department at 10:15 to await an answer for his latest—and last—proposal to Japan. Two hours later he had his answer: The Japanese envoys wished an appointment to deliver a reply. They would come in person.

Five thousand miles to the west, in Hawaii, it was still early morning. Soldiers at Hickam Field filed sleepily into the mess hall for breakfast. On the great battleships in the harbor, many servicemen prepared for a day of rest. At Wheeler Field fliers still lay sleeping in their bunks—none of them aware of the wave of violence thundering toward them....

By 1:50 P.M. on the sleepy Sunday afternoon of December 7, 1941, Washington's radioman Frank Ackerson picked up an unbelievable dispatch from Honolulu: "Air raid, Pearl Harbor—This is no drill!" Unbelievable but true. Just three minutes before, a Japanese dive bomber—first of a wave of 183 carrier-based planes—swept low over America's chief base in the Pacific. With blazing suns painted on the wings and grinning faces of the helmeted pilots clearly visible, dive bombers swept dangerously low to wreak havoc on Wheeler, Hickman, and other air fields. Within minutes, Japan had erased United States power there.

Bedlam followed. There was no time to think, little time to react, try as Hawaii-based men would. For at the same time great formations of bombers stormed in over the American fleet tied up in false safety, bobbing along Battleship Row. An armor-piercing bomb crashed through the second deck of the *Arizona*, triggering an explosion of hundreds of tons of powder in fiery horror. The battleship leaped in rigor mortis, cracking in half as it settled to the bottom of the sea. The *West Virginia*, afire amidships, sank. The *Oklahoma*, struck by five death-blow torpedoes, rolled over in shallow water and lay with breast buried, bottom pointing grotesquely toward a smoke-filled sky....

It would take a thousand books to tell the entire story, Marvel Harrington was to think much later. But praise the Lord that, even paralyzed by shock and horror, He had given her strength to pencil an outline—perhaps to maintain her sanity. And there was more.

That same afternoon, amid the stench of burning oil, the roar of flames, and the frenzied cries of the trapped, wounded, and dying, the Navy must tally losses of the surprise raid: 18 ships sunk or badly damaged... 188 planes destroyed... 159 more damaged. And then, grim-faced and retching, the *men*: over 2400 Americans killed... half buried in the watery grave of the *Arizona*... and 1178 wounded. Muttering, "This is war and war is hell..." an officer reported the losses. And a horrified president's Cabinet calculated quickly: about three times as many men perished as in the Spanish-American War and World War I (as it must be called now) combined. Damage could have been worse:... Japanese had ignored Pearl Harbor's invaluable oil facilities. And Admiral William Halsey's carrier force chanced to be away on special mission. Nevertheless, the sneak raid paralyzed the Pacific fleet.

* * *

The electrifying news reached Nebraskans as they sat down to Sunday dinner, New Yorkers when WOR interrupted its broadcast of the Giant-Dodger football game, and Californians as most came home from church. Bewilderment turned to rage when Americans learned that at the very moment Japan bombed Pearl Harbor, two smiling and bowing Tokyo envoys were smoke-screening in Washington under pretext of diplomatic negotiations.

The Harringtons had lingered after church service in a prayer for peace led by Pastor Jim and the deacons. Tension had hung over the congregation more heavily than the bittersweet aroma of fall asters from Snow and Rae Harrington's garden. Children, aware, clung to Marvel and Mary Ann after Sunday school. Even Mother's violin seemed to strike a minor key, Marvel thought afterward. Had she known the minister would follow to scream the news? *"Japan has bombed us! War. Oh, dear God—"*

20

Bleeding Hearts in Aftermath

The day after Pearl Harbor, employees of the Soil Conservation's office huddled near the radio. A sober-voiced announcer had interrupted his account of the brutal raid to say that the president would be speaking before Congress, his words aired. Mary Ann gripped Marvel's hand for support, shaken, unable to comprehend.

> Grimly, Franklin Delano said: "Yesterday, December 7, 1941, on a day which will live in infamy, Japan launched an unprovoked and dastardly attack on American soil. As commander-in-chief of the Armed Forces, I now ask Congress for a declaration of war. . ."

Marvel, wishing she could cry out against the cruelties of mankind, dropped to her knees. Mary Ann sank with her, face convulsing in a wash of tears. A few knelt afterward. Some drifted away in stricken silence. Others sought comfort in numbers, knotting in groups to whisper or whimper. Still others, staring over shoulders in their departing stalk, uttered words both bitter and profane. "How can anybody of sound mind pray—even *believe* in a God who let this happen?" One thing only did they, along with all other Americans, hold no illusions about the kind of war this would be. There were no cheers.

At home there was confusion. Daddy had been promoted to high rank—an excellent organizer, able to handle and maintain order, harried supervisors had told him . . . a necessity is establishing control over every code, creed, and color men . . . women, too, entering ammunitions plants, shipyards, and aircraft plants. ("Probably can't drive a nail straight," the man continued, "but wars bring booms, you know.")

No Dale Harrington didn't know. Well, he'd find out as superintendent.

To the family, Daddy said dazedly, "Imagine me—in *charge*."

"Oh darling, it's *easy* to understand. You're the right choice." Mother paused, before adding brightly, "Anyway, it won't be for long. The war won't last, we know that. Well, don't we?"

Nobody answered. In a silence thick enough for slicing, somewhere a pot boiled over. "Something's burnin'!" B.J. yelled, darting out.

He could manage. Marvel felt she was needed here in the living room. There was more to be said. She was right on both matters.

"Yuck! What's *this*?" he said moments later, holding out an elongated mass of what looked like wet wool yarn on a long wooden spoon.

"Spaghetti. I—I forgot to turn off the burner," Auntie Rae murmured. And then, spotting her son's tracks of frothy starch over the long stretch of carpet to the kitchen, she gasped. "Oh, I could cry—"

Uncle Worth held her to him, seemingly aware his wife's tears had nothing to do with the scorched pasta. It was the awfulness of a country at war. Not what it would do to her alone, but all others. And something more.

"There, there—don't cry. I can clean the pot or get you a new one. Want to hear about your husband before you freshen your makeup?"

It was so uncharacteristic of Auntie Rae, but she was still weeping as her head bobbed up and down, tumbling the dark curls. But then, everything was uncharacteristic now—a war of survival.

Uncle Worth's voice had lost some of its bravado, but he managed to blurt out, "It—my news has to do with Dale. There's— uh promotion—he needs a hand—hafta double production. I'll work, trust me—to meet his expectations—yours, hon—and, God willing, *His* too—"

The parents were crying, all four of them. It broke Marvel's heart. Signaling Mary Ann, she managed an undetected exit to her room. By force of habit she had checked the mailbox. It was empty.

Darkness came earlier now. Marvel moved quickly to switch on lights—all of them, including the desk lamp. "No shadows, Lord," she whispered. "Oh, please help me drive away all satanic darkness—especially from my heart. I must not surrender, except to You. To You I surrender *all*—yes, my dreams, my hopes, I trust to You." Then, in the agony of longing, she added, "Titus is in Your hands, too. Oh, *please* bring him back to me, even if he's changed, maimed. Oh dear God—"

Sinking into the desk chair, she gave way to complete exhaustion, hands shielding tired eyes from the bright light. Behind closed lids, Marvel saw him then—her Titus as he would ever remain before her. Faith was a wonderful gift. God had chosen this man for her. God alone could bring him back. Meantime, the Lord needed working people—people who participated in their own lives for His cause...not drifters filled with worry and doubt, only to reach a certain point realizing they had allowed their hearts to fill with failure and regret over tasks, callings, and dreams not accomplished. And He had armed both her and Titus with His love—for today as well as tomorrow!

And Titus deserved her best. For earthly love, no matter how pure and genuine, was a fragile gift. It demanded patience and nourishment—even protection—for survival. A husband and wife, as they would be someday, had seven days a week for those precious needs. But apart, the keen edge of their loving relationship could be dulled, finally fade. But only if they allowed it. Letters would help. *Oh, if only she could hear!* But denied that, she would find a way (just as Titus had promised he would do) to form a bond, keeping alive that spirit of warmth and closeness. Of course! Through their book...

Refreshed, she began making notes. Minutes later when she turned the desk radio on, it did not disappoint her. A newscaster said:

Repeating an earlier broadcast: Immediately following the president's appearance before Congress, a grim and angered Senate approved his request for a formal declaration of war following Japan's brutal attack on Pearl Harbor, voting *yes* 82-0...the House

388-1 . . . only one abstention—that of Representative Jeanette Rank of Montana. Note that this representative cast a negative vote in the war resolution of 1917. It is expected, according to White House sources, that both Germany and Italy will announce they are at war with the United States! This is another of those times that try men's souls, but united stand we against aggression. The sneak attack brought our country into fighting a war we did not invite or want, but has united our people as no other event could have. Americans everywhere are responding already with anger and determination. But we must turn a deaf ear to rumors . . . listen only to news releases directly from the White House sources . . . and interpretations from the Office of War.

Marvel scarcely heard the door swing open to admit a distraught Mary Ann, until her cousin spoke. "Oh Marvel, don't—not today! How *can* you—with the world tumbling around us? *Why* do you write?"

"Because I must. I promised God—and Titus."

"But there's been no word, and anything could have happened—*anything*! Don't you realize it yet—know I could have lost Jake?"

Marvel bit her lip before saying dully, "I realize. Don't you think I hurt, too? At least you're married while I—"

"Have only memories. Oh, if I've hurt you, cut my tongue out. It's my worst enemy. But I still don't see why you do *that*."

Waving a hand for Mary Ann to sit down, Marvel whispered, "My paper bridge—it's my way to the future with Titus—preserving all this which will be warped, misinterpreted by history. *Listen!*"

One day (the announcer continued) the president's foes are apt to claim that a kind of diabolical conspiracy within the administration brought on the attack on Pearl Harbor. There is no foundation for this view in spite of indications that Roosevelt aides may have bungled the relay to Hawaiian intelligence decoded from Japanese messages. But this is no time for rumors now or to be recorded as *fact* in history's pages. Put no stock in stories that commanders in Hawaii were negligent...did not take proper precautions. Tell that to the Navy...the Army...the Marines!

Marvel turned wearily to face Mary Ann. "Now do you see?" Downstairs, Billy Joe served to ease tension. "Any need for welders there at the aircraft factory, Daddy or Uncle Dale? Look, *I'm* qualified—that spaghetti was welded to the pot. I cleaned it!"

The cousins managed tremulous smiles. "I'd settle for an omelet. I make a mean one. Will—will that square things? I'm an escape artist."

Wordlessly, they embraced and stood motionless a full minute.

* * *

America did not storm the street waving flags and cheering men into battle—no new martial songs such as World War I's "Over There." Instead, advertisements changed overnight from immaculate young faces in immaculate uniforms to begrimed infantrymen plodding through war-torn villages. The country, alerted now, came to realize that this war would not end quickly or be fought easily. To dislodge Hitler from his iron control of the Continent would be a painful, bloody business, and the road to Tokyo would be paved with the bodies of American men. Peacetime draft ages could change. Some of that pavement could include younger boys in school, those previously protected by dependents—namely, wives and children, or those previously considered "too old." So far the horrors of war touch people at home "only indirectly," newscasters, now providing the nation with 24-hour coverage, said. Wrong! All were sacrificing, surrendering their loved ones—the hardest sacrifice of all.

Of course (newsmen hastened to explain) it all began long ago when roads were clogged by untold numbers fleeing ravishes of floods, droughts, and the Great Depression. More especially they came from the Dust Bowl of America's heartland seeking work—any kind would do...

some eked out a living by becoming "fruit tramps"...harvesting crops in season...gleaning fields. In sunnier climes, men could set food before their families, and so they stayed on. Others remained for lack of funds to take them home. But now the war boom has brought unprecedented prosperity to millions, including those who stayed on. Welcomed now are the "Oakies," the "Arkies," and the million men called "Tex!" Once turned away, the migratory laborers and the jobless, pariahs of the thirties, find their services much in demand. Employment offices comb the streets for enough to meet the quota, particularly on the West Coast where aircraft factories, busy long ago while the rest of the country slept, had stepped up production before the declaration of war. Henry J. Kaiser, having worked for the government—master-minding construction of Boulder Dam—is busy combing the country for workers, his talents now turned to shipbuilding. Kaiser and other West Coast titans scan the union to meet and exceed quotas set down by FDR. Many a Bronx boy who had never left New York area rushes to Seattle or Tacoma to take crash courses in sheet-work. Portland is filled to bursting point. San Diego's population doubled. Thanks to Douglas Aircraft, six plants now in California...and now hear this! The south itself is shaken by tremors of enormous migrations. Old Gulf Seaport of Mobile with its elegant tree-shaded colonnades and mansard roofs, having slept longer than Rip van Winkle—230 years, to be exact—took only two to wake up. Population of Key West, Florida, leaped from 13,000 to 30,000 in two years! In 1940, folks, there were only 90 shipyard workers in the state of Georgia. Now Savannah alone employs more than that number. This is a frightened but determined America...calling for more cooperation and adjustments than ever before—not to mention heartbreak.

* * *

Heartbreak. And that, thought Marvel Harrington, was the hardest to bear. She could cope with the other changes. Correction: She *had* coped, past tense. And *would* cope, future tense. But the present? How long could she go on hoping, watching, waiting—the not knowing?

A year had passed since Pearl Harbor—an eventful year. Marvel took notes both on press releases and comments of the media, watching all the while, with her usual sensitivity, changes in the faces around her. Of the 31 million men who registered for the draft, nearly 10 million were inducted ... 36 percent of registrants rejected (classified as 4-F) ... and shockingly hundreds of thousands turned down because of illiteracy. What an opportunity for teachers! And, she thought, wearily, that included all the Harrington women: Mother, Auntie Rae, herself, and Mary Ann. Count Mary Ann out. Her cousin was hearing regularly from her officer-husband now. Each day brought a letter addressed to Mrs. Jake Brotherton and marked "Postage Free."

"He's coming—or I'm going!" Mary Ann would announce, bringing back the lights which had faded in the early stages of the war. "Dimouts," the president had called darkened coastal cities in imposing the restrictions. Purpose was to diminish skyglow. That fragile light alone could be silhouetting Allied merchantmen at sea ... betray them to Nazi U-boats. In late April 1942, Broadway's Great White Way was blacked out and ordered to remain so for the "duration." That translated into the war's end. Along the Pacific shores, all leeward lights were first turned low, then painted black. Cars must drive with headlights on dim even after covering the glass with blue cellophane. Drapes were drawn in homes, lights were shielded, so that one must be careful not to stumble over furniture—or one another!

But Mary Ann, still carrying her heavy load and adding to it, went about humming to herself, "When the Lights Come On Again All Over the World," a song which sprang from what was now called the "blackout."

"Oh Marvel! I'm worried about you. You've *got* to get out some. You're living in self-imposed exile. Leave some of this—go to some of the swing-shift matinees," Mary Ann said, trying to cheer her.

Daddy overhead. "I agree, honey—fact is, we all should, but especially Daddy's baby bear. Listen, know who all's been coming in to raise morale among civilians in confined places? Orchestra conductor Werner Jansen for one, and your mother got to hear him! Bless her heart—she has so little time for her violin, working as she is part-time at the university, and now taking on that office job with me—"

Mother had an office job? Marvel was stunned and ashamed. Was she losing touch with *all* her loved ones? She rallied to fake a smile. How white, pale, and drawn Daddy looked. And he was to come to California for his health, Dr. Porter had said. How could he take advantage of the long days of sunshine—very long, "Pacific War Time" having gone into effect, setting all clocks ahead to conserve on electricity? But Daddy had no time to enjoy it.

Uncle Worth moved into their triangular conversation to add to his brother's account of visiting entertainers. "Flyer 'Wrong Way' Douglas Corrigan came in person and—"

He was interrupted by his son. B.J. had overhead. "Wow! Him? No foolin'? Now that's what I'm going to be: a pilot!"

"You'll do no such thing!" Auntie Rae's voice held an unnatural sharpness. "Your father and I will put our feet down on that. Why, the very idea! I'd think you'd know better after what happened to Duke."

"Duke?" Marvel gasped, heart throbbing in her chest. "Something's happened to Duke? You didn't tell me. Tell me now. Is he—?"

"You had enough on your mind, honey," Daddy tried to console. "And nothing's certain. You know his mother—how excited she gets."

"And with just cause this time," Auntie Rae whispered. "He's MIA."

Missing in action! Duke. Oh, there must be some mistake.

Mary Ann's eyes lost their glow. "I—I didn't know either—"

"You don't listen," B.J. accused. "Got a one-track mind!"

"Stop—please stop," Auntie Rae begged softly. "I can't have you two—not the children I love so much—at war. Maybe Snow's right, saying Duke'll show up—could be anytime. He had just applied for a transfer back to the States. She *is* right. I just know—"

"Then I can join up," Billy Joe said smugly.

The world was moving fast—too fast. Auntie Rae mumbled something about helping Mother. The two brothers remained to talk of other matters—how much they were all making and saving, most of it invested in war bonds. "Wise choice," Daddy said, "considering how much they'll yield." To which Uncle Worth added, "Not much choice really. Employers just take a percentage. Not that you and I'd object, looking to the future like we do." Daddy had agreed. After all, it was the patriotic thing to do and "we owe it to our fighting men and—"

Our fighting men and *women*. Thousands of women were serving directly as nurses in the armed forces, the Women's Army Corps (WAC) or other auxiliaries. And indirectly—just consider the number working with Daddy and Uncle Worth. Office workers, yes, but women serving with their hands alongside the men. "Rosie, the Riveter" might be a funny song someday. Not now. There was so little to laugh about in these uncertain times.

Remembered cartoons created by Gill Mauldin along with persuasive columnist, Ernie Pyle, marched before Marvel's eyes ... exhausted, and bitter, unshaven, once-immaculate uniforms now caked with mud and blood ... marching through war-torn villages, heads still high and Old Glory waving—symbol of what they were fighting for. Even now, somewhere out there in the street a loudspeaker blared: "Remember Pearl Harbor," almost but not quite drowning out another of radioland's attempts to cheer people on. "The Johnson Family" was signing off with "'Bye, 'bye—and buy bonds!"—reminders which canceled attempted cheer.

The vision cleared as Mary Ann tugged at Marvel's arm. "Let's go. What is it, Marvel—what is it? Your eyes are dry, but your heart's crying. Duke? Oh Marvel—my Jake—your Titus—"

"All of those," Marvel managed through stiff lips. Then she shared the frightening picture-memories ... and the realization of contributions of women in this painful, bloody business of war.

"I know—I know," her cousin sobbed as they climbed the stairs. "Then there are those of us who—who wait—live with dread, anxiety, praying for just a few stolen hours with our men. What were we born *into*?"

"The Apocalypse."

Mary Ann gasped, then said with a catch in her voice, "There's mail for you—"

21

When the Heart Cannot Accept

Mail—after all these lonely months of waiting. *Years* where Titus was concerned. How hard she had prayed for a word from the man she loved—just a single word. Only one memory linked her to his heart: memory of his telephone call, his proposal. Then silence. Silence, too, as the calendar turned end-on-end during the time she had tried to hear *of* Titus, since she could not hear *from* him. All efforts failed, leaving hope so hard to cling to.

And now on this April day when spring should be ushering in new hope, Marvel Harrington wondered if the letters would bring it. Or would one of them destroy it forever? She shuddered and found her mind was incapable of sending a message to her trembling hands to say that envelopes should be opened. She groped for a chair and watched helpless as they slid through her nerveless fingers. One . . . two . . . three. *Three* letters in one day.

She tried to pray and could not. The only way to reestablish contact with God at such a time was to clear the way, put herself in His hands. He cared—God always cared. It was so evident in the victory garden below. *Victory* garden—how fitting. Marvel found a new meaning to the title now, although it had originated when the government announced that there would be a shortage of food. It had begun with sugar, spread to coffee, then meats . . . and eventually other food would be rationed—probably all of it. "Grow your own" became the slogan. How beautifully Mother and Auntie Rae had responded, just as Grandmother Riley had

216

. said of her daughter, Snow. Looking down on the magic garden below, Marvel realized how proud Grandmother would be of Mother. Was Mother staying in touch? She must check.

But not now. For now, she wanted to clear her mind and very soul. So she concentrated on the spectacular display beneath her window. In a nest of leafy lettuce, crimson tulips were pursing scarlet petals after their all-day's yawn of hollow mouths in the warm sunlight. How beautifully God had arranged nature. The tulips did not mind the smell of green onions alongside them at all. If only mankind could be so wise. Well, Marvel thought with a sudden lift of spirits, the Depression followed by war had brought people closer...American people, anyway—maybe one day the whole world. Aloud, she said softly, "Did I have it all wrong, Lord—praying for more faith? If I talked things over with You more often, my faith would grow on its own. Forgive me. Let me pray morning, noon, and night—believing You will respond— *knowing* You will. In Your own way, in the name of Your Son, who made the greatest sacrifice of all..."

A little breeze shivered along the spines of the feathery asparagus. But Marvel no longer minded. Closing her eyes, she let nature caress her skin, its pungent smell penetrate her nostrils. The *victory* garden!

She could open the letters now:

There was one from Kate Lynn Porter. *Finally*, she thought with a smile, remembering how the doctor's daughter had postponed geometry assignments. A second letter bore a Texas postmark but had no return address...strange. The last of the three came from the sanitarium, where Elmer Salsburg— declared criminally insane—was institutionalized for life. What did they want of her?

Marvel scanned the three letters briefly—too briefly to comprehend the words in her rush or note that a clipping had fallen from one of the envelopes to the carpeted floor. Her subconscious mind said they smacked of confusion, disappointment, and something else. Shock? Heartbreak? *Be calm*, she scolded herself. Kate Lynn's letter first. Her friend just might have news of Titus through Bill.

My dear Marvel: So much has happened to break my heart that I'm not at all sure how to write...not

even sure if I'll send it when I finish. I won't if it's too
morbid. We thought the Depression was tough, but we
could work together—*be* together. Nobody *died*—
like now. We were not "war wives." (Nobody even
knew about war or "isms" except students like you.
Your thinking impressed Daddy so much, please remember that. Daddy loved you.)

Impressed, loved—past tense? Something was wrong, very
wrong. Marvel read page after page of Kate Lynn's rambling
letter—*wrenching* pages which proved her fears were justified.
Dr. Porter was dead.

Oh, the awful ordeal of anxiety and anguish of waiting
(something I'm reliving now while trying to comfort Mother
and myself). It's all so senseless—Daddy, a *doctor*, able to
patch up others, but not himself. We waited and waited,
haunted by dread of receiving that telegram beginning,
"We regret to inform you...." Mother blames herself for
leaving Daddy. But, oh Marvel, she *had* to when he went
into the thick of things. Even before, she'd had to live in
high-rent hovels—anywhere to be with him. It's all so
senseless. Does anybody ever win a war? The war to end all
wars, they tell us—to make this world safe, in a brave new
world.... What's the good if there's nobody left to enjoy it?
Certainly, Daddy won't be here.... Oh, I could cry my eyes
out. I'll never forgive those brutes who destroyed our
peace—*never*! I know Christ suffered. He asked for water
and they gave him vinegar, gall, or whatever it was. He had
come to heal and to save and was crucified. So I know *He*
understands that Daddy had the same experience...but *I*
don't understand! Oh, I wish I could accept all this horror...be good, be compassionate. But I *can't* say, "Father,
forgive them; they know not what they do." They *do* know!
And Bill said they—the Japs—are sly and treacherous, but
not as smart as they claim...that maybe we committed
some blunders, but theirs was the greatest of all. I don't
understand this, but Bill does, and he says if the idiots had
penetrated Southeast Asia instead of attacking Hawaii, they
could've found the resources (what *were* they looking for?)

without provoking America to war. Oh, if only... Still, maybe we're luckier than we think. Bill says intelligence sources admit they possibly could have creamed us, we were so unprepared, peaceful. Under their rule? Oh, God took pity on us, after all.... If we were under the rule of those crazies—know what they're doing now? Dive-bombing, that's what—droves of them strapped in bomb-filled planes and *meaning* to crash. Yes, they sure enough are. "Suicide Squads," they call the pilots—so misguided they think they're coming back after death, having died for the emperor and the Land of the Rising Sun! Don't say I didn't warn you. This is a mess, something *I* had to get off my chest—and I've tried to dodge what I'll say next like guys who dodge the draft. "Draft Dodgers," they're called. Right mean, I guess, but it *is* unusual to see draft-age younger men in "civies." And to think my Bill up and volunteered. I'd rather he'd have dodged. Oh, how can I tell you. He—Bill—is out there somewhere, heaven knows *where*... news blacked out... no mail allowed. And even before now, his letters were censored. He never did hear from Titus. But you can know he's safer than Bill—I mean, aren't reporters safer than pilots? Sure, they are. They can practice their craft on the ground, while flyers ride *their* craft up in those firey skies. So now while I cry for a father who'll not be coming home, I wait for one of those terrible telegrams saying: "We regret..." not knowing how that sentence will end: "missing in action" or the death sen-tence. You can't know what it's like. So talk to me, keep me sane like you always did. I'm afraid to blink, the world changes so fast—one blink and it's shifted. Tell me about the glamour there. Is it prettier than here now? It's rained and rained, so the fence rows are tangled with *living things*. There I go again. Tell me about hairstyles—and clothes... can't change much, can they? I mean, the Depression pre-pared us for all this. "Wear it out. Make it do"... if anything can prepare us for loosing those we love....

Marvel felt ill, the words swimming before her crazily. Dr. Porter—dear, sweet, caring Dr. Porter who had pulled her family through those awful illnesses without pay, just a labor of love.

Bill Johnson, Titus' cocaptain in football, seeing active duty. Such a close friend to Titus, but he had heard nothing either. An aching awareness of Titus made her skin prickle, come alive with his remembered warmth, his gentle voice, and his *vows*! And Kate Lynn thought Marvel couldn't know the agony of waiting? *Oh, dear God, help me! At least she and Mary Ann have tasted the joy of belonging....*

Reading the letter from the sanitarium was easier—easier to read, but not to comprehend. Marvel looked at the words blankly, wondering what it all meant—other than to tell her that her stepcousin had "expired." She could feel no sorrow other than that which one feels on hearing of the death of any fellow human being—even a subhuman like the poor demented, tortured Elmer Salsburg. It was merciful that the Lord had taken him, considering his condition as described by the sanitarium's representative.

That representative was no longer a part of the institution, she read. He had left under "less than favorable conditions." Or, "as service personnel would refer to such a situation: 'dishonorably discharged.'" (Marvel felt a gnaw of surprise and disapproval at the lack of taste. Why overexplain and in such terms?) She read on. His dismissal accounted for the long delay in notifying Miss Harrington of her relative's (*relative*?) demise. Also, in auditing the books following the administrator's departure, it was discovered that a misappropriation had led to near-bankruptcy. Now with government aid, they were able to meet the deficit... distribute funds according to terms specified by Frederick Salsburg, deceased father of the late Elmer Salsburg. Since the will was most complicated, it would be advisable that Marvel Harrington, executrix of the estate, appear in person to serve the long list of heirs—the most sizable legacy going to the executrix... other monies to be distributed according to terms. An attorney would handle the matter were Miss Harrington unable to attend....

Miss Harrington was! Immediately, Marvel signed the form attached and sealed it in the envelope provided. It was puzzling, ambiguous, and more upsetting than she cared to admit. Why make mention until she knew the terms of the document? It would be a relief to set the matter to rest. Memories of Elmer were less than pleasant. But she would handle the situation with dignity—and a certain bond Uncle Fredrick had tried to establish between him and his stepfamily. God had given her the power to love the unlovable man who surrendered his soul on his last day on earth. She rejoiced for that....

Contents of the last remaining letter surprised her most of all. At first, Marvel smiled. The signature sparked that short-lived smile. It gave way to shock at the contents. It was like Editor Corey to be hurried, curt, and somewhat disorganized, brilliant man though he was—like him, too, to forget an identifying return address. But the message was *unlike* him. Trained to be objective, the man who had befriended her used innuendos of emotion, reflecting more than words could say:

> Dear Marvel: All's chaos...whole blame world's gone to pot. Makes me sick...all this killing. Have to write this stuff about war—hate it—fighting enough battles as is...Battle of the Bulge (my own belly) ...trying to see over press releases piled over my head...*Head*, that's what the bell-bottom guys call the latrines these days—places to flush down the waste. Well, flush it all down for my money! Maybe it'll all end in the "unconditional surrender" FDR's asking for. But we got caught with our pants down, not our fault...so who am I to place blame? Just hope history records it like it is but who knows with all the blackouts on news, the censorship? Apt as not, some smart-alecky upstart'll call our emergency-measure internment camps where we feed possible betrayers better than we feed ourselves "concentration" camps like Hitler's torture chambers. In this war firepower counts for more than derring-do...battles won by the side massing most planes, warships, and artillery. Before the United States can defeat the Axis, we have to turn ourselves into a mighty arsenal—just what we're doing I might add...and when we do invade full-force, the Allies'll blast h—— out of Fortress Europe, taking the yellow race with them. Sounds corny, but I believe in a democracy...just hate all-out arms race on building more efficient ways of *killing*. That's why I want you to go on telling it like it is. Cover

the homefront. Don't quit on us now, Marvel. Bunch it all up and send it like you used to. You'll write that book. You *have* to. Titus would have wanted it that way....

Would have. A wave of apprehension shook the core of her heart. Mr. Corey was going to tell her more—something to do with what happened to Titus. *And I'm not able to bear it alone, Lord,* she whispered. *Stand close to me.* And with that agonized prayer, Marvel let the letter flutter from nerveless fingers onto her desk.

"I love you, Titus! Come back. You *have* to. You promised!" she shouted to the empty room. Then, amazed, she wondered if her words carried downstairs—or even onto the street. In any case, the force of her voice released a flow of adrenaline which allowed her to read on.

A. Thomas Corey had accepted the offer once turned down by young Titus Smith... took over publication of the Greenville, Texas newspaper... found unopened mail, "scads" of which came from the talented reporter. Return address marked in upper left of envelope... not unusual, all servicemen overseas were allowed only that. (*But Titus wasn't a serviceman!* Marvel thought with a gasp.) All censored, Mr. Corey explained briefly— most marked "Hold for future notice." Could be from sectors where news was blacked out (*in the midst of battle?*), but nothing more until this—"see enclosed."

But nothing was enclosed. The editor had forgotten. *What?*

Feeling weak and shaken, but still not knowing what the omission pertained to, Marvel was able to read the remaining lines—lines which touched her heart... lines which allowed her a brief reprieve in which she offered praise to the heavenly Father who had wrought another miracle.

P.S. The last war? Maybe. Unpublished rumors— classified info for "security measures"... same old jargon—of a secret weapon... bound on securing peace on earth. Huh! If it's all that powerful, couldn't we destroy it? Sounds like it could lead to the chambers of hell. Is it our weapon or the enemies'? Has to be one more war, according to a slip of a girl I once knew (*you!*). I don't know much about this Armageddon business, but seems like it's the war between good and evil, right? Thought you'd want to know I'm fighting my private one. Could be I'll make out with my own Private Weapon. You told me to pray, and praying *is* the only weapon against a holocaust. I'm trying to cross that gulf 'twixt me and Eden, thanks to you and Doc Holt. Remember his farewell to the grads?

Did Marvel remember? Even in her joy at the editor's words, there was the familiar ache of sorrow. It was not good that man be alone, God had said, after he created the earth. And the same was true of woman. Marvel, like Mr. Corey, wanted to reclaim that garden, help the Creator restore it, but not alone—not without Titus.

She glanced at her watch. Two hours had passed. Intending to go downstairs immediately, Marvel rose quickly. It was when she shoved the chair beneath her desk that a piece of paper fluttered beneath one of the chair's legs. The clipping!

Plainly marked "Hold until notification of kin," the newspaper headline spelled out the dreaded words: "Missing in Action."

Marvel knew then. There was no need—no need at all—to check the list. But, with a heart pounding so hard that the names blurred together, she forced a trembling finger down the alphabetical list, letting it stop on *S*. The walls closed in around her. She was a prisoner, held captive by mankind's folly, unable to accept her sentence.

Titus Smith.

* * *

Marvel never remembered going downstairs. But she must have managed on legs as dead as her heart, for Mary Ann was speaking.

"I was coming up for you. What on earth took so long? Hurry—no, wait! You look like you've seen a ghost. Don't answer that—just tell me on the way. Mother and Aunt Snow have gone to a class in first aid. I'm to cheer you up. We're going to a movie—"

Going to a movie—she was going to a movie. Don't think, just go.

Marvel unburdened her heart to Mary Ann concerning their mutual family friend, Dr. Porter, being a casualty of the war. Mary Ann was devastated—so shaken that she looked to Marvel for solace. Marvel was surprised to find herself able to measure up. Helping gave her the strength she had prayed for, and it spared her the pain of telling about Titus. Perhaps someday—but not now. It was too new, too painful.

The Civil War epic "Gone with the Wind" was not a good choice. Undoubtedly, Marvel thought as she tried to concentrate, the film served to brighten a drab time for Depression-weary Americans when it was released. People needed entertainment to help forget their troubles—either something lighthearted, romantic, glamorized by hints of innocent sex appeal...anything avoiding discontents and disturbing conflicts. Or something which reached too far into the past for moviegoers to identify with or care about. "Gone with the Wind" fell into the latter classification.

But a war picture now, no matter which era it depicted, was unbearable for Marvel—and, she suspected, for Mary Ann as well. It was hard to tell. Let her cousin choose.

Marvel tried to watch, closing her eyes when the scenes depicting war became too graphic. When perhaps the worst was over, she tried to watch Scarlett O'Hara (Vivian Leigh) behaving scandalously in attending a ball in Atlanta while dressed in mourning for her husband, a casualty of the fighting. Even worse, the beautiful black-clad widow was obviously enjoying her dance with the raffish blockade-runner Rhett Butler (Clark Gable). *I'm doing the same thing*, Marvel's anguished heart cried out. Was there no escape?

"I've seen enough of this compost heap!" Mary Ann whispered.

Marvel rose with her and they made a hasty exit. Outside, she inhaled gratefully, thankful that Mary Ann found relief in a flow of words.

"I don't give a flip of my finger how many awards that long-winded 'Wind' won. For me and my money it wasn't all it was cracked up to be! I didn't see it—who had the price?—but I remember something critics said about it being 'designed for escape into another era.' *Escape?* It was too real. Bad as 'The

March of Time' newsreels were that used to come in a double-feature ticket—showing war in other countries or—or that awful crash of the *Hindenburg*. What was that German thing—a *tank*?"

"Dirigible. I'll need to include that when I—I go back to writing."

"You mean you *stopped*? That's not like you. *I'm* the scatter-brain."

There was a silence—a silence Marvel must fill before her cousin asked questions. "All right, so 'You're My Darling Scatter-brain.'"

"Thanks, Marvel—you make me feel better. Only I still hate that movie, or what it made *me* feel—worse than that hoax Orson Welles pulled on radio! Remember when he scared us to an early grave with that terrible science-fiction thing, without telling us it was make-believe—saying some characters from outer space had landed *here*? Alarmed the whole world, I guess. And that movie did that to me—af-after hearing news about Dr. Porter. That's hitting too close to home. Oh Marvel, I want to see Jake! That's mean. I know you feel bad too. We'll talk at home—"

They didn't, as it happened, for the war had struck again—struck even closer this time.

No lights blazed as they once did when there was a crisis. Air-raid wardens saw that the imposed regulations were kept. But even as the cousins groped their way through the darkened hall, something warned of trouble. The hum of excited voices, though pitched low, said all family members were talking at once. Both girls stopped.

"Oh Dale, it's awful. I—I don't know what to do. Can't there be some mistake? That's it—a mistake. They're just excited—"

"No mistake this time, Snow," Daddy's voice was grim. "I know—"

"I know, too—both of us talked to Emory. He's matter-of-fact. Eleanore's the hysterical one—already fearing about Thomas—"

Auntie Rae interrupted, which was unlike her. "Worth, I worry, too."

"About *me*? Oh, corncobs!" B.J. burst out. "When I go—"

"*You* are not going, Billy Joe!" his mother said sharply.

"Oh, Marvel!" Mary Ann's whisper echoed down the hall. "Is it—?"

"Duke? Yes." The words closed around Marvel's throat like long fingers in the dark, but she forced herself to continue. "We must go in."

"Well, whatta you know! The Misses Hollywoods," B.J., suffering wounded pride, burst out. "Your dress's too short, big sis. 'As you show, so shall we peek'!"

"That'll do," Uncle Worth growled. "You're not too big to be taken out to the woodshed!"

The boy, whose voice was cracking with adolescence, hesitated, obviously wanting to seize the opportunity of reminding his father there was no woodshed. If so, he thought better of it.

Daddy hastened to Marvel to place a supporting arm about her shoulders. "Are you all right, honey? You're so pale. You heard?"

Marvel could only nod.

Mother joined them. "We're all so upset, not knowing what to do. I know your aunt and uncle need us, but there are our jobs, and you—and everything. I guess the aircraft factory will allow time off. Do we know, Dale? I guess *you'd* know—but Marvel? You decide it."

"You decide, Mother," Marvel said gently. "I have to be here. There are reasons why—important ones. But I can manage, believe me."

"Good girl," Daddy's voice broke. "We'd better go. Only I don't want you here alone. It's unsafe now. Things are different."

Mary Ann squared her shoulders. "I'll stay with her."

B.J., eager to make up for his behavior, said manfully. "Me, too!"

"God bless you all," Uncle Worth said humbly. "Great kids."

A calm settled in around them—everywhere perhaps except in Marvel's heart. She moved about, helping Mother pack a small case, even managing a smile as she reminded her to take her last pair of nylons. The men would break news of the emergency and arrange for bus tickets, making small talk of having to ignore the mocking sign at the terminal which demanded: "Is this trip necessary?"

Suddenly, they were gone. A hush closed over the great house.

* * *

First things first. Marvel Harrington must remember that, put some order back in her life. So thinking, she wrote responses to Kate Lynn and Editor Corey. Three times Kate Lynn's intended letter of condolence ended up as a crumpled ball in the waste-basket. The completed one was little better, but it would have to do. Marvel was deeply pained to hear of Dr. Porter's becoming a casualty, but such a dear self-sacrificing man would live forever in the hearts of those who loved him, she assured his daughter. "And put me at the very top of that long list," she ended the paragraph, with an aching heart.

> I know a bit what you and your mother must be enduring, my dear. Even as I write, my own parents and Mary Ann's have gone to Oregon to console Duke's folks. You'll remember Duke from our high-school days (a million years and World War II ago?). Try, as I am trying, to trust God to bring only good news of Bill. Waiting is an agony all its own. How can I find the words to tell you about a puzzling list of MIA's I received? Safe, you said of Titus...*safe*? Kate Lynn, reporter or not, his name was on that list.... And so I, too, wait...prayerfully. Mary Ann waits—like you, unable to hear the facts regarding Jake (I *did* tell you they were married by proxy?). The whole world waits ...I guess even our president....

She was unable to continue—just repeated the feeble attempts to comfort and add her love. "And of course I'll pray, dear friend!"

Writing to Mr. Corey was even more difficult. Congratulating the editor on his new position presented no problem. He was obviously happy—and yes, she promised, the column could be continued. It was just a matter of picking up where they had left off—first, to digest materials collected, put them into some sort of sequence. Life had kept her too busy, Marvel went on to say, quickly telling him of her educational pursuits. What else did I say? she was to wonder after posting the letter. Ditto...ditto ...about mixed feelings concerning the war. How could killing ever be justified? And yet, there was duty to country...unprovoked attacks. "I guess you are right, sir, in feeling that the roots of war lie within our own hearts. God's holy Word tells us that we are not to be overcome by evil but to overcome evil with good. Jesus Christ has walked into your life without knocking—Jesus (not the money-changer), the changer of hearts! We still have a choice. We can destroy ourselves and this world, or help our Creator restore the Garden...."

The book? Yes, yes, Marvel promised. She would write and keep on writing—praying with every breath she took that Titus Smith would return. It was imperative. Marvel stopped short of letting an outsider (dear friend though he was) know what she had not revealed to her own family. America must know, must *care*, lest that "secret weapon" he mentioned blot the very stars from the sky. Mr. Corey *would* keep her informed about Titus? Surely there was some mistake.

With trembling hands, Marvel turned full attention to the printed accounts she had saved as history unfolded. Already Titus seemed closer.

In many aspects of American life, the war quickened the tempo of change—that she knew and had known even before World War II began. But were the changes always for the better? Which reporter said: "Looks like this war has sped up every kind of process, both good and bad in America?"

Well, she thought with a sigh, it had quickened the tempo in employment and accelerated educational pursuits—both for debatable reasons. Weapons were for killing ("God help us all, the allies and the enemies!") And education? One had to wonder if some young men used college as a shield against the draft. That, too, would pass. Already age limits were lowering, martial status questioned.

There was social ferment, but maybe it worked just the opposite—allowed good to come of evil. "Unless a grain of wheat falls into the earth and dies, it remains by itself alone; but if it dies, it bears much fruit," according to the gospel of St. John. *Amen*! Marvel Harrington was seeing a vision all her own: the book that must be written.

Unemployment had vanished. The growing need for workers had encouraged vast numbers of Negroes to emerge from the Deep South. They had suffered from the Depression and some oppression "back home," but they were forced to suffer more in the "Promised Land." Wherever the black people went they met special kinds of humiliation which told them they were "inferior." When they donated blood to the Red Cross, the blood was segregated. War plants cried for "all kinds" of help, but Negroes often found themselves turned away at the factory gate. Oh, they could serve in the Army, but they were segregated in barracks and mess halls (Jake had written about that). When white soldiers boarded troopships, the band played "God Bless America." When the uniformed black soldiers marched up the plank, the band switched to "Darktown Strutters' Ball." But (and Marvel would want Fanny to read this section of the book to her family so they all could "bust with pride"!) Negroes refused to submit passively to the denial of their rights, being told that they were not Americans. The National Association for the Advancement of Colored People, heretofore a "silent minority," swelled 500 percent after Pearl Harbor... the number of Negroes employed as skilled craftsmen and foremen doubled (Daddy had told her what a wonderful one such supervisor the man working alongside him and Uncle Worth was). Marvel stopped at that point to thumb through her files excitedly in search of supporting information. Oh, here it was: the good and bad!

There must be a dragon lurking in every garden—sad but true. The assertion of Negro rights inevitably accelerated racial tension—even now... everywhere, she realized in horror, reading on... not just here in Los Angeles where, according to newspaper clippings, 3000 beat and kicked and slurred Mexican-Americans. Would that it were only local, but on a sultry June night the worst race riot in a quarter of a century erupted in Detroit. All-night mobs roamed the grimy Negro slum of Paradise Valley. At dawn, black and white mobs halted streetcars, hauled off workers... and officials did nothing until an uninvolved middle-aged Negro was shot by whites "just for the hell of it" one boasted. By then hundreds were injured... dead: 25 blacks, 9 whites.

In Beaumont, Texas, Marvel read in humiliation, white workers burned two blocks of Negro homes, while across the nation in Harlem a riot did a million dollars' worth of damage. But these eruptions marked a turning point, thank God. Sobered by the display of racial hatred, governors called for antidiscrimination. Citizen's banded together for a good cause, "gulfing barriers between the two races."

Slowly the Negroes were given a chance to prove their worth. All America was waking up after a long, nightmarish sleep. Could this be due to seeing at last an embarrassingly similar credo overseas where Nazi doctrines of "blood" and "race" were leading to torture chambers? The rest was good news. Oh, how proud Fanny could be of the all-Negro 99th Fighter Squadron which won commendation in Europe and the 93rd Infantry Division which was rapidly distinguishing itself! "And, hear this, Fanny! Your people (and that means *ours*—we are one family!) are now commissioned *officers*. Georgia's considering repealing its poll tax. Supreme Court is giving consideration to outlawing white primaries in all 48 states! Liberalism is beginning!"

Lost in her private world of writing, Marvel had lost all count of time. She hardly heard Mary Ann's call: "Come on down, Marvel! Hurry! I've got something important to— Come on! Oops, the phone again!"

Marvel had expected to see a glowing Mary Ann, judging by the excitement in her cousin's voice. Instead, the rounded face was twisted in pain, which turned to sudden anger. "Oh, why did you call me, Jake?" she screamed, pounding the wall with hard-clenched fists. "You ought to have gone—not said a word! First, you say we can be together—"

When her cousin paused, exhausted, Marvel said gently, "What is it, Mary Ann? Tell me—and stop beating the wall as if it were your husband's chest."

"Husband?" Mary Ann tasted the word and, pushing back the dark curls which had fallen forward, murmured, "He is, isn't he? Oh Marvel, what would I do without you—without *Jake*? Oh, help me, will you. I have one hour—just one to fight my way through priority-travelers—service personnel first—Well, what about wives? Is this trip necessary? Mercy on us, we don't even want to *go*. Then *that*!"

"You'll have to calm down, Mary Ann. I can't help without knowing my job description," Marvel said as lightly as she was able.

At last the pieces fit. Jake had called, thinking they would have a lengthy time before his orders came through. Correction: orders just arrived . . . but they could have the weekend—*there*! There? Oh, Santa Maria Air Base. Billy Joe had called Greyhound . . . had to have *bus* reservations—imagine that! Oh, she couldn't make it. She *couldn't*!

But she did. Marvel and B.J. walked the short distance to the terminal with her.

"Oh, thank God for you both!" Mary Ann cried. Emotional tears welling up in the great brown eyes, she hugged them in turn (too tightly for her brother's comfort until she whispered, "You're not *always* a pest!").

Then, checking her watch as she walked, Mary Ann elbowed her way through a glowering crowd and swung aboard. The last they saw of Mrs. Jake Brotherton was her sitting at the back of the bus astride her overnight bag in the aisle. And she was waving a white hankie. *The white flag of victory!*

"Well," B.J. said, faking a sneeze to justify using a handkerchief, "they've all abandoned us. You and I are among the 'door-key children,' the 'eight-hour orphans'—only we're not *kids*. I'll do my share."

"You'd be doing your share, sweetie, if you never turned a hand," Marvel assured him. "You keep us smiling—something we'd forget how to do without you!" The youngest Harrington stood ten feet tall.

Marvel had intended going on with the change toward black Americans, but B.J.'s reference to latchkey children led to the homefront....

The reshuffling of population during WW II comprised the greatest short-term migration in American history (one item told her, going on to quote numbers). People swarmed defense towns where there were not enough family dwellings, parks, playgrounds, hospitals, theaters, cafes. People slept in cars, tents, concrete-floored garages, and refrigerator lockers. Greedy landlords exploited a seller's market all over the country, while pretending piety in such ads as: "Fur. Apt., no streetwalkers, home wreckers, drunks. Couples must show marriage certif." They lived in squalid trailer camps (one writer reported), in pestilential shantytowns with privies in back, or commuted 40 miles to and from work. Remember, all this was earlier and we know now....

This—why, this was worse than the Great Depression, Marvel thought in bewilderment. She wanted to lay it all aside, but couldn't.

Children raised in such mushroom cities found the war a time of confusing disruption...fathers inducted, working in defense, or "frozen to war-essential" jobs. Millions of women had gone to work, so children— wearing keys around their necks—entered empty houses when school let out. Result: "This uprooting led to a spectacular rise in juvenile delinquency... especially alarming was the rise of offenses by young girls."

America, which had spent years trying to cope with millions of unemployed, suddenly found itself facing acute manpower shortage. Western Union "boys" became elderly men. Women marched off to war or donned coveralls to work in aircraft factories, ship- yards, and munitions plants. War brought prosperity. America did what it had to do...but what price glory!

A depression-poor country now found itself faced with runaway inflation. The concerned and alarmed president named Supreme Court Justice James F. Byrnes to head a newly-created Office of Economic Stabilization. Byrnes was farsighted and tough. He took one look, saw the problems created by the panic of wartime and too much money, and imposed a mid- night curfew. "So I'm the home-front czar—just follow orders!" Hence the name "Byrne-out" by those accus- ing him of electricity conservation...but conserva- tion, yes...gasoline...tires. "If you haven't turned them in, do so *now*! Both will be rationed and soon ...next, probably coffee...sugar...possibly meat, even clothing—certainly shoes...which will create a dragon all its own: black market. There must be price control!" Which leads to now...

Resting her tired eyes, Marvel felt a helplessness creep over her entire body. "How sad, Lord—oh, how sad. Your heart must be bleeding like my own. Small wonder Your Son shed no tears for His own grief but sweat drops of blood for this world. Oh, to stop this senseless killing—this bloodshed for wrong reasons. And most of us are trying, Lord. You know we are—in the only way we know how, while those untouched by Your love seek another idol: *money*. Forgive them."

She was on the verge of putting the articles away, feeling she could stand no more, planning waffles for B.J. and herself. The self-appointed man of the house would enjoy that—so would she, except that something in her subconscious compelled one last glance.

Conservation . . . conservation. . . . She and Mary Ann worked with the Agricultural Conservation Association. Did this have to do with them? She knew the reasoning behind the gasoline shortage (U-boats were sinking oil tankers). To intensify the problem, Japan's conquests of the East Indies and Malaya cut off the natural rubber supply. No tires—why, Americans had forgotten how to move by automobile. All this the Harringtons knew, just didn't talk about—working and praying instead. But wait, here it was:

> The Department of Agriculture, which has been urging farmers to curb production, now turns its energies to persuading them to step up output . . . get back home to the farms . . . now essential to the war effort . . . cease draft of farmers. The once-active Agricultural Conservation Association will reduce personnel, change focus, move inland most likely. The great need now will be for workers in the Office of Price Control . . . issuing ration books. . . . a long fight ahead . . .

Marvel let the clippings flutter downward. Her mind was unable to function. All this coupled together was too much—too much. Duke . . . Jake . . . beloved friends . . . and *Titus*! Dropping her head onto folded arms, she was unable to pray. God knew that there were some things hearts cannot accept.

22

Another World

It was true. It was all true. With B.J. in tow, Marvel checked grocery shelves late Sunday night. The family was scheduled to be home early Monday morning in time to report for work (unless "bumped" by men and women in uniform trying to spend leaves or furloughs with loved ones—otherwise traveling on troop trains, planes or in convoys of olive-drab vehicles carefully spaced and paced at 35 MPH). Mary Ann's schedule was uncertain.

Small wonder the Office of Price Administration needed over-hauling. Originally, Marvel recalled vaguely, the agency groped blindly on piecemeal price-fixing, doomed for inadequacy. Later, the pendulum had swung questionably far (always under fire in case of controls) when replaced by a general maximum price regulation. That august body froze most prices and defense-area rents at their March 1942 levels. Daddy and Uncle Worth talked about it, but in general terms. "How fortunate we are to *own!*" they congratulated themselves. So the Harringtons had not been affected in either case. She half-smiled at the memory of the stumpy, cigar-puffing Leon Henderson, chosen by President Roosevelt to head the agency. He was renowned for his economic shrewdness, but had no real power to curb the rising inflation until now. What a difference! "General Max," the segment of society which howled at any restriction dubbed the man. Good or bad, control was essential. As one commentator said, "Tough, just plain tough, when you're caught betwixt and between, scared silly you won't have enough, scared to death you'll have too much. Sort of like the fix American farmers were in: Produce, don't produce! Now ladies, so I'm told, feel guilty if they still have nylon hosiery stashed away . . . families afraid to declare tires. Would cars have to run on rims? But scared not to. And now there are sugar and coffee shortages. Any coffee left over gets you the infamous title of 'hoarder'! While sugar—to declare or not to declare. New regulations say declare it, but fear of shortage tempts homemakers but robs honest folks of sleep."

Yes, Marvel remembered how Mother and Auntie Rae had struggled over that. "Now you can't tell me our government would want all that lovely fruit to go to waste. It has a right to be jelled!" "And you ladies have a right to be *jailed*," Daddy had teased when there was a mysterious knock on the door. Dear, conscientious Auntie Rae had rushed to the bathroom and flushed down their precious supply, without realizing that she was furthering the shortage. And the caller? A next-door neighbor begging to borrow a cup of sugar for her husband's lunch cookies! There had been some good-natured joshing from the Harrington men. It would be good to have them all home. . . .

"Why're you grinning, huh, Marvel?" B.J. asked in puzzlement. "Me, I don't like this—sort of creepy, looking at these empty shelves."

Marvel noticed him then. "It seemed to happen overnight, didn't it? I guess we knew it was coming, but when it hits—"

"Pow! Like Pearl Harbor! Will we have to form queues like they do in England? S'pose? Look: no sugar, no coffee—just a little canned meat. I'm gonna put sardines in our basket. And what about tuna for sandwiches? Oh look, Marvel!" his voice dropped to a whisper. "See that bunch of men—no, over there where I'm pointing my thumb—all lined up outside the cigar store across the street trying to buy cigarettes. Let 'em learn to roll their own if they're bound on smoking that filthy stuff. They need to grow their own like Old Uncle Ned used to. And look! I thought bootlegging was against the law—"

"It is, honey," Marvel hastened to tell her young cousin. "This way it's legal. Not that legal makes it right. Pick up some cheese."

"I wish these baskets had wheels. I guess they never will. Maybe after the metal shortage," he said, disappearing with the hand basket.

Within minutes he was back. "This was fun with you until—"

Looking into the still-unshaven face of the gangling boy, Marvel saw uncertainty and a sort of sadness. "What's wrong? Did something happen?" she asked quickly.

He nodded. "Two women were talking about stockings—accused our president of sending the only nylon ones to Europe. Said the government ordered it, using it as bait to spy over there while our mamas have to wear those tacky rayon things. It's not true, is it?"

"If it's true, there's a good reason, B.J. Just remember, we were cautioned to ignore rumors—told, too, that there would have to be sacrifices. My understanding is that nylon is in short supply because it's used for parachutes. Let's believe that, for I know *it* is fact."

"Parachutes!" Fascinated with the word, nylons were forgotten. Practically, Marvel folded the shopping list down the middle, placed it on a lifted knee, and tore it apart. "Here's your half," she told a grinning B.J. "Let's have a race!"

B.J. won. A muttering group of swing-shift shoppers, dedicated to the war effort, had grouped around a radio on the glassed-in meat case. An announcer was saying excitedly:

Repeating: Word has just come through regarding the death march in Bataan...not new, but news to America...and the atrocities and inhumane mistreatment goes far beyond that which was inflicted in the sneak attack on Pearl Harbor. We must rekindle the red-blooded American spirit, redouble our efforts, at whatever price! Become a *national team*, keep a stiff upper lip, be as uncomplaining as our baseball teams. The Boston Red Sox have just announced that they'll work out in Medford, Massachusetts; the New York Yanks in Atlantic City...not the usual spring training of old, due to travel restrictions. Those profiteering from war, while our dedicated young shed blood on foreign soil to protect them, should be put into solitary confinement! Yes, the black markets—and those who patronize them. For black markets flourish in every product in short supply. Cab drivers who once guided their fares to speakeasies now know where low-grade gasoline's smuggled in, which will result in rationing even more strictly. Bellboys turn their talent to procuring cartons of cigarettes. Bananas and chocolate, hard to lay hands on in stores, go to the highest bidder! And the largest black market ever looms just around the corner: meat and butter. OPA is arming....

Office of Price Administration! Marvel resolved to leave early tomorrow. Something whispered a warning of change. Her hunch was correct. The ACA office was aflutter with white-face excitement. Desks and chairs were piled high like barricades and employees were working furiously but with lack of organization. Some said there were rumors of sudden attack ... offices must be moved inland, perhaps to midwestern states. Who wished to volunteer? Others reported that the ACA would be done away with completely—no more jobs. Best get into defense—paid more, anyway. Even the supervisors knew little, other than that this office would be closed. Marvel hailed a harassed supervisor (tempted to grab onto his coattail, but restraining herself and running alongside him toward the file cabinet) to inquire what was best for persons like herself and her cousin.

"Oh yes—good morning, Miss Harrington. I remember you both as very hardworking employees—our best. All I can say for sure is that there's word from the top that this branch will merge, unless the entire program's discontinued. I just don't know. I—we—uh, over here with that file case, boys! What was I saying? Oh, you wished advice. Leave your mailing address, it's on file. No, better mail it to the main office. You have the address—checks will be mailed."

The man disappeared faster than Billy Joe had in the market.

"Take my advice," one of the other girls said in passing. "Put your paycheck in government bonds. It's for a good cause—purchasing weapons for our men on the fighting front, you know. I'll make any sacrifice for the man I had to see off to war. You, too?"

Marvel nodded. The awful pain came back. "I have some bonds—"

"Buy more! Give until it hurts. I'm fed up with all the gaff about the bond pressure's a hoax! The doubting Thomases yell, 'Foul play—just a ploy to snap up millions like a snapping turtle, millions to be spent on fighting inflation. They'll buy guns without our help!' Just think— Oh I shouldn't be standing here talking."

"Go ahead," Marvel said softly. "It will do us both good."

"Well, I get dreaming—dreams and faith are all we have to hold onto. Well, aren't they, Marvel?"

Marvel nodded again. "They're enough—love for our men and faith in our God to look after them, bring them back to fulfill that dream."

The girl—Marie, wasn't it?—looked up misty-eyed. "Beautiful," she whispered, "beautiful—like you. We all talk about your courage, determination, and a sort of glow like you wear a halo. Oh, how he must love you! And your name is right. But I knew you dreamed like me. Look what we'll have 'When Johnny Comes Marching Home' or 'Oh, Johnny!' and in my case, it *is* Johnny. I'll be Mrs. Johnny O'Neal, and we'll be in the money—right on Easy Street. Those bonds are refundable at ten percent when we win this war!"

Marvel wondered if Marie knew that employers were compelled to collect taxes on payroll deductions in a "withholding tax" and that, if the war dragged on, just possibly they would handle war bonds in the same manner. But that was only talk. And hopefully Mother was right and the war would end soon. Why borrow trouble? "Hold that line," she smiled instead. "Cling to those dreams and your faith. Oh Marie, wait! Have you heard where the OPA will be located?"

"Oh sure!" the red-haired Marie said airily. "Right here— moving in this afternoon, in fact." She paused to smooth the skirt of her tailored black suit. "You know, you gave me an idea. Maybe *I* should apply. A supervisor's coming, and I know about setting up files and all that. You *were* considering this, weren't you? And seeing that you, Mary Ann, and I've worked together—well, let's!"

Marvel agreed, glanced at her watch, and promised to return.

This time it was Marie who said, "Wait! Uh, Marvel, this *is* contributing to the war effort—helping get our men home? But well, what if Johnny wants me with him before it's over—when he's back at another station? Could I go if we're frozen on the job—"

"The way I understand *frozen* does not mean you can't leave, just not accept private employment. The government would try to place you in another position similar to this. We'll have to check. 'Bye now!"

* * *

Dale and Worth Harrington and their wives were home on schedule. Mary Ann Harrington Brotherton was not. This Billy Joe's hastily scrawled note told Marvel. No time to talk as they'd hurried off to work—as had he, with school afterward. "I had my report card—a really super-duper one—but nobody paid attention. Wanted to tell my daddy and mama that I kept my promise around this morgue, too. Well, maybe they'll listen to you—had their minds up yonder in Oregon. Didn't talk about that, too—or is it *either*? Tonight maybe? B.J."

The evening's talk buzzed around Marvel's ears with none of it making much sense unless one read between the lines, which she tried very hard to do. She must listen. She *must*. Never mind that two letters lay unopened, face-to-face, the way B.J. (who had developed a sudden recognition of others' right to privacy) had placed them. Marvel wondered briefly about the return address—wondered, too, if she could hope to accomplish in a lifetime what was expected of her at the OPA office. But first things first. The family deserved undivided attention.

"I do wish Mary Ann would show up," Auntie Rae kept saying as she packed lunches and put midnight coffee on to perk. "I'm in a state—"

"Of nerves. We all are after Duke's—" Uncle Worth could not go on.

Mother poured a cup of coffee, sloshed it onto a clean table-cloth, and mumbled something about its making no difference as the water wasn't even hot. "Aunt Eleanore can't talk sense, Marvel, but—"

"None of us could," Daddy said raggedly. "Your Uncle Emory is—is not able to take charge like he always did, honey. They're *so* bitter—even declare they'll refuse the insurance policy. I—well, I oughtn't say this, but I'm glad you're a girl. What am I saying? I was *always* glad—so proud of you. Why do you think I named you *Marvelous*? And now it's marvelous you won't be fighting. Oh, Worth, Rae, forgive me—"

"Because they have a son?" B.J. demanded. "Well, they'll be proud of me tonight—soon as Marvel tells how I've behaved. Huh, Marvel?"

"You've been wonderful," Marvel smiled. "And he has a good report card, too. As for Mary Ann, Jake will see that she gets home."

Did anybody hear? In their state of confusion, uncertainty, and fatigue, they were unable to sort matters out, make sense of what had become a senseless world to them. With that, Marvel could identify. In a shattered world, one found it hard to decide what mattered—*really* mattered—after all. Life was such a fragile thing....

The best she could determine, both families (Uncle Joseph's as well as Uncle Emory's) were totally disoriented, having come face-to-face with the reality of death—blaming themselves, accusing one another, cursing the world, saying God had turned His back on them.

Daddy shook his head in disbelief. "Nothing I said helped."

"It's too new," Marvel offered, her heart feeling deeply grieved for them all. "I loved Duke, too. And there's an emptiness inside us because a part—an important part—of us is gone. Oh," she went on to say with sudden inspiration, "about our Billy Joe's being a boy...Uncle Worth and Auntie Rae, be proud! He carries the family name—something Mary Ann and I must surrender. There are only two boys left."

Auntie Rae turned toward her, eyes full and warm, "Thank you, Marvel," she whispered. "We *are* proud. Come here, B.J. You're not too big to be hugged. And you can't go! See? Like Marvel says, you're to carry on the Harrington name instead of a rifle!"

Talk resumed then...warm talk...love-filled. They needed each other. There was even laughter, somewhat restrained but cleansing, as they "broke bread" together (a proud Billy Joe's chosen cinnamon rolls), tearing them apart in jagged chunks and dunking (for the first time ever!) in their steaming cups of coffee. Now they could talk freely.

"Your Aunt Eleanore's like a ping-pong ball, bouncing this way and that, Marvel," Mother said sadly. "Oh, how I pity her. One minute she's in a kind of stupor, and the next she's saying it's all her fault, like coming West had anything to do with losing Duke."

Marvel nodded. "Duke wanted to go. From where made no difference."

Daddy squeezed her hand. "Right as rain. No sense in blaming California. It's been kind to us 'foreigners,' as Oregon's been—"

Uncle Worth looked thoughtful. "Oregon's so green and lush. Reminds me of Texas—the way it was before the drought. And Alex Jr.'s struck it rich. You know," he said slowly as if the ideas were new, "I always knew we'd be going back, Dale. We talked all that out before leaving home. And even if we hadn't, Father's wishes would have counted."

Auntie Rae's eyes enlarged. "What are you saying, Worth. That we—"

"Aren't going? Not at all. I just think Emory may go, too. It may be that he'll have to—for Eleanore. I'd do it for *you*!"

Of course he would. So would Daddy. The family understood. And understanding, they only communicated wordlessly.

Prolonged silence was too much for B.J. Bothered more by all the goings-on, he gave voice to questions: "What about Thomas? Nobody's mentioned him. And the girl cousins—could they spare time to see you? Those three neither toil nor spin, but there are charity balls, so I hear. They'd like that! And about this going back business . . . Hey, if Uncle Emory goes home, I betcha Uncle Joseph'll tail him. S'pose?" He inhaled sharply, popping the lone remaining bite of cinnamon roll in his mouth. Promptly, he suffered a seizure of coughing. "Dry crumb—" he gasped. "Don't y'all care I'm *choked*?"

"On words," Uncle Worth laughed, whacking his son on the back after Auntie Rae handed him a glass of water. "Easy does it, sonny."

"Sonny" obliged by giving off a loud burp and mumbling, "'Scuse, please." Then he continued his monologue: "Aunt Eleanore hated Texas. Beats me why she'd want to go back . . . if she does?"

"That's a barrage of questions for one sitting," Daddy said, stealing a glance at his watch. "Better get a bit of shut-eye, then 'Heigh ho, heigh ho! It's off to work we go. . . .' No, I see you need answers. I guess we all do. Maybe I was avoiding facing them."

One by one the answers came as the family pitched in to tidy up. Thomas? Duke's young brother never did share his idol's passion for a service career . . . now "pretty broke up," hoping to avoid the draft. His father found "bankers" carried no more clout with draft boards than inhabitants of skid row. Cindy and Erin, both married now, lived back East somewhere. Little time to talk details . . . Monica, still in school. Didn't know Joseph's plans . . . not even Emory's for sure. As for, Eleanore, that was another matter.

"Your aunt's suffering, honey," Auntie Rae said softly, "like thousands of other mothers who've lost sons. First it was that lonely period of waiting, then—then, it was Duke's missing. I—I can only imagine the anxiety and uncertainty—and now the *knowing*."

"Don't—don't cry, Mommy," Billy Joe gulped, a little boy again. Regaining control, the little boy became a man. "Don't worry, I've about lost the stomach for bein' a Colonel Doolittle!"

Colonel Doolittle. Marvel's own tormented mind welcomed a side road. She would review notes on *Lieutenant* Colonel (wasn't it?) and his 1942 raid on Tokyo. As she recalled, dropping bombs inflicted little damage. But what a boost to American morale!

"And yes, there *is* something Duke's mother's obsessed with, B.J.," Uncle Worth was saying. Marvel dropped her thoughts to listen. "Nothing like raids on Rotterdam, Hamburg, Munich, and maybe on Tokyo itself. Hard telling with news blacked out. But in your Aunt Eleanore's state of shock—well, there's no reasoning. Seems a fishing party took some offbeat trail into mountain country, and one of the children picked up a Japanese bomb. Yes, a live one. Guess they managed to hoist several onto the Pacific coast on—would you believe?—*paper balloons*. Too bad several people were killed by the one the child found. Chances are it won't happen again, but try and tell *her* that!"

Mother said a little desperately, "This war has us all a little crazy. It'll end and we'll pick up where we left off. I—I'll (she was making a pathetic effort to restore their light mood) find that 'lost chord'—you'll see! Everything will be the same—*everything*."

Nothing will ever be the same, Mother!

All had risen. Someone turned out the light and opened the blackout shade in preparation for "calling it a day."

Billy Joe interrupted the procedure. His question well could have come from the tomb of the Unknown Soldier: "What if the world had a war and nobody came?"

* * *

Memories turned over in Marvel's mind, images rushing past in sequence of a carefully planned album. How long had it been since a whirlwind brought Titus to her, only to whisk her away in a renewed burst of fury? But most important were the pages between—their hours spent together paving the way to a lifetime of love together. But there could be no togetherness, no time at all, if the "Missing in Action" were followed by a "we regret to inform you ..." letter like Duke's parents received. But in a sense, she thought wearily, Aunt Eleanore and Uncle Emory were fortunate to qualify for the message. Marvel Harrington had no claim. She was not in the picture, according to the War Department's files. Titus Smith's "nearest of kin" was a sister. Or, was Lucille herself a survivor? Marvel's letter had come back marked "Addressee Unknown."

This kind of thinking was getting her nowhere—exactly what she had wanted to avoid. Escaping the family was easy. Escaping memories was not. The only fence around the world was work. Quickly seizing her notebook, Marvel worked behind the closed drapes of her bedroom, all else forgotten, until sleep's gentle fingers closed her eyelids as she had closed the drapes.

Was it by chance or Providence (Marvel queried) that U.S. aircraft carriers were on maneuvers when the carrier-based Japanese attack struck Pearl Harbor on December 7, 1941, knocking out much of the Pacific fleet? At first outnumbered ten to three, American flattops struck back boldly. Their plans softened up islands to be invaded ... supported assault troops ... later bombed Japan itself. And herein lies a story history must record. For memories must be preserved to rekindle and reawaken the American spirit, strengthen our resolution that war must not happen again. Taking off from the U.S.S. *Hornet* aircraft carrier, Lieutenant Colonel James Doolittle and his copilot of San Antonio, Texas (she wrote proudly), and roughly some 80 other aviators dropped payloads on Tokyo on April 18, 1942. Of the 16 B-25 planes, 15 crashed in or near China; the other landed in Russia. Seven of the volunteers died, including three who were executed by the Japanese. That bombing by a brave few represented the first time Japan was hit after its sneak attack on Pearl Harbor. Historians one day may claim it caused little damage, represented little gain for the Allies. Wrong on both! That run marked a psychological turning point for the war in the Pacific. Japan was shocked with disbelief, while American morale soared and the U.S.S. *Hornet* was made famous. Living up to expectations, the carrier went on to fight...

At that point, Marvel Harrington, (destined to become a celebrity herself by the Lord's time clock) had fallen asleep. Yes, the *Hornet* would go on to fight in a tide-turning battle on Midway, making its last attack off the Santa Cruz Islands when, after absorbing tremendous punishment, it sighed and sank to the bottom for a well-deserved rest. But its spirit rose from that watery grave. A new carrier bearing its proud name came out to meet the mounting threat of Nippon's kamikaze corps. Japanese pilots by the hundreds, seeking a death "as sudden and clean as the shattering of crystal," aimed their planes at U.S. warships. As many as one in four hit home, but the new *Hornet* managed to remain intact. Soon it helped to carry the war to Japan's very doorstep.

For reasons of national security, Americans would not hear of defeats and victories as they occurred. Later, however, they would read the glaring headlines followed by stories in brief: "The Carrier *Hornet* Shown Burning! Attacked by an enemy plane in the battle of Santa Cruz. Japan loses 100 planes plus use of two carriers...shattered plans to retake Guadalcanal. New *Hornet* Commissioned 13 Months After Its Namesake! The namesake carrier narrowly escapes a kamikaze in 1945. At Okinawa alone, suicide planes hit over 300 ships, killing thousands. But these are not the only fronts...take heart!"

None of this Marvel knew then, just as she did not know of the news awaiting her in the two unopened envelopes....

Marvel moved stiffly in an effort to rise from the cramped position at her desk. Something had startled her during that sleep of exhaustion—a vague sense of something unfinished.

And then she remembered the letters. Suddenly awake, an icy cold gripping her heart, without use of a letter opener she ripped the end off the thicker of the two envelopes. A sheath of legal documents dropped to the desk.

Feeling further depressed, Marvel scanned the contents, knowing the source without checking for signatures on the notarized pages. The sanitarium, of course. But what was this? In haste, she had read it wrong. There had to be some mistake. A more careful reading left her still unconvinced. "I don't believe it. I just don't," she gasped in shock. "This—why, this amounts to a fortune!" Her stepuncle had led them all to believe the first will had depleted all resources.

All the Harrington brothers were mentioned: Alex "for further holdings in the Northwest" ... Emory and Thomas "for shares in a bank of their choosing in Titus County, Texas" (a *bank*—back home?). Fascinated and awed, Marvel read on: Grandfather Harrington was to be in charge of "said bank," while Daddy and Uncle Worth (this *couldn't* be!) were to apply their even more sizable sum to restoration of the Harrington farm! Numbly, she noted that Miss Marvel Harrington, executrix of the Frederick Salsburg Estate, would be rewarded for executing duties "listed below." The amount was staggering. Alexander Jay Harrington, Esquire and Leah Johanna Mier Riley for purpose of maintaining hotel ... church to be completed or refurbished ...

Marvel's mind could absorb no more. Daddy and Uncle Worth must make her understand ... maybe a lawyer. Oh, why did she feel so depressed, so apprehensive? And then she knew a very real fear inside her heart. In near-delirium, she groped for the remaining envelope.

There was no signature. The note enclosed with a lengthy newspaper clipping needed none. The hasty scrawl of Editor Corey was easily recognizable. Somehow she knew she stood at the gates of another world.

Marvel (he scribbled): You're to go on writing—hear? Still waiting for promised material. Need it. Want to know what you showed me? Dignity of work, that's what! And something else—leastwise, you hacked out a path where I could have a confab with the Editor Upstairs. Work—most folks in this business see it as a curse. God taught me it's a blessing, but I need help—yours and His. Let's you and me form a T.G.I.M. Club—trash this stupid T.G.I.F. stuff. Work, Marvel—Titus would want you to. Keep that cute little old chin up and say, "Thank God It's Monday." You'll make it alone!

All brightness vanished from Marvel's world, replaced by a tyranny of black-thought clouds. "I knew," she whispered. "All the time I knew." Staggering to her feet, she let the list of "Those Brave Young Men Who Gave Their All" fall to the floor. Then she crumpled to lie beside it. If only she could cry, feel the welcome release of cleansing tears. But her tear ducts were dry, her heart empty. Everything blessed had been taken away. For Titus—her Titus—was *dead*.

And Marvel had died with him—a strange kind of death which had made God into a stranger she could not reach with words. Never before had faith faltered. Marvel had been sure—so sure—that faith could see her through anything: the Depression . . . the drought . . . the humiliation to which she had been subjected . . . the loneliness . . . the waiting.

She longed to kneel at the entrance of the gate which locked her lifelong faith away, confess her helplessness, her hopelessness to the One who could tenderly lead the way back. But that, like the tears, was denied. All Christians knew that one day the King would command the Spirit to be freed from the body. But how could it be that the Spirit lay dead while the body went on functioning? For function she must.

A splash of cold water, a change of clothing, a fluff of the hair, and Marvel Harrington tiptoed out in dutiful ritual. Feeling nothing . . . for nothing lay ahead. She would never be Mrs. Titus Smith. . . .

23

Wedded—Through Union or Separation

"Wear it out. Make it do." "We can. We *will*. We must!" "Is this trip necessary?" The three FDR slogans greeted Marvel above the maze of boxes and files heaped in the small, poorly ventilated room designated to be the OPA office. People rushing to and fro in that labyrinth screamed to make themselves heard above the noises created by objects being shoved against walls or into corners—anywhere to gain an intricate passageway. This place must be open for business *tomorrow*. Already gawkers had gathered to grumble.

"We can't make it," the red-haired Marie said in what she planned obviously as a little aside for Marvel's ears only.

Unfortunately, two clerks, backs against a heavy metallic case, paused in their tortuous push to catch their breaths simultaneously. In the sudden quiet, Marie's wail reached the ears of the ever-frowning chief clerk, a middle-aged lady whose yellowed gray hair needed a rinse.

"The word *can't* is not in our vocabulary!" Mrs. Harper (who had exactly the right name, Marie was to say of her later) said sharply. And with that she pointed to the slogan: "We can. We *will*. We must!"

Marvel sensed the mood of the place immediately. And what few questions remained were answered in the boardroom marked "Do Not Enter" to which only Mrs. Harper had access. The head clerk, however (she told Marvel, with obvious pride), could usher other persons in on business. The seven businessmen, all volunteers, rose formally when the lady appeared with the needed applicant. The interview was brief.

Could she type? Was she willing to work long hours? Did she at present have—or had she lost—a husband or close relative in the service? Four yeses meant she was a natural as far as the busy board was concerned. Marvel would serve as a window clerk (together with a dozen other wives, sweethearts, or close relatives of servicemen). With the blindness that blesses all inexperienced, she accepted the position without question and went through the rigors of being fingerprinted and bonded. She was accustomed to hard work and pressure. This should be no different. Anyone could see that there would be more pressure and longer hours. But unlike those around her, Marvel would welcome that. It was essential to her sanity. As for pressure, she would not be affected. How could she be when she could feel nothing—nothing at all?

The windows went up promptly at 8:00 A.M., Mrs. Harper told the new girls, and stayed up until 5:30 P.M., at which time outside doors would be locked. "However," she added darkly, "you girls are to remain and serve those waiting inside—long day, long week."

Yes, long was a short word for it. Marvel saw the other girls grimace. Some muttered among themselves. They were the more experienced.

"I listen to people who bought a car, or sold a car, or demand their 'fair share' whether or not they own a car, till I feel like I could leap a car in a single bound," a war-wife from New York moaned.

"Kansas City Kate" as she came to be called as the crew became better acquainted, agreed. "Except you can't escape that way, kid," she said knowingly. "You're frozen on the job, remember?"

"How could I forget? And long days . . . is the madam kidding! The 40-hour workweek disappeared with nylons—emergency measures, you know."

Marie sneezed, "Don't know if it's the dust somebody's swishing around over there or the feather duster itself— Sure's no draft—well, the cold catching kind—in this place. But I wanted to share a secret. Better yet, I'll demonstrate. Follow me to the community restroom down the hall. I need to wash up anyway, don't you?"

Marvel nodded. In the bare-bulb light of the beehive-like facility, Marie proudly exhibited the leg makeup which "looks exactly like hose," she claimed, and was a "heck of a lot better than those one-size-fits-all baggy rayons."

"I'm impressed," Marvel said truthfully, drying her hands on a handkerchief (paper goods being in such short supply). She was about to leave when Marie detained her.

"You're the writer. We all recognized your name back there in dear old ACA. So you'll be taking notes here, too, hm-m-m?" Without waiting for an answer, the talkative girl (who used rapid conversation as an outlet for her fears) rushed on. "I've had it up to here with garter belts—we all have. My one and only met its fate in this very place. Are you listening? Well, one of the elasticized stays popped off just about the same time the light bulb did the same thing. And there I was crawling around on my hands and knees in the dark looking for the pesky thing when in walked the janitor with a *flashlight*! Write *that* down. Someday it'll be funny," she ended on a near-sob.

Yes, someday it would. Marvel gripped the other girl's hand and attempted a smile. Someday, God willing, she would find her sense of humor, her will to live, her ability to feel—and to pray.

For a moment too brief to measure, there came a flash of lost hope. Like the fragment of a dream, it was hard to grasp, to hold onto, but there seemed to be a whisper—or was it recollection of a prayer? "Maybe it was both," Marvel's heart murmured. "Didn't you ask God to return Titus—no matter what the circumstances or the condition he was in?"

No! She *dared* not hope. It would only prolong the agony. But in some private chamber of her heart there was an echo of Mother's deep, mellow "lost chord." It faded, but gently, like remembered smells of Grandmother Riley's roses, the nearforgotten notes lingered long enough to untie snarls of despair and start the long process toward unraveling the sleeve of care.

* * *

Mary Ann had returned. The big house on Elm Street hummed with her cousin's presence. Everybody was talking in subdued tones, laughing and crying at the same time. "She's back!" B.J. announced unnecessarily. "Only it's *Mrs.* Hollywood now. But it's stupid to *cry*!"

"Sometimes we cry when we're happy," Marvel said, busying herself with locking the door behind her. If only she could act natural.

"And laugh when you're sad?" he persisted.

"Something like that. Don't try to understand, honey. *I* don't."

Billy Joe sighed and muttered something about "older people" having "bats in the belfry." Then, with an exaggerated sigh, "Oh well, come on. Meet the new Mrs. Jake Brotherton. Oh yeah, I know. Big sis was married a'ready, but she claims this is *different*—the ring maybe? Brace yourself to be ignored. She won't even see us come in!"

He was right at first. Mary Ann was giving an emotional account of the trip. Jake met the bus, could stay at the hotel, took her here, took her there . . . to the commissary operated by military personnel . . . big discounts (didn't the sparkle of her ring prove that?) . . . found chocolate. "Imagine *chocolate* bars! I got some for 'the pest,' but don't tell him. I'll use the candy to coax him into something." Meals? Oh (airily), at the officers' club. They went to a big USO show, featuring none other than Betty Grable, and the star had her hair done "like I *tried* to do, but it don't—*doesn't*—look right on me, her being such a bombshell of a blonde. The style'll look great on Marvel and you, Aunt Snow. But Mother and I are stuck with these black curls. Still, Mother, we could wear the curls piled on top, swept up in back like the actress'."

Mary Ann's tone changed when she told of Jake's assignment. Yes, overseas, but who knew where? Some combat zone—letters to and from him would be censored. "Are all the rights and privacies guaranteed by our Constitution gone?" Uncle Worth's effort to tell her preservation of those rights were what the men and women were fighting for was ignored. "We're supposed to believe in ourselves and our cause? I've heard all that before. Supposed to claim it's *the* war—the war to end all wars! Well, this war has *not* ended on schedule. Maybe it never will. Maybe it *is* the last war—Armageddon! And I—I—I had to send my Jake smack dab into the middle of it—remembering D-Duke."

"Go ahead and cry, darling," Auntie Rae said tenderly, moving quickly to hold her daughter close. "Don't hold it back like your Aunt Eleanore. We're keeping in close touch with her. Healing takes time."

Daddy offered his handkerchief when Mary Ann's tears were reduced to whimpers. "Th-thanks," she hiccupped. "I should have a towel—"

B.J. went for one, his wink at Marvel saying that his reward just might be one of those candy bars. Uncle Worth moved closer to the still-clinging mother and daughter. The family needed to be alone.

Marvel, seeing her mother busy with peanut butter sandwiches, went to offer a hand. "Oh Marvel!" Mother greeted her happily, "I didn't see you. We all stay so busy. Sometimes I wonder if it's right. Then I know it is. It won't last forever. Then we'll find a better life, one with more time together, doing what we loved—"

"We *are* together," Daddy said and added a little fiercely, "we always will be, God willing! Here, let me measure the coffee, Snow White. You look tired—and so do you, honey," he said, looking at Marvel.

"Don't we all?" she managed, looking at her father's ashen face.

"We're out of jelly," Mother said, closing the cupboard door as if trying to close the world's greater problems out. "The sandwiches need it. Just think how our fruit went to waste. Remember when there was so much sugar and we couldn't afford it? And now, there's something called *inflation*—whatever that is. Lots of money, no sugar. Life's just not fair—not fair at all."

Marvel looked at her father, their Harrington eyes locked in understanding. There was something deeper troubling Mother. Marvel was surprised to find herself being first to speak. "There'll be jelly for the next crop, Mother," she promised, going on to tell of hearing that sugar for canning would be available to those applying for the special coupon. "I'm working with the OPA now—no chance to tell you."

"See what I mean? We don't get to talk! I still say it's unfair!"

"You're right, sweetheart. Life *is* unfair, but God is good!"

Yes, God is good. I will never lose sight of that, even though there is no power left in me for prayer. Life is unfair? Sometimes, Marvel admitted from the world into which she had drifted. Or was she unfair to life? An answer must have come, for suddenly and achingly sweet awareness of Titus crowded out all other thoughts, and something resembling a prayer came from her agonized lips: *Oh, please let memories remain. Spare me that loss at any price....*

"It was all so wonderful and so awful," a tearful but glowing Mary Ann burst out later in the privacy of Marvel's room. "I feel married now—really married by union. And before I was married by separation. Make any sense, honey? Not now—but it will sometime. It will!"

"It does now," Marvel murmured. "The marriage by separation—"

"I don't understand. Oh you—you—*you're not*! Oh Marvel—"

The world was unreal. In the real world she would never have given voice to feelings. *Feelings?* How, when there were no feelings left alive in her dead heart? But she found herself saying numbly: "No ceremony—no. But married, no matter how Titus and I are separated. Even," the last was a whisper, "*death* cannot destroy love."

"Don't *say* that!" Mary Ann cried out. "Not when our honeymoon was so perfect—almost—except for that threat. I won't think about it... I *won't*!" Gripping Marvel's hand, she talked rapidly then.

The trip home was a nightmare, knowing Jake was gone, missing one bus, then two. Bumped twice for a load of nurses carrying orders for overseas duty. Feet swollen, those ankle-strap shoes cutting off circulation, and scared stiff when a bunch of drunken sailors loaded in, vomiting all over the bus. No lights, and those balloons overhead like clouds. Why, what if a bus instead of an enemy plane hit one of those cables? Nothing to fear but fear? Well, that was enough!

"I ignored that mocking sign, thinking nothing mattered since—since I said that final good-bye. And in a way, it didn't. I was too numb to feel the trampling of spike heels on my insteps, hear whimpering children, or smell stale lunch boxes. My husband was gone—leaving me nothing but a frightening insurance policy and a rock for a heart! But I went on alert when those sailors took over, until I remembered my Jake's telling me to be brave, not to cry! Well, I deserve that medal for bravery. I do because I didn't—didn't cry, I mean. The pain went too deep for tears. Can you imagine f-feeling th-that way?"

"I can indeed," Marvel said with a kind of finality. And then, without thinking (would she ever be capable of organizing thoughts again?), she handed the list of MIAs bearing the name of Titus Smith to Mary Ann. She was never to remember Mary Ann's reaction. Blessedly, pain blotted it out. But one thing she knew: She would remain his "beautiful lady in blue."

* * *

Marvel's confiding in Mary Ann gave them both enough courage to report to work the following morning. Mary Ann even pulled herself together enough to ask how she should dress.

"Is there much choice?" Marvel asked. "You know, 'Wear it out.' So all the girls are suited out—tailored. Good that styles don't change, and choice of blouses, frilly jabots, or ties at the neck."

She told Mary Ann about the leg makeup then, and they decided to stop by the five-and-ten to check on its availability. Life was falling into shape without a pattern.

In the confines of the handkerchief-size office, Marvel was surprised to be greeted with the news that she was to report to the boardroom on arrival. The chairman, a Mr. Stockwell who owned several oil wells—all pumping "up north," one of the girls had told her—stood, straightened a floral necktie, and said formally, "You may be seated, Miss Harrington—gentlemen!"

With a murmured thank you, Marvel slid gratefully into an oversized leather-upholstered chair. There she heard the startling news. Based on her records, Mr. Stockwell said, she had been chosen as custodian. That explained the finger printing and bonding. She understood? She must have nodded, while wondering of what she was custodian. Soon enough she would find out.

Clearing his throat, the chairman explained briefly: "It will be your responsibility to go into the First National Bank's vault and lock the coupons there for safekeeping at the close of each workday. With two bodyguards accompanying you, of course—their job being to strong-arm racketeers, black market being at its zenith. This is no absolute guarantee of your safety, so we advise that you keep a sharp eye out for suspicious characters."

Nothing to fear but fear? Maybe Marie was right. Someday this would be funny. Marvel doubted it.

"Nobody asked me," she mused to Mary Ann on the way home after that first grueling day. "I'd never so much as issued a coupon book."

Mary Ann gave a rapid account of her own experiences in a nonstop paragraph, pausing only occasionally to giggle from fatigue and delayed reaction to the backwash of tensions. "Somebody handed me a sky-high pile of A-books for gasoline. Somebody else equipped me with an enormous roll of B-coupons. I never did know where the C's came from. It was my duty to accept the applications and pass 'em along to the price panel, that august body of dignitaries, including his honor, the mayor. And there I was bogged down in transportation again, wondering, 'Is this trip necessary?' Oh well, I guess you got a crawful, too, so stop me at any point. No, *don't*. I need all those points, learned about them, too. Wonder how this definition fits into that theorem? Whew! Never before have I seen such a thriving business, such a long day, or such short tempers on both sides of my window. Nobody had time to show me the ropes, so I— without you there to help me!—had to figure out all by myself that everybody who owned a car received an A-book, since in some mysterious way of bureaucracy, somehow the book belonged to the car—not the owner—right?"

The long stream-of-conscience ended with the question. Ahead was the variety store they had planned to stop by to check on the leg makeup, so Marvel nodded toward its sign. Inside, a very young girl with lips painted in a cupid's-bow, chewed gum while saying, "Yeah, we got 'em—*liquid stockings* they're called. Wan'na try 'em?"

Marvel and Mary Ann paid the girl and left her to chew her gum. "Shortage on help as well as all else. They scraped bottom to find that one. But, oh Marvel! I love this stuff. I'm so happy I— I—I could cry!" And suddenly she did just that. "I can't go on. I guess we'll get through this, but I don't even want to. What can we do—*what*?"

"I'm going to see our minister," Marvel heard herself saying, although she had not planned the words.

"I'll go with you."

"No, this I must do alone, Mary Ann. It's personal—"

"I'll go with you," Mary Ann repeated.

Marvel tried a deep breath. It caught in her throat, ending in a dry sob. "You don't understand. I've lost touch with the Lord. I can't go on with my church work feeling like this. I can't even pray."

Mary Ann stopped, tears rolling unashamedly down her rounded cheeks. "I—I c-can't either—God help me. I *have* to tell somebody—you, Pastor Jim. But I can't tell God. You will let me go—you *have* to."

Marvel took her cousin's hand and pulled her forward. "Yes," she said.

* * *

At home Marvel's father met her at the door. "I need to see you—alone," he said. His face was serious, and he carried a business-size envelope. The sanitarium—of course those named in Uncle Fred's will would be notified. *I've been unable to concentrate*, she thought foolishly. *Was I the one named executrix? That was a lifetime ago, I'd have answered.*

Daddy led her into the cool, shadowy room the family shared as a library. Books lined the walls: the classics (studied)... the textbooks (still in use)... encyclopedias (for reference)... *The Grapes of Wrath, Tobacco Road* (as yet unread)... and—Marvel's eyes stopped, shame and remorse washing over her—the *Holy Bible* (neglected, when its pages should have come first in her life. She *must* see Brother Jim!).

"Have you seen this—did you know? Your Uncle Worth and I can't believe it. Is it true? I'm talking about the will. Honey, are you okay?"

Yes, she knew. No, she was not okay, but what she said was, "It's true, puzzling as it is. All Harringtons are heirs—Grandfather, too."

In a flat voice, without emotion, Marvel explained the terms.

"This isn't real to me, baby. I—I feel like I'm hearing another person—some stranger's life story. It's too much for you, but knowing you, you'll try. Me? I feel like all the air's knocked out of me."

Daddy's voice sounded far-off, puzzled and sad. But did she imagine that slight intonement of excitement? Maybe. She couldn't be sure about anything anymore. "We'll have to have a lawyer look at the entire layout. By now the others will have been notified."

He sounded understanding, so she must have made sense. Patting her affectionately on the shoulder, Dale Harrington said humbly, "How did God ever give such a daughter into our care? No wonder my stepbrother chose you to handle things. He loved you. We all do. And how very proud of you the Lord must be—"

Oh no, Daddy, no, his daughter wanted to cry out.

He took her hand and lifted her to her feet. Even so, Marvel's legs trembled, threatened to give way beneath her. "Banking, you say? Your uncles are—are to go into that? Well, Father got his wish." Then, as if to himself, "I wonder if this'll be the answer—without Duke—"

"Daddy," she said, startling herself by the sudden change of subjects, "do you have a ration book? Gasoline—we drive so little—"

Yes, he had one B-book for carpooling, Daddy said without interest.

* * *

Back in her own room, Marvel felt drained. Helplessly, she tried to pray. The words seemed to hang overhead, going nowhere. She might have been praying from the grave. Did anybody believe the dead prayed? A momentary dirge whispered within her. Then it, too, faded.

Brother Jim took her call in person. The moment had arrived. What was there to say? Somehow he seemed to understand. It was wonderful to hear her voice. And of course she and Mary Ann could come in. No appointment. "The truth is that I need to talk too, my dear...."

Afterward, Marvel felt a need to dismiss the will and the urgent need to talk with the man who was still in touch with the Creator. Idly, she picked up the blank A-basic mileage ration book that there had been no time to study. It looked innocent enough on the cover. All day she had repeated like a broken record, "Name, address, and serial number"—all very *service connected*. But something inside must have been responsible for the fading of the initial elation once the applicant opened the cover. She was soon to find out.

The warnings were numerous and frightening: The coupons in this book are not valid unless the lawful holder has signed the certificate below. "I, the undersigned, do hereby agree I will use this coupon book

only in accordance with the rules and regulations of
the Office of Price Administration. Each use of the
book will constitute a representation in the OPA that
the book was lawfully acquired and being lawfully
used. Violators of the gasoline rationing regulations
are subject to revocation of the rations and criminal
prosecution under the laws of the United States.
IMPORTANT INSTRUCTIONS: 1. Coupons can be used
only in connection with the vehicle described in the
front cover. Detached coupons are *void*."

"You *must* go on writing," Mr. Corey's letter had stated. "Titus
would want that." Yes, the writing would hold his memories
warm and alive within her forever. "I must record every detail,"
Marvel's heart said for her. "Maybe Marie's right. Someday it will
be funny, if there's laughter in heaven."

Without realizing the thought was contradictory to the per-
suasion that she was alienated from God, Marvel reached back to
feelings expressed by those with whom she worked... varied,
still closely aligned.

"Ha!" Marie had said in frustration after reading the warnings.
"Not that the A-book would get its holder far. Each coupon allows
such a smidgen that the gas tank would be dry before a driver
finished filling in state, license number, and mileage and paid the
bill—unless he remembered to turn the motor off! Travel's about
as unsavory as public transportation anyway, what with lights on
dim, street lights blacked out—real spooky—and road clogged
by those olive-drab convoys and camouflaged catcalling, "Does
her mama know, soldier?"

"Yeah," Annette from Alabama chirped, "'bout like finding
grit in th' spinach, if y'all don't go likin' spinach to begin with!"

Marvel had gone on working but overheard the Bronx accent
of Naomi, who looked more Spanish than Hebraic, although she
spoke constantly of the decadence of the German-Jews, her
relatives. "*Madre mia!* I know the ropes—been in charge of tire-
rationing before at David's other bases, you know? Last move I
had to leave in a rush. Forgot to surrender one remaining coupon
in my A-book. Owned a secondhand car then and sold it to some
fast-talking draft dodger out to make a quick buck. Bit all my
fingernails off on that blunder. Me—the expert on gas and tires,

holding an illegal ration book in my purse! Every time that train made a whistle stop, I was sure the FBI would come looking for Naomi Heinbeck!"

Talk buzzed around her then, as one by one the weary girls would take turns at the windows and work through the stack of applications. Every day was precious, they agreed... made more so by the uncertainties of war. News sparse... weather reports discontinued for national security... frequent news blackouts from combat zones... letters censored.

Marvel had heard it all before but wedged time in to jot down ideas—anything, *anything* to hold onto, pull her from the mental quagmire into which she was sinking... deeper... ever deeper.

* * *

One week passed. Then two. True, there was a state of inflation in a time of price control. People held a handful of worthless stock (blue chips as change from canned-food stamps and red from meat stamps). Ceilings clamped on rent, but the Harringtons managed, having their own home and the experience of the Great Depression. Imagine "125 a month"!

Marvel pasted on a smile which she didn't feel. And then, at last, she found courage to look at the list of MIAs the editor had sent. Oh no—*oh no*! Through a white maze, she forced her eyes to focus. And there it was: the name Bill Johnson—Titus' cocaptain in high school football... Kate Lynn's husband. First Dr. Porter—now Bill.

How could she write to her friend? *How?* What was there left to say to a former classmate who had lost both her father and her husband?

Mary Ann was married by union. Marvel was married by separation in death. While Kate Lynn—Kate Lynn was married by *both*—

"We must see Pastor Jim tomorrow," she said tonelessly to Mary Ann the next day. "Here, I'll feel better if you read this."

It was a mistake to share the MIA list, Marvel realized immediately. What a thoughtless thing to do when Jake was overseas—possibly involved in D-day which whispers said was in progress. A clock struck 1:00 P.M. Pacific War Time....

But the expected tears did not come. An ashen-faced Mary Ann shook her head in shock, unable to comprehend. "We must, yes—today." Then, incoherently, she asked, "The papers—did Uncle Dale tell you?"

About the will, Marvel was sure she meant. "Yes—all papers are signed. Daddy helped. And yes, we'll stop by the church tonight. Yes."

* * *

Something big was in the air. Previously nobody brought a radio to the office. This day a minuscule model, tucked behind files, brought whispered news:

> Late, due to a blackout of news, we bring you this special report. On this third anniversary of Pearl Harbor, be advised that last June 6, 1944 came the invasion of Western Europe. The invasion of Normandy was the mightiest defeat of its kind in military history. Simultaneously, we can report that it succeeded. All following was inevitable. We are sweeping east to Paris... thence to the low countries... so far locked in brief but bitter combat... hopefully and prayerfully proceeding to meet the westward-driving Russians. Support our brave men and women to ultimate "unconditional surrender"! in this war of violent contrasts: devastated towns, liberated and joyous cities... bodies, ours and theirs, paving streets... children hiding from a rain of death, starving, but coming out to accept a handful of chewing gum from Allied forces. But we *will* bring the war home to Hitler... and soon! Now, do you know what we're fighting for? Next target: Tokyo. You'll pay for that sneak attack in '41... that death march of '42! You took no mercy on U.S. forces in that 85-mile march in Bataan... leering as hundreds died of exhaustion and brutality. We will take no mercy now! United we stand. Naught can separate us.

24

Mysteries of the Mind

"Look," Marvel said without inflection as they passed the college campus where an after-sunset glow lingered briefly in the windows. "I see no boys—not one. Of course, it's late," she amended quickly, for lack of something better to say. Mary Ann feared the mission ahead.

A convoy passed. There were the usual whistles, then one teasing call from a lad who undoubtedly was homesick and afraid. But he was well-trained. Enough already of having some red-faced sergeant yell, "Whatcha want, huh, soldier-boy—lace on them panties?" But even a sergeant recognized that his men had to let off steam by "girl watching." No harm in that. So, uninhibited, the youngster in uniform's words came back on the evening's sea breeze: "Must be recess in heaven, men! Lookit them angels!" And the jeeps rolled on—probably toward another H-Hour.

But neither "angel" heard. "Boys will be back to school when we're all through k-killing each other—if anybody's left," Mary Ann mumbled from her own private world. "Sodom and Gomorrah are beginning to s-sound good by com-comparison. Oh, the church—I can't go in. I'm not worthy. I've committed blasphemy—punishable by death. I'm *lost*!"

"We both are in a sense. That's why we're here." Marvel took her hand.

Dr. James Murphy, the man of gentle humility who preferred to be called Pastor Jim, sat waiting—tips of his forefingers pressed together and pointing upward like the steeple of a church once they were seated in his office. Years of preparation had left him unprepared for the home-front casualties of war. Now, three years after Pearl Harbor, he had seen sorrows of a lifetime. His face reflected the melancholic expressions of those within his prayers.

"Marvel—Mary Ann—" he began then, as a fleeting expression of weariness and pain crossed the caring face which looked older than his years, James Murphy changed tactics. "I feel a need to pray."

The prayer was brief. Neither girl found voice for an *amen*.

Somewhere a warning wail cut through the silence. Air raid or curfew? There was an air-raid shelter in the basement, as there were in all buildings considered safe, with appropriate arrows pointing the way for the man-on-the-street. But none of the three within the church moved.

"Knock and it shall be opened," the minister paraphrased in soft, melodic tones which echoed against the locked chambers of Marvel's heart.

Something inside her opened in response. And in an unknown tongue the story poured out: the hurts of childhood . . . the shattered dreams heaped on like burning coals from the Great Depression . . . the humiliations . . . the trials of decisions and indecisions . . . the dedication to parents, friends, and God— most of all, *God*. And she had kept those promises even beyond the dreams, as need after need presented itself on the migratory trip West. But always there had been Titus, her plans to be reunited with the man she had pledged to marry. And now—now there was nothing . . . nothing at all. Titus was *dead* and her heart had died with him, and there was an ever-widening gulf between her and God.

"I cannot cross it," Marvel ended her soliloquy tonelessly. "I am separated from God for eternity. Titus is gone. I cannot cross alone."

"No—no, you can't. So let God carry you."

Marvel felt nothing—nothing at all. A wrenchingly familiar song drifted from a radio speaker:

> I'll never smile again—until I smile at you—
> I'll never love again—I'm so in love with you—

> For tears would fill my eyes—my heart would real-
> ize
> That our romance was through....

No. The scream of denial within her came out in wounded whisper of repetition: "No, it isn't possible."

"Nothing is impossible with God," Marvel heard the minister say, and knew that he had gone back to the wide chasm. "I was thinking," he said conversationally in an effort to reach a common ground, "if Mary Ann's brother were here, he'd find the right way to say it."

"Billy Joe?" Mary Ann surprised them both by saying, "You remember B.J.?" But how could you forget the—the pest?"

Pastor Jim managed an affectionate chuckle. "Sure and I do! He hasn't told you I see about his work here. Quite a boy, that one—helping on the grounds. Such a shortage of help these days. Anyway, B.J.'d say, 'So what the heck. Let God tote you piggyback!'"

The hoped-for smiles did not come. Instead, some mystery of the mind was unlocked within Mary Ann. Little Billy Joe . . . now a gangling giant . . . always unkempt . . . clothes forever too large. But he would make it. B.J. would be handsome, own a suit (by then cuffs would be back) with easy elegance. Cuffless pants would be outdated—like uniforms, but he'd still be that newborn baby Daddy had placed in her arms to hold. He was so beautiful she used to tiptoe in to count the shadows of each curling lash when those blue-veined eyelids closed in sleep. How could such tissue-thin lids close out the teddy bear night-light? A miracle in pink-and-white poreless skin. Babies! Oh, how she loved them . . . how she and Jake dreamed. But bubbles burst....

"Like Marvel, I'm lost. God has turned His back—"

James Murphy rose, closed the drapes, and flicked on a dim light. "God never turns His back. We are the ones who turn away, my child. You aren't lost, except in your own mind. Our Father gives gifts and never, ever does He want them returned! He loves us too much."

Mary Ann's head shot up, the sweep of her dark curls cascading behind her. "Then how about this war! Don't tell me it's a holy war. I won't buy that. Do you justify this killing? *Do you?*"

"Not morally—no. On the other hand, isn't our right to say, 'Praise the Lord' to be preferred over Heil, Hitler! I reckon so."

Time was ticking past. They must go with nothing settled.

"You two precious girls are suffering battle fatigue—every bit as real as that of the fellows on foreign soil. You've worked and planned, only to live in the worst of times, tried to bring happiness to so many. And you're paying the price we all pay. Can you believe that?"

They could. But neither could serve in the church anymore. It would be hypocritical.

Did he chuckle, or was it a sob? "Hypocritical? What does that make *me*?" Dr. Murphy might well have been questioning himself instead of the two agonizing in his office. "Once upon a time in divinity school, I knew all the answers. My faith was untested, untried, so secure behind a protective cloak of my doctrine that Satan could never touch me. Ah, life's hard school fills up with pop quizzes, midterm exams—which is about where I am now. And," he sighed, "it's the *final* that counts."

The final exam. A chill swept over Marvel's being. Her neck was stiff. And now her legs, like her heart, had lost all feeling. But something compelled her to look up for the first time, eyes locking with this man of God who was confessing his own misgivings. There must have been a question in her eyes which his words were answering.

He sat erect, correct, as preparation for listening had taught him. *Listen . . . be prepared to console, to guide, to back up all else with quotations regarding God's grace.* But James Murphy was back "down home," his soft Southern accent blurring the edges of his words. The kindly eyes were squeezed together behind his glasses as if to close himself away from fighting the hurts around him—and inside.

"I've had to close the books on some of my training, what with people coming to me for help that school didn't prepare me for: how to cope with other creeds, codes, doctrines, foreign to mine . . . baptisms differing from our practices . . . condolences where there seemed to be no hope . . . suicides, departed souls whose lips had made no profession of faith . . . and—and last rites. Know about those?" He addressed the question to Marvel.

"A little. Go head, Pastor Jim. What did you do?"

"What I felt God willed: executing my duties such as would be required of me were I a chaplain on the battlefield. So, back to you, Mary Ann. Yes, in a way we *are* engaged in a holy war—with Satan!"

Wearily his lifted hand pressed over his eyes. But he was in control when the next words came: "Hypocrites? No, neither of you is that. Strange thing about hypocrites: They don't think that of themselves, any more than saints think of themselves as saints! Cast your burden on the Lord. His shoulders are wide. Don't you think He's had enough experience to understand? Forget fretting over prayer. Let Jesus intercede. There's a way to bring happiness to others when we are unhappy ourselves. Just know that and all else will be provided."

Pastor Jim had leaned forward then. His eyes held a new gleam. And in his voice there was a sort of conspiracy. He had an idea, he said, and he would not take a *no*—absolutely not! Marvel and Mary Ann were to take charge of the upcoming Christmas program...use children. Mary Ann's mother *would* provide refreshments? ("See that she does!") And of course Marvel's mother would play. The Deacons Harrington would help. And shouldn't there be serving of the Lord's supper?

Mary Ann was crying soundlessly. Marvel found herself too weak to protest taking charge of the children's nativity scene.

Instead she said, "Mother plays the piano, too. But about the congregation: Aren't we supposed to avoid crowds in case of—"

"Bombing? Yes, but I've violated so many rules, why not one more? As for the unlikely attack, there's an air-raid shelter below—remember? And thank you, but my wife plays the organ"—yes, Mrs. Murphy, the whip-thin lady who looked too tiny to coax out such deep-throated music.

"Either way, my mother says that all she can play is in a minor key these days. Sorry."

"Tut, tut! That's the job you two are assigned. Happiness produces a major key of joy! You'll witness a miracle—I feel it."

The two guests stood. Did they thank him? Marvel remembered how warmly he gripped her hand and how softly he said, "God bless you," as if he were the mouthpiece of the Lord Himself.

Out in the street darkness had gathered. The girls walked into the silence of the night—a silence Mary Ann was to break. From the shadows of dusk she said, her words as soft as the whispering palms, "This is the time of day I feel most lonely—as empty as the streets."

Mary Ann's desperation fueled Marvel's own anxieties and uncertainties, the bleakness. She spoke only to relieve the raw silence. "How did you feel in there with Pastor Jim?"

"Sorry for him. His face was so drawn with fatigue and pain—and yet trying to find two lost lambs. But something happened," Mary Ann added suddenly, as if the words were a delayed revelation. "When he mentioned the nativity scene," she said slowly, "I guess I was tuned in on the same station, ready to listen. Did I sound foolish, going into that rigmarole about Billy Joe's birth? I—I think for a minute I got caught up and saw the Baby Jesus. Silly—go ahead, say it."

"It was beautiful. I was feeling so—so— How can I say it? Sorry for myself? Abandoned? Hideously decomposed? And then when the pastor's thinking took him home, mine did, too. But not to those Christmases, wonderful as they were," Marvel said with a catch in her throat. "Something else—strange, but it had nothing to do with our talk. Or did it? I was whisked back into the persimmon grove before the leaves were stripped away. It was just a flash, but I saw a cardinal go winging past. I was always enchanted by—by that omen of a needed spring, an anchor after the long, harsh winters. It eclipsed the darkness."

"Maybe there's hope—" Mary Ann began and stopped.

"For you, of course, there's every hope."

They were nearing home. Mary Ann made a gallant effort to console. "Maybe it's a case of mistaken identity—a mistake about Titus."

"No!" The denial was instinctive and complete. She dared not go on hoping. It would only prolong the agony. And yet the memory came back to haunt her: She had begged God to send Titus back...no matter how. *Just let it be!* Did she believe it could happen? Dare she?

At the door, Mary Ann whispered, "We have to fake it—remember? We—we'll have to try that happiness act on the family first. Oh my sakes, God'll have to carry me over the threshold l-like Jake did."

* * *

James Murphy had said he felt he would witness a miracle. He did.

Inspired by their daughters' enthusiasm (and pathetically relieved, their exchanged glances of parental understanding said, but the girls failed to see), the senior Harringtons agreed without question. B.J. volunteered beyond the call of duty. He'd clean the church 'specially well, he declared—before and after. Decorate, too—"me and some of the guys."

Marvel was tempted to relive the past, opening her box of souvenirs of a broken heart to remove the treasured letter Titus had written to describe his first Christmas in Austin and decorate accordingly. But something warned against it. B.J. and his recruits could live up to their promises.

There would be little time for preparation. The family, like all other participants, had frenzied schedules. Somehow Auntie Rae managed fruit cakes, hoarding rations of both sugar and time. Billy Joe and "the guys" explored the church basement and found decorations of Christmas past. Then declaring that the faded dyes wouldn't show in candlelight, they looped them on branches of a scrawny tree. Marvel and Mary Ann invited the girls at the office, then regretted it. The nativity scene was doomed from the beginning—dress rehearsal proved it. The holy family was miscast (Joseph being a head shorter than his espoused. Well, why not? he reasoned. "So's my pop!"). Mary forgot her lines, so they finally were forced to omit dialogue. The band of angels could not sing in tune, their only talent being to giggle.

"We're in over our heads, out of our depths. 'Out of the depths, oh Lord, hear my prayer'!" Mary Ann cried angrily. "Happiness? Hah!"

"The original manger scene was unrehearsed," Marvel mumbled, sick with frustration. Her heart grieved for them all, but not for herself.

Christmas Eve! The curtains were to part promptly at half-past seven. Behind it, Marvel checked her watch. The very hands on its tiny face seemed to tremble. *One hour late.* "I can teach *reading*," a desperate Mary Ann whispered. "How come I can't cope with angel wings and fit shepherds into bathrobes too long for these boys' daddies?"

It didn't matter. It didn't matter at all. Mother filled the once-elegant auditorium with soft, sweet strains of violin music of unbridled joy. Surely, *surely* it must have passed from the throng of God's angel band to lodge in her heart. Transfixed, Marvel peeked from back of the curtains to the spellbound audience, each buried in a private Christmas memory, melting into the first Christmas—the one not seen by the eye but by the heart, born of faith and renewed hope. Mother, her wonderful mother, had given them back a near-forgotten gift. Marvel scanned the audience quickly, noting the dark blur of double-breasted suits blending in with carefully correct service uniforms—some with striped sleeves indicating rank of enlisted men, others with gold bars or oak-leaf clusters to distinguish officers. In the flickering glow of candlelight, a reflected glint shimmered and danced to join the gleam in the musician's pale gold hair...the expectant eyes of small children...and, for one moment, in Marvel Harrington's heart.

The curtain parted hesitantly. At the unrehearsed cue, Snow Harrington came back to the real world and, professionally lowering her bow, ended the rhapsody. But the melody lingered in remembered echoes which covered all imperfections of the statue-still members of the cast on stage: a too-tall Mary, a too-short Joseph—the mother looking down and the father looking up at the unlifelike doll held in the mother's arms, each in adoration. *Beautiful.*

And then the unbelievable!

Mary stooped to lay the babe to rest, and the improvised cradle swayed due to her stage fright. When Joseph reached up to help, the sleeve of his robe became entangled with the hay-filled bed, and one of its legs gave way. But what was this? An oversized *male* angel on borrowed wings descended from some unseen realm and, with a carpenter's skill, righted the cradle. Then as if it were a part of the unwritten script, the man-sized angel folded his hands as if in prayer, and seemed to ascend to his realm. *Billy Joe!*

Nobody found it amusing. There were tears instead—tears which lingered throughout Dr. Murphy's reading St. Luke's account of the holy birth...candlelight communion (with two soldiers kneeling, crossing themselves, and asking to partake) ...refreshments...and the organ-accompanied recessional.

Healing would not happen in a twinkling, but the delicate pieces were taking shape. Mary Ann whispered in awe: "Who can know the mind of God."

25

New Year, New Life—
New Love

Exhausted and exhilarated, Marvel had collapsed on her bed, too weary to undress. The image of her mother floated before her. Behind closed lids, the dresden skin took on an ethereal glow in the pale gleam of flickering candlelight. Snow Harrington looked like an angel, played like one, and performed with a kind of stage presence her daughter had never known she possessed. *We have all grown*, Marvel thought foggily, remembering the children in the nativity scene... Billy Joe's miraculous shift of the episode from the ridiculous to the sublime... Daddy and Uncle Worth's unprejudiced acceptance of the unorthodox communion—the two deacons saying only, "We serve the needy, but need Father know?" As for Mary Ann and herself...

But the thought remained unfinished. She drifted into a restless dream where exhilaration gave way to exhaustion, and despair's waiting figures clutched at her throat. In that netherworld state, Marvel saw herself in a mirror of her past, one filled with tormenting ghosts. In the darkest segment of that nightmare, she stood teetering on the bring of a great gulf... straining... straining to reach the hand she could never quite reach. At last she fell, awaking with a start and the stifled scream of "Titus!" on her lips...

"Oh dear God, help me!" Was she praying? Marvel was unable to answer, to differentiate between fact and fiction to find *truth*. Light and darkness were one. She only knew that the ache within her had enlarged to an agony so profound it could not be borne alone.

"Strength is made perfect in weakness," Marvel said, and believed it. If she could not reach God, He could reach her. But she must have the patience of the persimmons. They did not ripen overnight....

Sleep was impossible after that. Rising, she went into the bathroom to splash water on her burning face. Returning, she took up her pen and wrote almost fiercely what she knew would be an enlightening view for her book:

> Never before had our country fought a war like World War II... Americans battled in jungles of Burma and desert sands of the Sahara... in the frigid Aleutians and the torrid Solomons. American pilots swept the skies over Java and Libya, bombed Crete, dodged deadly flak over Tobuk and the Ruhr. American sailors and merchant seamen steamed past fiords of the Vikings and the ancient ruins of Carthage...died in the Indian Ocean, and the Baltic, and within sight of Atlantic City.
>
> Yes, it is amazing how Charles Dickens wrote a century ago words (repeated by Somerset Maugham in the twenties) which are true of today... For it truly is "the best of times and the worst of times" as history will bear out one day. The best? Yes, if one calculates in terms of currencies...the breakthroughs on new fabrics and medications ...with modes of world travel moving people at awesome speed, leading one to wonder if one day there'll *really* be a man in the moon! As to an atlas on this brave new world we hope to create, even the mapmakers must be undergoing a cultural lag—drawing and rubbing out overnight. Maps must be drawn on an installment plan, such in terms of purchases not verboten... money used instead to purchase war bonds. The worst? The terrible price we pay. So how does one bring together the best and the worst? Never by some grand alliance between good and evil. That was settled *in the beginning*. We must fight on toward ultimate victory, remembering always: "In God We Trust."

Perhaps we slept too long. For almost a century the United States had been fortune's child, in spite of setbacks, enjoying the benefits of world power without having to meet the obligations of alliances and standing armies. Americans of the forties paid the price. They died on foreign shores and distant seas...young men and women who were just beginning to get on their feet after more than a decade of hard times.

For some who might otherwise have lived quiet, uneventful lives, the war brought a kind of excitement and glory. America had its share of martial heroes: Major Richard Bong, all-time air ace; boyish Audie Murphy, the country's most decorated soldier; Sam Dealey, commander of the sub *Harder*, which sank four craft but never returned; Dorie Miller, a Negro mess attendant who coolly fired a machine gun from the deck of the *West Virginia* as it burned at Pearl Harbor; a young PT-boat commander named John Fitzgerald Kennedy, vessel shattered by torpedo but succeeding in saving his crew, though badly injured himself. The list is inexhaustible. But for many, war was mainly a time of monotony and routine. Some made supply runs to nearby areas of the Pacific, traveling endlessly, like the crewman in Thomas Heggen's book *Mr. Roberts*, from "Tedium" to "Apathy" and back. Others spent long, tiresome hours standing watch on Coast Guard cutters, or endured the loneliness of the Arctic tundra, or were simply stranded at dreary communications posts on bleached coral islands, or were simply shunted from post to post in America... waiting, always waiting for their names to appear on shipping-out lists or for letters at mail call—letters which never came. It was a time of loneliness, disenchantment, and despair. Little did they know that they, like those on the homefront, also served. Indeed, waiting may be the hardest part of all.

Not so with their brothers in combat. Theirs was a war filled with tension and fatigue which rendered them impervious to pain. "This war," wrote correspondent Ernie Pyle, "consists of tired and dirty soldiers who are alive and don't want to die...of long darkened convoys in the middle of the night...shocked-silent men wandering back down the hill from battle...chow lines...Atabrine tables...foxholes...burning tanks...Arabs holding up eggs...rustling of high-flown shells...jeeps and petrol dumps...smelly bedding rolls...C rations...and of graves and *graves* and GRAVES."

But they believed in a cause, *the* cause greater than themselves...knowing that love is stronger than death, and that many waters cannot quench it.

Laying her pen aside, Marvel Harrington wondered where the words had come from. Oh yes, from each clipping collected—hers, Titus', and foreign correspondents—and from hoarse-voiced radio announcers who rasped out hurriedly such news as General Douglas MacArthur's departure and the fall of Manila simultaneously (two weeks late, when the news blackout was lifted). But the other—the recaps, the editorializing? Startlingly, she was to realize later some of it was prophecy. And how did one test prophecy? Wait and see if it happened, according to Pastor Jim. Marvel would know then that the words expressed this Christmas morning came from a higher source. But for now the whisper was gone. Sleep was gone from her eyes. And a new day was dawning. She rose, feeling refreshed and at peace, the program and her writing past tense.

The long rosy fingers of breaking day greeted her as the drapes of night were parted. "Oh, say can you see—by the dawn's early light—what so proudly we hail—in the twilight's last gleaming?" Somewhere Old Glory striped a smoked-filled sky with red, white, and blue—while within her heart, a flag of victory went up. The war was not over, but a battle was won. Marvel had been struck by Satan's flak but not mortally wounded.

From downstairs there drifted a blend of beloved voices, the smell of freshly perked coffee, and a first whiff of roasting chicken. And above it all came the muted sound of "Joy to the World!" No matter how low the radio might be turned, it could not drown out the triumphant message of the ancient Christmas carol....

* * *

Back at work, Marie's greeting was to say she was among spectators at the Christmas program. There was nothing but praise. Yet in it Marvel sensed a certain longing. She was right. "It reminded me of when I was a child. I was in touch with God then—in His grace, as that preacher put it. We called it salvation then, I wish I hadn't lost it like I lost that silly charm bracelet. I miss 'em both!"

"Then come back. You'd be welcomed."

"By you, yeah, but not by Him. I guess," Marie said, as expertly she unwound a roll of B-coupons, "I'm that rock He created and can't lift."

"There's no such thing," Marvel said with conviction.

Marie's red head bounced up as if about to take leave of her shoulders. "You mean like the old song 'Love Lifted Me'? *Ooops!* Two minutes to go before we open the windows—and act *graceful!* I can't. God lifted me once but dropped me. I'm that rock, I tell you—a real heavyweight sinner, that's what. He gave up on me."

Time was of essence. Marvel Harrington was to bring happiness whether or not she herself was unhappy? It was easier than she thought.

"God didn't give up on you or me, Marie. We gave up on Him," Marvel said quickly. "We're all struggling these days. Just know that once He gives a gift, He never takes it away."

"Who said *that*?"

The crowd on the other side of the window was growing impatient. Marvel rose hurriedly, pasted the accustomed smile in place, and inhaled deeply. "The Bible," Marvel heard herself reply. Then, patting her friend reassuringly on the shoulder, she added, "Pastor Jim had to remind Mary Ann and me too. Just be our Marie. We need you."

Hurriedly opening the window, Marvel looked over the sea of scowling faces. "Good morning!" she said brightly, "I hope you all had a great Christmas. Now put me to work. There's very little left of 1944."

Faces relaxed. A few returned her smile. And Marvel felt better.

* * *

Marvel awoke early on New Year's Day. Somewhere church bells were softly repeating the echo of last night's guarded welcome to another year's struggle. But inside herself a bell was chiming its own song, a song of faint hope—softly...falteringly...with silences between each note. But enough to let her feel a certain anticipation.

Mary Ann must have felt it, too. "Marvel, are you awake?" she half-whispered, giving the doorknob a prolonged shake.

Once inside, her cousin said in a rush of words, "Let's slip out for a quick stroll—beaches'll be deserted. Hurry!"

Marvel hurried. Minutes later they were padding along in the mists of early morning. The tide had not come in and the quiet beach was a miniature city of children's sandcastles whose architecture would be washed out to sea within the hour. Neither girl spoke. There seemed no need. The two of them shared a special relationship which Mary Ann said was preordained, what with their being birthday twins. Marvel doubted that. Relationships needed nourishing, else they would die. But today she felt they both knew they had come to say *good-bye* to old thoughts and reach out hopefully for the new. *Good-bye.* Marvel tasted the word and found it had the same bite as the salt air—or the unshed tears within her. There ought to be a better word. There had been too many *good-byes* already. The word was too sudden, too final.

The gulls came wheeling in then, breaking the silence around them. A foghorn warned hoarsely and the mist-obscured jetties creaked and complained with the aches of another day. Were they, too, attempting to unload the flatsom of their inanimate lives? There was little time left for speculation. The heavy mists of early morning were parting, giving right-of-way to silvery wisps resembling clouds, come down to visit. In that new setting, the gulls dipped and darted, increasingly noisy in their search for food. In unspoken agreement, the girls turned.

One more block and they would turn to Elm Street. And then Marvel stopped short, heart beating unmercifully against her rib cage.

A brisk breeze moved in and Mary Ann moved with it, holding onto her wind-tossed curls with one hand and attempting to keep the box-pleated skirt covering her bare knees with the other. "Should've worn our slacks," she called over her shoulder, the words sucked up by the stiffening wind. "*E-e-eek!* Watch out for that palm frond. Marvel?"

When there was no answer, she turned back and, seeing Marvel standing transfixed, ran to her, ignoring all else. "Marvel—Marvel, what is it? My word! You look like you saw a *ghost!*"

"Something—somebody—" Marvel gasped breathlessly through frozen lips. *A ghost of the past*, she wanted to add. But her voice was gone.

"Where—what?" Mary Ann coaxed, reaching out to grasp her hand.

"There—in that cloud. He was there," Marvel whispered. "See?"

Mary Ann's dark eyes searched the quiet beach. "No *he* there—not even a cloud," she laughed. Given ordinary circumstances, Marvel would have taken pleasure in that laughter, withheld like her tears. But this was no normal circumstance— not normal at all.

Marvel allowed herself to be towed along, glancing occasionally over her shoulder to make sure her cousin was right. The clouds were gone. The breeze had gone back to the palms. They were alone on the beach. But her heart went tumbling back to another time, another place. A whirlwind had brought Titus to her, only to whisk him away. . . .

Breakfast was waiting. Waffles! "Happy New Year!" the family greeted Marvel and Mary Ann.

"Didn't even know we sneaked out," Mary Ann whispered from the corner of her mouth as they joined hands for prayer.

"Um-m-m," Marvel murmured. "Best waffles—best coffee—"

"Best family," Mary Ann added to everyone's delight.

"Best Be the Tie That Binds," Billy Joe added impishly to call attention to his wearing a white shirt and bow tie. With his forefinger he loosened the collar.

Uncle Worth reprimanded his son with a glance. But there was a twinkle of amusement in his eyes. Daddy covered beautifully by commenting that B.J. was more "on the beam" than the rest of the family. "Better eat up there, girls—early church, remember? Mother Riley always said 'What you do on New Year's you're apt to do every day thereafter, so make it good!'"

Mother poured more coffee, stooping to brush Marvel's forehead with a kiss as she passed. Auntie Rae announced: "No more waffles—save room for meat loaf. Cost a pretty penny in red tokens. I'll frost it with mashed potatoes, maybe ruffle 'em for you, B.J.—honoring you for that great performance on Christmas Eve!"

A little embarrassed, the boy teetering between manhood and boyhood dropped his head, sending a hated curl across his forehead. He brushed it away impatiently. "Can I slurp?" he asked concerning fluted potatoes.

"Of course you *may*," Auntie Rae smiled with proper emphasis.

"Any more hallucinations?" Mary Ann grinned as they hurried upstairs to dress for the New Year's worship service.

"No," Marvel said truthfully, longing to add that it was not a hallucination in the first place. "See you in three shakes of a sheep's tail." Use of the near-forgotten Southern expression brought a smile from Mary Ann—and more. She used up one of the five minutes in a Pollyannish burst of "glads": She was glad Marvel's words reminded her to get at the book...glad she *wanted* to go on with it...and glad, *so* glad to see Marvel being Marvel again.

Was she Marvel? Looking at herself in the mirror, Marvel wasn't sure anymore. She only knew that there was a glow in her heart—a glow which must reflect in her face. Blue, something blue—yes, a scarf...

The service was beautiful—made more so by Marie's being in the congregation. After the benediction, Marvel elbowed her way to where the guest stood, and hugged her warmly. "Welcome to a new beginning."

"Oh, thank you for that—thank you—*thank you*. I feel so wonderful inside. You're right—God never forgot me. He stood right beside me today. And that's not all! I prayed and prayed last night and He heard—He heard every word! My Johnny's on his way home. Maybe he's here already, sleeping off that long voyage home, dodging subs. His captain's already here, but being a commissioned officer got him on a plane. My Johnny's his tailgunner but a non-com. Oh, I'm bustin' with excitement. Hi, Mary Ann. Marvel'll tell you. I gotta see the pastor—"

Marie breezed away. Marvel explained. And the bells rang louder.

Auntie Rae's meat loaf would have done a disappearing act had she failed to slice it thin and refrigerate half for warming up the next day. "Wonderful invention, these refrigerators—and they love their job, ours humming while it works," she commented as she shelved the meat loaf.

"Well, we'd better hope it keeps on the job," Uncle Worth said a little grimly. "Like cars, there'll be no more for the duration."

The sober moment passed when Mother brought out a raisin pie. "No scolding now. This pie sweetened itself from the sun-dried raisins I saved from our vines. No butter in the crust. Who could afford coupons for that? Well, I did cheat just a teeny-weeny bit by using what few bacon drippings we're supposed to turn in—for *what*?"

"Ammunition," Daddy said, then quickly turned the matter aside by taking Mother's pie and, licking his lips, cut it in seven wedges.

"Yummy good," B.J. said with his mouth too full. He swallowed, then went on: "I'm sorta put out though. *I* helped dry those raisins—picked the grapes anyway—and get no credit. That's me all over—a Sad Sack!"

"Sad Sack?" his father repeated and stopped chewing. "What's that?"

His son assumed a superior expression. "I thought *everybody* knew. Read George Baker's cartoons. Sad Sack's a dismal-looking dogface, a guy who works hard and watches somebody else get the promotion—like me."

Mary Ann looked at him in exasperation. "You! Why, you hog the show—always did. Better stick with words listed in the dictionary!"

"I do," B.J. said smugly, filling his mouth again. "Sad Sack *is* in the dictionary—some of 'em anyhow. So, Big Sis, let me define it for Mrs. College Co-ed! 'Sad Sack: a hopelessly inept person; a ludicrous misfit.' Convinced?"

"Very!" his big sis replied. " 'Sad Sack' you are."

There was a round of laughter. It was a lovely day, made more so by a call from Grandfather—a first. Daddy took the call and reported.

"Wow! Do *I* have news!" Daddy said, looking a little dazed. Mother hurriedly drained cold coffee from his cup and refilled it. His hand trembled in accepting it. "Thanks, sweetheart. All's well at home. Mother Riley's writing. But our father, Worth, is shocked out of his skin over this Salsburg will. Seems Marvel's letter went astray—got there the same day his check came, along with a letter from Emory."

"He'd heard, too—Em, I mean. Received word, money, what?" Uncle Worth leaned forward to ask when Daddy paused to finish his coffee.

"All of the above—lock, stock, and barrel. I—I guess the sum's tremendous." Shaken, Daddy leaned back and stared emptily into space.

All seemed to inhale at once. "But what else did Father say? How did he sound?"

Angry, Daddy said. Didn't their father always use anger as an overcoat? No surprise, but it had taken his sons years to know it was a bluff. Piece by piece, Dale Harrington fit the puzzling conversation together. Alexander Jay Harrington, Esquire was pleased as punch—anybody with one iota could hear it in his voice. Man! what he and the Duchess could do—and *would*: restore the hotel, make it a regular tourist attraction . . . add onto the church, refurbish . . . landscape . . . and start the search for the just-right shareholders for the Harrington Bank before Emory and Joseph got there. Frederick already held controlling stock of Cohane's bank. Might as well call it that. The skinflint *thought* he owned it—and half of the booming Culverville as well.

Cohane—Amanda's father! Marvel and Mary Ann looked at one another in cousinly understanding of matters their parents knew nothing about.

"You mean—you mean," Mother stammered, "they *are* going back? I mean *now*? Your work's not finished—and have you listened to the news? You both—Rae and I are afraid you'll be drafted—older and younger—"

Daddy's expression changed. "Yes, we listen, my sweet. Fathers and sons are going together. But we're not going *anywhere*—not now."

Mother relaxed. No longer did a gray sky press down over her day. "The bank's for *them* then—not us. Oh, did you wish them a happy '45?"

Did the family exhale in unison? It seemed so. The day resumed its sheen, war clouds forgotten, and they journeyed back easily into the lap that love establishes.

"So," Mary Ann said tentatively at the close of the day, "back to the salt mines *mañana*. Suppose we *are* heading for a happily-ever-after?"

"Nothing would surprise me," Marvel said secretively.

But something did.

* * *

The day began quietly—too quietly. Was there something in the making—something secret having to do with war? Marvel had not listened to the news for several days, feeling the need for a holiday with her family. She must get back on schedule, complete some material for Editor Corey, respond to some letters, work on her book. But for now the stack of applications for ration books, mileage records, and additional stamps must be sorted before it toppled. Touching the blue scarf at her neck gave her needed courage—and more. There was a tingle of sweet days remembered beginning along her fingertips and traversing her spine. Unexplainable as the quiet, the sensation hung there waiting.

Was there a sound? Something accounted for her upward glance.

And there he stood: the face in the fog!

Move...she must move else he would vanish and she would know without Mary Ann's reminder that she was hallucinating. The room spun around her and the walls were singing love songs...louder, louder...and such a rush of warmth surged through her veins, Marvel was sure her legs would not support her. Oblivious to all around her, she rose tentatively and moved forward, lips parted expectantly, blue eyes riveted to the beautifully familiar face. *Alive, he's alive. Now I feel alive again.*

"Titus," she whispered. The name held its usual magic.

The finished application lay between them—untouched.

In the brief silence that followed, Marvel's sweeping glance reviewed the features she knew so well: those gray, gray eyes now wine-dark, as they always were when focused on a single subject which shut out the rest of the world...the patrician nose...the finely chiseled mouth. How gentle it could be in less serious moments than this, and how boyishly appealing when curved in a seldom smile. Oh, how long, how *very* long it had been since that tall, lithe figure strode into her life!

"Speak to me, Titus. Reach out and touch my hand. Let me know this is not a dream!" her heart cried out. But she was unable to speak.

Swallowing hard, Marvel hated herself for the slow blush she felt staining her cheeks when she realized that she, too, was under scrutiny—yes, as she had been years ago. It was all being played out exactly as before, history—no, a love story—repeating. The slight lift of the classic eyebrows above those thoughtful eyes was quizzical.

She wanted to speak to this stranger who was no stranger at all, differing only in the fact that he was in uniform. At first a detail which went unnoticed as one saw few young men in civies anymore. Was it sight of the two bars on the officer's cap lying beside the completed papers at Marvel's window which put her on alert? Captain . . . so Titus held the rank of captain. But when . . . how? The walls were singing an old refrain now: ". . . a lifetime was spent—in one little mo-ment—with the beau-ti-ful la-dy in blue. . . ." It had been only a moment now, as she waited for him to speak, explain himself, pick up where they left off. But it seemed a lifetime indeed.

He spoke then, just a single breathless, "Oh!"

"You remember—but of course you do—" There were drums now—drums drowning out the melody within her, drowning out her voice.

Eyes growing darker, he nodded, too mesmerized to speak. "On the beach—in the fog—"

The voice, once so deeply resonant, sounded faraway, distant, because of the drums which Marvel now knew were the unmerciful beatings of her heart. *You Tarzan—me Jane*, she thought, giddy with happiness. *Captain Titus Smith, meet Miss Marvel Harrington.*

"We were never strangers—were we?" she managed, wondering if others were watching, listening. And then it did not matter.

"No—never strangers. I'd waited all my life."

The male voice was deep and pleasant, but unfamiliar. A feeling of uneasiness gripped her. And it grew as he continued softly, "Remember the old song of the thirties, back before all this commenced? 'I didn't think I'd know you—but my heart said, *Leave it to me!*' Which only goes to show you—how smart a heart can me. Remember—uh," he leaned forward, so breathlessly close the clean, pungent scent of shaving lotion mingling with sunshine captured in his beige uniform tangled in her nostrils, "uh, *Marvel?*" he read from her identification badge. "Jove! That's a love of a name. *Marvel Harrington*, correct?"

Jove? Love? Had Titus' assignment led him to Great Britain? And why didn't he remember her name? Something was wrong—

very wrong. Shell shock, Grandfather called the loss of memory—now battle fatigue. That was it. Patience...she must have patience. It would all come back. There had been recognition in his eyes. And if it didn't? Tonight she would pray a long, long prayer, thanking God for answering her prayer. She had asked only that Titus be returned, no matter in what condition, what form. She would take him marked down to any price.

There was noise around them, now. They were not in the world alone.

"Oh, good morning, captain!" Marie's voice. Marie had dared invade their world. "I'm so sorry, sir. I promised to watch for you—take your application," she said, obviously flustered. "I see you two are friends. I didn't know you'd met. But you know each other—"

"We were never formally introduced." The charming smile came easier than Marvel remembered fleetingly as Marie made the introduction. Johnny's captain—her Johnny was tail-gunner, the girl rushed on. And the captain needed emergency gas for his short leave.

Did I acknowledge the introduction? Marvel wondered as her eyes caught sight of the application for which Marie's freckle-sprinkled hand reached. "Wait, there's some mistake. You have the wrong one," Marvel said quickly. "The name here's—" she paused to reread the printed name on the top line, "Prinz, Philip?"

"Philip Prinz—last name first, I believe?"

"But—but I don't understand," Marvel stumbled.

Marie came to the rescue. "I do, Marvel. Here, I promised Captain Prinz I'd help—not that I pack any weight in the right places."

There was a shared laugh between the two. Marvel did not join in. The popular song came back to taunt her: "I'll never smile again—Until I smile with you—I'll never laugh again—What good would it do? For tears would fill my eyes—My heart would realize—That our romance was through...."

Oh Titus! her tortured heart cried out. *I'm so in love with—YOU!* But this man was an imposter. How foolish—what purpose would there be? There was a law against impersonating an officer, Marvel found herself thinking disjointedly. But what of another man—a civilian, as far as she knew—being impersonated by an *officer*? This *had* to be explained.

"Are you waiting for my military I.D.? Is that the normal procedure? Regulations are that we wear dog tags: name, rank, and serial number. We're government property, you know." Almost playfully—Was he laughing at her?—he reached toward the buttons on the light wool shirt. Behind that military press hung the metal tag.

"Oh no!" she protested, feeling the blush again. Involuntarily, her hand reached out as if to stop the American officer with the English accent—*Titus*, it had to be Titus—from baring his chest.

Immediately a warm hand closed over her cold one. "You're behaving as though we were strangers," he said softly. "We are not strangers at all. You—why, you are the girl I want to be my wife!"

He let go of her hand then, looking stupefied at his own words. "Have I offended you? I thought you knew. Oh, let's begin this bloody conversation over. Please forgive me, Marvel—uh, Miss Harrington. Of course I plan to change that. Oh, there I go again!" He bowed comically from the lithe waist. "May I have the honor of your company for dinner this evening?" The voice lowered intimately, while keeping a proper manner of respect. "I will explain everything then. *Please* say yes."

Marvel's heart leaped, even in her embarrassment. "You've made no mistake," she began formally. "I have." But some compelling power raised her eyes to meet those gray-black ones, and Marvel knew she was unable to refuse him anything. She had prayed. Here stood her answer.

Mutely, she nodded. The officers' club was all right? She nodded again as they agreed on the time and place. No matter by what alias, it was Titus to whom Marvel Harrington said *yes*.

Lines at the window lengthened, voices grew louder. "Sold down the river...the Yalta agreement? Are you outta your mind? Meeting of the minds in the Big Three at Yalta? Allies we need...combine Stalin's relentless determination with Churchill's humor—and FDR's personal charm'll beguile 'em both anyway...exaggerated...miscalculating. You'll see. Shut up, all of you, *shame*. Look at what's happening now, *victory!*"

So something *was* in the air? Marvel thought dully. For better or worse, her legs had simply crumpled. Sit down she must. And when she looked up he was gone. A dream? A mistake? How did one redeem herself, make right regretted words, when it was all a dream—a senseless daydream?

But it was no dream. Mary Ann's stance erased that thought. With a pencil clenched between her teeth and arms akimbo, she stood before Marvel totally deaf to the din of voices.

"Did I hear what I thought I heard?" Mary Ann lisped, chewing hard on the precious pencil—one of the few remaining with erasers. "Who was he—that officer you limped to meet? Promise to tell me, huh? Was that— No, I heard Marie. It couldn't be *Titus?*"

I don't know. He had proposed, and she didn't know his identity? True, anything could happen in this war-torn world— anything but that.

"Things are getting rough out there," Marvel managed. "We'd better report to our command posts. I—I'll tell you about it tonight." *Providing I can figure it out.* Had she dared encourage this Prince Philip? Philip Prinz? Worse, it was she who initiated this with him. *Him?* The name was not Smith. Titus did not have an identical twin. It *was* Prinz. . . .

How much to tell Mary Ann? That dutifully she had sent him away—or the truth, that she would be seeing him this evening? Seeing him and knowing that he would propose a second time— no, a *third*!

Wrestling with a decision was unnecessary. Mary Ann was detained because of a telephone call. It was not unusual. Applicants often asked for the girl whose name appeared on their ration books. But it *was* unusual for Marvel to go home without her cousin. She needed the time to be alone, sort out her feelings, decide what to wear on this, her first date.

Mother was separating iris tubers from clumps along the walk. "I was considering crimson salvia for spring—" she stopped, shoved the trowel into loosened loam, then wiped a gloved hand across her brow. "Hot for January— My goodness! Time for supper—then work. Are you all right, honey?"

More than all right . . . ecstatic. The very palms seemed to reach infinity. The moment passed, and Marvel calmly told of the evening's arrangements. Mother was glad she had met "someone" at last. She needed out more. Period.

Mary Ann burst upon them. "Jake's in *Oregon*—me, too, nearly. *Help* me!"

26

In Iron Tears
Where Answers Lie

There was plenty of time. Why, then, did she feel hurried? Marvel asked herself, while sorting through her limited wardrobe for a right blouse to compliment the tailored navy-blue suit. The white blouse was too severe. The polka-dotted voile, too fussy. The pale blue—no, she could not bring herself to wear blue. Red was not her color. Why had she bought it? Hastily, hanging them all back, she chose a dainty pink and laid out the long-neglected fuchsia pillbox hat with the nose-tip veil. Somewhere, buried beneath the folded-away garments in her cedar chest, was a pair of matching gloves. Gloves brought back memories too painful to remember, but too lovely to forget: Mr. Bumstead, the grateful school bus driver, who gave her the red woolen mittens in appreciation for her taking roll for him ... *and Titus*, she thought slowly. *Do you remember how many lunches you sacrificed, how many miles you walked to save bus fare in Austin—all to buy me the beautiful kid gloves. Do you?*

Dismissing the memories or burying them deeper into her subconscious, Marvel ran into the shower stall. Where was the soap? It had a way of disappearing—traveling from shower to tub to wash basin, shared as it was between Mother, Daddy, and herself. Soap was scarce—they must conserve. And even so, Americans were more fortunate than the Europeans who had no soap at all. The Japanese? Who knew?

She padded barefoot to the basin, found the lilac-scented soap only to drop it three times. It was slippery, hard to hold onto when her hands were trembling. Surely her heavy page-boy-styled hair was soaked! Well, she would look a mess—and that was that.

Not according to the admiring glance from one Captain Philip Prinz. A little embarrassed, Marvel dropped her eyes before his scrutiny while the Jeep, driven by one of the non-coms, waited for the two of them to leave the shadows of the columned wraparound porch.

"Good evening, captain," Marvel said a little primly, but could not bring herself to add *Prinz*.

"Philip," he corrected softly. "And may I call you Marvel?"

She looked at him a little sadly, leveling the penetrating blue eyes to meet his. "Of course," she said with gentle dignity, longing to cry out, "Didn't you always?" How long was he going to keep up this game? Or had he forgotten, lost his memory? If so, seeing her seemed to have poked at the ashes of the past and found a tiny last spark remaining. Was that too much to ask, to hope for? In her state of confusion, Marvel's heart reached the zenith of the celestial sphere of her pent-up emotions, only to plummet to the darkest nadir. At the lowest point she wondered if Titus could have been assigned a totally new identity—or worse, been taken a prisoner of war, brainwashed, and tortured until nothing remained. Mary Ann would have said, "Nertz! You've been seeing yourself in some B-movie!"

Mary Ann! Behind them, Marvel heard hurried words and movements in preparation for her joining Jake to be with his family again—*as his wife*.

The pain within her deepened, even as she took her escort's proffered arm and felt his other hand close over her fingers possessively.

The junior officers rose to their feet quickly when the two of them entered the mess hall of the officers' club, saluting smartly and remaining at attention. The captain, hat in hand, returned their salutations politely and murmured a courteous "As you were." The men relaxed.

They sat in a secluded corner. Some part of Marvel's mind noted that there was steak, butter, coffee—all scarce, but made so by the needs of the servicemen. The other part concentrated on the familiar eyes-turned-black in which she was drowning helplessly. *Titus!*

He lifted a hand and hesitated. Was that hand to close over her own again, render her helpless with a touch? The hesitation was momentary, and then the lifted hand passed over his face.

"You are not eating," the captain chided gently. "Shall I cut your meat? I say, this is a bit less tender than in normal times."

Normal times? When was that? Marvel sighed unconsciously as she picked up her fork and picked away at the salad, mind buried in the past.

"I do not know where to begin. Dare I hope you will help me?" he asked.

Marvel smiled slightly, wondering if the curve of her lips reflected more sadness than joy. "Just begin where we left off."

It was a wrong thing to say. His definition of the past was *today*.

"Ah," Captain Smith—Prinz—whatever the name would prove to be—said hopefully, "my proposal! I spoke too quickly, but leaves can be canceled. Our time together is short. Just know that my intentions are strictly honorable—"

"I never questioned that. But I'm waiting to—to hear it all."

"I wanted to take you home with me—as my wife, of course. *Home*—beautiful word, stable, convincing. We could see my sister—"

Home . . . his sister. It *was* Titus!

Marvel nodded, wondering if her eyes reflected her inner glow. "Lucille," she said breathlessly. "Texas—tell me all about it."

"Lucille?" Again the look of puzzlement. "Victoria," he said haltingly. "You placed me in Texas. Does my British accent sound Southern, Midwestern or wherever that single-star state is?"

"The heartland," she said a little stiffly, ignoring reference to the flag. "You sound like a stranger in our home state."

Not *our*, *your*, he smiled, then added that it was understandable—drawn together as they were—that the two would expect common backgrounds and memories. Marvel asked no more questions, preferring to hang onto his every word. There would be a slip . . . there had to be. And then she would force the truth.

But there was no slip, no flaw, no falling into the trap. Her host recited his lines well, as if rehearsed for a final performance. No boots and saddle, no (and he sang this part softly) "spurs that jingle, jangle, jingle—as I ride merrily along." And no desire for a ten-gallon hat, thank you very much!

"Stop stereotyping us!" Marvel wanted to scream out in protest, feeling a burst of unexplainable anger. Tonight would not be repeated!

No rural background, no interest in agriculture—as he gathered she had? At her nod, he leaned forward, almost pleading to be understood. Then surely his native Boston would hold appeal. Lovely countryside for *riding*—sans dust, migrants, tinsel, and *Japs*! Oh, Marvel must see it all for herself. The war would end soon and they could begin a new life together there. On the other hand (thoughtfully) he could remain in the military—another promotion in rank would be coming shortly. That would please the family. All their men were in the military—traditional, unquestioned. Philip—yes, this man was Philip now—had never bucked the system. His father and grandfather before him had been Annapolis men with all its pomp and circumstance, but had understood when he preferred the "silver wings in the moonlight"—*loved* that plane. Oh, the Prinzes were Americans—Polish descent he believed. His mother was English—married his father in World War I, left a young widow who preferred "the continent" to the "colonies." Refused to come to America even now during the *blitz*.

"Am I talking too much?" The face became boyish, eager to please, and Marvel caught herself falling beneath his spell again. "It—it seemed so important that you know everything," he said haltingly.

"It is important," she agreed without inflection.

Immediately he was inexorably transformed. The service wasn't so bad once a man made it through training, let the powers-that-be take him apart piece by piece, then put him on his own in putting himself back together...knowing his mind, gait, posture, and vocabulary were changed—his whole identity, in fact. And as an officer a man was to act superior (never mind how he felt) until he *was* superior.

"You feel that way, Ti—uh, Captain Prinz—Philip?" Marvel burst out, not caring that she stumbled or that dessert had come.

"Not really," he said a little humbly. "It's a game I must play."

A game. Life was a game? Marvel stared stonily at the wedge of pie.

Playfully, the captain reached across the table to pick up her fork and place it in her hand. But he did not let go of the hand. Instead, he gripped harder. "So, which should I do?"

"That must be your decision. You'll find the answer."

He leaned closer. "I can't make it alone now that we've found one another. Don't you know that? You felt it, too. I could tell!"

"I don't know." She felt pressured. "I don't know what I feel."

I feel a certain animosity, a jealousy, Marvel thought darkly. No, not that. I feel that you've assumed a place that rightfully belongs to Titus—therefore, to me. You have stolen my sacred memories. And I am left with nothing but emptiness. You've even pushed God away....

"I think you do know." His voice was soft, his manner tender. "But I promise now to give you space —and I wish I could add *time*. But time's rationed these days. Just know that my words were not spoken lightly. And please don't answer now—*please*—" Philip pleaded.

The resolve within her weakened. She would see him again—maybe on a friendly basis. That was impossible. Why promise herself anything so foolish? She owed him an explanation, Marvel realized—an explanation which would have to come later. Now she was too shaken.

They talked on, trying to find a common ground. Marvel was unable to recall the conversation later. Movies, books, church—yes, well yes, Philip Prinz considered himself a Christian. He was a baptized Catholic. But if the matter meant so much to her—

It did. But submitting one's will to God must be personal, not based on the desires of another. He would give it thought—yes, pray.

When they parted, it was all arranged. Yes, same time, same place tomorrow evening. And perhaps she would invite him in for coffee. Then when Marvel bade him good-bye, she was saying the word to Titus. Although whether there was an implied "until tomorrow" or "forever," her heart refused to say. Life once so simple had turned complex....

* * *

Los Angeles was basking in unseasonable mid-January heat. Hot Santa Ana winds blew in from the desert to bend the palms leeward and whisk the smog (a new word coined from the blend of fog, heavy snow with smoke from chemical fumes belched from increasing industry) to sea. But remembered snow swirled the circumference of Marvel's heart. And the scorching winds whistled in icy breath. Mother's new plants were wilting, but Marvel shivered anyway. How then, she asked herself later, did she bring herself to go on with the writing promised rashly to Mr. Corey? Titus would want her to, the editor who loved them both had said. There would be no mention of the strange events, the questions they aroused—just the work. For yes, she was continuing to see this reincarnation of Titus—or was it Titus himself? The "short leave" extended, unless it was canceled, now that Captain Philip Prinz no longer planned the trip to Boston—?

"I can't go. I can't so much as entertain the idea," Marvel had said, meaning every word but hoping he would remain here. He did.

"And I can't entertain the idea of leaving you," he had said.

Feeling a need to talk with someone wiser than herself, Marvel considered seeing Pastor Jim again. But what was there to say? Mary Ann was the leaner. But deep inside, her cousin was of tougher fiber than she saw herself as being—and she made Marvel laugh. Oh, what a comfort it would be to have Mary Ann tease her out of this trance, call it "small potatoes." Fortune had smiled on her birthday twin, however. Jake—according to one breathless telephone call—having served in numerous air raids (places and dates "classified information") was in Ft. Lewis, Washington. The newlyweds could be together...could visit with Jake's parents in Oregon, call on Mary Ann's relatives there, too—all this and *more* if Marvel would get her "off the hook" at the OPA...arrange a leave. All too soon the telephone conversation ended.

"How was your date with—er—the young man?" Mother asked once while checking her grocery list. "I declare there's a shortage on *everything*!"

Date. Singular when it should be plural. Would Mother understand that there was no shortage on pain? Her daughter's driving need to find answers—answers to ease that pain, bury those oscillating emotions which blinded her to all else—had led to several dates with the "young man." Her—Marvel: the stoic, the steadfast...

No, she was alone—totally alone. Well, one thing was certain. If the Creator Himself couldn't lift her, she certainly could not lift herself. How senseless! God had no time for such utter nonsense. Neither did her Mother. Everybody was too busy—when she most needed them.

She and Mother talked of small matters as Marvel helped pack lunches, and then about Mary Ann. "Your Auntie Rae's concerned about her job. I told her you'd take care of it," Mother said, folding a last paper napkin.

"I tried to explain," Marvel said, choosing her words carefully so as not to increase household anxiety. "You know how those things go—not enough help anywhere. So the chief clerk reminded me that there was a war on! We suspected, didn't we just?" The question intended to be light hung there without a supporting smile. "They replaced her."

Auntie Rae came into the kitchen, carrying a stack of freshly folded sheets. "Mary Ann will find another job. There's no shortage," she said with assurance. "Um-m-m, sheets smell of sunshine. Well, as they say down home, 'I hate to eat and run,' but—"

"Duty calls," Marvel finished for her, "which reminds me of mine."

"Oh, you're leaving? Going back to that typewriter? You push yourself too far. Of course, look who's talking. Don't we all? Marvel, take a little time for living, maybe going out with the young man again or someone else. There are so many nice ones at church. But you're bound on writing—I see it in those eyes. Tell me, do you put any stock in the talk about the Yalta meeting? What do you think, hon?" Mother said.

"I think," Marvel said, slowly edging her way to the door, "that's what I hope to cover tonight."

* * *

Back on the familiar turf of journalism, Marvel's fingers flew across the typewriter keys and her mind went into the black-and-white print of fact-collecting. Pencil between polished teeth, she recapped:

In 1942 Germany was winning the battle of the Atlantic. Allied strategists stepped up preparations for a great attack across the English Channel, taking necessary precautions. In early 1943 the battle of the Atlantic reached a turning point. It is well to remember that in January of that eventful year, President Franklin Delano Roosevelt—having held from the beginning of WW II global conflict required global diplomacy—disappeared from Washington, D.C. only to reappear in North Africa... the first president to leave the nation in wartime... the first since Lincoln to visit a war zone. Little did he know as, writhing in pain as he labored over terms drafted by himself, Winston Churchill, and Joseph Stalin which offered the Axis nothing from the Allies, demanding instead "unconditional surrender" that critics would argue later that the Yalta conference did more harm than good... a "great mistake... stiffening Germany to greater resistance..." others more moderate saying that the historic event had little or nothing to do with subsequent developments.

And what are those developments? Mr. Roosevelt undoubtedly knew that war had its own way of shaping the peace. And so it was that, although March saw terrible losses, Admiral King had developed an extensive program to cope with the U-boat menace... the convoy system improved... and hundreds of "guardian angel" escorts added. Radar and sonar proved invaluable as submarine spotters. Monthly losses were sliced in half by May... by summer the vital Battle of France was waged without loss of a single Allied vessel... and the Allies had command of the seas! There was supremacy in the air as well. With British planes conducting mass night bombings of German industrial targets and American Flying Fortresses and Liberators striking by day, Germany's transportation system reeled on the verge of collapse... and D-Day was at hand.

Marvel paused, wondering how many of those reading her column would remember. None, she calculated, none at all—unless some caring person like herself recorded it while it remained fresh and new.

Inspired by the thought, she continued, giving no thought to sleep:

It was shortly after midnight on June 6 that three air-borne divisions dropped behind German lines. Each young volunteer paratrooper carried some $10 worth of newly-minted French currency, a tiny U.S. flag stitched onto the right sleeve, and a dime-store metal cricket to signal at night. Out they tumbled, those brave boys—some right on target in Normandy... some scattered miles from planned objectives... and sadly, some to drown in flooded lands or in the sea... but proudly wearing the flag... and often clutching a copy of the Holy Bible, their manuals to live and die for... so poignantly pointed out by the dedicated chaplain: *"To die is not the end—it is to die without God."*

Had Marvel Harrington written that? And who was this un-named chaplain she, the columnist, had quoted? His identity seemed important—as if when she knew the source, the other answers would come. Flexing tired fingers but feeling wide awake, Marvel knew then that she would have that long-postponed talk with Pastor Jim. Strengthened by the decision, she scanned her notes. Going on seemed important.

At daybreak our mighty armada approached France... cold, weak, seasick (and aching with homesickness), the heavily laden troops clambered down cargo nets to the small craft bobbing in heavy seas. Everything seeming to go dead-wrong in the murderous fire of battle. But we are Americans! Mile by hard-won mile, our men fought on to join forces with British and Canadian soldiers. On July 25 invaders raced for the French capital. One month later Free French forces rode through the boulevards of the liberated city to the cheers of joyous Parisians. And when one day your own son asks "What did *you* do in the war, Daddy?" Tell him this: "Ten days before that celebration, the American army, led by Lieutenant General Alexander Patch, had invaded southern France to join forces with General George Patton whose troops stormed south from Normandy." Ah yes, and tell him more. By November the rapid Allied advance cleared Germans from France. There was hope that the European war might end by Christmas!

But Satan held an ace. His servant, Adolph Hitler, had one final surprise stored in that sick mind. On December

14, 1944—Remember?—some 250,000 Germans launched a savage counter offensive, catching hopeful Americans by surprise. On the third day of that bitter siege, when battle-weary soldiers were surrounded by the enemy, overconfident Germans delivered an ultimatum. A command came from out of the smoke-laden fog: "Surrender or face annihilation!" General Anthony McAuliffe sent back the one-word classic response: "Nuts!"

So as we Southerners would say: "How do y'all like them apples?" Or, "Put that in your pipe 'n smoke it!"

The day after Christmas, one of Patton's armored divisions drove into the bulge from the south to break the siege of Bastogne. From the north, First Army units drove to meet him. By late-January the bulge had been wiped out. No longer could an Allied victory in Europe be denied! Can we say—*dare* we say—that the meeting of the minds of the "Big Three" was in vain?

Meantime, the war in the Pacific followed the same pattern. Let all America look over its shoulder now early in 1945.

One day soon a review of that important theater must be completed, but not now. Marvel was too drained, while at the same time exhilarated. Captain Philip Prinz had shown little attention to her mention of the book in progress. But this column would reveal something she suspected lay buried behind his military mask. Yes, this writing Marvel would share, but not until she had met with Pastor Jim.

* * *

The minister sat quietly throughout Marvel's story. It had been hard at first, revealing her innermost feelings. But Dr. Murphy's calm acceptance lent her courage. And once the words began, they were as impossible to stop as the incoming tide. Nothing could have restrained them.

Borrowing from his tranquility, Marvel leaned back and relaxed, noting only that early-February skies were purpling with twilight. Shadows danced through the minister's office, obscuring his features. The thought did not trouble her. Exchange of

confidences seemed more natural, because that was the outcome of the conversation. Eventually it would be the sharing
which led to Marvel's decision.

"I suppose," Pastor Jim said at last, "that you have looked into
this, exhausted all the resources, making sure there's no mistake?"

Marvel nodded in the dimness. "Yes—yessir, I have—all
except the military. And you know how they close ranks."

"Yes," he said tiredly. "I do. I see so much—hear so much, and
my heart goes out to all of you. I just want you to be sure—"

"That the two men—if there *are* two of him—are identical? I
am sure, very sure—every look, every gesture. I wish," she said
miserably, "I had a picture of Titus, and you could meet Philip."

"That wouldn't help," he said quickly. "Supposedly, each of us
has an identical twin somewhere. Not that I buy that, you understand. I doubt that God needed to duplicate! But appearances are
deceiving. I've heard no such claim about the inner person.
Think on that aspect. And then, Marvel," his voice dropped,
"what about feelings—yours, I mean? How do you feel when
you're with him?"

"Miserable," she said without hesitation.

"And apart?"

"Miserable."

His sigh seemed to fill the office. Dr. James Murphy's face was
eclipsed by the shadows, but Marvel Harrington was all but
certain that he brushed a tear from his cheek. His voice gave
further indication of emotion. And when he spoke, she thought
of him for the first time as a man torn by the conflicts of life, not
just as her minister.

"I identify with you, my dear. I, too, have lost. And I remember
the torture, the torment, the pulling away from the world—both
worlds, in fact. It was—it was our child," his voice was husky with
such emotion that Marvel felt herself wanting to grasp his hand,
offer condolences, the reassurance she had come to seek.

"Tell me about it," Marvel encouraged softly. "How you felt—"

He felt, the beloved pastor said, as if time had stopped. All
clocks had died, never to live again. All hands were frozen, the
hour hand and minute hand locked at the point of their infant
daughter's last earthly breath. They had such hopes, such
dreams for that God-given gift—an extension of themselves,

their immortality. How could a merciful God do this? *How*? In a sense, he stumbled on, his was a sin far greater than Marvel's. It was understandable that she would be confused, uncertain. Not so with himself! He *knew* . . . and yet continued to deny. It was not true, it couldn't be. And so he lapsed into a world of his own making—searching every face for the lost child, and finding her everywhere. Comforting? No, it was a mockery—a pit of escape Satan so cleverly designed and into which he entered willingly. Oh yes, he identified!

"And now?" Marvel whispered, wondering if he knew how much depended on his answer. Her question must have reminded him he was not alone.

"Oh—oh, now?" Pastor Jim said quickly. "I am at peace. It was during that life-and-death struggle that I met God, came to really know Him, and knew that I must serve those who had suffered as I had. But not until—Well, tell me this, dear child: How long has it been since you let go completely—broke down and wept?"

Marvel was taken by surprise. "Wept—I—why I *never* weep!"

"Jesus did."

"But—but—" she faltered, rising to go, feeling weak-kneed.

"Purge yourself—shed those iron tears. That's how answers come."

27

In His Image

It was half an hour before Marvel took her leave, although she had intended leaving when she rose. Was it the music which detained her—the soft melody reaching through the walls from the choir room? The world seemed to be spinning in tune with the music, or the words the minister had spoken. The music and the words were one—layers of new meanings blending with those of old. *Mother*. It was Mother playing the lead violin, rehearsing for Sunday. And the words? Pastor Jim was saying more. Listen—she must listen to him. Or was it the voice of God? It had been so long since she heard that Voice....

"What was that you were saying—about God's image?" Marvel asked haltingly as she sat back down. She wanted to cling to every word said by this man who had revealed so much of his secret soul—a part he had held prisoner as she herself had done. "I think of my mother as being that—and my father—and—and"—there was a catch in her voice—*"Titus."*

"We all are created in God's image, Marvel. What we—all of us—must guard against is trying to fit Him into *ours*, create a god of our own making. Now," he chuckled in the dark, the sound seeming to light up the room, "you're going to get more than you bargained for, young lady! I'll push my luck a bit, give some advice. I know you love the other young man—"

"More than I ever dreamed it was possible to love another human being. More than I can ever love another again. We are joined together like Siamese twins—heart to heart. And what

God has joined together, let no man put asunder!" Marvel burst out passionately.

"I understand. It is a wholesome sign that you can give voice to those feelings. But about that image— Well, I still have some advice, so take it. It's free—no luxury tax."

Marvel felt a laugh begging for release. Without warning it surfaced, its unfamiliar melody blending with the music. "No ration coupons either? Go ahead, Pastor Jim. I'm listening with both ears—and my heart." The laughter threatened to turn to tears.

"Consider this. Supposing, just supposing there had been no Titus—no love of your youth? Don't answer, honey. (Unconsciously was he advising the daughter who would now be a young woman?) Just mull it over in your mind. Would Captain Prinz have cast the same charm? Look at him in a new way. See him for himself instead of fitting him into the image of someone else. The answer is there."

"In iron tears!" Marvel said with a lilt in her voice.

This time when she stood, she left. "Can you find your way?" Dr. James Murphy called after her a bit anxiously.

"I already have," she said with certainty.

* * *

Daddy met her at the door. "I was coming to look for you," he said, holding out a light jacket as proof. "Are you all right, sweetie? Your mother's at rehearsal—your aunt, cooking. Billy Joe's doing a rain dance with excitement over a straight-A report card. Oh, come on in. I'm talking too much, but I see you so seldom."

It was true. Marvel felt a twinge of guilt. Admittedly, she had avoided (neglected was a better word) the family for fear they would ask questions she was unprepared to answer. Now that it mattered less, she realized that something else was paramount in their minds. The inheritance had come!

"I refused to believe it until I actually held the check," Daddy began. Then all were talking at once.

"For the first time in our lives, Dale, we can make choices—no more being pushed around," Uncle Worth said with satisfaction. And what were those choices? Auntie Rae wondered aloud as she plopped buttermilk biscuits into the gas oven. Time would tell. Hadn't they always planned to go back...and do what? Something somebody else wanted, expected? Their father? Their two older brothers? Yes (at Marvel's question), Emory and Joseph had headed to East Texas with "dollar signs for eyes!" No escaping the lure of silver and gold, even if it had to be handed out through a teller's cage. Banking was in their blood. "Well, that's better than some things," Billy Joe interjected mysteriously. What things? "Oh, some of the guys got peeved at me because I made the baseball team. Said if I had a blood test, it was bound to turn out 99 percent pea juice. But boy. Just wait'll they see my report card! I may have to bloody some noses before we leave here. We—why, we'd be rotten-egged outta town if they had their way, the snobs!" But California had been kind to them, Mother managed, having returned to find her home in a state of commotion.

Daddy filled her in quickly as he took the musical instrument from her arms. Auntie Rae checked on the biscuits and told of another call from Mary Ann. Jake's parents were staying on in Oregon—bought the Texas-bound brothers' property. She and Jake would decide for themselves. One thing for sure, her husband wouldn't be yanked around by the nose by them or anybody else when he mustered out. Reenlist? Not on your life. It would take all the "zoot suiters" (referring, Marvel knew, to the closest thing Los Angeles had to organized gangs—4-F'ers who strutted the back alleys in flashy suits styled with baggy, heavily padded shouldered coats, peg-leg trousers, armed with trace chains which they promptly dropped when somebody yelled, "Th' fuzz!") in this world to keep him in the service, rating or no rating! Uncle Alex could use him. But—well, the next two months would tell. If the war *did* end on schedule in Europe—

"Of course, it'll end!" Mother said. "Decisions can wait, right?"

Snow Harrington looked at her daughter, but it was B.J. who spoke. Marvel was glad. Sometimes decisions could *not* wait. Mother and Daddy must make their own like Jake and Mary Ann. (She must find out just when her cousin planned to return, as there was another opening.) But she was relieved at B.J.'s contribution to the "war effort." It was best to close the conversation on a light note, postponing heavier talk.

"It'll be kinda good to get back. I never took a shine to labels— like that pea-juice stuff, like being from Texas was *bad*. And, you know what? I didn't like people going outta their way for me just because the name was Harrington! Works both ways, but I was a punk kid then—a pest, that's what my big sis said. Hey! I wish I could see her even if she *is* bossy. If she and Jake can stop the smoochin' long enough to bother— Mother, if you'll butter me another biscuit—"

Billy Joe had the floor and was not about to lose it. Quickly stuffing the second half of the biscuit on his plate into his mouth with one hand, he fished in his pocket with the other. "Gotta note here—something I tore from a paper— Oh, here it is. And about that name business, I was gonna say it'll be good *being* a Harrington when we get back home. I'll *be* somebody then—we all will. Yep! War's over. Here's the proof. We're sniggerin' at ourselves already! Let's pass this around—take turns readin' and chewin'!"

"What to Do in Mopping Up After a Last Air Raid," Uncle Worth read aloud, then smiled and repeated, "A *last* air raid. I like the sound of that. Eat up, family. I'll read first, then you share the honors."

What they shared and Marvel was to include in her book was:

1. Buy a whistle. If sirens blow, blow right back at them!
2. Find a bomb? Run—no matter where, just how fast.
3. Never miss an opportunity. In case of a die-hard raid, *grab*:

    A. In a bakery? Grab a cake (sugar'll be scarce!).

    B. In a tavern? Grab a bottle!

    C. In a movie? Grab a blonde!

4. Oops! Hand grenade? Pick it up, shake it hard so it will not explode and hurt somebody later. If firing pin is stuck, heave it in the furnace. The fire department can save part of your house.
5. If the fire department is late in responding, douse the place with gas (if you have any A-coupons left). That way, you can collect full insurance.
6. Act excited, scream. It will scare heck out of the kids and they'll run to Mama—clearing the street so you can get to the air-raid shelter ahead of the others.

7. If that siren continues to blow, drink alcohol—even if you're a teetotaler; eat onions, sardines, and Limburger cheese to guarantee privacy in case you opt for shelter.

8. CAUTION: If you're hit by flying debris or trampled on by mobs of sillies, don't fly apart. Pull yourself together; keep your head—it's the only one the government issues!

It sounded funny, put in past tense. Those at the table laughed during that hurried meal, battle fatigue gone for the present. And in its place, Marvel thought in the inner sanctum of her writing-mind, was the gyro that somehow sees Americans like the Harringtons through all crises—the inevitable sense of humor and a deep and abiding faith that set the nation back on course. The world looked better already.

"Well now," Uncle Worth said, wiping his eyes (from tears or laughter?), "thanks for sharing that, son. Proud to be a Harrington, are you? Well, we're mighty proud to have you!"

Auntie Rae squeezed both her men's hands.

"Pull yourself together," Mother repeated, starting to stack the dishes. "The war *is* going to end. Our men will come home and, whatever we do, we'll live happily ever after!"

"Us three bears," Daddy said dreamily as he rose to help his "middle-size bear." He paused to glance at Marvel, looking a little uncertain. Was he apologizing—afraid he had implied his daughter was destined to spinsterhood and not certain how to correct it?

Marvel smiled and saw relief spread over his face. His sensitivity was one of the things about him she loved so much. She was welcome—always would be. Even more than welcome—they needed her, just as they always had. And, loving her, they must be prepared to let her go.

But for now, "baby bear" rose to help her mother. And her father, checking his watch, said to them all: "Well, it's been a good day! Let's look forward to Snow's concert Sunday, and know that she's right in saying the war'll end, our boys will come home, and we'll live happily ever after! Man, oh man, what a day of rejoicing when we can say 'It was—they did—and we *are*!'"

"Yep," his brother agreed. "And thanks again, son. And to you, stepbrother of ours, where you are: You've restored my day—

like the Lord restores my soul! On your mark, get set—exit, family!"

Could victory be this near at hand? The air smells of it, but our commander-in-chief has reminded us often enough against the dangers of overconfidence. It has been long, hard, and brutal. And now that the blackout on news alerts us to another front, we wait . . . not ready to celebrate. We will never be, according to our president. Rather, he says, "We will emerge from this victorious, yes, but not in celebration as much as the grim determination that it must never happen again!" And so (an excited neighbor's radio blared on) we depend on previous reports. While the Nimitz was cleaning out the Central Pacific—it is assumed that listeners recall details leading up to that point—MacArthur and his pugnacious Admiral William "Bull" Halsey were leapfrogging through southern seas . . . bypassing Japanese strong points, assaulting less-fortified places to serve as springboards to the Philippines . . . making it possible for General Douglas MacArthur to fulfill his promise to return. The Japanese made what the free world prays was a last frantic attempt. Will we ever forget Commander David McClintock's gasp of astonishment, his exclamation of horror?

"My God—my God! The whole Jap fleet!"

And in that battle for Leyte Gulf, Japan risked everything—and lost. When the shooting was over, the blackout ended. Only then did America know. When? January 1945—this new year. And now February ends. The war-torn Manila is free! Losses are staggering, we know, although for security reasons, figures cannot be released. We only know that it required house-to-house fighting to flush out the enemy who ruthlessly bombed a sleeping Pearl Harbor . . . sent in suicide bombers to destroy our ships of mercy, even though the unarmed Red Cross flag clearly stated their mission . . . captured and tortured our medical personnel . . . made prisoners of newsmen. . . .

Pressing her body against the impersonal wall, Marvel paused on the shadowy stairs. Red Cross ships . . . newsmen . . . Was there a clue here, something that had not occurred to her before? For a moment, insight seemed close. When it faded, she stood, unable to move or think except to will its return for completion. But it was gone. She heard only the remaining fragment of the news. Then it, too, was gone—leaving the rest to speculation:

> During the reconquest of the Philippines, the Allies very well may be carrying out a war of attrition aimed at Japan itself—behind that protective cloak of secrecy. We do know that we promised Tokyo Rose, that sweet-talking Oriental female with the low, seductive voice who tried to trick our war-weary servicemen into betraying America, she would get her answer in March... arriving special delivery by B-29 bombers. "We can—we *will*—we MUST!" *We are Americans!*

"Americans—and Christians," Marvel whispered feeling that she stood on the threshold of discovery. The answers were as yet unrevealed, because the door of her heart had been closed. Soon—very soon—it would swing open, just as it had swung open in childhood. Life had seemed so simple then, surrounded by love, ready to receive. When the Sunday school teacher, dear Mrs. Key, led the little song: "Behold, behold! I stand at the door and knock, knock, knock..." four-year-old Marvel Harrington had sung from the open door of her little-child heart and envisioned Jesus stepping from the painting on her Sunday school card and walking in—to stay. Pastor Jim had reminded her that once Christ entered, He remained, that silence made no difference. She should wait upon the Lord. The thought was comforting.

Walking on up the stairs, Marvel realized that some discoveries she had made already—and some decisions as well. She had come to grips with the self inside her that had known little beyond self-denial—blaming herself for a world she did not create, giving but not receiving. Willingly she had entered a dark wood that, while she did not plant, she had made little effort to escape—shutting away others instead, for fear of being hurt again as she had been hurt so many times before. What would she be, allowed to make a choice? Titus had asked so long ago.

Herself, she had answered without hesitation. But was that true—completely true? Who am I?

"The truth is," Marvel said slowly, "that I was not completely true to myself—not the self God wanted me to be. But oh, I loved Titus. And I'll always love him. Stop trying to forget. I'll remember, knowing that as long as I remember, Titus will be alive in my heart. But I must not stop living and laughing and loving just because the world is the way it is." She hesitated, wondering then if the words she whispered to Titus' memory were intended for the ears of God as well. "I'll never stop loving you, even if I am silent—"

Inhaling deeply, Marvel let herself into her bedroom, moving quickly to draw the drapes and turn on lights here and there. Meantime, her thoughts ran on, there was Philip—alive and waiting. Waiting to be discovered—

Discovered? Yes, the heights and depths of himself—not in the image of another. A shrill ring of the telephone interrupted her thoughts.

* * *

The evening skies lit up with crimson scarves of color as the sun dipped beyond the sea. Marvel had made good her promise to meet Philip at the secluded little restaurant, one of the few which remained open along the shore. Robbed of the view, what did they have to offer? restaurateurs wondered among themselves. With help scarce, *nothing*.

Captain Philip Prinz thought differently. "Privacy," he said to the head waiter, "behind that potted palm. We'll order later."

Now, seated in the tiny stall, shielded from other diners by the plants, "all the ships at sea" (Foreign Correspondent Boake Carter's phrase so often quoted by Americans in these days of war), and by drawn drapes, they looked at one another across the small table separating them. Philip's voice had sounded urgent when he called. Now that urgency reflected on his face.

"We have to talk. Oh," he moaned, "stop looking at me like that." He raised a uniformed arm as a shield against whatever emotions Marvel must be unknowingly communicating. "I can't think," he added with a kind of wistfulness. Then lowering his arm, the words came tumbling out. "Have you ever given any thought to modeling as an angel? That mass of golden hair, those innocent violet eyes, and now the curve of that chin, upturned now as if—as if I didn't bloody well know better, I would say inviting a kiss. Oh, Marvel—Marvel, don't *laugh!*"

"I'm not laughing," she said quietly. "I'm thinking, Philip."

He sighed. "That's why we're here—to think. Time is short."

He could not conceal his surprise when her fingers touched his lips gently. It was her first time to touch him, and it had touched his heart as well. The intake of breath was sharp, pained when she spoke.

"Please—no mention of the future. You promised, Philip. And I know about time. I listen to the news. But there is talking to do—getting acquainted. We don't really know one another at all. No! Don't stop me. I promised an answer to a stranger. Let's begin where we should have begun—*would* have begun without the frenzy of war."

"And where is that?" His voice was a whisper.

"As friends" was all she said.

"As a friend," the man across from her, looking so heart-breakingly like Titus, repeated, seeming to puzzle over the words. "I'm not sure I can make the transition. Still, it has a nice ring. It has been far too long since I had a friend—one in whom I could trust completely, not be afraid to let go of my fears and misgivings, feelings of ambivalence about this whole devilish war. Officers can't do that, you know. The men in our squadron depend on us. And there's a carryover into private life, childish as it sounds—this conviction that we have to look and act in charge. Otherwise, we'll lose whatever we're trying to hold or to gain—be a *failure*. I—I shouldn't be admitting all this. I don't know what came over me. You'll see me as a weakling and walk away—" Philip paused helplessly.

Marvel looked at the handsome officer—so tall, lithe, and (she had thought) so confident, always seeming to march when they walked together. And something more: a longing to be understood and, yes, an affection in his straightforward eyes that amounted to a proposal.

"You could never be a weakling, Philip. And I will not walk away."

For a moment, he looked bewildered and then fierce. "You want to hear more?" he asked almost angrily. "You mean how soft inside I am, how vulnerable to hurt, how scared I was when bombs exploded all around me in Madrid? You look surprised. See? I've shocked you!"

. Marvel shook her head in denial. His openness had not shocked her. At least, not in his sense of the meaning. Where he saw a weakness in himself, she saw strength—a strength which gave him courage to reveal himself. And one day she would tell him that the revelation had brought him closer, not pushed him away.

"It was mention of Madrid. I never knew you were in Spain."

It was his turn to be surprised. "You know about Spain? Had someone there? I guess you're right. We really *are* strangers."

Not anymore. Marvel felt her own breath rise up in a little gasp of realization. But what she said was, "I wrote about it. I told you about the book we—I—want to complete from the columns (*and yes, I had someone there!*)." Pushing the thought aside, she fished in her bag for the column to share with Philip, found it, and spread it before him. "Look at this, and then tell me everything."

Philip obliged and, as he read, Marvel saw his expression change, fill up with flares of passion and fire she had not suspected. When the waiter peered from behind the screen of greenery cautiously, then quick-stepped to their table, Philip seemed unaware at first. Then, still reading, he murmured, "Lady's choice— Oh, make it the specialty of the house." The waiter, who confided to Marvel that he spoke eight languages, shook a bushy head, and seemed unable to cope with one.

Not meeting her eyes, Philip Prinz began to speak at last. Yes, he had been in Spain . . . and the memory made him angry. Could he ever forgive, forget? He had wanted to run then and he wanted to run now. He had seen too much of killing—on both sides. And if only it could have ended there . . . but no, from one front to another . . . covering every front. Surely, there could be no more! Forgetting rank, thinking of survival . . . forgetting *self*, just pulling one another through. Anything, *anything* to outwit the Axis powers, get the blooming thing over.

Sir Winston Churchill was wrong—dead-wrong—in dubbing the English Channel the "soft underbelly" of Europe. Only the good news crept out to raise morale of the Allied forces. "Radio detecting and ranging" sounded good, described as it was by the sing song in Garbriel Heatter's melodramatic versions. "Ah, yes—there's good news tonight, friends—no smile on Hitler's face now!" ... as soothing as Bing Crosby's crooning...kept the world buying bonds. But behind the lines faces were camouflaged by masks, a mixture of mud and blood, one lost battalion after another hacking their way through brush to get at machine-gun nests...knowing—all the while *knowing*—that eventually they would be captured, forced to do the enemy's commands.

"Remember, corporal?" Captain Prinz murmured in address to a lost buddy (obviously having forgotten Marvel's presence in the painful archeological diggings of the subconscious). "Remember how you had to take over a detachment, rely on your own resources—getting us through but paying with your life and your men when your truck brought up the rear?"

Nazis cracked every code. German language? Who knew it? English they knew as well.... It took the resourceful kid from Tennessee to get them through when the Jerries (short for German) moved in to take over the silent American convoy, ordering them to keep moving—moving (*God help them!*) behind their own lines, betraying their countrymen by showing identification, behaving normally after Nazi rifles and machine guns were aimed at their backs from the owners crouched in the rear of their vehicles. He had prayed then—*oh, how he had prayed*. And that was back in the days when God took pity on the dying and *answered!* Corporal Hayes behaved like the easygoing guy he always was, allowed the enemy to pass through, then from the back of the last truck yelled to warn Americans on guard in something called "Pig-Latin from down home": "*-erry-Ja's in th' 'uck-tra!*" Allies swarmed in from all directions, captured every conniving one—shook the truth from cowardly officers. But Corporal Hayes and his detachment were blown to bits. *Forget?*

Marvel's throat ached with compassion and understanding. *What was happening to her?* she wondered. She was mixing the sacred memory of Titus with the reality of the new man before her, when the sole purpose was to separate the two. It was impossible to be in love with another man after the sweetness, the gentleness of the man to whom she was committed—actually *married* to by separation. The face swimming before her blurred to separate into three men: her beloved Titus, the cock-sure Captain Philip Prinz, and now the new Philip who had emerged in another image all his own—a vulnerable human being who decried the awfulness of war. Then the three merged into one again. How long, how very long she had waited for Titus to declare himself, to say a definite "I love you—Will you be my wife?" And across from her sat the man who proposed at a first meeting. They were alike. No! Not alike at all. They were at opposite ends of the spectrum. And yet—

Marvel toyed with her salad, watched sightlessly when the disgruntled waiter removed the plate and replaced it with an entree neither she nor Philip touched. Looking at the man across from her now, Marvel saw that he seemed as confused as she felt—a kind of desperation. She must escape—now . . . this minute.

"What is it, Marvel—this war within you?" he murmured. "You have sat through all this senseless rambling, said nothing. *Please*—"

"Explain? I will—tomorrow night," she whispered.

Outside, she asked him not to accompany her home. Just hail a taxi. They would complete this conversation tomorrow night.

"There may not be a tomorrow night—" Philip said haltingly as he tucked her inside the door of the waiting taxi. "I—I—"

"Want an answer now—but I'm unprepared. Tomorrow night!"

This time she did not object when he leaned forward and brushed her hot forehead with a light kiss. It could be their last, she knew.

* * *

It was late, but Marvel found Mary Ann waiting for her. Otherwise, the house was empty. So it was startling to see a crack of light beneath the door of her bedroom. Assured of a welcome, her cousin had taken the liberty of letting herself in. She held a glass in her hand.

"You scared me out of my wits," Marvel gasped from Mary Ann's tight embrace. "How did you get home?"

"By Greyhound," Mary Ann giggled, hugging harder after slamming the glass down. "Jake, my husband—*doesn't that grab you!*—is out on maneuvers . . . just a three-day thing and close, but I had to see you. I *had* to!" she said breathlessly.

"Is there something wrong with you, the family—what?"

Mary Ann released her. "I wondered the same about *you*—out at this wee hour *alone*. Or were you—alone, I mean? You look different, Marvel—something's happened. Sit down. Drink the iced tea I fixed—"

There was no choice. Mary Ann was pushing her into a chair.

Gratefully, Marvel sipped the cold tea. The room was stuffy, and she realized suddenly that she had eaten nothing at the restaurant.

"You *do* look different—more alive in one way, more dead in others. Oh, go ahead—tell me that's wrong, that something can't be *more dead*. It's either dead or alive. Say something, *anything*. You *are* alive?"

"I'm not sure," Marvel murmured, wanting to tell Mary Ann the whole story but unable. Instead, she pressed the cool of the sweating glass to her throbbing temple. "You talk first. I'm ready to listen."

Something akin to pity came into Mary Ann's dark eyes. Pity—why? The other girl seemed to weigh something in her mind before taking over the conversation. Then, reaching a decision, she covered the ground quickly. Being with Jake was heaven-in-one-room. They couldn't bear a minute apart, except in a circumstance like this (her voice thickened with emotion). And when they got home—yes, home in Texas—on that they were agreed, provided Marvel went—Marvel and Titus—

Titus! How could Mary Ann be so cruel? She knew he was dead. Why make him more dead? she thought foolishly.

"Don't—" she whispered, the word rising up to choke her.

They sat in silence, the tick of the clock seeming to shake the walls. "You've had no word—heard nothing, Marvel?" Mary Ann asked quietly at last. "You have to know. I have to tell you—"

"There's nothing to tell. I do know!" Marvel felt a burst of anger, heard her voice rising without power to control it.

But Mary Ann was not offended. Her voice was unusually gentle when she spoke. "Titus could be—probably *is*—alive, Marvel. Jake saw him. He remembers Titus in high school. I never met him—"

"He can't be—that's impossible!" Marvel cried out in denial. "You know the circumstances—you *know*! Oh, why are you doing this?" Never in her 20 years on earth had she felt so enraged.

Mary Ann was more patient and understanding than Marvel had thought possible. Pulling her chair closer, she wrapped a protective arm about Marvel's trembling shoulders. "Miracles do happen. You listen."

Marvel listened, knowing that what Mary Ann told her could not be true. And when her cousin finished, she was all the more convinced.

Lieutenant Jake Brotherton had seen action all over the globe... still as tense as a coiled spring, with enough ribbons pinned on his chest to paper a wall, Mary Ann explained. He took part in everything, absolutely everything everywhere, except in that unspeakable death march in Bataan. Food ran out, along with medical supplies, and men ate mutton three times a day ... then mule meat. Time lost its meaning... rank meant nothing... thousands died... as many surrendered. But somewhere out there in that fiery furnace of hell (hell, yes—worse than Dante could have imagined in his version of *Inferno*. Did Marvel know about the extermination of the Jews—that it was true, *really* true?)... somewhere—yes, somewhere, where *was* it?— Jake met Titus.

"Where?" Marvel asked tonelessly. "You've jumped all over the globe, and it was not Titus. We both know that. But where did he think—"

"I don't know," Mary Ann admitted helplessly. "It could have been anywhere. He doesn't know either, except that it *was* Titus ... mud-caked and hungry like all the others... crawling on his belly, trying to help Dave Breger. Remember him? Wrote that column that kept us sane?"

Marvel nodded. "G.I. Joe," she said through tight lips. Then the tightness relaxed to form a reasonable facsimile of a smile. Watching, Mary Ann noted that it did not reflect in the sad blue of her eyes. "There's one of Breger's comic strips on our bulletin board—satire on the endless red tape of bureaucracy, like we put up with at OPA. An order to arrange a stack of documents in alphabetical order, then burn them." Marvel sighed then said practically, "When are you coming back to work?"

It was Mary Ann's turn to explode. Leaping to her feet, she glared down at Marvel. "How can you ask such a stupid question. *How?* After what I've told you? You, why, you're *unworthy* of a man like Titus Smith! And you claim to love him—promised to marry him. You're just a martyr!"

"Stop it!" Marvel, too, was on her feet. "I can't stand any more! I did love him. I *do* love him. I'll always be in love with Titus, but

I—I have to get on with my life. I'm trying—and now you come back and destroy it. I've met another man—the stranger on the beach that day."

"Then your heart's not dead, after all. I remember—you turned—Oh, you're confusing me. You're seeing him, that's all? It *has* to be all—"

Marvel shook her head. "He's asked me to marry him—brought me to life."

"There's some doubt about that! We'd better sit down and talk."

They sat back down and Marvel poured out the whole story, while an astonished Mary Ann listened, transfixed.

"I'd give a big horselaugh if you weren't so serious about this crazy mix-up. That guy—Philip Whosit or whatever—has to be some kind of nut, or spy. English, my foot! Sounds fishy to me. I'm surprised he didn't try and sell you some bill of goods, pretend he was royalty. Wait a minute. Did you say a *prince*? A counterfeit, I betcha!"

Marvel felt herself smile. Mary Ann was Mary Ann again. That made her feel more like Marvel. Mary Ann smiled with her, then sobered.

"Whatever his game is, this prince—"

"Captain Philip Prinz—and it's no game."

"Marvel, come to your senses! Haven't you heard a word? Jake saw Titus. He doesn't make mistakes—can't afford to and hope to live!"

Marvel sighed deeply. "It would have been easy for Jake to make the same mistake I made—and I guess it was a mistake. But Mary Ann, they're identical, Titus and Philip. It's shattering. I'm trying to sort out my feelings. I no longer doubt Philip. I question my own feelings." Her voice lowered because of the lump in her throat. "I have to separate them, see—Philip—not the image of a d-dead love."

"Dead! You said your love would never die. Titus didn't either!"

Marvel's head began to pound again. "There is no proof," she said wearily, adding silently, *I wouldn't believe it anyway*.

"There's proof." Mary Ann's voice was positive. Hurriedly, she rummaged through a bag, muttering, "Candy bars for B.J., some soap—*here*!" Triumphantly, she drew out a rumpled envelope.

"No time to write—said you'd understand. Titus told Jake to send this to me. He's doing something—lots of somethings, all secret, can't send messages—"

With her heart pounding unmercifully, Marvel tore open the envelope and gasped as a faded four-leaf clover dropped to the floor. A lifetime ago, she and Titus had combed the Bermuda grass beneath their tree searching for the elusive good-luck charm that they never found. Neither would she find Titus again.

28

One Leaf Is for Hope

Managing to look fresh in spite of a sleepless night, Marvel Harrington arrived at the Office of Price Administration an hour before opening time. A puzzled guard opened the door, remarked on a feel of spring and victory in the air, then pointed to the telephone. "It'll be for you again—might as well take it."

Tempted to ignore the black instrument, she moved to straighten her desk. When it continued to ring, her "good morning" was crisp.

"Marvel? You sound so businesslike. I was thinking about last night and all it meant to me, your letting me bare my soul the way I did. But we do need to understand. Only, Marvel, I realize that I did all the talking, and I know nothing about you—" Philip said.

You know a lot. Haven't you listened—listened with your heart? Aloud she said, "My turn comes tonight—remember?"

There was a groan at the other end of the line. "There'll be no tonight," he said in disappointment. "That's why I called: There's retreat and we officers have to inspect. Then we, in turn, must attend orientation. You know what this is leading up to. We just don't know what theater. And I can't leave you. I *can't* without an answer—"

There was a plea, a caress in his voice which set her pulse racing. Could she love this man? True, the new feeling she had for him was as fresh as the rapidly approaching spring. But the winter had been long, so long. Time . . . it would take time to love

311

again. Even now, touching the black instrument with her finger-tips gave it life, brought him closer—just a breath away. It would be so easy to let herself melt with the warmth of his presence. No!

"I am unprepared to answer now," Marvel said softly, not recognizing the *yes* in her voice. But his sharp intake of breath said Captain Philip Prinz had heard, had Marvel taken note.

"But we know—we both know, don't we?" When she was unable to respond, he rushed on, "The Provost Marshal's coming in, just routine—checking on your safety, has to supervise the M.P.'s you know—see that they're guarding you and those bloom-ing coupons. *I* will be your protector for life." Philip's voice shook with emotion. "But for now the P.V'll pick up extra rations. You know what that means. We're all on alert. Keep that under wraps. And unless I'm restricted to the base, I'll do my best to wait until tomorrow. All right?"

Replacing the receiver, Marvel shivered. She was not cold, just confused, uncertain—and frightened. Someday, she thought dully, possibly people would wonder why the urgency, the need to push ahead of the clock. But the entire world had spun out of control, leaving time behind.

Friday—today was Friday. Sunday morning Mother's concert was scheduled. If only Philip could hear her play, and Marvel could watch his face. That would tell her something she needed to know. Just what was vague....

Events of the next two days were blurred in Marvel's memory. Thankfully, the family was too deeply engrossed with Mary Ann's presence to note Marvel's own behavior. Everything seemed turned around, looking backward at one level, forward in an-other—like a photograph reversed in printing. Did she make sense at the family dinner table or at her work window? Didn't she start speaking and find herself unable to hold onto the thought and complete it? When the Provost Marshal came, she went to the files for application blanks and closed the drawers to return empty-handed. Some deeper level of consciousness must have prompted her to react normally. Was she too much in love to care, or not in love at all? At a different level, Marvel knew life could not be capsulized, lived all at one dose. God knew the answers. Why didn't He share?

Only once did Mary Ann get too close for comfort. "I'll be leaving Sunday right after church. Want to talk? Tell me what you've decided?"

"I haven't," Marvel said slowly. "Oh, I know Titus is dead. I faced that reality long ago. The clover could have been anybody's—and you yourself don't know where or when Jake got ahold of it—"

Billy Joe had interrupted then, unwilling to let his sister out of his sight. He had money for chocolate bars, and wouldn't that be a nice surprise for Mother's Day? And Mary Ann *had* to see his report card.

Marvel had hurried away, but something was more clear in her mind now. Of course she would check Mary Ann's story with Philip.

* * *

"I would like to meet your family," Philip suggested when he called for Marvel the following evening. "If they're to be my family, too—"

"Oh—we—aren't we jumping the gun a little?" she objected, hoping her voice reflected no panic. "It's a poor time, Philip. My cousin came home unexpectedly. Everybody's talking, and—and besides," she finished coyly, "I want to have this time all to ourselves. You Englishmen are supposed to move slowly, go by the book. Wow! What other people don't know!" Grabbing his hand playfully, Marvel skipped lightly toward the waiting taxi— anything, *anything* to avoid questions and add concern to her father and mother's busy minds and schedules.

Neither was hungry, they said, so they settled for a small cafe which appeared almost empty. From a rear booth (the only one, the waitress confided, boasting drawn curtains for privacy), Philip ordered grilled sandwiches and fed nickels to the jukebox, selecting "Harbour Lights" and pressing "repeat" five times. He leaned across the table then, eyes sparkling unnaturally. "Yes, Marvel?"

The sandwiches came in the nick of time, sparing her an answer. Careful to keep her hands busy, Marvel said quickly, "There's so much I want to say, Philip—to ask you and hear you

314

say. About my cousin first. Does the name Jake Brotherton mean anything to you?"

Philip looked puzzled. "Brotherton? A serviceman? No, but look! We didn't come to talk about your cousin—or this chap."

"Please, Philip, it's important—"

He sighed and shrugged. "Name, rank, serial number? I met millions in those fiery furnaces, those valleys of dry bones. You know I wouldn't remember one G.I. Joe. We lost all identity out there—"

His voice had gone back to the battlefields again, just as Marvel had hoped. Gently, she led him farther back, naming fronts in both European and Japanese theaters which Mary Ann had mentioned. Yes, to them all—Captain Philip Prinz had been there. Then it *was* possible the two had met. Marvel stopped in mid-thought then. This was purposeless. It did not explain the pressed clover.

But now it ceased to matter. As Philip talked, it was she who leaned forward, hanging onto each word as if adding another jewel to her priceless strand of pearls. He was revealing more and more of himself, carrying her into his world. More—she wanted to hear more.

"I was injured, you know—hospitalized later. But at the time I was desensitized, felt nothing after crawling through muddy snakepits running red with Japanese, American, British, and Russian blood. I could feel nothing save the void inside me where the heart used to be—anger at the world, wanting to cry, and convinced it was unmanly. All sides were desperate, but we couldn't shut our eyes to the ruthless killings . . . make-believe it didn't happen. So we fought on and on . . . wading water up to our armpits . . . learning to hate, while feeling compassion, then nothing—*nothing at all*! Survival—oh, dear God!"

Philip remembered one incident in particular, and as he talked (again seeming to forget her presence), Marvel's mind wrote:

American soldiers learned to adapt to barbaric warfare in which no quarter was given by either side. The worst of the jungle fighting was the strain of battling an unseen enemy. Marines, sailors, infantrymen, airmen—all of them—engaged in fierce combat—rank meaning nothing, fighting to preserve their lives and the men around them. An American would fall mortally wounded. Enemy soldiers would appear and from the black nowhere scream, "*Banzai*, you die!" stabbing the stench-filled air with satanic laughter. Then the Japanese, knowing Americans would care for their own, would infiltrate by night and induce Americans to expose themselves by whispering from the tangled jungles: "Marine, I'm one of you! Wounded. Joe, Joe, where are you? *Help* a dying Marine...."

When he paused, Marvel whispered, "And that is what happened to you—how you came to be injured? You went to the rescue?"

"Fool that I am!"

"Oh no!" Marvel cried out in compassion. "*Hero* that you are. You care. Oh, this is exactly what we need, my darling—exactly what we need for our book, Titus."

"*Book—Titus?* I don't understand. And that's twice you have mentioned the name. Who—what? Am I not entitled to know about *you*?"

Yes. Yes, he was. The whole story came tumbling out then, haltingly at first, painfully, then in a wave of such strength it refused to be dammed up, held back by walls of restraint. Beginning with childhood in the Great Depression... going on to the drought... the mass exodus... all of it and the feelings of the times, the commitments. And Titus? Yes, Titus Smith was real, very real—or had been.

"*Had* been?" Would she have told him more, including Mary Ann's report which she had dismissed, refusing to return to a world of hopeless hoping, had there been no question from her companion?

Marvel could thank him for the interruption. She had given him far too much of an inside glimpse already—something to be held in sacred memory. "Dead," she said. "Another casualty of war."

"I'm sorry, and yet jealous of the past. But there is room in your heart for me, a living love? Jove! Hand-to-hand combat's one matter, but competing with a memory's quite another. Friends? We can never be that, surely you know." In a sudden gallant gesture, Captain Prinz uncurled her clenched fingers and kissed the palm of her hand.

What did she feel? Marvel was unsure, her smile careful, thoughtful. "I wish very much that I could feel what you profess to feel—"

"But you do," he said positively. "You'll not just walk away, Miss Harrington, no matter what you say! 'Oh, your lips tell me *no, no* . . . but there's *yes, yes* in your eyes. . . .' Remember the song? That's *you!*"

Oh how could he handle the matter so lightly? *How?* Love was all-consuming, electrifying—yet *spiritual*, perfected by God alone.

Marvel told him about her mother's concert then, pled with him to come. Concert, violin? He knew nothing of music. Like art, it was *Greek!* Why search for hidden meanings in melodies without words?

"I'm no musician either," she tried to explain. "But I can appreciate without creating—except for the words. I create them—well, not really. The words come from inside to send my soul soaring—"

Philip interrupted with a soft laugh. "Oh Marvel, even you are struggling for words. Why bother when we have our own language? Hear that music?" Yes, she heard. Glenn Miller's orchestra, his vocalist singing: "I watched those harbour lights . . . How could I help if tears were starting? . . . Goodbye to tender nights . . . beside a silver sea. . . ."

Beautiful, yes, but different—of the flesh, not of the spirit.

The waitress came back with the check. The cafe was closing, she said.

Philip objected. "We have more to say. You love me, Marvel, but I have to hear you say it. *Those* are the words *I* search for!"

Marvel rose. "Yes, Philip, I love you," she said softly, reaching for her bag and carefully avoiding the hauntingly familiar eyes. "But wait! No celebrating just yet. Honor my wishes. Allow me to go home alone. There's something I must do be-before I answer your proposal. I know time is precious. I should— I've lost so many I love—"

"So what's one more?" he rasped out fiercely. "Just another statistic! We love each other. I don't understand. Don't toy with my heart!"

Again, Marvel leaned down to touch gentle fingers of hush to the finely chiseled lips. "I don't play games. Don't try to understand. Not now—I must go, and I've a feeling you have things to do, too."

Yes, he admitted, things to do. Important matters—which ruled out the concert. But he would meet her afterward, God willing.

"He will be," Marvel said with sudden confidence. "God *is* love."

She left him staring after her in silence and bewilderment.

* * *

There was something she must find. A poem she had clipped from a magazine long ago, intending to send it to Titus as a reminder of their search for the green trophy of youth. Unable to locate Ella Higginson's 1862 verse, Marvel resigned herself to its loss and decided to store the faded clover away with the souvenirs of her past. Choking back tears, she opened the chest, inhaled deeply of the faint fragrance of lilacs, and placed the faded leaf on top. And then she saw it...read the words, tasted their aching sweetness, and copied the words for Philip (wondering if poetry held no more meaning for him now than music). Yes, she would share the words of "The Four-Leaf Clover." But the leaf she must keep for herself.

Rising, Marvel closed the chest, and walked from the foot of the bed to the side. There she dropped to her knees, burying her face in the silence of the down comforter Grandmother had given her.

It was late, very late, but there was a greater need than sleep: a time to be alone with her thoughts, to have the luxury of time and space. In these brief hours before church services, Marvel Harrington must make the most important decision of her 20 years: say *yes* to a new life with Captain Philip Prinz or cling to the innocence of girlhood and its dreams. But there would be no good-byes. One could not bid farewell to memories folded away temporarily with those dreams...dreams made with Mother and Daddy...promises—actually commitments—and dreams spun out like cobwebs in youthful exuberance with Titus Smith. And the greatest commitment was to God Himself whom she had silenced in her selfish grief as she had attempted to silence Philip's declaration of love.

"Dear God," she cried out in the darkness of self-imposed exile, "You know my needs, my loneliness. Bring me back into the fold of Your purpose. My soul belongs to You. I place this decision and my life in Your hands!"

The tears fell then—the iron tears, Pastor Jim had called those tears held within the heart until the ducts are dry and one forgets how to weep. There was pain, agonizing pain, so all-consuming, Marvel's frail body shook with its intensity. Then, in her exhaustion, there came a soul-cleansing flood of tears so great that the comforter was wet beneath her hot face. But there was release. She was purified, joy-filled.

Rising on legs made steady and sure, she opened the window. A little breeze was rising to toy with her ash-gold hair and lifting the fog from the bay, stroking her rounded, still-rosy cheeks with gentle fingers to bring God so near she could touch His shining raiment. From overhead came the feel of warmth on her upturned face—a warmth born of a triumphant sunrise, and warmth sent back to earth from the throne God had ascended to occupy. "You can do it alone now," His voice seemed to say. And yes, she could. Marvel knew now what her answer to Philip would be.

* * *

Philip met her after church as he had promised. How like Titus he was, looking at her in silent adoration as she descended the steps—an idea she must abandon. Philip was *not* Titus except by the strange quirk of nature which had given the two men a physical likeness. Or did her heart bear the responsibility? Clinging to the mistaken identity was unfair to both the man before her and the man declared dead.

"How charming you are in that blue suit, my dear," Philip said in admiration. "And the veil of that whimsical hat!"

The whimsical hat. Yes, it was safer to concentrate on that bit of trivia than go back to colored memories of "the beautiful lady in blue. . . ."

"Thank you," Marvel smiled, accepting his outstretched hand.

He fell into step beside her, uniformed shoulder well above her own. "Where can we go to be alone?"

"To the beach? Yes—the beach. I can't promise we'll be alone—"

"But away from people who care—except for each other."

There was no time to answer, for Philip rushed on. "I hope you can walk in those heels. Otherwise, take them off and I'll carry you! I've seen the chaplain, made arrangements—all subject to your approval."

"Oh, but you shouldn't have," Marvel murmured. Her protest went unnoticed, partly due to the screech of dipping, darting white seagulls, but mostly because Philip was not listening.

"Bloody brazen of me, but timing is everything these days. My orders can come, so I took the liberty of looking at rings."

Marvel stopped. "Philip, no—"

"No? No ring, or no, I should make no selection?"

"Neither of those" she said gently. "It's no. I cannot marry you."

"You don't mean, you cannot mean that is your answer!"

The look of hurt in his eyes reflected in her heart. Philip Prinz was no longer the self-assured officer in command. His handsome, masculine face was now that of a little boy denied what he would have died to possess. She had hurt him, hurt him deeply. But he deserved no less than the truth. Someday he would thank her. But now pain was too new, coupled with wounded pride, uncertainty, and desperation.

"It is *no*, Philip. It has to be. Deep in my heart, I guess I always knew. But I was confused, buried in my loss, searching—making you into another man's person. It was unfair. *Please* forgive me!"

Remorsefully, but sure of purpose, Marvel stood on tiptoe in the shifting sands to touch his face with gentle fingers. Desperately, he grasped her hands and held them to his heart, not seeming to have heard her words. "I don't understand—I just don't. I prayed."

"I prayed, too, Philip," she whispered above the lap of the waves. Some part of her noted that the tide was coming in.

"But God didn't answer," he said, still unable to understand.

"God always answers, but we must accept that sometimes His answer is no."

"You were exactly what I wanted—the girl I never expected to find. Oh Marvel, my dear one, it can't end like this—without love, without hope," he groaned, oblivious to the crowds sweeping past.

"I do love you, Philip, in a very special sort of way. I love you too much to marry you when there is a destiny to which I am committed. And hope? There is always hope. Christ gave us that."

Philip nodded. "For the world? For mankind? You and me?"

"All of those—when 'The Lights Come on Again.'"

"But us—all for naught? Our togetherness has meant nothing?"

"Wrong, dear Philip! Our togetherness has meant everything. It put my world back together, mended my heart—jarred me into a world of reality."

"But took away our dream world. How can you say there is hope!"

Marvel drew a deep breath. "If I had said yes, I would have married a dream," Marvel said with a kind of reverence. "And the hope we have with us forever, as long as we remain in His hands."

In His hands. And into Philip's outstretched hands she placed the poem.

* * *

Marvel Harrington walked away, not daring to glance back at the lonely stranger on the shore who stood looking until the girl of his dreams became a blue dot in the distance. She would never hear his repeating her words "in His hands." She only knew that she felt sad, but happy. She would miss Captain Philip Prinz, whom God had chosen as the tool of His original plan. In the beginning was the Word....

The salt air was bracing, the sky turquoise-blue. Marvel was released from her prison. She had made her exodus. She had crossed that great gulf....

From overhead came the screeching of wheeling, diving gulls, seeking their daily bread. There was today—*today only*. God taught so much through nature. Marvel had learned a valuable lesson from the aquatic birds: to accept...to endure with no thought of yesterday or tomorrow...to take a day like today, without flaw whatever direction she looked. This was a day which the Lord had made. She would rejoice and be glad in it. The future was in His hands. With a tremulous smile, she repeated the words of the poem:

I know a place where the sun is like gold,
    And the cherry blossoms burst with snow.
And down underneath is the loveliest nook
    Where the four-leaf clovers grow.

One leaf is for hope, and one is for faith,
    And one is for love, you know,
And God put another in for luck—
    If you search, you will find where they grow.

But you must have hope, and you must have
    faith,
    You must love and be strong—and so,
If you work, if you wait, you will find the place
    Where the four-leaf clovers grow.

HARVEST HOUSE PUBLISHERS

For the Best in Inspirational Fiction

RUTH LIVINGSTON HILL CLASSICS
Bright Conquest
The Homecoming (mass paper)
The Jeweled Sword
This Side of Tomorrow

June Masters Bacher
PIONEER ROMANCE NOVELS

Series 1
1. Love Is a Gentle Stranger
2. Love's Silent Song
3. Diary of a Loving Heart
4. Love Leads Home
5. Love Follows the Heart
6. Love's Enduring Hope

Series 2
1. Journey to Love
2. Dreams Beyond Tomorrow
3. Seasons of Love
4. My Heart's Desire
5. The Heart Remembers
6. From This Time Forth

Series 3
1. Love's Soft Whisper
2. Love's Beautiful Dream
3. When Hearts Awaken
4. Another Spring
5. When Morning Comes Again
6. Gently Love Beckons

HEARTLAND HERITAGE SERIES
No Time for Tears
Songs in the Whirlwind
Where Lies Our Hope

ROMANCE NOVELS

The Heart that Lingers, *Bacher*
With All My Heart, *Bacher*
If Love Be Ours, *Brown*

Brenda Wilbee
SWEETBRIAR SERIES

Sweetbriar
The Sweetbriar Bride
Sweetbriar Spring

CLASSIC WOMEN OF FAITH SERIES

Shipwreck!
Lady Rebel

Lori Wick
THE CAMERON ANNALS

A Place Called Home
A Song for Silas
The Long Road Home
A Gathering of Memories

THE CALIFORNIANS

Whatever Tomorrow Brings
As Time Goes By
Sean Donovan

Ellen Traylor
BIBLICAL NOVELS

Esther
Joseph
Moses
Joshua

**Available at your
local Christian bookstore**
